John Murphy and Company

# Life of Blessed John Gabriel Perboyre,

Priest of the Congregation of the Mission

John Murphy and Company

**Life of Blessed John Gabriel Perboyre,**
*Priest of the Congregation of the Mission*

ISBN/EAN: 9783744653688

Printed in Europe, USA, Canada, Australia, Japan

Cover: Foto ©Raphael Reischuk / pixelio.de

More available books at **www.hansebooks.com**

Blessed John Gabriel Perboyre,
*Missionary, China*, 1835.

# LIFE

OF

# BLESSED JOHN GABRIEL PERBOYRE,

## PRIEST OF THE CONGREGATION OF THE MISSION,

Martyred in China, September 11th, 1840.

*Translated from the French, with the permission and blessing of*
THE SUPERIOR-GENERAL OF THE LAZARISTS IN PARIS.

---

*Non judicavi me scire aliquid inter vos nisi Jesum Christum, et hunc crucifixum.*
(1 Cor. ii, 2.)

For I judged not myself to know anything among you but Jesus Christ; and Him crucified.

---

BALTIMORE:
JOHN MURPHY & COMPANY,
1894.

# APPROBATION OF THE FRENCH EDITION

BY M. ANTOINE FIAT,

*Superior-General of the Priests of the Congregation of the Mission and the Sisters of Charity.*

---

Having examined "*La Vie du Bienheureux Jean Gabriel Perboyre,*" printed on the occasion of the Beatification of the Venerable Servant of God;

And having personal knowledge of the contents of this "*Life,*" composed for the most part from the very words of the Blessed Martyr,

With all my heart I approve of it and very willingly authorize its publication. Everyone will find in Blessed John Gabriel Perboyre a perfect model of all the virtues of the Christian, the religious, the priest.

After having led many souls to God by the perfume of his virtues and power of his doctrine, Blessed Perboyre fulfilled a short but glorious career as a Missionary in China. Apprehended through hatred for his religion, he submitted with heroic patience to the horrors of a long captivity, the refined cruelties of inhuman executioners, and the tortures of a most painful martyrdom.

I can recommend no book that contains a life and death more honorable to the Church and to the Congregation of the Mission.

A. FIAT,
*Superior-General.*

PARIS, *November* 10, 1889.

---

IMPRIMATUR:

FRANCIS CARD. RICHARD,
*Archbishop of Paris.*

PARIS, *November* 7, 1889.

# TABLE OF CONTENTS.

## BOOK I.

### FROM THE BIRTH OF BLESSED PERBOYRE TO HIS DEPARTURE FOR CHINA.

## BOOK II.

### FROM HIS DEPARTURE FOR CHINA TO HIS MARTYRDOM.

## BOOK III.

### VIRTUES OF BLESSED JOHN GABRIEL.

## BOOK IV.

### ACCOUNT OF THE BEATIFICATION OF THE VENERABLE SERVANT OF GOD, JOHN GABRIEL PERBOYRE.

# LIST OF ILLUSTRATIONS.

# LIFE OF BLESSED JOHN GABRIEL PERBOYRE.

## BOOK I.

### FROM HIS BIRTH TO HIS DEPARTURE FOR CHINA.

### I.

#### BIRTH OF BLESSED PERBOYRE.

At the beginning of the nineteenth century, in a hamlet amid the fertile vineclad hills of France, a child was born, for whom the virgins and martyrs were weaving a crown and preparing a high place within their ranks. Forty years later, people visited with devotion the place where he first saw the light of day; many, thousands of miles away, recommended themselves to him; while others prostrated themselves at his tomb to implore his mediation with God, because from all sides came tidings of the miracles granted through his intercession. The Sovereign Pontiff, Gregory XVI., received with pleasure a picture of him, had it placed in his modest oratory and loved to invoke the humble missionary;—but why this veneration? Because this child grew up in the practice of all the virtues and crowned a holy life by a glorious martyrdom.

His father, Pierre Perboyre, and his mother, Marie Rigal, though not rich, were in easy circumstances; they lived as true servants of God and cultivated the modest patrimony received from their parents. Contented with their state, they envied not those more abundantly provided with the goods of fortune. It was not their ambition to leave much wealth to their children; they strove rather to inspire them with the love of God, the richest of all treasures. They were full of simple faith: peace and union reigned in their hearts: never had there been the slightest misunderstanding between them. Their lives recalled the simplicity of the days of the patriarchs. Through a pious zeal for the practice of the Christian virtues, they watched carefully over their family and strove to train them in piety more by example than by precept. Therefore, God showered His blessings upon them. They had eight children, two of whom remained in the world where they died Christian deaths. Three daughters consecrated themselves to God. One died when she was about to enter a community; the others became Sisters of Charity, one of whom was among the first Sisters sent on a mission to China in 1847. Three sons entered the Congregation of the Missions. John Gabriel who was martyred in China; Louis who died at sea on his way to the same country; and Jacques who survived his brothers.

John Gabriel Perboyre was born at Puech, parish of Mongesty, diocese of Cahors, in 1802, on January 6, the day on which the Magi, guided by a miraculous star, came from the East to Bethlehem to

House where Blessed John Gabriel Perboyre, Priest of the Congregation of the Mission, was Born, January 6, 1802.

adore the Infant Saviour and to offer Him in person the first fruits of the Gentiles. The star of God arose also for him on this day and faithfully conducted him in the straight path of wisdom and showed him the kingdom of God. He not only found Jesus in the crib, like the Magi, but found Him upon Calvary, where he had the happiness of dying for Him. The Feast of the Epiphany seems a fitting birthday for one destined for an apostolic career, to evangelize heathen nations and to shed his blood for Jesus Christ.

The next day, he was baptized and with the name John Gabriel, received the robe of innocence which it is believed, he preserved spotless until death. From his earliest years and during his whole life, he was crowned with graces, and the goodness of God was manifested in him by his constancy in the pursuit of perfection, and was especially displayed in the firmness with which he confessed the name of Jesus Christ among infidels and endured the most horrible tortures.

---

## II.

### HIS CHILDHOOD.

THE childhood of John Gabriel did not display the thoughtlessness of ordinary children. Piety seemed natural to him. Every one was edified at the eagerness with which he learned his prayers, and the fervent way he recited them on his knees, with his hands clasped. Nothing was more touching than to hear him pronounce the Holy Name of Jesus, whom he had already begun to imitate, and the name of Mary, whom he regarded always as his mother, and who had him under her special protection during his whole life. When but five years old, he was remarkable for his modesty and for a gravity far beyond his years. When his older sister committed some slight fault, he would reprove her gently and tell her she should not act so. He had a great horror of sin and was deeply grieved if any one said or did anything to offend God. He would not permit his sisters or nearest relations to fondle or embrace him; he could hardly bear these marks of affection even from his mother. It seemed as if he already understood the great privileges, as well as the delicacy of chastity, whose brightness the slightest breath can tarnish. As he had a pleasing countenance, his family loved to gaze upon the little angel and caress him, but it was painful for him to submit to these affectionate demonstrations. It is true that his father disapproved of such things and this alone was sufficient for him; but it was plain that John Gabriel himself firmly resisted anything of the kind. When his parents told him anything was wrong, they could rest assured that he would not do it again; for he would never intentionally commit the slightest fault.

This docility became a source of blessing to him and kept him from many dangers. So exactly did he practise obedience that he seemed never at fault. All his tasks were done in a way that pleased his parents, who could not but admire his perfect submission and the intelligence with which he did everything.

When he went to church he was noted for his modesty and piety. Everyone was struck with his recollection. He did not look around or talk to his companions. Those who saw his respectful posture could not help admiring him. Strangers visiting the church of Mongesty, were surprised: they invariably asked who the child was who prayed so fervently, and envied his parents the possession of such a treasure. No priest could have been more respectful: nothing could distract him or withdraw his attention from the presence of God. It mattered not what happened in church.—People used to say, you might walk over him and he would not heed it.

Like St. Vincent, he showed from his earliest years a great love for the poor. As soon as he saw a beggar at the door, he would appeal to his parents for him, saying: "There is a poor man in rags; we must give him food and clothes." He would himself go to get him an alms, and his face would then beam with happiness.

He was but six years old when he was given charge of a little flock of sheep, and he faithfully discharged this duty. Neither the bad weather, nor the animals straying away caused him the least ill humor or impatience.

At the age of eight, he was sent to school, and his master soon discovered his more than ordinary talent. In a few months, he had outstripped many of his companions older than himself. His teacher delighted in praising his sedateness, his application to study, the sweetness of his disposition and his gentle conduct toward his school-mates. When the teacher was obliged to leave the class, he put John Gabriel in charge; for he had observed that the precocious virtue of this child commanded the respect of the others. He went to school but six months in the year but this time was well employed. He arose early and if sometimes his mother forgot to awaken him he was much grieved. Always attentive and studious, he did not engage in games and foolish conversation in going and returning from school. On his return, he would offer to help his father, and if there was nothing for him to do, would go back to his books. Without being disagreeable or unkind, he was always sedate and reserved and never became familiar with any of the children. Though friendly with all his companions, he much preferred the society of the most pious of his school-mates.

When he went to school he began to attend the instructions in catechism. His pastor, like his schoolmaster, was delighted with his good conduct and ability. He admired this child, whom every one called little angel or little saint, which shows their opinion of his virtue. Listening to the word of God with earnest attention and readily understanding the explanations of the catechism, he was never at a loss for an answer when questioned; and when any one made a mistake, the pastor would ask the little doctor and his explanation was always correct. When the priest left the class, he asked John Gabriel to continue the questions, and on his return found everything quiet and in order. The catechist then modestly resumed his place and took no pride in the confidence bestowed upon him.

Every evening was employed in reading the lives of the saints, particularly St. Vincent's, and other books of piety. He taught catechism to his brothers and sisters and the other children of the neighborhood who came to be instructed by him. All admired how aptly and modestly he explained to his companions the instructions he had heard. One of his sisters being slow to learn, he redoubled his care and patience and gave more time to her than to the others. Sundays, on his return from church, those who could not assist at the sermon asked him to give them an account of it. He complied with their request with such ease and unction that he might have been taken for a divine. One day his father, astonished at the way he spoke of the things of God, said, smiling, "Since you preach so well you should be a priest." The child lowered his eyes and burst into tears.

The pastor of Mongesty, who saw the piety and zeal of John Gabriel, admired in silence the virtues which shone in the holy child, but was particularly struck with his great devotion to the Blessed Sacrament of the Altar. When he was in church, he would remain sometimes half an hour with his eyes lovingly fixed upon the tabernacle. Already, he understood the great love of Jesus Christ for men, and his heart, penetrated with gratitude, wished to respond to the love of his good Master. For this reason, his venerable pastor decided to set aside the prescribed rule in regard to First Holy Communion. The custom was not to allow children to make First Holy Communion until they were fourteen or fifteen and, sometimes, even sixteen years old. Although John Gabriel had not attained his eleventh year, he was allowed to make his First Holy Communion and no one complained, for all considered him worthy of the favor.

Great was his joy when he heard the good news.

He thanked God for so great a grace and reflected earnestly upon the advice his pastor gave to prepare him for the reception of the Holy Eucharist.

The good priest, for his part, neglected nothing to assist the operations of the Holy Spirit in this young heart: he saw his words fall on soil well prepared to produce a hundredfold. He noted the purity of his conscience, his earnestness in going to confession and his progress in the practice of virtue.

Upon the eve of his First Holy Communion, before retiring to rest, he went to his parents and, prostrating himself at their feet, with his face bathed in tears and his hands clasped, he asked them to pardon him any trouble he had caused them. It was difficult for them to give him what he asked, for they could not remember ever having found him at fault: they could hardly restrain their tears when they saw humbly kneeling before them, their son whom they regarded not as an ordinary child but as a little angel that had been confided to them.

After his First Holy Communion, young Gabriel hastened to join the confraternity of the Blessed Sacrament, established in his parish, and he fulfilled its obligations with fervor and punctuality. He often approached the sacred tribunal of penance, and it is needless to add that he had the holiest dispositions; he received Holy Communion with great fervor every month and on all great Feasts. On Sundays, he assisted regularly at the recitation of the rosary in the parish church and never neglected to attend any of the services. His happiness was to pass this holy day in prayer at church. or in pious reading at home.

His constancy in the path of perfection never varied.

Church of Mongesty, Diocese of Cahors, in which Blessed John Gabriel was Baptized and received First Holy Communion.

The missionary charged with collecting the account of his early years asked his parents if at certain times, they did not notice that he was more diligent at prayer, more fervent in the service of God and more exact in the performance of his duties than at other times: they replied that they had not. "If he had not been so uniformly good," said they, "we should have found him better at certain times; but he always left us nothing to desire." His were not fleeting transports of piety, or momentary outbursts of fervor which show an inconstant mind. He advanced with even pace, profiting by every grace; and his perfection continued to increase as God communicated to him new lights. Though nothing singular or extraordinary was remarked in him, yet, to observing people, his constancy and progress in virtue were astonishing in a child.

During the summer, he remained at home to help his father with the work in the fields, and his industry was indefatigable. He was made overseer of the workmen, an office which caused him much annoyance at first. The workmen often blasphemed the Holy Name of God, spoke against religion and used improper words. John Gabriel's heart was torn with grief; he confided his troubles to his father, telling him what the men said and how much such things pained him. "Well," said his father, "you must tell them it is wrong and that they must not do it." "I dare not," replied the child, "I am too young." Later, he acted on his father's advice and his firmness and modesty made the workmen more careful in their speech.

As to himself, he never allowed the least improper expression to escape his lips, never used even a light word in conversation, and had a decided repugnance for everything that savored of lying or artifice. Kind and pleasant to all, he had great affection for his brothers and sisters, and was always ready to do them any service. He devoted himself to them with a sincere and tender affection, strove to withdraw them from evil and bring them to good. His advice to his brothers and sisters was given with such discretion and affection that it was always well received. This caused his father to say, "Death may overtake me when it shall please God. My children will not be orphans; John Gabriel will be a father to them."

If, on the one hand, his parents admired his prudence and wisdom, on the other, they were no less flattered to hear what others said of him. Every one spoke of him with praise and congratulations; the people of Mongesty proposed him as a model to their children and regarded him with a veneration which always increased the better they knew him. Well could they apply to him what was said of St. John the Baptist: "What a one, think ye, shall this child be?" *Quis putas puer iste erit?* (Luke i, 66.)

---

## III.

### JOHN GABRIEL AT THE PREPARATORY SEMINARY OF MONTAUBAN.

JOHN GABRIEL had a younger brother named Louis. Every one was edified by his piety, and his parents saw with pleasure that he followed in his elder brother's footsteps. Louis manifested a desire to enter the ecclesiastical state and his father sent him to M. Jacques Perboyre, his uncle, superior of the preparatory seminary at Montauban. But, as Louis was delicate and extremely timid, John Gabriel was sent with him to help him to become accustomed to this new kind of life. Besides, it was thought a short sojourn at Montauban would help John Gabriel to acquire the knowledge suited to his condition. They did not intend him to learn Latin, for he had never expressed any such desire; they thought he would be obliged to remain at home with his parents to whom he would be a support in their old age. The two brothers now left the paternal roof for the first time. It was a sad, tearful day for the family, but they consoled themselves with the thought that John Gabriel would not be long absent. They were deceived: God had His designs upon this child who did not return to Mongesty for some years.

John Gabriel was then in his fifteenth year. He came to Montauban with Louis, and M. Perboyre, at the first sight of his nephews, whose good qualities charmed him, resolved to keep them both. As this worthy superior was the instrument which Providence used to train them in ecclesiastical virtue, permit us to give some short details of his life. M. Jacques Perboyre was born April 10, 1763, and when very young was received into the Congregation of the Missions. Remarkable to relate, he, at first, desired to preach the faith in China, but the revolution of '93 hindered the execution of his design. This privilege was reserved for his nephews. While only a deacon, he was made professor in the seminary of Montauban and was soon raised to the priesthood. Afterward, he was sent to the seminary at Alby, where he remained until July, 1791, when political troubles forced him to leave the institution. He returned to his family, but was soon obliged to hide, to escape the fury of the enemies of religion. The damp cave which served as a refuge for the holy missionary and where he contracted severe maladies, may still be seen. Sometimes, he left his retreat to sustain the courage of the other priests, who, like himself, were every day exposed to great privations and still greater dangers. With the help of a disguise, he exercised during the night the duties of his holy ministry and well-nigh perished a victim of his holy zeal.

The Congregation not being re-established at the restoration of religion, he was appointed by the Bishop of Cahors, pastor of a district where the priest received a salary. The missionary whose disinterestedness was as great as his fervor, represented that it would be better to confide this post to an ecclesiastic whose age and infirmities made it necessary for him to receive government aid. Being young and able to work, he could take charge of a parish which others might accept with repugnance. Upon this, they made him pastor of Valaire, one of the poorest villages of the diocese. Here he faithfully fulfilled the duties of a good shepherd. The character of the parish soon changed; little by little, disorders disappeared and gave place to the practice of Christian virtues; soon, prejudices against religion vanished; thanks to his patience, gentleness and disinterestedness, he at last completely gained the confidence of his flock; the alms that came to him from all directions permitted him to help the poor, for whom he had always a paternal affection.

The zeal which animated Jacques Perboyre had not sufficient scope in this parish, so he left it and returned to Montauban where he had been sent before the revolution. Interested in the welfare of this diocese, he opened a school to prepare young men for the priesthood. In this work he was assisted by two other priests noted for their zeal and piety. This undertaking presented grave difficulties; for he and his assistants found themselves deprived of all human resources; but Providence, on whom they relied, did not fail them. After their many trials, Our Lord blessed the pious undertaking; the number of pupils increased so much that he was obliged to procure a larger building. He wished to obtain the old monastery of the discalced Carmelites, but lacked the necessary funds. Nevertheless, putting his confidence in Him Who is never invoked in vain, he installed himself in the new house which was soon filled, though much larger than the one he left. The pupils always felt for M. Jacques Perboyre the greatest affection and deepest gratitude. Their affection was well deserved, for he treated them with the kindness of a father. Those who applied for admission to the seminary were never refused on account of poverty, when possessed of good dispositions. His whole desire was to make himself useful to the church and to society. Being poor when he came to the Carmelite house, he was poor when he left it. Consequently, the Bishop of Montauban, who honored him with his confidence, begged him to accept a canonry, which he did with the permission of his superiors. His last years were a succession of sickness and cruel sufferings, which he bore with extraordinary courage. Death did not take him by surprise, for he often thought upon it; and, for more than twenty years, he slept every night in a coffin. He saw the approach of his last hour not only with calmness, but even with joy. His life had not been sterile; he left in the diocese of Montauban a great many priests whom he had trained; but what contributed most to the happiness he enjoyed at this supreme moment, was the thought that he died poor. He was regretted by all who knew and appreciated his merit. His death occurred March 8, 1848.

After doing homage to the missionary whose memory has long been venerated, we return to John Gabriel. As he seemed destined to remain in the world, he wished to acquire only the knowledge suitable to his future position. He studied grammar and arithmetic and the rudiments of geometry. The first letter he wrote his parents has been preserved and we produce it here, because it shows the affectionate candor of the child.

"May 9, 1817.

*My Dear Father,*—It has been a long time since I have heard from you. I long to know if you all enjoy good health. I wished to write to you, but as I have never either read or written a letter, I dared not take up a pen. It is but right, my very dear father, that you should have the first fruits of my knowledge. You will see that I am not yet very learned, though I have applied myself as much as possible. My brother is very well; we have not had the slightest ailment.

We need clothes; have the kindness to write me word if you wish my uncle to buy us some. I embrace you. I also most tenderly embrace my dear mother, my brothers and sisters.

I am with much respect, etc."

John Gabriel did not lose a moment. When he had fulfilled his task, he employed his time in copying books; but chose, through preference, edifying books and in these, the passages best suited to nourish and increase piety. His progress was rapid and shortly after writing the letter we have just read, it was thought he was sufficiently educated and that he should not remain longer at the seminary; so his father was requested to send for him.

This news filled the place with sadness, for they already appreciated his talents and virtues. The professors thought it would be a pity to let a child leave the seminary who possessed dispositions so rare. They said he must be let stay and pursue his studies. His uncle desired it as much as they did, but he thought that his parents would not consent to part with a child so dear to them. His father having arrived meanwhile, the professors informed him that it was their opinion that his son was not intended for farm work, that his talents and virtues made them think God had other designs upon him. Influenced by these views the father asked his son if he wished to study Latin. The boy said that if he would leave him a short time at the seminary he would examine before God what state he must choose. Having obtained permission to remain, young Gabriel implored the light of the Holy Spirit and discerned that Our

Lord called him to the ecclesiastical state. He told his desire to his uncle who was eager to aid the designs of Providence. A few days after, John Gabriel wrote to his father to obtain his final consent. The letter shows with what care he sought to learn the will of God, what he did to know it and how pure his motives were.

"June 16, 1817.

*My Dear Father,*—Since your departure I have reflected upon your proposition about studying Latin. I have consulted God upon the state I must embrace to be most certain of going to heaven. After many prayers, I believe that our Lord wills I should enter the ecclesiastical state. Consequently, I have begun to study Latin, intending to abandon it, if you do not approve. I know you need the little help I could give you; my only regret is that I can not assist you in your great labors, but if the good God has called me to the ecclesiastical state, I can not take any other road to eternal happiness. I shall continue what I have begun till I hear from you. If you agree to my continuing my studies, I shall have to order new clothes. You will be so kind as to send me the money to buy them. I think that uncle's purse is not sufficiently well stocked to permit him to advance me the money. I embrace you all, particularly my dear mother. I am, etc."

His father having received this letter, resigned himself to the Will of God which was so clearly manifested. He answered John Gabriel that, since God called him to His service, not only he would not oppose it, but that he was disposed to make every possible sacrifice to help him to follow the course that Providence had shown him.

---

## IV.

### PROGRESS AND VIRTUES OF JOHN GABRIEL AT THE SEMINARY.

JOHN GABRIEL was fifteen years of age when he began to study Latin. At first, he was given a special professor under whom he made great progress. He had been, at Puech, the model of childhood; at the seminary, he was the model youth and scholar. His masters never observed the slightest disobedience in him. The exactness with which he fulfilled every point of the rule was not through habit, but from a spirit of faith and the desire to please God. Masters and pupils watched him well and could never find any fault in him. Often his schoolmates tried to make him speak during silence time; it was pains lost, for he would only give them a smile. Sometimes, he would say to them kindly, "Don't you know talking is forbidden?" He had so great a fear of displeasing God that he would have endured the greatest injuries rather than offend Him.

He watched affectionately over his brother Louis, whom his parents had confided to him. It was a saint rearing a saint, a martyr forming a confessor. They were united by the same tastes, the same inclinations, still more than by the ties of nature. Aided by such a guide, Louis soon made great progress in knowledge and piety. John Gabriel exercised his influence upon several of his cousins who were then at the seminary and whom his uncle had placed under his care. How often a sign or the glance of a friend cast by stealth has checked the thoughtless pranks so natural at this age.

In his intercourse with the other pupils, he was always friendly, full of kindness, and ready to do them any service. However, he never joined in the sports when they were at all boisterous. "Never," said his professors, "have I observed the slightest levity in him or the least dissipation." He knew how to combine the maturity of age and the charms of childhood. His piety had nothing sad or morbid about it, every one liked to talk to him for his conversation possessed an irresistible attraction. If sometimes a schoolmate made himself disagreeable, he showed no ill humor but spoke to him with as much affability as if he had done nothing to him. His patience was often put to rude proof which served only to show how solidly he was established in charity. One of his classmates several times tried to wear out his patience pushing him and pinching him till the blood flowed to make him speak, and to draw from him some angry expression, but John Gabriel answered only with an affectionate and conciliating smile, which seemed to implore his neighbor to let him listen to the lesson. "What admirable patience!" said his persecutor afterward, "I doubt if his sufferings among the Chinese cost him more." The tricks they played upon him proceeded more from mischievousness than from malice, for they loved him sincerely; it would have been difficult to dislike a companion who was so good and obliging to everybody. Never did he find fault with any of them or use the least word that could wound or displease. No pupil ever made the slightest complaint against him. He endured every trial, forgot everything except the services done him. His uncle, under whose care he developed these good qualities, sometimes sent him in the refectory some delicacy that the other pupils did not have ; but this distressed John Gabriel, who would either refuse it or share it with his neighbors.

From his entrance into the seminary, his virtues gained him the esteem of every one and he was dispensed from the many trials to which new comers are generally subjected. He was called little Aloysius Gonzaga, or little saint John; and very often the Holy Child, not only on account of his pleasing, innocent face, but especially because he practised the virtues of the Child Jesus. Having early learned that Jesus is the model of Christians, he endeavored to imitate Him with all possible fidelity. One day, some one complained to him that his bed was so uncomfortable that he could scarcely sleep. "Do you not think," said he, "Our Lord had a worse bed on the cross?" Another time, during vacation, he was told "You work too much and go to bed too late." "Our Lord has worked much more for us, and I have plenty of time for sleep."

His love for Our Lord was very affectionate. When he thought himself alone, he often cried out, "O my Jesus! O my divine Saviour!" words said by him with an unction that proved they came from a heart inflamed with love. After Jesus, Mary possessed all the affections of his soul; he had a truly filial tenderness for her. He was delighted to steal some moments from his studies to go and kneel at Mary's shrine. During vacation he was nearly always seen with the rosary in his hands. While at school, when not with his companions, he was sure to be found before the Blessed Sacrament or Mary's altar. Jesus in the Divine Eucharist had a particular charm for him; his sweetest moments were passed before the tabernacle; the fire which burnt in his soul shone in his face and animated it with an expression of happiness and love. His modesty in church and during divine service struck all beholders. He knelt as immovable as a statue with his eyes fixed on his prayer-book or gazing at the holy tabernacle. When he served Mass his fervor excited the celebrant's devotion; priests thought themselves happy to have him perform this office for them. When he received Holy Communion, people said that Our Lord was not hidden in the sacred species to him; that the veil which hides Him from us, was torn away and that he contemplated his Saviour in His human form. Then would his face express faith, peace, joy, gratitude and piety. During his thanksgiving, he seemed all absorbed in God; his soul opened to the rays of divine justice, and received an abundance of celestial favors. He communicated every Sunday and on all feasts; his happiest days were those on which he received Holy Communion, for he had a great hunger for this heavenly manna.

It will scarcely be believed, but it is well attested by those who knew and studied him at this age, that he had made such progress in the interior life that he always kept himself in the presence of God while engaged in exterior occupations. "It is said," remarked the Vicar general of Montauban, who was his class-mate, "that he had the gift of a double nature, one absorbed in study, the other absorbed in God. This was always the case, whether he was in class, at study, or in recreation."

This holy youth could not relish the frivolities of childhood, and, without condemning, took no part in them, except to be accommodating; the only pleasure he found in them was in mortifying himself and obliging others. He seemed to have no attraction but for God and all his happiness was to converse with Him. During the optional recreations, he walked about alone with a book in his hand, or he would converse on useful and edifying subjects with his companions. It was astonishing to see him so recollected in such a crowd of giddy, restless boys. Nevertheless, there was nothing melancholy or fault-finding about him.

It is not surprising that prayer was his delight. While still young, he had understood its necessity and advantages. Though he had a singular love for work, the exercises of religion were his first attraction. During the vacations which he passed at Montauban, he went out but little and nearly always with his uncle. Generally, when not employed at study, he was occupied with prayer and pious reading.

He loved to meditate; and, when asked to give an account of his prayer, he did it briefly and with charming simplicity. He possessed a special talent in choosing resolutions, not general and vague, but practical and drawn from the subject.

If he entered the study-hall after the others were assembled, which only happened when his masters detained him elsewhere, he began by imploring the light of the Holy Spirit; he knelt upon the floor and not upon the bench, as was often the custom of the pupils: he said his prayers with a recollection which edified every one. The sign of the cross, which many of the students made through routine and with careless haste, was for him a deeply religious act, which showed the faith and respect which animated him: this piety was evinced everywhere—in church, in class, at study.

His conduct was so well regulated that the slightest failing could not be discovered in him, and even the most severe were constrained to do him homage. "If I had not known that he was a child of Adam," said one who was a long time with him, "I would have thought that he had never sinned, because there never was anything reprehensible about him." According to the testimony of one of his schoolmates, his life was so perfect that if they consulted all the pupils one after the other, not one of them could have remarked the least imperfection. "Name the virtues," said one of his professors who had closely observed him for many years, "he had them all; name the defects—I never found any in him; he went to confession very often but I do not know of what he could have accused himself."

His progress in science corresponded to his advance in piety; though he passed rapidly from one class to another and nearly always had the first place and the first prize, no one was jealous of his success. but did justice to his merit. This superiority in talent would have become for others a cause of self-love, but not for him; he regarded himself as the last of all, never presumed upon the confidence of his masters or the respect of his companions, but sought to efface himself and to hide himself in God.

As to his mortification, every one who knew him in his youth, said that he watched so carefully over his tongue that he was never heard to utter an improper word. Wherever he was, he always walked with his eyes cast down. His uncle had a servant who mended the linen and who had a sort of authority over the nephews. When they were sick she took care of them like a mother. One day, observing John Gabriel's attitude, she said to him sharply: "Lift up your head, now, and look at me." The child, as if he did not hear her, kept his eyes fixed on the ground. "I do not remember," she used to say, "that he ever disobeyed me in anything but this." He imposed upon himself the pious practice of fasting on Fridays and Saturdays to unite himself to Our Lord's sufferings and to honor the Blessed Virgin, his dear Mother. During the most severe winters, while the other pupils would press around the fire, he stood apart engaged in study, enduring the cold with patience, rejoicing at having something to offer to God. He was never exacting to the servants and showed much gratitude when they did him a favor. During vacation, when he walked in the garden, he never touched a fruit or smelt a flower. He was continually occupied with prayer, reading or meditation.

His reading always had a serious aim, to sanctify his soul and to acquire the means of working one day with success to procure the glory of God and the salvation of his neighbor. By this wise course, he avoided the dangers so common in colleges: and, far from losing any of his piety or fervor, he continually increased it.

From his earliest years, he was noted for his great compassion for the poor and this disposition developed as he advanced in age. Often, at breakfast or luncheon, when he received his piece of bread, he would steal out of sight of his companions and either give the bread to the beggars at the door, or put it in the basket for the poor. The servants who often saw this charitable act, would say to him: "To-day you have not breakfasted, and now you have deprived yourself of your luncheon to give it to the poor." Then, he would blush to find himself discovered and answer modestly: "Pardon me, but I never make a better breakfast or luncheon than when I give my share to the poor who are in so great need. Besides, I have no great merit in this, because I can easily do without it."

John Gabriel distinguished himself no less in philosophy than in the preceding classes, for he possessed correct judgment, and quickness of perception. When he learned metaphysics, he fathomed the most abstract subjects with a penetration which astonished his professors. While he was making his course of philosophy, his uncle sent away a teacher who was rough with the boys. To replace him, he selected John Gabriel, who willingly took charge of the class. The pupils loved their new teacher, who always treated them with kindness. Thirty years afterward, they could not speak of him without tears. As an instance of the veneration they had for him and for anything that belonged to him: one of his pupils to whom he gave a certificate of good conduct had it framed, wishing, he said, to preserve it as a relic of his master whom he regarded as a saint.

We shall end this chapter by a letter from M. Thyies who was his professor during the greater part of his studies. It is written to his uncle, M. Perboyre.

"*Rev. and Venerable Friend*,—You ask me to give you all the details I can remember of your illustrious nephew, John Gabriel Perboyre, while at the seminary at Montauban. It is a great pleasure for me to accede to your request and to return to the most peaceful time of my life, where the kind, pleasant face of this dear child has left an unfading memory. I will pass a pleasant half hour in talking with you about him.

"If I remember aright, when he first came to the seminary it was not to stay, but only to accompany Louis, who came here to school. John Gabriel, himself, was soon to return to the paternal roof. I can see him now; fair, fresh and rosy, with bright, intelligent eyes. He walked along the enclosure during recreation beside Louis, not at all affrighted at the strange faces and sights that met his gaze. This child charmed us all; we desired to have him go through the course of study. You objected at first; you said one of the sons ought to be left to cultivate his father's vineyards. You were right: they were both to cultivate no other vineyard than the vineyard of Our Lord. You consented, and John Gabriel soon had a Latin grammar. He showed the happiest dispositions and, in a few months, learned the rudiments of the Roman tongue. When vacation came, you wished me to give him special care. I worked upon good soil and he made rapid progress. What an ardor he had for study! How attentive he was, when I explained anything difficult to him! A fault once pointed out, never appeared again. As he was devoted to his teachers, they, too, were attached to him. I shall never forget the look of gratitude he used to give me when, examining him on what he had learned during the week, I made him understand that he had made real progress. The amiable child wished to attribute this improvement to me, but it was really due to his zeal and talents.

"At the close of vacation, about six months after he began his studies, he entered the fifth class; and, at the first examination, obtained the second place in class and, soon after, the first, which he always retained. At Easter, he passed to the fourth class, where he had the same success.

"When vacation came again, John Gabriel returned to my care. We resumed our lessons with pleasure. I was so well satisfied with my pupil that I would not give him up to any one. When school opened again in November, he went into the second class where I taught; then to rhetoric, where I again had charge. Here, he had to compete with students who to-day are not the least distinguished in our diocese. He came forth from the struggle with honor. His class-mates loudly applauded him at the distribution of prizes—they loved him so much. I must say more, they had a veneration for him and gave him no other name than that of the Holy Child. Sometimes in class, his neighbor would tease him to see if he could not be distracted. He would reply only by a half smile and a sweet, imploring glance and return to his lesson. Why a smile and a beseeching look instead of a rebuff? Because he wished to disarm his mischievous neighbor wounding his feelings. There is, in souls intimately united to God, a delicacy of charity which they feel without understanding. This kindness made his companion return to his duty, and his teacher, who quietly observed this manœuvre, did not interfere.

"This is all I can recall of these years, so pleasant to me. John Gabriel was a model of piety and application to all his school-fellows. While devoting himself to his studies and the practice of virtue, he cherished a design which he communicated to me when I first taught him. Just after hearing a sermon by the Abbé de Chiezes, who gave that most fruitful mission in 1817, he said to you: 'I wish to be a missionary.' You laughed at his desire; do you laugh now? Oh! no; you weep with love and admiration. He has been a missionary; he has been still more—a glorious, generous martyr! I remember that, at the end of his course of rhetoric, at the public exercises just before the distribution of prizes, he read an essay he had written during the year. It was full of strength and fire and was entitled, 'The Cross, the Most Beautiful Emblem.' Some time ago, in looking over a bundle of old papers I came across it and read it over. I put it on file again with some others. I shall look for it and show it to you. In one part he said: 'Ah! what is more beautiful than this cross, planted amid heathen nations and often watered by the blood of the apostles of Jesus Christ?' He did not know that he would one day give the cross this divine beauty, and that we, his friends, would thrill with joy and pride at the thought that we had known and loved this martyred missionary."

---

## V.

### BLESSED JOHN GABRIEL IN THE NOVITIATE.

In the Congregation of the Missions founded by St. Vincent de Paul, the interior seminary is the name given the time of trial which all must undergo before they can be admitted. Shortly after John Gabriel's arrival in Montauban, he felt himself interiorly urged to enter the Congregation of the Lazarists, as they are usually called, and to go to preach the faith to the heathens in China. However, fearing to deceive himself, he prayed fervently to God, the better to learn his will, and made a novena in honor of St. Francis Xavier. Scarcely had he finished it, when he felt that his prayer was heard. God made him understand that he would one day go to announce the faith to the idolators of China. He hastened to speak to his uncle, who then attached but little importance to his desire, but after years proved that this was no vain dream. John Gabriel persevered in his resolution of entering the Congregation of the Mission; the superiors admitted him and he began his novitiate at Montauban, December, 1818.

He passed through this probation with all the perfection that might be expected from a young man who gave so many proofs of consummate virtue. Yet, it must be said that he made his apprenticeship to the religious life at a most unfavorable time, and it might have compromised a vocation less firm than his. The director to whom he was entrusted, though very virtuous, was little suited to his office, which was only given him by circumstances, as they had not yet fully organized the novitiate at the mother-house of the Lazarists in Paris. The Congregation, victim of the outbreaks of violence during the revolution, had scarcely arisen from its ruins. Besides, Blessed Perboyre taught a class of younger pupils and, at the same time, went to class himself, because he had not finished his studies. All these difficulties did not prevent his making his novitiate with such perfection that he is proposed as a model of all novices.

Our saintly youth had a companion who intended to embrace the same state, but who withdrew afterwards, thinking that God had not called him to be ecclesiastic. It is to his kindness that we are indebted for the following details, given in response to a request for his recollections of our martyr. "It is with a sweet satisfaction, dear sir, that I give you the desired information about John Gabriel Perboyre. I have jealously cherished his memory in my heart. I can not think of him without recalling the virtues of which he gave so lovely an example. It would be easy to write, without my aid, the history of his novitiate. You would have only to picture to yourself the ideal of the perfection of a novice; then, apply to John Gabriel all that you have imagined most perfect: you can be assured that it will all be true of him.

"His obedience was so great that I think no one could carry self-renunciation further; he gave up his will entirely to his director. He observed the rules so exactly, that if St. Vincent himself, who made the constitutions, had been on earth he could not have practised them with more scrupulous exactness. At dawn of day, at the first, stroke of the clock, he started from his bed with admirable promptness; at the first sound of the bell for any exercise, he left everything to go to the place where he was called by the will of God. One day I said to him: 'I am sure that in imitation of those religious of whom Cassian speaks, you leave a letter half formed when the bell rings.' 'Well,' he answered, 'what is there astonishing in that? We only do our duty!' In fact, he never failed in this and I assure you I several times examined his work and frequently found an incomplete phrase, part of a word or an unfinished letter. As to the rule of silence, I cannot remember that he ever once spoke without necessity.

"You ask me if during retreats, we remarked anything special about him. The only thing I noticed at such times, was the long periods he spent upon his knees. I could not understand how he could kneel so long. His recollection was so great habitually, that it could not be more perfect during a retreat. His modesty was all that could be desired and wherever he was, his conduct was conformable to the rules laid down by the saints. Even when alone in his room, he allowed himself no liberty; this I could often observe, for every time I entered the room which I shared with him, I found him at prayer or studying in a respectful posture, entirely absorbed in the presence of God. The crucifix was always before him and he gazed on it with an expression of deep and loving devotion.

"As to his mortification, I have always been convinced that he never allowed any occasion of practising this virtue escape him, thus depriving himself of a satisfaction, overcoming some repugnance, or renouncing his will and inclinations. I do not remember seeing him take breakfast once the whole time I was with him. Sensuality had no part in his repasts. When he helped himself, he skilfully took whatever was least agreeable. If any food was not palatable, far from seeming displeased, he was delighted. He ate only through necessity, without observing what he took; or, if he did observe, it was only to practise some mortification. Sometimes, his uncle or director would take us and the other students to a religious celebration in some convent, and if after the ceremony, they offered, as was customary, some refreshment to those who had taken part, John Gabriel did not even look at the delicacies; and to their urging would respond with a modest, polite refusal.

"He carefully guarded his eyes, and walked always with them modestly cast down. One day during a walk I said to him: 'I do not understand why you deprive yourself of the pleasure you would enjoy in contemplating the beauties of nature. Do you think it would be a sin to raise your eyes? What harm would it be to look at a meadow decked with flowers, to admire such marvels of the power and wisdom of the Creator?' He answered, 'I agree with you and, far from thinking it wrong, I believe the sight of such marvels can contribute to the elevation of our soul to God, if we consider them with a spirit of faith, after the example of the prophets and saints who from them took occasion to bless Him who created them.' Thus, he did not blame those who considered the works of God; but he deprived himself of this innocent pleasure so that he could offer Him some act of mortification. Besides, he had no need to seek God in creatures, because, like St. Augustine, he had found Him in his own heart.

"It might be thought, perhaps, from what has just been said of his modesty and recollection, that his virtue was stiff and severe. Not at all; he was gay and very agreeable in recreation; he took very well the jokes I sometimes played upon him. His conversation was never frivolous; it was solid and, above all, pious. He was well informed for one of his age. When I met with any difficulty in the study of the scriptures, especially of the psalms, I consulted him rather than any one else, because his answers were more satisfactory. His kindness to me was admirable: when I felt sad and disheartened, he would console and encourage me; he would remind me of the tribulations which God sends His saints, and he would say, 'We should be happy at not having to suffer greater trials.' Contempt and humiliations were precious gems to him: it sufficed to have injured him to receive from him some testimony of cordiality or affection. There is one occasion I can never forget. I told him one day of an action I did in a moment of gaiety, which was against the rule. He told me respectfully, but with frankness, that I had done wrong. A little piqued at this response, I said curtly, 'Do you think every one has a virtuous disposition like you?' My remark was wounding, but I saw that his face did not even flush. He was no less calm and smiling than if I had paid him a compliment. I felt that I had done him an injustice, for he was of a lively temperament and I knew that if nature seemed to have so little empire over him, it was owing only to his vigilance, to his efforts, and to the numerous victories he had obtained over himself; so I hastened to apologize. The same day he proved to me that he had entirely forgotten my words. Having used my knife carelessly in cutting my quill pen, I made a deep cut in my hand; the pain made me cry out; he hastened to me, showed much sympathy and dressed my wound with the tenderness of a mother.

"No one could see and know him without thinking: 'There is a pure soul that a breath of evil has never touched.' The love of God was the only motive of what he did; each of his actions was an act of virtue. His heart turned as naturally towards God as the sunflower turns to the sun. Upon one occasion he said to me; 'To conceive a great sorrow for sin, I do not see that it is necessary to meditate on the chastisements which are reserved for it. If we think of the love God bears us and the pain that sin caused Him—this thought will be sufficient to give us a great horror of sin.' He made everything an occasion to raise himself to heavenly things, as the following fact will show. One day I heard a hand organ whose music delighted me. When he saw the pleasure it gave me he said, 'If the music of earth gives us such satisfaction, what joy will we not feel when we hear that of heaven!'

"I never saw any book in his hands that would not increase his spirit of recollection and piety. St. John Climacus, St. Bonaventure, St. Bernard and St. Teresa were the authors on whom he feasted. He read the lives of the saints with great pleasure, but his delight was in the holy Gospels and the Epistles of St. Paul, which he learned by heart. The life and writings of St. Vincent were also very familiar to him.

"During the whole time I lived with him, he was constantly my wonder and admiration. I observed him well, even spied upon him, and I could never find anything reprehensible. I felt somewhat aggrieved at seeing him so perfect. I will confess that several times I put him to the test, but he always was invulnerable. I do not think it possible for a novice to be nearer perfection."

---

## VI.

### JOHN GABRIEL'S VOWS.—HIS DEPARTURE FOR PARIS.

THE days of the novitiate passed and the pious seminarian silently grew in fervor and the practice of virtue. To prepare himself for the life of a missionary, he studied to form in himself the spirit of Our Lord and of St. Vincent de Paul. At last, the much desired time of holy vows came: he prepared for it by a scrupulous fidelity to all the obligations they imposed; obedience had become natural to him—chastity had always been much loved by him—poverty was his greatest delight; he felt himself inflamed with the desire of devoting himself to the salvation of the heathens.

On December 28, 1820, his wishes were fulfilled when he took the four vows of the Congregation of the Mission. It would be difficult to express the happiness he felt. This is the day on which the church celebrates the memory of the Holy Innocents; he too, presented to God a victim pure and spotless, being but a prelude of the holocaust he would afterward offer Him in China. The day of his holy vows was always as dear to him as the day of his baptism.

After entering the Congregation of the Missions, he was sent to Paris to begin his theological studies. Before his departure, he had to make some necessary visits. Everywhere he went with his uncle, he excited admiration by his piety and modesty; he sought to hide his virtue, but a perfume of sanctity was exhaled from his person, which baffled his humility. When he left a house those who had seen him said, "Oh what a holy young man! His modesty is ravishing." Though this was many years ago, the remembrance of his virtues is preserved to this day.

The act of humility which he performed when he presented himself at the city hall to obtain a passport, must not be forgotten. When the secretary asked him what was his father's employment, he replied that he worked in the fields; an answer which made the secretary suppose he meant a field hand, working on other peoples' lands. M. Thyies, his former teacher, who accompanied him, said: "Tell him that your father is a proprietor and works in no fields but his own." All those at the office were edified at hearing this; his modesty had already made a great impression on them; his humility gave them a high idea of his virtue. Upon their return to the seminary, M. Thyies hastened to relate to the other professors what had occurred at the city hall. They were not astonished, as they were accustomed to find in dear John Gabriel frequent examples of humility.

His virtue and perfect detachment were shown still more at the time of his departure. He loved all his relations, but he had an especial affection for his parents. Though he desired to see them before leaving, he thought it would be better to sacrifice to God this very leg timate pleasure. To his uncle's proposition to go to see his family, he replied, "St. Vincent went but once to visit his relations and he regretted it; if you will permit me I will offer to God this sacrifice." His uncle, not wishing to hinder an action which excited his admiration, let him do as he pleased. It was but a short trip, for John Gabriel, in going to Paris had to pass through Cahors, and from Cahors to Puech was but three or four hours' journey.

This sacrifice was the more agreeable to God as it cost more to the heart that made it. He was, in fact, deeply sensitive; the least services rendered to him excited the deepest gratitude, and he hastened to show it by his words and manner, as the servants at the seminary often noticed; they loved to serve him. He said to the person who fixed his clothes for the journey: "Really, I know not how to thank you for all you have done for me and my uncle. I can give you nothing, because I have nothing; be assured I will not cease to pray to the good God for you, that He may recompense you for all your kind services."

He was poor; he had an especial affection for poverty and desired to practice it in all its extent. When they wished to make him new clothes for his journey, he consented to it with repugnance. "Our Lord was poor," said he, "St. Vincent recommends poverty to us and practised it himself with much perfection; all my desire is to be poor like them." When packing his trunk, it seemed to him that more things were put in than were needed, and he complained of it. "What is the good of so many things which I do not need? In entering the community I embraced poverty; is it not just that I should practise it?" The only answer was that his uncle had ordered it. Then he submitted, stifling his inward repugnance. Noticing that they put in the trunk a small purse containing some money, he felt still greater pain. "What do you wish me to do with this money?" he cried, "are you not afraid of drawing down upon me the malediction of God?" "Your uncle has ordered it," was always the reply. He would have been glad to start without provisions or resources, so as to practise more perfectly the poverty of Jesus Christ.

At last, came the time to say farewell; a time of deep regret to his uncle and to all the professors, because the angel of piety who had edified them so much would leave among them a great void. He started, and, in a few hours, stopped at Cahors, where he passed two or three days. His uncle ordered him to stay with his confrères who had charge of the seminary in this town, and his parents came there to see him. The joy they felt in embracing this child of benediction, after so long an absence, was tempered by the thought that they saw him again only to part with him. In vain they urged him to pass some time with his family: he would not. When they showed him the road to Puech he said, "It is not the road to Heaven; to go *there* we must make sacrifices." Notwithstanding their generosity, his parents felt great sorrow. His heart was also touched, but, rising above the feelings of nature, he said to his mother, who did not wish to leave him an instant: "My good mother, we must accustom ourselves to giving up each other; you know that the good God has called me; we must begin to answer the call by parting." The time of separation having come, he embraced his parents and, mastering his emotion, he got into the stage coach without shedding a tear. He had already disappeared and his mother, still weeping, fixed her eyes on the carriage which tore from her, her beloved son.

---

## VII.

### JOHN GABRIEL PERBOYRE STUDYING AT PARIS.

THE presence of John. Gabriel at St. Lazare was like the box of perfume which Mary Magdalen poured upon the Saviour's feet at Bethania—the house was filled with the odor of his virtues. *Domus impleta est ex-odore unguenti*, (John xii., 3.) Every one was charmed with his piety and modesty.

He applied himself with much ardor and success to the study of ecclesiastical science. Not satisfying himself with the surface of things, he searched into all the subjects he had to study, and he understood them so well that he could explain them with precision and astonishing clearness. The Summa of St. Thomas was his favorite book and, at the end of his studies, the doctrine of the great doctor had become familiar to him. His only aim in studying was to please God and to acquire the knowledge necessary to make Him loved. He had a horror of vain glory, the spirit of contention and the desire of show or display.

The time of study, so dangerous to those just out of the novitiate, made him lose none of his fervor. He was not one of those ardent characters who, carried away by a desire to learn, are occupied only with their studies; their science becomes a fatal rock for their piety and ends by stopping the flight of a soul made only for God. Nor was he one of those, who, under the pretext that piety is useful for all things, neglect ecclesiastical science. He knew that a priest has need of both. St. Thomas was not only his teacher but his model, also; and, like him, he went often to the wounds of our crucified Saviour to obtain heavenly light and the ardent flames of charity.

The Angel of the schools once gave a young man counsels full of wisdom upon the way he should study. John Gabriel had read them and reproduced them so faithfully in his conduct that it seems we are but writing his life when we transcribe them.

"You ask me," said St. Thomas, "what is the true means of success in your studies and the sure way of obtaining wisdom. The counsel that I give you is not to occupy yourself at first with difficult questions, but to raise yourself to them by degrees. The knowledge which you acquire of the most simple truths will insensibly conduct you to the knowledge of the most profound. Do not hasten to say what you think, or to show what you have learned; speak little and never answer hastily. Fly from useless conversations; by them you lose time and the spirit of devotion, as well. Always preserve purity of conscience with great care; never do any thing that can sully it, or make you less pleasing to God. As to prayer, let it be continual. Love to be alone in order to give to prayer, reading and meditation all the time you would fruitlessly employ in conversation with creatures. You will be admitted to the secrets of the Spouse, if you know how to converse with Him in this retreat. Let not solitude make you crabbed or fretful; show yourself always sweet and affable, but without too much familiarity with any one, for familiarity is usually followed by contempt. Let each one attend to what belongs to him and do not disturb yourself about what is said or done in the world. It is of infinite importance to you to avoid traveling and useless visits. Call to mind the life and actions of the saints, walk in their footsteps as much as possible and humble yourself, if you can not attain to their perfection. Preserve always the remembrance of the good things you have learned and where you have learned them. Be not contented to receive superficially what you have heard or read, but try to understand and to fathom all its meaning. Never remain in doubt about what you can know with certainty. Labor with holy ardor to enrich your mind, store in an orderly manner, in the apartments of your memory, all the knowledge you can acquire; do not overtax the talents you have received from God; seek not to penetrate what is beyond you.

"If you follow exactly the counsels that I give you, doubt not that you will obtain according to your desire the possession of wisdom; your life will be filled with flowers and fruits. You will make the vineyard of Our Lord fruitful all the time you bear the yoke of Our Saviour."

Such was the rule of conduct St. Thomas gave to young students. Blessed Perboyre was careful to observe these rules well. He loved to relate some traits in the life of this great saint, but there was one occurrence which especially touched him and which he delighted to recall. It was when Jesus Christ said to the Angelic Doctor: "*You have written well of Me Thomas! What recompense do you wish?*" Every one knows the beautiful reply of the saint, "*Lord, I wish but Thee.*" An incident in regard to this is related by a worthy ecclesiastic who knew John Gabriel at Montdidier, shortly after finishing his studies.

"One day, having the honor of taking a walk with him we conversed a long time on grave and pious subjects; then the conversation turned upon St. Thomas, the Angelic Doctor. John Gabriel told me such touching things about him and his voice assumed so expressive a tone when he spoke the words of Our Lord Jesus Christ to St. Thomas when he had written his admirable works on the adorable sacrament of the Eucharist: *Recte locutus es de me, Thoma et de meo sacramento, quam me cedem accipies?* that the tears came to my eyes and I shall never forget it. I can see him now as he spoke those words, and it seems but yesterday."

Allow us to recount another anecdote which is still related of his sojourn at Montdidier; it shows how well he employed his time in Paris and in what spirit he studied. "The ecclesiastical conferences of the province of Montdidier were held at the college;" says an eye witness, "all the priests and professors took part in them. John Gabriel, though only a subdeacon, was invited to assist at one of them, and the subject of discussion was grace. After the orator had spoken, each person was allowed to make comments and correct errors, if any were observed. I remem-

4

ber that our young confrère, doing violence to his modesty and timidity, regardless of the impression he would make, asked permission of the president to submit some observations. He was heard with silence, mingled with respect and admiration, for his reasoning was just and true and his face and language expressed the uprightness of his soul. His speech was the gem of the conference and no one had anything more to say. The impression remained with each of us, not only that he was a theologian, but that he had had practical experience about grace, through his intimate relation with his divine Master; and that, consequently, this subject was extremely familiar to him. I remember, too, with what attention we listened to him when, during our recreations, we discussed theological subjects. He was often surnamed, in jest, Master of Sentences or little St. Thomas of Aquin, for every one saw that he was clever and learned in this science, which he seemed to love so much."

The same thing was observed about him while he studied theology, when he answered in class or proposed questions, or if, in recreation, the conversation was upon such subjects. His mind was solid and judicious, and it was evident, too, that piety ruled his work and that he spoke as a man who studied, not only to become learned, but still more to learn to know God and to love Him. He knew that it was only by prayer and humility that one could make useful progress in the sciences. This is why, when writing shortly afterward to his brother who was making his studies, he addressed him these truly remarkable words: "Try to avoid a rock which students in philosophy so often encounter; they grow accustomed to speak of God with an almost disrespectful freedom which insensibly weakens that religious feeling which the idea of the adorable Majesty should inspire: faith suffers and so does piety. Humility and prayer procure more knowledge of God than conceited reasoning. You must work in every way to grow more and more in this knowledge, and remember what the Apostle says: 'We cease not to pray for you, and to beg that you may be filled with the knowledge of His will, in all wisdom and spiritual understanding . . . . increasing in the knowledge of God.'" *Non cessamus pro vobis orantes et postulantes ut impleamini agnitione voluntatis ejus, in omni sapientia et intellectu spirituali—crescentes in scientias Dei.* (Col. i, 9.) John Gabriel knew how to avoid the dangers against which he warned his brother. His piety injured not his studies, nor did his work lessen his fervor. The more he learned to know God, the more he applied himself to love and serve Him. When he wrote to his parents, he never failed to give them wise counsels, either about the salvation of their own souls or their duties to their children. It will not be amiss to cite the following letter which he wrote his father at this time:

"*My Very Dear Father,*—No, you deceive yourselves; your memory is always present to my mind. I think of you every day and, indeed, of all my relations. I had thought of you, not half an hour before I received your letter. It filled me with joy. For sometime, I have intended writing to you and I admit that I have been too negligent.

"I have spoken to my uncle about my little brother Antoine. I think that it would not be wrong to send him here for a while to learn the first elements of divine and human knowledge; but, I implore you, my very dear father, to beware of inducing him by word, or in any other way, to enter the ecclesiastical state. for if he embrace this state without being called, especially if from human motives, he would commit a horrible sacrilege; and this would be for you and for him, the greatest misfortune. All that I desire is that he learn to live as a good Christian and not become so devoted to the things of earth as I was at fifteen. Though I am not ignorant of your care and vigilance to preserve in all your children purity of life, I tremble continually for his innocence, knowing that you are often obliged to lose sight of him and that he spends most of his time with the servants and workmen, whose mouths are full of improper and evil words, and you know better than I do, my very dear father, that these people are not so reserved in your absence as in your presence. I doubt not that you exhort them, from time to time, to fear God; and that you strongly reprimand them when you learn that they have offended Him.

"I embrace you and my dear mother,
and am for life, etc."

The pious student practised an unbounded obedience to those who held the place of God in his regard. His affection for all his confrères was so cordial that each regarded him as an intimate friend, sincere and devoted. Nevertheless, he had a great respect for all; nor did he ever permit any familiarity. He participated in the charity of Jesus Christ, his Divine Model. He shared equally in their joys and sorrows; when

acquitted himself with enlightened zeal of the duties that were confided to him, obtaining the most wonderful success.

"It was easy to see that he drew his science from its true source, the holy scripture. He had learned by heart the admirable Epistles of St. Paul to his well-beloved disciple; he took delight in them and regarded their precepts as if they had been written to himself.

"He was pious, yes, very pious; his piety was sweet, attractive, angelic. He was most edifying, especially during his frequent visits to the Blessed Sacrament and his thanksgiving after Holy Communion. During these precious moments, his face reflected the pure and holy joy of his soul. What then passed in his heart? He was like the seraphim; his soul felt all the emotions and raptures of those holy spirits.

"At the time our edifying confrère was sent to Montdidier, a retreat had just been given to the pupils. Fervor reigned among them. The little ones, always gay and happy, worked well; but they had not, like the older pupils, any special confraternity to maintain their piety, and to nourish and strengthen it. They desired to have an association with rules, feasts and privileges, so they chose the Sodality of the Holy Angels, whose director would be one of their teachers and whose prefect, one of themselves. It is needless to say who was the professor chosen by the unanimous vote. It was John Gabriel; the children thus gave themselves an angel to lead them under the banner of the Holy Angels.

"In complying with the desire of these young pupils, the new director felt a great responsibility. It is im-

exaggeration. Though there was nothing singular about him, there were no defects; the more you considered him, the more you would be astonished to find him perfect, everywhere and in all things."

---

## VIII.

### JOHN GABRIEL AT THE COLLEGE OF MONTDIDIER.

AFTER finishing his studies at Paris, John Gabriel was sent to the college of Montdidier. We limit ourselves to the documents which have been given us about this period of his life: "This holy young man was a sub-deacon when he came among us. His name, Gabriel, his face expressing frankness and modesty, his sweet, gracious smile, everything about him, prepossessed us in his favor; but that is saying too little; we were enchanted with him. We must not neglect to thank the superiors of the Congregation for the splendid missionary they sent us. What a blessing for a house to possess a professor whom every one regards as a saint!

"Our young confrère was not sent to us by his superiors for any special studies; this was left to the wisdom and discretion of the president of the college. Though his modesty made him careful to hide his talents, it did not prevent our discovering that he had made his studies with great credit and that he was well versed in literature. Always most submissive to his superiors, he awaited his task in the community-work with holy indifference. He accepted with equal pleasure a lower class or a course of philosophy; and acquitted himself with enlightened zeal of the duties that were confided to him, obtaining the most wonderful success.

"It was easy to see that he drew his science from its true source, the holy scripture. He had learned by heart the admirable Epistles of St. Paul to his well-beloved disciple; he took delight in them and regarded their precepts as if they had been written to himself.

"He was pious, yes, very pious; his piety was sweet, attractive, angelic. He was most edifying, especially during his frequent visits to the Blessed Sacrament and his thanksgiving after Holy Communion. During these precious moments, his face reflected the pure and holy joy of his soul. What then passed in his heart? He was like the seraphim; his soul felt all the emotions and raptures of those holy spirits.

"At the time our edifying confrère was sent to Montdidier, a retreat had just been given to the pupils. Fervor reigned among them. The little ones, always gay and happy, worked well; but they had not, like the older pupils, any special confraternity to maintain their piety, and to nourish and strengthen it. They desired to have an association with rules, feasts and privileges, so they chose the Sodality of the Holy Angels, whose director would be one of their teachers and whose prefect, one of themselves. It is needless to say who was the professor chosen by the unanimous vote. It was John Gabriel; the children thus gave themselves an angel to lead them under the banner of the Holy Angels.

"In complying with the desire of these young pupils, the new director felt a great responsibility. It is impossible to tell what success he had in implanting virtue in the young hearts God had committed to his care. He seemed the guardian angel of each child, and he really fulfilled that office. He did immense good among these little associates and gained among them as much merit before God as he received praise and admiration from men.

"I must now speak of his devotion to the Blessed Virgin. If it is true, as St. Bernard affirms, that devotion to Mary is a sign of predestination, all of us who were at college with him can, from what we know of our confrère, declare, without hesitation, his eternal happiness and proclaim him blessed. His room was a sort of sanctuary ornamented with statues and pictures, recalling to him the different titles under which the Mother of God is honored by the Church. As to the veneration he had for her, it was something more than devotion; it was a filial affection, a boundless confidence and an entire abandonment of himself to her care.

"A devotion so enlightened, so tender and persevering, could not fail to attract the love of her who was the object of it. We are certain that Mary had a special predilection for John Gabriel from his earliest years; that she watched over him with a maternal solicitude, obtained abundant graces for him from her Divine Son and guided his first steps in the path of virtue. The perfect fidelity with which he followed her guidance along the true way of happiness and glory, led him to a double triumph. Upon his forehead shine today and forever two beautiful crowns of immortality. Formerly, he called Mary his mother: now he honors her as his queen under her two most glorious titles, *Regina Martyrum, Regina Virginum.*

"Our young confrère's virtues were singularly augmented by his frankness, kindness and simplicity. His countenance delighted every one who saw him; there was an indefinable something about it that made us all love him; it was the reflection of divine grace, the outward expression of the beauty of his soul. In Blessed Perboyre, the soul predominated. All his senses obeyed him, or, rather, were held in strict slavery. He was a soul that scarcely touched the earth; who lived amid the feebleness of humanity like an angel who borrowed a human form to come here below to accomplish a heavenly mission.

"He possessed angelic modesty and virginal chastity; the effect of the fidelity with which he observed the compact of the holy man, Job; his eyes rested on no object capable of exciting the inclinations of the old Adam, or of troubling the peace of his heart. His was a privileged sanctity and the holiness of predilection. At this time of his life, God attracted him more by sweetness and consolation than by trials and combats. Divine Providence reserved them for another time, and we know with what courage and constancy he triumphed over them. Good as he was, if his confessor had allowed him to practise corporal mortification, no doubt he would have macerated his flesh as if he were a criminal. As his love for mortification was extreme, he was ingenious in satisfying it by a host of little painful things, which were not forbidden him by his director and by which he satisfied himself, as he could not follow his thirst and zeal for greater austerities.

"Apart from this slight difference between him and his confessor, his direction was easy. He went to confession every week and received Holy Communion several times a week. I do not know that he ever failed to approach the sacrament of penance and the Holy Table and he showed always the same punctuality, the same fervor, giving greater and greater edification.

"In his habits of life and his intercourse with others, he was of an even disposition, never laughing aloud but always with a gracious smile upon his lips. Full of sweetness, attractiveness and amiability, he was a faithful copy of his Divine Master. One needed only to look attentively at him, to be forced to say, 'See how good Our Lord is! how sweet His yoke! how light His burden! Learn it more by the example of His servant than by reading the holy text.'

"Shall I speak of his obedience and regularity? It was easy to see that he had a perfect submission to all who had authority over him. He saw in obedience and submission to men, the obedience and submission of Jesus Christ to God, His Father. This, doubtless, is why he never permitted himself the least murmur, the least disapprobation or even a reply to his superiors. He made sometimes, some slight observation; but then he was always careful to accompany them with so much respect and with such submissive apologies, that it was impossible not to agree to them and receive them gratefully.

"For a long time, it had been the custom at Montdidier to say Mass on Sundays and feast days for the prisoners, to visit them twice every day for morning and evening prayers, and to discourse on the truths of religion; then alms and food, and sometimes clothes were distributed to the prisoners. The food was generally what was left from the table; the scholars frequently added a part of the dessert of which they deprived themselves with much pleasure to aid so good a work. Often the provisions were too abundant for the prisoners, so they were divided, one part for them, the other for the poor of the town. No sooner had John Gabriel arrived, than, relying on his prudence and zeal, they gave him charge of these distributions. His ingenious charity soon gave this work a larger field, as he knew how to multiply the resources so as to meet the new demands. Devoting to this good work the means obtained from the fines imposed on the pupils for some slight fault or neglect of neatness and order, he formed a fund for the poor, which he skilfully managed, foreseeing the needs of a bad season.

"Every day at the noon recreation, he started out, eagerly followed by the pupils bearing the baskets. He directed his steps, sometimes to the prisons and sometimes to the suburbs. These distributions were made with much wisdom and were always accompanied by words of piety, resignation and encouragement. He returned loaded with the blessings of the poor, and filled with holy joy, 'because,' said he, 'I have just done what our holy Founder did.'"

We shall add but one word to this edifying recital. Some priests of the diocese of Amiens, directors of the Seminary of Montdidier, had a special veneration for John Gabriel; when they spoke of him in conversation they often called him "little saint."

After staying two years, Blessed Perboyre left the

college, leaving by his piety and modesty an impression and a memory which time has not effaced.

---

## IX.

### JOHN GABRIEL AT THE SEMINARY OF SAINT FLOUR.

HAVING arrived at Paris whither he was recalled by the will of his superiors, John Gabriel was told to prepare himself for the priesthood. This announcement filled him at the same time with happiness and fear; for if, on the one hand, he appreciated the advantage of going up every day to the altar to offer the Holy Victim and nourish himself with the Bread of Angels, on the other, he feared that he was not well prepared. But whilst he humbled himself before God, his superiors and confrères congratulated themselves on his elevation to the priesthood, knowing well that his entire life was but one long preparation for this sublime dignity. He possessed a great knowledge of the truths a priest must teach others, and his conduct displayed the eminent virtues the Church demands of those who are called to holy orders.

There is no record of the dispositions or feelings with which he received tonsure and the orders which precede deaconship. This omission is to be regretted, for the edifying life which Blessed Perboyre always led, leaves us no room to doubt that he prepared himself for the different orders so fervently that this young and virtuous levite could have been held up as the model of those destined for the priesthood, who might learn from him in what manner they should mount each of these holy steps to the sanctuary. We can, however, affirm that when he took Our Lord for his portion, he applied himself more and more to the concentration of his affections upon God; after his subdeaconship, he recited the divine office with angelic fervor; when he received his deaconship, he displayed all the virtues which St. Paul exacted of those who aspired to this dignity. He often read the writings of M. Olier on Holy Orders, and loved to meditate on the different degrees of the ecclesiastical hierarchy as described in the Pontifical. We know, also, that his eyes were always fixed on the model of priests, Our Lord Jesus Christ, and that he strove to follow His maxims and example.

Before receiving ordination, he recommended himself to the prayers of his relations and friends. Here is a fragment of a letter he wrote his father on this occasion: "It is decided, my dear father, that at no very distant day Our Lord will put upon me forever the yoke of the priesthood and that day will be the happiest of my life. What a happiness if I could receive ordination with all the dispositions it requires! What a source of grace for me and for others! How great must be the mercy of God to choose for His ministry one so unworthy! You know how little I have merited this favor. Implore Our Lord, I beg you, that I may not abuse the graces which He wills to give me. In a month, that is, on September 23, I shall be a priest. I hope you, my dear mother, my sisters and all my relations will unite in prayer to draw down upon me the benediction of heaven. I recommend myself especially to the prayers of my aunt Rigal. You will be amply repaid when I have the happiness of saying Holy Mass, not indeed, in virtue of my prayers, but by the merits of Him who offers Himself to His Father through my hands."

Before ordination, the young deacon passed some days in retreat. Two other confrères prepared themselves to receive the same grace: they both said afterwards that they had only to look at John Gabriel to feel an increase of devotion. He was ordained September 23, 1825, in the chapel of the Sisters of Charity. The next day, he offered for the first time the holy sacrifice of the Mass; with what fervor and transports of love, God alone knows. From that time, he worked with new zeal to strip himself entirely of everything human. The thought that a priest must be another Christ, *sacerdos alter Christus*, was always present to his mind, and he endeavored to form in himself the image of his divine Saviour.

Soon after, he was sent to Saint Flour where he taught dogmatic theology. To judge from his appearance, he was very young for so important a charge; he fulfilled it, however, with great success, for in him science and wisdom outstripped his years. He had to explain two very difficult tracts, Grace and the Incarnation. The pupils who assisted at this course have cherished the memory of their professor's instructions. His decided taste for metaphysics helped him wonderfully to explain clearly and exactly the abstract subjects of Grace and the Incarnation. What astonished every one was the extent of his knowledge, the correctness and depths of his arguments. He knew well how to impart the knowledge he had acquired by study and meditation upon the Holy Scripture, notably the Epistles of St. Paul. "I shall always remember," said one of his pupils, "a splendid introduction he made to the tract on the Incarnation by simply explaining the following text from the first Epistle to Timothy: 'And evidently great is the mystery of godliness, which was manifested in the flesh, was justified in the spirit, appeared to Angels, hath been preached to the gentiles, is believed in the world, is taken up in glory.'" *Et manifeste magnum est pietatis sacramentum, quod manifestatum est in carne, justificatum est in spiritu, apparuit angelis, prædicatum est gentibus, creditum est in mundo, assumptum est in gloria* (1 Tim. iii., 16).

His teaching had nothing dry or abstract about it, because he prepared himself for it more by prayer than study. He greatly relished those great truths which, besides the new food they offered each day to his piety, helped him to raise himself and others to heaven. He could not consider the greatness of God, and the marvels of His love without being ravished with admiration and penetrated with gratitude; and he had the secret of making others share the sentiments with which he himself was animated. His pupils left his class instructed and edified; they found in theology the double advantage of strengthening their faith and increasing their devotion.

Often, fear would seize upon his soul when he considered the importance of the duty he had to fulfil; he understood that if the priesthood was so sublime that the Fathers of the Church teach that it would be a formidable burden for the angels themselves, those should tremble still more who are appointed to train priests. For this reason, he neglected no means whatever to lead the seminarians to the practice of the virtues required by their holy state. A good many of them chose him for the director of their consciences, and it was for these principally that he had to exercise his zeal. But he knew, also, that he who plants and he who waters is nothing, that it is God alone who gives the increase; consequently, he prayed much to draw down upon his penitents the blessing of heaven.

He was the first to give the example of the virtues which must distinguish a holy priest. In the confessional, those who addressed themselves to him saw Our Lord in him. If the seminarians came to his room, he received them with so much kindness that they always left with regret, attracted to him by the cordiality of his manners. To-day, even after so many years, those who knew him then, remember the impression that he made upon them. In recreation, he showed himself affable without descending to familiarity; during his meals his modesty charmed every one. What attracted special attention was the manner in which he celebrated the holy mysteries. "How well he said Mass!" said one of his confrères, "what fervor at the altar! our seminarians called him the little Saint. In the pulpit his mind and heart spoke together; but it was a mind full of sanctity, a heart burning with divine love. He detested affected language; his eloquence was drawn from philosophy and the holy writ, like that of the doctors of the church; for he was profund in discourse." "I remember," said one of his pupils, "an excellent conference he gave us one Sunday on charity; never have I heard explained in a more solid manner, the unity of the double precept of love of God and of our neighbor; I can scarcely understand how it was possible for him to speak with such maturity and force at the age of twenty-five."

His confrères were no less edified by the virtues he displayed in every day life; and they willingly manifested their admiration. "See M. Perboyre," said one of the professors to a pupil, "he is indeed, a saint, a favored saint. I have no doubt that he has preserved his baptismal innocence." The superior of the seminary congratulated himself upon having such a co-laborer; but he did not long possess this advantage, for, at the end of the scholastic year John Gabriel was sent to a new post to which we must follow him.

---

## X.

### JOHN GABRIEL SUPERIOR OF THE SCHOOL AT ST. FLOUR.

THE ecclesiastical school of St. Flour, now a preparatory seminary, was then at its beginning and went through the painful trials to which God generally subjects the works of which He is author.

M. Trippier, whose name is long remembered in his diocese, founded and directed it for many years amid difficulties and obstacles of all sorts. Towards the end of 1827, John Gabriel was sent to replace him; many plans were made and abandoned before they thought of confiding this post to him; but events proved that he was the man destined by Providence to secure the preservation and prosperity of this important work. He found himself at first with inexperienced assistants; the house was deprived of all pecuniary resources; most of the pupils were still much in fault before the good spirit returned and M. Perboyre lacked not enemies from without. It was thought that the youth of the new superior was against him; and those most interested in the prosperity of the house had grave fears. But soon the sterling qualities of the young professor made them forget his youth; ill-will was disarmed at the sight of a young man whose virtue exercised an irresistible sway over all; the confidence of parents who had at heart the proper education of their children, was easily acquired: in a word, he proved by his example that Rollin spoke truly, when he said in his Treatise on Study, "A house is happy when God gives it a head who has the spirit of government, a genial disposition, solid judgment, humble and prudent docility, and perfect disinterestedness;—who comes to the place through religious desires and not from human motives." Such was Blessed Perboyre.

Scarcely had he entered the establishment when everything was changed; the pupils, whom we have said, would scarcely bend to the yoke of discipline, soon found themselves animated by better dispositions, without understanding what had made the change in them, or perceiving the mysterious ascendency which subjugated their wills. The school at first had only thirty scholars, but received more than a hundred at the beginning of the following year. If it is asked how the new director obtained this happy result, the response is easy; his virtue which, notwithstanding his great humility, struck all beholders, drew to him the respect and veneration of the pupils; his kindness and sweetness gained their affection; his prudence, his firmness, and, above all, his prayers did the rest.

As a superior must answer before God for the conduct of those confided to his charge, he kept an exact account of the good and evil done in the house and then took the most opportune measures to improve things. He had an eye to every one; knew everything that occurred, and watched and kept guard during the night to preserve from all danger the children so dear to him. He treated them with fatherly affection, but had no preferences. If sometimes one of them received a special mark of affection, this partiality, it was remarked, was always shown to the poorest among them. When they were sick, he took care of them with great solicitude; he frequently visited them, giving them encouragement and consolation and delighting them by his kind words which taught them to sanctify their sufferings and to endure them for the love of God. If they felt any distress, they were sure to find in his words a healing balm that made them forget their sorrows. If he had to reprove a pupil, he used no harsh or wounding expression, but spoke to him in a compassionate, impressive tone, and made him feel his misconduct and how much his faults displeased God, Who loaded him with benefits. Sometimes he would kneel down before the crucifix and make an act of reparation in the name of the pupil, whom he required also to ask pardon of God, and the culprit left him with repentance in his heart and tears in his eyes. When Blessed Perboyre undertook to reform a scholar, his conversion was assured; for if he yielded not at the first assault, the pious superior prayed, mortified himself and returned to the charge, pressing it with more vigorous efforts and, in the end, obtained a complete victory.

When he gave a reprimand, it was with so much kindness and sweetness that it took away all bitterness. Sometimes, however, but rarely, he took a severe tone and spoke to the pupils with so much authority that he overwhelmed them; his words made the greatest impression; even the professors themselves trembled with fear at such times so great was the power and efficacy of his language. If he had to punish any one, he did not draw back from this painful duty, but it was easy to see that he did violence to himself, and the culprit was more grieved at the sorrow it caused his master than at the punishment itself. The greatest chastisement the professors could inflict on their pupils was to take them before the superior, so much they feared to displease him.

In the instructions and counsels that he gave, he insisted particularly upon unity and concord. If there was a misunderstanding between two pupils, he called them to him to represent to them the obligation of mutual pardon, and he did not allow them to leave his room until they were reconciled.

This will show with what facility he could conciliate different minds. After the vacation which followed the revolution in 1830, the students returned with their minds filled with political ideas about which they conversed in recreation. Some defended the fallen family, others took the part of the younger branch which then occupied the throne; and in this conflict of opposing opinions, the discussion became a little more noisy than it should have been. The professors told the superior about it. The next day, after

Holy Mass, he went to the study-hall, with rather a dissatisfied air. He began by complimenting them on their application and the silence they observed in the morning; then as if to divert them, he related the fol lowing anecdote: "Two days ago, our servant and the barber met in my room. The servant while dusting the table found a Greek book and showed it to the barber; both men examined it with curiosity and tried to decipher something in it, but they did not know where the page began or ended; about that, even, they had opposite opinions; one pretended that it was in such a way the book should be held, the other maintained that it should be held in a different manner, though neither of them knew anything about it; each, nevertheless was anxious to have his own opinion prevail. The contest grew animated; they called each other injurious names, threatening to come to blows, so I was obliged to separate them to prevent a battle." Nothing more was needed to make the pupils roar out laughing. They supposed he invented the story of the servant and the barber for them. Then he skillfully applied this account to their case and made them understand how incapable they were of speaking competently of politics. The reflections which he made were so much appreciated by his hearers that there were no longer any political discussions among them and they began again to live in as perfect harmony as before.

In the tribunal of penance he had a particular talent for leading to piety those who came to him. His kind, impressive, charitable words worked marvels. "I used to think my confessor was not a man, but an angel," says a worthy priest who was then his penitent.

If an unruly child took him for his director, a marked improvement was soon observed in his conduct. So when the professors did not know what to do with a pupil, their last resource was to speak to the holy director, knowing the influence of his virtue upon the roughest and most stubborn characters. Here is an instance. There was in the house a pupil whom no one could control and who was so untractable that the majority of the professors were of the opinion that all efforts to improve him would henceforth be useless. They decided that the only thing to be done was to dismiss him from the school and send him home to his family. The superior, putting his confidence in God, concluded to take special charge of this young man and so completely changed his conduct that to the surprise of both teachers and pupils he became in a short time an edifying scholar: "It would be necessary to know him as we did," said one of his assistants, "to form an idea of what means he employed to accomplish a reform; now, he used a firm resolute tone; again, he was kind and more loving than a father; again, he tempered both together according as he judged it best to obtain the desired end."

When a pupil became harmful to the others, he was sent away immediately, and in this case no consideration could prevent it. Although he was adept in discerning characters and in understanding those with whom he came in contact and knew the way to lead them, he did not rely on his insight but on the grace of God, which he unceasingly implored by the most fervent prayers. "When I am at prayer," said he to one of his professors who asked how he performed this holy exercise, "I begin by giving homage to God;

then I reflect on my own needs, the needs of my teachers, pupils and those who belong to the house; then I beg God to bestow on each what he needs."

"Upon one occasion I was wonderfully impressed," said a young man who had deserved a severe reprimand, "I was in his room; suddenly he turned toward the crucifix and said to me, 'What sad moments you have made me pass at the foot of the cross!'" In fact, when a pupil was not virtuous, it was before Jesus crucified that Blessed Perboyre begged the conversion of the sinner, and he did not leave off praying until he obtained the asked for grace.

When the students were about to take their vacation, he never failed to give them wise advice about spending it well. The parents were pleased at seeing the interest he took in their children, but they were no less delighted with the affability with which he spoke to themselves; they always left filled with admiration for the little Angel, as they called him. Those who came from a distance to see their children, always asked to see him, and if they did not succeed at their first visit because the Servant of God was engaged with duties which he could not interrupt, they returned before leaving town, for they could not go home without seeing the master who was so holy, and so affable to every one.

His pupils had for him a wonderful affection and a boundless admiration. Here is what was written about him by one who was under his charge: "During nearly six years, the good M. Perboyre was my superior and father. I delighted in admiring the splendor of his eminent virtues and in enjoying something of the sweet odor he exhaled around him. For no one could approach or see him without being touched, attracted, enchanted by his angelic sweetness, profound humility and marvellous charity, and by all the virtues which made him a holy priest visibly predestined, and a living image of Our Saviour Himself. I must also say in his praise that I feel still and shall always feel the deep and happy impression he made upon me by his fatherly counsels, because they bore the impress and seal of divine wisdom."

---

## XI.

### HIS CONDUCT TOWARDS HIS PROFESSORS AND THE SERVANTS.

We have seen what his conduct was toward his pupils; John Gabriel was no less perfect in his intercourse with his co-laborers, young ecclesiastics of the diocese who, animated with a sincere good will, faithfully discharged their duties. They formed one family, united by the bonds of charity; the respectful esteem they had for their superior made them forestall his least desire. For his part, he lived among them as with beloved brothers and applied himself to forming them still more by example than by precept, to the practice of all the duties their position prescribed. "Far from taking advantage," they said, "of the authority to which he was entitled, he wished only to be among us as the first among equals, *Primus inter pares.* Each of us found in him a tender father, a sincere friend, a wise master, a faithful, loyal counsellor; in a word, all that could be desired of a good superior. He must have learned well how to obey, to command as he did. Never a harsh word, never an imperious tone to us; he listened to our complaints and recommendations with unalterable kindness. Whoever had done wrong, on going to our superior, was sure to find a kind, affectionate welcome. If he had to give a reproof that he feared might not be well received, he brought his eager charity to bear upon it. Assuredly, he cherished us as the apple of his eye. No matter what caused our distress, not only did he compassionate us, but he had a particular talent for consoling us."

His reserve was extreme when anything was said or done which could compromise the authority of his professors. When he perceived that any of them had acted in too hasty a manner, he gave them counsels in private, but before the pupils he said nothing that would make them suppose he disapproved of or blamed their action. He took upon himself all that was painful in the office of superior. The refusals of signatures and all corrective measures he, himself, willingly undertook. Every one was constrained, nevertheless, to love him, for all were certain that he never acted through precipitation or passion. His condescension to his assistants was so great that if the prefect, for any reason whatever, could not take the pupils out for a walk or preside at studies, or if a professor was hindered from going to his class, not only was he ready to replace him, but often even anticipated his desires.

When there was any trouble which interrupted the usual regularity of the house, he blamed no one, accused no one but himself. "It is my fault," he said. "If I had done this or that, such a thing would not have happened." The health of the professors was for him an object of special solicitude, and when they were sick or indisposed, he lavished on them every care. By his words full of faith and charity, he strove to maintain and increase the zeal with which he saw them animated. "Oh, how worthy is childhood of our love and respect!" he said to them. To bring them more successfully to the cultivation of good dispositions in their pupils, he often reminded them of the affection which Our Lord showed for children when He was on earth, how often He recommended to His disciples to do nothing to scandalize them. M. Perboyre did not advise them to give long discourses to children. "Avoid speaking too long to them," he said; "this can only weary them. Children are like a vase whose opening is very narrow: if you pour in the liquid in too great abundance, it falls outside and the vase is not filled; on the contrary, you fill it without losing your liquid if you pour it in drop by drop."

As the establishment was prosperous the number of pupils increased day by day and, as there reigned among them an excellent spirit and decided love for work, Blessed Perboyre could not help being delighted when he contemplated these consoling results; but, far from being dazzled by thoughts of self-love, he attributed all to God and considered himself capable of drawing down only the malediction of heaven on the work.

He endeavored to inspire his professors with the same sentiments and feared nothing so much as to see them take pride in their success. "Let us often recall," he said, "these words of St. Paul: 'Neither he that planteth is anything, nor he that watereth; but God who giveth the increase.' (1 Cor. iii, 7.) Our predecessors have sown; we gather the fruits of their labors. It is more difficult to grub up and cultivate a field than to gather the harvest when it is ripe. You rejoice at the good you have done, but what assures you that it is not due to the prayers of some good woman, hidden in the village, or, perhaps, of some good Christian in China, who has drawn upon us these blessings? Be careful to refer all to God, for He will punish us if we have self-complacency."

One feast day, all the students having approached the Holy Table, the professors congratulated themselves on this great act of piety and one of them said to Blessed Perboyre: "Oh! how pleased you must be; all our pupils have communicated to-day with remarkable fervor." "Yes, let us be pleased," said he, "if God is. But let us fear, also, that He is not so well satisfied with us as He should be; for if it should happen that He comes willingly into the hearts of our children, perhaps He finds in our hearts what He does not desire to see there."

"He was the implacable enemy of self-love," said one of his professors, "because he considered it as the great enemy of God. This is why he combated it unceasingly and could not perceive it without immediately attacking it. 'God alone!' he often repeated, 'God alone!' When he spoke on this subject he reminded them that Our Lord reprimanded the vain complacency of His disciples and said to them: 'I saw Satan as lightning falling from heaven. But yet rejoice not in this, that spirits are subject unto you: but rejoice in this, that your names are written in heaven.'" (Luke x, 18, 20.)

The charity of the good superior was not exercised

only upon the pupils and professors; he had a particular care of the servants. He provided for all their spiritual and corporal needs with a paternal solicitude. He watched that they fulfilled all the duties of religion, had them instructed and instructed them himself. During vacation, he would leave his room to teach catechism to a single servant or he would read spiritual books to him.

Among the servants was a woman who did the cooking and bought the provisions. He never held any conversation with her but what was indispensable and he did not allow her any unnecessary words when she gave in her accounts. Good and charitable to all the servants, he took care that they wanted nothing that was necessary and if they were sick, he lavished on them all the care they could wish. When he observed any fault in them, he reproved them with kindness and firmness, and inspired them with a great horror of the sins by which God was offended. Never did he find fault with them for what concerned himself personally. Whether he was well or badly served, he was always satisfied. He knew how to bear with their peculiarities, encouraging their efforts, and striving to maintain union among them; but if they had any serious faults, he sent them away without mercy.

When he spoke to them, it was less like a master using his authority than a servant addressing his superior; for when he asked for anything he always did it with humility, kindness and charity. "Ah! the holy man," one of his servants still says, "how sweet it was to work under his orders! How well he knew how to console us in our trials! What a touching interest he took in all that concerned us! At

Saint Vincent de Paul,
*Founder of the Congregation of the Mission and the Sisters of Charity.*

whatever time we came and knocked at his door, we were sure of being well received." "I often had occasion to disturb him," said the porter of the house, "and never could I discover in words or manner that he was the least annoyed by these interruptions." So his servants had for him the greatest affection and the deepest gratitude.

---

## XII.

### HIS VIRTUES AT THE ECCLESIASTICAL SCHOOL OF SAINT FLOUR.

During the five years he was superior of Saint Flour, John Gabriel perfectly fulfilled the duties of his charge. Obliged to be, at the same time, superior and steward of the establishment, he must have felt a repugnance for entering into the multitude of little material details with which he had, however, to occupy himself when he had to provide for the needs of all; he did it, nevertheless, with an attention which left nothing to be desired. He had to put the house in order, with all possible economy; nothing suffered, because nothing was neglected. He regarded himself as holding the place of Providence, who watches with so much charity over all His creatures. Though he often lost his rest to regulate affairs, he always rose at four o'clock: and, if the porter failed to call him, he reproached him and strongly urged him to be more faithful in executing his orders.

Extremely reserved in speech, never was the least slander heard from his lips. He conversed with the pupils only when necessary. Never did he speak unfavorably of those whom he was obliged to send away. His conduct showed that he understood the precept of charity in its fullest extent. In his eyes, his neighbor was not only a creature like himself, but a friend, a brother, a member of Jesus Christ and, on this account, he received every one without exception with the greatest cordiality.

It was especially towards the poor that he showed his charity; he gave them always the first place in his heart; he received them and spoke to them with much respect because he beheld Jesus Christ in their person and he took much pleasure in talking to them. He taught them to bear their privations with patience, telling them that Jesus Christ made Himself poor to sanctify their state and that if they were resigned, God would give them one day a share in the riches of heaven. Never would he allow a poor person to go away without an alms; if sometimes his purse was empty—and then only did he feel the inconvenience of poverty—he would go in quest of the professors, telling them he had nothing; that he had come to implore their charity for Jesus Christ; and his professors, knowing the pleasure it would be to him, hastened to respond to his appeal.

When he became director of the establishment, he found it with thirty-four pupils and without resources. Instead of complaining of this state of things, he thought of the poverty of Our Lord and, as he was always satisfied, he made others share in the joy that filled his heart. If they represented to him the destitution of the house, "Oh, well! what do you wish?" he would reply, "we are happy in being like Our

Lord, Who was in want of everything; Who had not even a stone whereon to rest His head; and, nevertheless, He was master of the world." In his room he had only what was strictly necessary: some very poor furniture, a crucifix, a picture of the Blessed Virgin, and of St. Vincent. As to his clothes, he often had them mended, and if any one said to him, "Sir, these are worthless: you must buy new ones," he replied: "They are too good for me."

He regarded the office of superior not as a source of power, but as a veritable servitude, and whilst by position he occupied the first place, in spirit he put himself in the last. He thought others were more agreeable to God than he was himself, and that he deceived others by an appearance of virtue. Flatterers were most unwelcome, because he could not help abhorring them. The greatest sorrow they could give him was to speak of his person with eulogy. One of his professors having deliberately said to him, "I am tempted to believe that you were conceived without sin for I never see you commit a fault;" the sorrow of his countenance showed that these words had deeply wounded him. "Do not say that," said he, "you must know but little about me; but God sees all. He knows my abominations." Through the low opinion he had of himself, he thought he was incapable and unworthy to preach the word of God. One day, when he least expected it, he was asked to speak to the pupils; he refused, alleging that he could not; it was urged, and insisted upon, and he at last yielded. Arrived in the chapel, he recollected himself for an instant, and, taking for his text these words of the prophet, *Pax multa diligentibus legem tuam,* 'Much peace have they that love thy law,' (Ps. cxviii. 165) he spoke to them with so much unction of the peace obtained by Christian conduct and of the happiness enjoyed by the true children of God, that he excited the admiration of the people. "I know not," said one of the professors on this occasion, "where he obtained such beautiful, sublime thoughts."

His confidence in divine Providence was wonderful, and though it was often put to severe trial whilst he was superior, he never faltered in his trust. When means were needed for the establishment, he was not disturbed. "Our Lord is rich enough," said he; "He will give us what we need." In fact Providence never failed to come to his aid. Notwithstanding the difficulties that he experienced, the location being inconvenient and unhealthy, he intended to build a more suitable establishment upon a more spacious and healthful site; but he encountered insurmountable opposition from the municipal council and was obliged to give up the project. He pronounced then the words which every one regarded as prophetic. "It does not matter; the gauntlet is thrown down and others will take it up." Some years after he left, the establishment was built on the site he had chosen.

Amid the most trying circumstances, there could never be discovered in his face or words any indication of discouragement. He possessed always a profound calmness which is only obtained by an entire abandonment into the hands of God; he was another Abraham hoping against all hope. In the most afflicting circumstances, he preserved so cheerful a bearing that often it was enough for his professors to see or hear him, to be relieved of their despondency and to share his confidence.

In 1831, a rival school was started in his neighborhood. Many people feared it would injure the prosperity of the seminary. Far from being affrighted, he showed almost joy. "I am rather glad," said he, "we will be incited to do better. After all, provided the good is done, it matters not who does it."

Always greatly desiring to live the life of Jesus Christ, he labored to learn more and more the practice of mortification. Though he was of a quick, sensitive disposition, the least impatience could not be observed in him. Having been one day struck severely on the head through the carelessness of a pupil, he did not complain or show any displeasure and hastened to soothe the pain the child felt at the awkwardness. The most unexpected things could not surprise him or find his amiability at fault.

His mortifications having seriously affected his health, he was nearly always suffering; but he did not relax any of his austerities or occupations. During the severest winters, he seldom approached a fire. As to his meals, it was impossible to know what was to his taste, or if one kind of food was more agreeable to him than another. When he was alone during vacation, he scarcely allowed any food to be prepared for him. The doctor ordered him to take a little tea after dinner; but the cook, not knowing how to prepare it, boiled it in water and served it to him that way. Several months after, a lady who had one of her children at the school, having seen how the cook prepared it, asked why he did not put a little sugar in the tea. "I did not know it needed sugar." "Did not M.

Perboyre show any repugnance when drinking the tea prepared this way?" "No, madam, he never remarked it." The cook, better taught, prepared the beverage properly, but the servant of God, whether he perceived the change or not, did not act as if he noticed it.

He long and earnestly studied Jesus Christ crucified and at His feet sought light and strength, weeping for his own sins and the sins of others, forgetting everything, forgetting even himself, was transported, as it were, into another world. "'Often," said one of his servants, "when I came and knocked at the door, he heard nothing as he was all absorbed in meditating on the sufferings of the good God." Weary of waiting, the servant would enter and find him weeping and sobbing at the foot of the cross. It was necessary to come close to him and to speak louder than usual to bring him back to himself; then he would be ashamed and blush at being surprised in this state. But if the cross had such powerful attractions for him, the tabernacle where Jesus remains for us had equal charms. From his room to the chapel there was only a small passage to cross; he profited by its proximity to pay Our Saviour frequent visits. Scarcely had he risen, when he would go to converse with Him; during the day, he came often and with renewed joy; his duties and business alone could tear him away; in the evening he came again and prolonged his prayer far into the night.

He had filled the diocese with the good odor of his virtues; the priests spoke of him only with much esteem, and now his memory still lives in the hearts of all who knew him. The Bishop of Saint Flour, who often consulted him, was grieved at his departure and would hardly let him go when he was recalled to Paris. All intelligent people considered him a most able superior and a saint. The Vicar General hastened to praise his conduct; the superior of the higher seminary, the director of his conscience, a man able to discern merit and but little inclined to pay compliments, said of him: "M. Perboyre is the most perfect man I know. He is a man all for God, Whose presence he does not lose sight of for an instant."

The priest who lived with John Gabriel shared the same opinion. "If I had to state the faults that I have observed in him," said one of them, "I declare that I would be embarrassed, because I never discovered the slightest imperfection." A certificate drawn up and signed by all his professors contains a passage which we must repeat here. "We have carefully examined all his actions and we have found that he always seemed to have acted under the inspiration of the spirit of God, that ineffable spirit which, without changing nature, diversifies itself in many ways according to different circumstances. Now, it was gift of counsel and strength, now, all the other gifts which we saw shining through his profound humility. Rich in all the virtues which St. Paul in his Epistle to the Galatians calls the fruits of the Holy Ghost, he knew how, like this great Apostle whose writings were so familiar to him, to make himself all in all to gain all to Jesus Christ. He knew how, under the powerful influence of divine grace, to accomplish his end with strength and to dispose all things sweetly after the example of eternal Wisdom, which he studied continually and copied in all that he did."

## XIII.

### DEATH OF HIS BROTHER LOUIS—VISIT TO HIS FAMILY.

In the beginning of the year 1832, John Gabriel Perboyre received tidings which plunged him into deep affliction. His brother Louis, who had sailed for China more than a year before to preach the gospel to the heathens, had died at sea before obtaining the object of his desires. We give an account of the life and death of this pious missionary, the details of which may be of some interest.

From his earliest childhood, Louis Perboyre strove to imitate his brother and, like him, pursued the paths of virtue. When at the preparatory seminary of Montauban, he was considered the model of the other pupils. His success was no less brilliant than was John Gabriel's. When he finished his studies, he entered the Congregation of the Missions and went to Paris for the novitiate and to acquire ecclesiastical knowledge. During all the time he was there, he was a consolation to his superiors, who congratulated themselves upon seeing him give the same edifying example that his brother had given. He showed remarkable talent for his years, and every one was astonished at the facility with which he acquired the knowledge necessary for his state. Of extreme amiability, exemplary modesty and tender piety, he charmed every one by his good qualities. This is the testimony of all who have known him.

During the course of his ecclesiastical studies, he felt himself inspired to go to preach the faith to the idolators of China. Meanwhile, four young missionaries from this kingdom arrived in Paris; Louis Perboyre was appointed to serve them as "guardian angel" and preceptor; he discharged this office with great zeal and their progress was rapid. His pupils, in their turn, taught him the language of their country and the young teacher profited so well by these lessons, that he acquired in a short time an extensive knowledge of the Chinese tongue. In 1830, he was ordained priest, though he had not completed his twenty-fourth year, and started for China with his four Chinese pupils who were joined by two others who had come to Paris a short time before. They embarked from Havre, December 3, 1830. They had with them four young priests of the Foreign Missions, who, "filled with the apostolic spirit," started across the seas to spread the sacred fire with which their hearts were inflamed. Among them were MM. Delamoth and Boric, who some years after, shed their blood for the faith and M. Verolles who was afterward raised to the episcopacy. It is to his kindness that we are indebted for the interesting details about the voyage and death of Louis Perboyre which are found in the following letter:

"*Rev. Father*,—I am happy to be able to give you some details about M. Louis Perboyre, one of the companions of my voyage. It was in the year 1830. We remained in Havre the whole month of November and, on December 3, we set sail. A thick fog soon robbed us of the sight of the shores of France. In the Gulf of Gascony, opposite Rochelle, we were assailed by a violent tempest for three days; but on the 8th, the Feast of the Immaculate Conception, calm succeeded the storm. We continued our route, though very slowly, being baffled by the winds. We passed Porto Santo, Madeira, Palma, the Cape Verde Islands, Cape Vaches at the extremity of Africa, and, on March 17, we arrived at the Isle of France. Some days afterwards, our ship anchored at St. Denis in the Isle of Bourbon. We stayed there eight days; instead of waiting for our ship which was to remain here a month, Louis Perboyre thought, like the rest of us, that it would be better to go on a ship from Java, which came from the Cape and returned to Batavia. We expected thus to arrive sooner and more easily in China. The winds opposed us; we returned to the South to seek more favorable winds which would permit an easy sail to the East. From the Isle of France to Bourbon, the heat was excessive. Some days after our departure, the temperature suddenly changed; the wind from the south pole chilled us. All the eruption of the skin was driven in; a fiery rash from which M. Perboyre suffered, ceased suddenly. We had already passed St. Paul and Amsterdam when malarial fever, and soon delirium, seized upon our dear Louis. His disease was cerebral fever.

"What were we to do? In the first place, neither doctor nor medicine was at hand: upon this coast-ship we had nothing but castor oil. We gave him a foot bath. We needed ice for his head but where could we get it? We prayed, we made a novena to save our precious confrère, but he was ripe for heaven; the good God received the pious and fervent desires for the apostolate that consumed his heart. Consciousness returned for a short time; he went to confession, and received Extreme Unction from his confessor, M. Delamothe, afterward a generous martyr for the faith. M. Delamothe died ten years later in 1840, in chains, rent and torn in shreds by rack and pincers, in the prison of Cochin-China. It was impossible to celebrate Mass. Louis Perboyre rendered his soul to God after a week's sickness on May 2, 1831; I remember it well. We were sailing toward the north, not far from the coast of New Holland.

"He could not be brought to church, so we did our best to supply its place. He was clothed in his sacred vestments and enclosed in his hammock. We recited the office of the dead, and with the cross at our head walked in procession to the stern of the ship. All the officers and passengers, though Protestants, took part in this sad and mournful ceremony, and after having blessed the ocean over whose abyss we had travelled five months, and which was for one of us the last resting place, we let him slip from the fatal plank and the waves of the sea buried him in their depths. O Father, what a heart-rending blow to us! how often we repeated with the prophet, *Abyssus vallavit me, pelagus operuit caput meum, et terræ vectes concluserunt me in æternum.* "The deep hath closed me round about: the sea has covered my head . . . the bars of the earth have shut me up forever." (Jonas ii, 6-7).

"This unexpected death overwhelmed us; the venerable Boire, one of the companions of our voyage, told me he never felt a death so sensibly. We all loved Louis cordially, because he was so amiable to every one. He possessed a sweetness, a condescension, a suavity, a candor, an innocence, a simplicity which drew all hearts to him; a happy union of qualities, no doubt supernatural, which we constantly admired in him; he never swerved from virtue a single moment. He was bringing back to China six Chinese pupils who had begun their clerical education in Paris; this charge was rather painful on account of the difficulties of the voyage. We had on board our ship forty passengers, of whom the greater part blasphemed from morning till night, and sang continually the '*Marseillaise*' and the '*Parisienne*.'

"Louis Perboyre, always self-contained, preserved amid this turbulent crowd, the serenity of his soul; he pursued his work, the education of his dear Chinese, and every day as far as sea-sickness would permit, held with them conferences and the exercises of St. Lazare. It was an edifying contrast to the noisy dissipation and impiety of our passengers.

"Often have I conversed privately with him, as I well remember. He was learned, very sensible, and had keen penetration; everything about him showed that he would have been a distinguished missionary. His solid and affectionate piety, his fervor, his zeal for souls, his love for Jesus Christ and His holy Mother, his filial devotion to St. Vincent, etc., so many eminent gifts of mind and heart are still, to-day, after more than twenty years, present to my mind and renew my grief that we lost him at the beginning of his career; and that so many fruits of salvation which he would have gained in the East have thus been stifled by the death of one who made so good a beginning and raised so great hopes. Can he not help us from his throne in heaven?—Allow me, etc."

It may be judged from the preceding letter how much John Gabriel must have loved a brother in whom God united so many rare qualities. He bore him the most tender affection, and it could be said of them, as of David and Jonathan, that his soul was knit to the soul of his brother. This union had not its source in flesh and blood; it came from grace which had given them both the same taste, the same inclination for virtue. When Louis was about to go away, his brother went to see him in Paris; in congratulating him on his mission, he envied him his happiness, and when bidding Louis adieu, expressed the hope that he might one day join him. Louis recalled this circumstance during his sickness; when it was regretted that he should die before having labored in China, he replied that he left a brother who would soon take his place.

After paying to Louis the just tribute which he owed him, John Gabriel wrote to his parents to console them. We transcribe the letter he wrote on this sad occasion.

"*My Dear Father and Mother*,—Let us mingle our tears, let us unite our prayers; for our dear Louis is no more. What sad news for you, for me, and for all the family! Last year when he left France, we were overwhelmed by the weight of the sacrifice which imposed on us so hard a separation. But we did not think, amid our regrets and desires to accompany him across the sea, that his death would so soon complete our desolation.

"Alas! in His impenetrable and adorable decrees, God has reserved this trial for us. You could not lose a better son, nor I, a better brother. Nevertheless, my dear parents, do not give up to excessive sadness; we have motives for consolation. We may believe that Louis preserved his baptismal innocence. From his earliest years he has been sheltered from all occasions of evil which so often prove fatal; he has been carefully raised in the shadow of the altar. A short life has gained for him the prize of a long course: in the flower of his youth, he was judged ripe for heaven. He must be already enjoying the recompense of his beautiful virtues. How great must be his glory! Our Lord, faithful to His word, is pleased to bestow upon him the ineffable happiness promised to those who leave all for Him: father, mother, brothers, sisters. Let us not worry about his last moments; Our Lord, the Blessed Virgin, his guardian angel, his holy patrons lavished on him more assiduous, loving care than a father, mother, brother or sister could have done. The providence of God is kind and admirable to His servants and infinitely more merciful than we can conceive. Let us bless Our Lord, Who has taken two of the elect from among your children,* to place in heaven two protectors for all our family. Their example should instruct us. Let us despise the world, detach ourselves from all things of earth and attach ourselves to God and His service alone; we gather at death only what we have sowed in life.

"I shall often offer Mass for Louis and Mariette: you must have some Masses said, too. We do not know in what they may have to satisfy divine justice.——"

* He speaks of one of his sisters who died an edifying death in the flower of her youth.

Two days later, he wrote his uncle the following letter, in which he depicts, in a touching manner, his great desolation and also the sentiments of faith which animated him.

"*My Very Dear Uncle,*—O no! you could not tell me any more afflicting news than Louis' death. What have I among men dearer to me than this poor brother? I am inconsolable; my heart is torn with anguish, my tears continue to flow. Every day I water with them the altar and his letter, the last tender token which I received from him when leaving the Isle of Bourbon, March 30, a few days before his death. Ah my dear brother, in less than a year, thy body is buried in the depths of the sea, and thy soul reposes in the bosom of the Deity! Repay us for our sorrow by thy blessed protection and obtain for those who weep for thee, the grace to share in thy glory and happiness. I do not doubt that he now enjoys the glory of heaven and, thinking this, I say to myself, 'Why art thou sad, O my soul? and why dost thou disquiet me?' *Quare tristis es, anima mea, et quare conturbas me?* (Ps. xlii. 5,) but nature mourns! Yes, my very dear uncle, you have trained Louis to be one of the elect of God. All the pains you have taken with us have not been entirely lost. After leading an angelic life under your care and having drunk at its source the spirit of his state, consumed with zeal for the salvation of souls, he travelled across the seas, seeking a martyr's death. He found only that of an apostle. May I prove worthy to fill the place he has left vacant, so that I may expiate my sins by the martyrdom after which his innocent soul sighed so ardently. Alas! I have already lived more than thirty years which have passed like a dream and I have not yet learned how to live. When shall I learn how to die? Time disappears like a slight shadow; without our perceiving it, eternity arrives. *Verumtamen universa vanitas omnis homo vivens.* 'And indeed all things are vanity, every man living.'" (Ps. xxxviii. 6.)

The same sentiments were expressed in a letter which he wrote his brother Jacques, who was then making his philosophy in the College of Montdidier.

"*My Dear Brother,*—What sad moments have I not passed since I received your last letter! Judge of my sorrow by what you felt yourself at the news of Louis' death. Could we lose any one dearer or more amiable? It was an angel God gave us in this brother. He wished to take him early from earth. Do not let our affliction entirely absorb us. Let our desolated souls turn towards God, to seek in Him true consolation. Let us confess that God is all good and all merciful. He has crowned Louis with graces during all his life and accorded him the happiness of dying the death of the saints. What a beautiful death in the eyes of faith! In exchange for this sad life, which he sacrificed generously for Jesus Christ, he enjoys a divine, eternal life. He Who assures us of this, is the Truth, as well as the Resurrection and the Life. Though we have the sweet confidence that our brother is already in the bosom of glory, let not our humble suffrages cease to ascend to the throne of grace; they will always return to us, changed into heavenly benedictions."

Thus John Gabriel Perboyre showed how efficacious the truths of religion are in sweetening our greatest trials. Far from allowing himself to grow tepid, he took occasion to attach himself more firmly to God. Not satisfied with fulfilling the duties of a good superior, he applied himself also to learning the virtues of a missionary. Though alone, and left in some way very much to himself in the house, having no other confrère with him, he followed the rule with scrupulous exactness and for all the exercises he could not make alone, he went to the main seminary, so as to be united with his confrères. These same rules he observed no less faithfully in travelling; for a priest who accompanied him when he returned to his family, said the most fervent novice could not have been more regular.

During the vacation following the death of his brother, Blessed Perboyre went to see his parents to console them for their loss. "I found him there," said the professor who accompanied him, "just as I had seen him at Saint Flour, always self-possessed, humble, recollected, full of kindness, edifying and detached from all things. During the ten days he passed with his parents, he ceased not to prove to them that he loved them in God. The man of God revealed himself in everything. It is said that St. Vincent wept when leaving his parents; as to him, he shed not a tear, though he saw them for the last time."

The zealous missionary then announced to his family his intention of going to China; that God interiorly urged him to go, and that he would do all that he could to respond to His will. They wished to turn him aside from his purpose, making him consider the dangers he would have to incur, the privations and persecutions which awaited him; but he only smiled at these objections and replied they were precisely the object of his desires.

Before returning to St. Flour, he went to Montauban to see his uncle; there also, he spoke of his project of going to China. He, too, tried to shake John Gabriel's resolution as they did at Puech. "You are so feeble," he said, "that you will die on the way, like your brother Louis." "I hope to be more fortunate than he." "But if you go to China, nothing awaits you there but martyrdom." "That is all I wish. Since God has wished to die for us we must not fear to die for Him."

After having paid his respects to his uncle, he resumed his journey to Saint Flour; everywhere he was admired for his recollection and modesty. There was nothing strained or forced about him. Having observed that one of his travelling companions felt a certain embarrassment in his intercourse with persons of the world, he said to him privately, that it was not contrary to modesty to raise the eyes towards the persons who spoke to him, provided he did not fix his gaze upon them, that if he had too constrained a manner, it would produce a bad effect and cause piety to be decried.

Scarcely had he returned to the ecclesiastical school, when he received a letter recalling him to the house in Paris. This was not surprising, for his health grew feebler day by day; he wrote to his superiors telling them he feared the establishment would suffer because of his infirmities. As soon as the news of his departure was known in town, it could be seen how much he was esteemed by the Bishop of St. Flour, who knew how to appreciate him and who consented only with difficulty to his leaving the diocese. The event was regarded as a great calamity by his pupils and their parents. Indeed, the students wept as if they had lost a father or mother. As to himself, notwithstanding the tender love he bore them, he remained calm and resigned and started to accomplish elsewhere the will of God.

---

## XIV.

### HE IS MADE SUB-DIRECTOR OF THE NOVITIATE OF THE CONGREGATION—HIS CONDUCT IN THIS OFFICE.

APPRECIATING John Gabriel Perboyre according to his merits, his superiors thought it proper to appoint him sub-director of the interior seminary or novitiate. This was not what he desired; he would rather have obtained permission to go to China, towards which all his aspirations tendered. Though in a secondary position, he directed almost alone all the seminarians, the director being scarcely able any longer to fulfil his duties on account of age and infirmities. He acquitted himself of his new charge with all the prudence and zeal they expected of him and his efforts were crowned with the happiest success.

In entering upon this new and important charge, he began by humbling himself before God and implored Him to give him the wisdom necessary to correspond to His designs. He considered attentively all the duties he had to fulfil and the means he must take to procure the glory of God and the advancement of those confided to his care.

Persuaded that this duty demanded much vigilance and care, he had his eyes always fixed on the seminarians, to reform in them whatever was defective, and to lead them by degrees to the perfection of which each was capable. Able to discern spirits, he made himself all to all, and conducted each in the way that suited him best. His zeal had nothing precipitate about it: he knew how to wait when it was necessary and to close his eyes to many imperfections. Sometimes, if it seemed expedient to speak and act with firmness, he did it, but in such a way as not to wound anyone.

He required scrupulous exactness in regard to obedience and he would not allow the least fault against this virtue; but his charity knew how to reprove without coldness. It was recommended to the seminarians not to touch the flowers at the country house; one day he perceived one of them pluck several. He said nothing; but, gathering a flower, he looked at it a moment, then dropped it saying, "It has been forbidden to gather flowers; I should have thought of it." The lesson was successful.

What charmed his seminarians was the kindness with which he received them. The most timid had no difficulty in opening their hearts to him. When a postulant came to him, John Gabriel showed him such affection in the first interview that he readily gained his confidence. Having also to direct the lay brothers, he put himself on their level, speaking to them with great simplicity and using comparisons to make them comprehend better what he said.

His kindness did not degenerate into weakness or hinder him from trying the seminarians, so as to form them to solid virtue. One of them having a sister, a Sister of Charity in a hospital of Paris, went to see her, and found the Superioress distributing pictures to the sisters. One was offered him; he accepted it and returned to the seminary. He asked the sub-director's permission to keep it. With every appearance of displeasure his novice master told him he must return the picture to the Superioress and make an apology to her for the bad example he had given the community by accepting a present without authority. This order was quite wounding to self-love; yet the young man submitted and started to obey. He had only gone a few steps when Blessed Perboyre recalled him and said: "Wait and go at two o'clock," knowing that he could not see the Superioress then. At the appointed hour, the seminarian went to the hospital, where he learned that the Superioress had been gone some time. He returned and gave an account of his trip to his director who expressed the satisfaction his good will gave him.

Like all the saints, John Gabriel had no love for the parlor, and when one of the seminarians was called there, he generally gave him but ten minutes to receive the visit. He was grieved to see any one making acquaintance with outsiders, thinking that all who entered the Congregation should find their happiness in it, and not expose themselves to lose the spirit of their state, perhaps even their vocation, by frequent intercourse with strangers.

In recreation, he showed himself benevolent and amiable without losing his grave manner. He spoke little, and, through charity as much as through modesty, let the seminarians talk, reserving to himself the judgment of their propositions, rectifying them when they were incorrect. It was then he appeared a man of sure judgment, the prudent and enlightened theologian.

He had charge of a course of Holy Scripture, given to the seminarians and students. They all still remember the impression he then made upon them. He began with the gospel according to St. John. He treated the subject in a most elevated manner; in explaining the first chapter, he spoke with such admirable depth and clearness of the eternal generation of the Word and of His divinity, that his charmed auditors hung upon his words.

Far from trying to distinguish himself by high conceptions, he hid, as much as he could, the great knowledge that God had given him of His adorable mysteries. But whatever precautions he took to master the feelings which agitated his soul, he could not always succeed; and in the conferences and the explanations of Holy Scripture, often his voice became suddenly vibrating and piercing, his face flushed, his eyes were raised toward heaven. "Everything about him," says an eye witness, "told us that he was moved by an inspiration of the Holy Spirit; all proclaimed the ardor of the divine fire with which he was consumed when he thought of the mercy of God to His creatures."

In the explanation of the Epistle of St. Paul to the Romans, no difficulty embarrassed him; he explained the most profound and obscure passages with the same ease as the simplest and clearest texts. It was not only in class that he so well expounded the writings of the Apostle; during recreation, when the conversation happened to fall on these subjects, he astonished every one by the learned manner in which he spoke. An ecclesiastic who lived with him said: "No one can express to what degree he understood the admirable logic of St. Paul. He was in his element when he spoke on this subject. Often has he delighted us, as much by the elevation of his thoughts, as by his facility in expressing them. His speech faltered when he spoke of common things, but his words poured forth when treating of the deep truths of this great Apostle."

With his great simplicity, he never sought, in preaching, to strike the imagination or captivate the hearts of his hearers; still less, to make a vain display of learning, which would have been easy for him, nourished as he was by the Holy Scriptures and the Fathers of the Church. He used but few texts, but they were well chosen and perfectly developed. The object of his instruction was to inspire a great detachment from the things of earth, a great contempt for the world and for all that it loves. Union with Jesus Christ was one of the points on which he insisted most, saying that it was the most efficacious means of acquiring the perfection which God requires of a missionary. The love of Our Lord for us, the love that we must have for Him, were the subjects of which he most preferred to treat. After the example of the Beloved Disciple, he unceasingly recommended charity and union of hearts, saying that we must avoid with care anything that can lessen the esteem for our neighbor in others' minds or in our own; because this union depends in a great measure upon the opinion we have of our associates. He prepared his instructions at the foot of the cross, more than from books. When you entered his room, you generally found him kneeling on his modest *prie dieu*, and when he rose to receive his visitor, often his eyes were bathed in tears.

In the holy tribunal of penance, he was kind and patient, speaking little; but the few words he said breathed forth a sincere love of God and a vehement desire of making others love Him. A person leaving him felt enlightened, cheered and disposed to do everything to please God.

Although endowed with a great talent for encouraging others, he did not lavish praises on them; he liked flattery no better for others than for himself. He would have feared to be the occasion of self-love to his seminarians, as self-love is so natural to mankind and does them so much harm. He labored energetically to inspire them with a profound contempt for themselves and a love of humiliations. A student being ordained priest, he called him to his room the day after his ordination and requested him to perform a very humiliating action; he obeyed without hesitation; then he returned to Blessed Perboyre, who gave him precious counsels about the practice of humility and obedience. No less did he instil into the students a great esteem for their vocation, showing them its many advantages. He taught them to bless and thank God for this grace of preference, which he refuses to so many others. If, on account of ill health, any seminarian was obliged to go for a short time to the country, he received his letters with much interest and hastened to write him, in a spirit of faith, counsels most suitable to his condition. Here is what he wrote one day to a seminarian :

"*My Dear Sir*,—Many thanks for your promptness in giving me news of yourself ; they are not so agreeable as I would have desired, since your health is in so bad a state. But the spirit of faith which reigns in your letter, your resignation and submission to the disposition of divine Providence, have edified and consoled me.

"Courage then, my dear sir ; fear neither sickness nor death ; say only with St. Paul, 'For I know this will turn to my salvation—According to my expectation and hope ; that in nothing I shall be confounded : but with all confidence, as always so now also shall Christ be magnified in my body, whether by life or death. For to me, to live is Christ ; and to die is gain' (Phil. i, 19-21). The repugnance that you feel, the spirit of the world amid which you live, will serve but to detach you more and more from it, and make you sigh unceasingly to Our Lord like the prophet : 'Woe is me, that my sojourning is prolonged ! I have dwelt with the inhabitants of Cedar : my soul hath been a long sojourner.' (Ps. cxix, 5, 6.)

"Your soul will be more pure, you will more ardently desire to leave this world and be re-united to God ; the more you feel this desire, the more you will strive to purify yourself. 'For in this, also, we groan, desiring to be clothed upon with our dwelling that is from heaven :—Knowing that, while we are in the body, we are absent from the Lord.—Absent rather from the body, and to be present with the Lord.

And, therefore, we labor, whether absent or present, to please Him.' (II Cor. v, 2-9.)

"Not to keep the messenger waiting, I shall close, embracing you with all my heart."

John Gabriel had the gift of consoling the afflicted, of calming and dispelling temptations, especially of discerning what came from God and what was the effect of the imagination or a deception of the demon. The seminarians were happy to make him share their spiritual trials, to consult him upon their resolutions and their projects for the future; they received his decisions as oracles.

Often, both in public and private, he spoke of the greatness and goodness of the Blessed Virgin, striving to inspire all with a tender devotion for this good Mother. The necessity of having recourse to St. Joseph to acquire the interior life, the utility of honoring the holy angels to claim their mediation and to testify our gratitude, the recommendation of invoking the guardian angel everytime we left or entered our rooms,—a pious practice to which he was very faithful—were the subjects upon which he frequently discoursed. A seminarian, assailed by great sadness, accompanied by doubts of his vocation, because he knew of his mother's serious sickness, addressed himself to John Gabriel to find strength and consolation. When he told him his sorrow, Blessed Perboyre said to him: "My dear friend, if I go myself to console your mother, will you be satisfied?" "Indeed," replied the seminarian, "I would be delighted." "Ah well!" replied the director, "you must address yourself to some one who will discharge the duty better than I can. I promise you to send her your guardian angel and to implore hers also, to help you in this trial." The young man retired, satisfied, and all his doubts disappeared.

Sometimes, a word from him sufficed to pacify the greatest troubles and to calm the greatest temptations. A seminarian felt the greatest disgust for his vocation; persuaded that he had not the courage to persevere in a state of life where everything displeased him, he went to his director and told him the reasons that he thought sufficient to make him return to his family. Blessed Perboyre heard him with much calmness and said to him, smiling: "What! Is that all that frightens you? return to your retreat; it is nothing." The seminarian withdrew, much astonished at this brief response, but he was more so when he perceived that all his fears were dissipated by these few words.

Another seminarian had conceived so great an antipathy for John Gabriel that he could neither see him, hear him or think of him without feelings of aversion. Suffering from this distress, he disclosed his feelings to his director, M. Perboyre, who listened to him with a smile upon his lips, then, embracing him with affectionate kindness, he said to him: "You are right; as to myself I do not comprehend how they can support me; if they knew me they would have a still worse opinion of me." The seminarian retired, his heart touched by this kindness and humility; and from that time he felt only affection and esteem for his holy director.

The following fact will show also, that he possessed the secret of tranquillizing souls. A priest of the Mission had a nephew who made his studies in the higher seminary of his diocese. This young man distinguished himself by his talents and piety; the career which he had embraced pleased him and he worked with ardor to acquire the knowledge and virtues his vocation required. Suddenly, he felt himself assailed by a great sadness and he fell into extreme melancholy; he no longer had any relish for study or his religious exercises; every thing became insupportable to him; his conscience was consumed with scruples and tormented by despair. However, his conduct was very regular, so that his superiors had observed no change in him, because he suppressed his sorrow and confided it to no one. In this cruel trial, he wrote to his uncle that he was entirely discouraged; that he could learn nothing and felt an invincible disgust for all exercises of piety. His uncle, thinking that a trip would be advantageous, made him come to Paris, and confided him to the care of Blessed John Gabriel, who treated him with so much kindness and intelligence, that his scruples and melancholy were dissipated; the young man recovered his happiness, his love of his vocation, his taste for study and for piety and returned to his diocese perfectly cured.

---

## XV.

### EXAMPLE GIVEN BY BLESSED PERBOYRE TO HIS SEMINARIANS.

It was not only by his instruction and able direction, but also by his example, that John Gabriel formed his seminarians to the virtues they must practise. If he exhorted them to perfection, his life showed much more sanctity than he demanded of them. The young men admitted to the seminary were struck with his modesty and recollection, and felt a great veneration for him. It is interesting to read of the impression he made upon a student at his entrance into the Congregation. "The first time I saw him," said this missionary, "he was with M. Etienne, who was then procurator General of the Congregation. They were both standing in front of me. Blessed Perboyre had so humble and modest a bearing, that I took him for one of the lay brothers of the Congregation, engaged in the lowest work of the house. What astonished me was that M. Etienne paid him much attention and seemed to have great regard for him. However, this Brother so poor, so silent, seemed to remind me of Our Suffering Lord, and this first impression was increased the more I knew him. After he left the room, I was surprised when M. Etienne told me that this man, so poorly dressed, was the director of the interior seminary. I had seen him only as a Brother servant; it was not long till I saw him as Master of Novices and heard him, too; for he had not spoken in the other interview or, if he did speak, I do not remember his words; only I seemed to see in his person all the virtues of which I have read in the lives of the Saints. For many years, I had desired to meet a saint; it seemed to me that if God accorded me this grace, it would be a great help to my sanctification. No one I had seen until then, fulfilled my idea of a saint. In seeing M. Perboyre, it seemed that God had granted my desire. He was, in fact, so holy that I found no fault in word or action, though I purposely observed him during the six months I passed in the greatest intimacy with him. All virtues were so natural to him that they seemed to be born in him and to grow up with him; he practised them without apparent effort; he had but to yield to the habits of his life, like the waters of a river which flow naturally onward, so that nature could not be distinguished from grace in him—so well did they seem to be mingled. Sanctity seemed natural to him; I know not if he could have been more saintly. I have several times heard his confrères say before he was martyred, 'You will see that John Gabriel Perboyre will be canonized.'"

Though placed above those whom he had to train, the humble director put himself beneath them and regarded himself as their servant. In the first conference which he gave them, he spoke in a simple, familiar manner; he declared he had only been put in this important post, to place himself entirely at their service; this he proved by his conduct, being always ready to listen to them and to aid them when they needed his counsels. The students had a great opinion of his humility for when they consulted him on theological difficulties, he would have desired them to consult some one else. His charity prevailing, however, in a few words he enlightened their doubts and generally profited by the occasion to incite them to the study of theology, as the basis of true and solid piety.

In a conference which he gave the seminarians, he told them that certain persons, by their position, are especially obliged to give edification; that all do not fulfil this obligation, but this, nevertheless, does not authorize the relaxation of those who do not receive the example to which they have a right. One of the seminarians, thinking that, perhaps, the director wished indirectly to give him advice, examined in what manner he fulfilled his office; but, not finding matter to reform, went to Blessed Perboyre and desired to know in what he had disedified his confrères. What was his astonishment when he answered him: "You are deceived; in all that I said I had reference to no one but myself."

Another day, as the same student cleaned the corridor, John Gabriel left his room and, not perceiving him, the seminarian threw the sweepings on him. Looking up, he was much ashamed and hastened to apologize; he received this reply: "Do you not know that I am the sweepings of the house?" Once in conversation, some one interrupted him, and, with great haughtiness, told him some painful facts. John Gabriel, far from being troubled at this rude conduct so underserved, replied with a sweet smile and words of approbation. "You could see," said a missionary who witnessed the scene, "that he relished humiliation and found his delight in it. He who treated him thus, cherished him with even great esteem; but, knowing the humility of Blessed Perboyre, wished to give him an occasion to satisfy his great love for humiliations."

"Charity," says St. Vincent, "is always in proportion to the humility of a soul." According to this, some idea may be formed of the charity of the fervent director for his students. His kindness at their first arrival made a great impression upon them; they delight in recalling it even to this day. He often recommended this virtue of charity as the only means by which a missionary can make himself agreeable to God and have much success in his ministry. "Among all his conferences," said one of those who lived under his direction, "there was one I shall never forget; it was upon kindness. After showing the difference between natural and Christian kindness, he explained how precious the latter is; how dear it had been to St. Vincent and how rare it is, even among those who apply themselves to devotion. He reminded us of these words of Jesus Christ, 'Blessed are the meek: for they shall possess the land.' (Matt. v, 4.) I felt what he said was true, for I knew his kindness had gained my affection."

One day, when returning to the country house with the students, some children began to insult them by impudent words and, huddling together, they closed up the passway. One of the seminarians asked him to rebuke them, but Blessed Perboyre answered: "Come this way; we will take another path; it would be better to step aside than to give them an occasion to offend God." They passed into the field that adjoined the road. A man who perceived the misbehavior of the children said, "You should have walked right over them." "We have done better," said John Gabriel, "we have passed them by."

He profited by his recreation-days to exercise his zeal among the poor, or among the children who ran after him; stepping to speak to them, he distributed to them medals, pictures, books and other objects of piety, teaching them to honor God, to pray, to go to confession and to be respectful to their parents. Upon arriving at the country house, his first action was to prostrate himself before the statue of the Blessed

Virgin to invoke her aid for himself and the seminarians. After a short prayer, he divided his time among his various duties, reading some work of piety, reciting the breviary and the rosary, and in directing the young men.

He had greatly at heart the practice of poverty; he did not content himself with watching to have it well observed—he took every occasion to recommend it. His room, his clothing—everything—recalled this virtue. He dreaded to get new clothes; he used a great coat so ragged, that his confrères laughed at it and said it was no longer fit to be worn. He discarded it, for he did not wish to make himself remarkable.

The zeal which he had for the amendment and perfection of his seminarians, made him offer himself every day as a victim, and pray fervently in order to draw down upon his work the blessing of heaven, for he expected nothing but from God the source of all grace. "There is no real good done in souls," he used to say, "except by prayer." When he had cause to study closely a postulant whom he thought injurious or without a vocation, he addressed himself to God and had the students make a novena before some feast of the Blessed Virgin; at the end of the novena, this student would leave the house, after taking part with the others in the exercises of which he had been the occasion and object.

Such was the director whom Providence gave to the novitiate of St. Lazare. "There came from his person," said a missionary whom he trained, "a sanctifying influence which made a deep impression upon those who approached him. He was a saint and had the gift of making saints. No one dared commit the least fault before him, not only on account of his authority, but still more because of his sanctity, which condemned all imperfections. Rarely did he reprove, in words, those who misbehaved; his manner was not that of a reformer, but was peaceful and quiet. He allowed some faults to pass unnoticed; he preached in the manner of St. Francis. He often urged his students to study the primitive spirit of the Congregation in the first members, especially that set forth in the life and writings of St. Vincent; he frequently implored Our Lord to increase His spirit in the whole Congregation, persuaded that to preserve and extend it, the same means should be used as had been employed in the beginning to establish it. That is why he so much esteemed and practised amiable simplicity, which is so blessed by God and so agreeable to men. His pupils, witnesses and admirers of his virtues, were forced to strive to serve God with more fervor, and to follow more faithfully the holy practices of the rule. "It has been sixteen years since I left him; his memory still speaks to me, *defunctus adhuc loquitur*, and teaches me, as if he himself were present, simplicity, humility, meekness, mortification, zeal and especially recollection and the interior life.

---

## XVI.

### JOHN GABRIEL PERBOYRE OBTAINS PERMISSION TO GO TO CHINA.

Blessed Perboyre thus trained apostolic men who would announce the good tidings of the gospel to the whole world and lead to God many stray souls; but one thought pursued him everywhere; he, too, had desired, for a long time, to labor in foreign lands. He knew that God had called him and he had done everything to correspond to his vocation. But the same God Who called him and Who urged him so strongly on one side, restrained him on the other. His superiors and directors, learning his desire, always said it was not to be thought of; that his health was too feeble to resist the fatigues and privations; that he would not be able to stand even the difficulties of the journey. The unexpected death of his brother Louis was the decisive argument with which they opposed him. He could only repeat that the voice of God interiorly urged him; his words seemed but the pious illusion of his zeal. Days, months, years passed and the accomplishment of his desires was always delayed. Nevertheless, he submitted without accusing any one, blaming only himself. He humbled himself before God, pouring out his tears, thinking that his sins hindered the realization of his desires. This he showed on several occasions. One day, speaking about vocations, he said there was not only a general vocation for the Congregation which must be preserved with care, but also a special one for a particular duty that the least infidelity might make one lose. "As for me," he added with deep sadness, "I have certainly lost my special vocation by my infidelities." "For fourteen years, I have asked to go to China," said he on another occasion to a student, "I had this vocation before I joined the Mission and it was for this I entered St. Lazare."

The motive that urged him to go to China was

the desire to work for the glory of God and the salvation of souls, with the hope of obtaining martyrdom. For more than six years, he asked Our Lord every day at the Consecration, the grace of shedding his blood for Him. To be a missionary in China was but a means to attain this end. He loved to speak of the Venerable Clet who died for the faith in that country. "What a beautiful death was that of M. Clet!" said he to a novice, "beg God that I may die as he did." Having one day assembled the seminarians in the conference hall, he showed them a rope and a coat stained with blood, and told them in an animated tone: "This is the coat of a martyr—this is M. Clet's coat and this is the rope with which he was strangled; what happiness for us if we could one day have the same fate!" As he left the room, he took one of the students aside and said to him. "Pray, then, that my health may be strengthened so that I can go to China to preach Jesus Christ there, and die for Him."

To show the relics was a rare favor and only allowed as an exceptional recompense. "Who can express with what respect and veneration he exhibited these venerable relics?" says one who had seen them. "He made us notice the spots of blood with which they were embellished, and which adorned them like precious stones. If we sought, in touching them, to feel some of the virtue that is hidden in everything that belongs to a Servant of God, it moved him with an ardent desire of martyrdom. Then his face would glow, his words and bearing showed the burning desire he had of shedding his blood for his Divine Master."

At last, one day the students saw that he was troubled; he seemed to have some important business on hand, and to demand some great grace, for he prayed more frequently than usual and with particular fervor. As he knew his desires were opposed on earth, he wished to do violence to heaven and to implore God to change the disposition of his superiors in his regard.

He had just learned that they were going to send missionaries to China, but he was not of the number. Moved by a mysterious inspiration, he went and cast himself at the feet of the Superior General and implored him, with tears, to put no more obstacles to his vocation. The venerable superior, deeply touched, promised him to speak of it in the council, but the majority of the members declared that it would be an imprudence to let him go; that he would do more good in France than in China; besides, seeing the bad state of his health, it would but give him his death. However, M. Etienne, then Procurator General, combated these objections; and, in regard to the health of the Servant of God, he asked them to obtain the opinion of a physician. The doctor being consulted, said at first that if M. Perboyre started, he feared he would die on the way. After this decision, everything seemed settled. It was not, however; Blessed John Gabriel continued to solicit the much desired favor from Him Who holds the hearts of men in His hands; he implored Mary, his good Mother, not to abandon him upon this important occasion. The same day, the doctor, having reflected upon his decision, feared he might be deceived; he felt so great remorse that he could not sleep that night and could regain his tranquility only after resolving to revoke his decision. In fact, the next morning, he went to St. Lazare to say that he no longer opposed M. Perboyre's departure, and that he conscientiously thought he would not die on the way, but that the sea voyage would improve his health. The members of the council agreed to this opinion and decided that John Gabriel should go to China.

He, hearing this happy news, hastened to prostrate himself before God to offer Him a thousand thanks for so precious a favor. Then, he informed several of his relations, but only the letter which he wrote his uncle can be found. It is reproduced here:

"*My Dear Uncle,*—I have great news to tell you. The good God has just favored me with a very precious grace of which I am very unworthy. When He deigned to give me a vocation to the ecclesiastical state, the principal motive which induced me to respond to His voice was the hope of being able to preach to the heathens the good tidings of salvation. Since then, I have always had this project in view, and the thought alone of the mission to China made my heart palpitate. Ah! my dear uncle, my desires have to-day at last been granted. It was on the Feast of the Purification that permission was given me to go to China, which makes me think that in this matter, I owe much to the Blessed Virgin. Help me, please, to thank her and to beg her to thank Our Lord for me. I will go with two of our young confrères and several priests of the Foreign Missions.

"We must sail from Havre about March 10, perhaps some days later. I will try to write you a few words again before my departure; I cannot express to you how delighted I am with so admirable a vocation. No doubt you congratulate me yourself. I hope you will have the goodness to pray unceasingly for me, that God may deign to bestow upon me the graces I need for a happy voyage; to live, suffer and die as a true missionary. I have just written to my parents; I hope they will know how to make the sacrifice, like good Christians. I wish you would, when you have the opportunity, console and help them by your good advice, etc."

As soon as the news of John Gabriel's departure for China was circulated at the mother-house, there was general astonishment, and enthusiastic admiration for his course. If he had desired to take the students and seminarians with him, all would have esteemed themselves happy to follow him. All regretted not having asked for this mission. For some time, it was the only subject of conversation. As to himself, he was always calm and recollected and seemed to experience no new emotions, continuing like his usual self. His preparations were made by prayer. To make himself agreeable to God, he wished to renew his general confession. Though he loved his parents with great affection, he did not think of going to see them. Knowing that he would never see them again in this world, he showed on this occasion the detachment of an apostle. One of his cousins who lived in Paris, having come to see him, tried to dissuade him from his project. "What," said he to him, "do you not dread the fatigues, privations and dangers which await you among these heathens?" "My dear cousin," he replied, "what is our body? A little clay.—Must it be prized so much? Does not heaven merit much greater sacrifices?"

Our holy missionary had inspired so deep feelings

of veneration that many people desired to have some souvenir of him; but his poverty was so great that he had nothing with which to buy pictures. One of his confrères offered him some money, but he refused to take all that was given him, contenting himself with what was strictly necessary; he thought that, having made the vow of poverty, he could not give costly things. Presenting a medal of the Immaculate Conception to one of his relations who came to see him, he said: "My dear cousin, I beg you to accept this medal; it is a trifle, no doubt, but you know I am poor and that I have made a vow of poverty; that is why I ask you not to consider the worth of the thing itself, but to accept it as a memento from a person who is very fond of you."

The following fact will show the impression Blessed Perboyre made on those, even, who saw him for the first time. Before starting, he was obliged to go to the ministry of foreign affairs, and the clerks were struck with the air of sanctity which shone in his exterior; they felt great esteem for him; several of them sent him pictures, asking him to write his name on the back. His humility was grieved, but he dared not refuse them this pious desire.

"The day of departure having come," said an eye witness, "he assembled together all the seminarians to speak to them for the last time. When he entered the hall, his face showed at the same time joy at going and sorrow at being obliged to separate from his dear seminarians, whom he loved so much and who so cordially loved him. He mounted the pulpit to make his last farewell; in the assembly, solemn silence reigned; each was eager to hear the last loving words, but his heart was too full; scarcely had he pronounced the first words when emotion choked his voice, and, at this moment another thought besides his farewells pre-occupied him—it was the deep sense of his miseries and infidelities; it was regret for the scandals he had given them. Abandoning the pulpit after saying a few words, he prostrated himself in the middle of the hall and asked pardon of the seminarians for his negligences and the bad example of which he had been guilty. The spectators of this affecting scene, urged by an irresistible impulse, fell also upon their knees and replied only by sobs and groans. He remained long in this humble posture, annihilating himself before God, imploring Him to pardon his failings. When he arose, the seminarians asked him to give them his blessing before leaving them; he refused at first, not thinking himself worthy of blessing them, but his charity triumphed over his humility and he blessed them with fatherly affection, begging Our Lord to preserve them inviolably in His love, recommending himself to their prayers, promising never to forget them before God and, after some simple, loving words, left the seminary. I shall never forget this touching scene, nor the blessing of him who left us to go to martyrdom."

The last adieus of the community were given in the court yard, at the entrance. All the members of the Congregation who were present wished to receive his blessing. The venerable Superior General, Very Rev. Dominic Salhorgne, notwithstanding his infirmities, came to embrace, once more, one of the noblest of his children. The community was moved to tears, and implored his prayers, like the early Christians who recommended themselves to the prayers of the martyrs when they went to execution. At last, he must go; and, after pouring out his soul before the Blessed Sacrament, after invoking Mary, his tender mother, St. Joseph and St. Vincent, whose venerated relics he left with regret; after putting himself under the protection of the Holy Angels, John Gabriel Perboyre started for Havre, whence he would embark for China.

# BOOK II.

## FROM BLESSED PERBOYRE'S DEPARTURE FOR CHINA TO HIS MARTYRDOM.

---

### I.

#### VOYAGE FROM HAVRE TO BATAVIA.

BLESSED John Gabriel arrived in Havre, March 16, 1835, thence he wrote his uncle the following letter.

"*My Dear Uncle*,—I have been here in Havre since the evening of day before yesterday. Our ship, the 'Edmond,' is already laden and only awaits a favorable wind to set sail. This is why I hasten to send you my last good-bye. As I told you before, eight missionaries full of courage and hope now set out together. I again claim the help of your holy prayers. You know how much we need the assistance of Our Lord. Ours is the same vessel that last year brought M. Baldus to Batavia in three months. The officers are really polite gentlemen, and the sailors are very respectful to us. There are no passengers besides the missionaries. I will send you news the first opportunity I have at Batavia, Manilla or Macao. Thanks to the kindness of our pastor at Catus, my parents after having wept much, have become perfectly reconciled to my going. I left my brothers and sisters very well. May God grant them every blessing!

"The weather has just become fine and urges us to start. On Friday, March 20, we embark. Remember me again to all those who are interested in me. I recommend myself to their prayers and yours, united to whom I am for life—"

The travellers started March 21. Three months after they arrived in Batavia, whence John Gabriel wrote the following letter to M. Salhorgne, Superior General.

"BATAVIA, June 29, 1835.

"*Very Honored and Dear Father,*—Happily arrived in Batavia, we hasten to give you the news which in your tender solicitude for us you have long expected.

"You know we started from Havre the 21st of last March. We left our much loved France in the same peace of mind we felt in leaving Paris. I rejoice at the good dispositions God has given us. I was suddenly reminded of a sad, though peaceful remembrance which came to me as a heavenly thought. It was that it was not yet five years since my dear brother Louis embarked upon the same voyage that we have undertaken, and that he received his recompense and crown before obtaining his desire. I felt inspired to place our voyage under his protection; my soul was raised to him in confidence; my eyes were filled with tears, but with sweet tears of delight.

"Two days after our departure, we advanced at full sail through the English Channel; a favorable wind facilitated our voyage, but the continual and violent rolling and pitching of the vessel made the new passengers so sick that for a week the ship was really a hospital. It is needless to recall what the missionaries suffered. By the grace of God, this trial though very inconvenient, served like all others, to exercise and increase more and more our courage, instead of abating it in the least. However, He Who rules the powers of the sea and moderates the movements of the waves, accorded us relief and consolation. On the 29th, we came in sight of Madeira; the tempest ceased and good weather gave us new life. I could say Holy Mass, which we did each in turn nearly every Sunday and holiday. Oh! how happy we felt upon this vast desert of the ocean, ever and anon to find ourselves in the company of Our Lord.

"For a long time, our progress was very slow. It was Easter Sunday when we crossed the equator. The usual ceremony of this occasion was postponed until the next day. A piastre, which each of us gave the sailors, exempted us from any other role than that of simple spectators. A month afterwards, we doubled the Cape of Good Hope, 38° south latitude. We had to change the ideas we had obtained of this locality. We had been told that the sea would be fearful but we found it as calm and placid as at the Canaries. God spared us in this passage, generally so dangerous, that we would be better able to sustain the fatigues of crossing the Indian Ocean.

"On May 31, between 60° and 70° east longitude from Amsterdam, we experienced a new tempest. Our captain, who has sailed thirty-six years, had never seen one so terrible. It lasted for twelve hours in the fiercest intensity; enormous waves mounted to the top of the mast, then beat upon the deck and everything not firmly fixed to the floor rolled from side to side, pell mell. One wave, after giving our ship so violent a jolt that all the ballast was thrown upon one side of the hold, suddenly reversed, and threw upon the poop two men who held the helm, and then bore off a boat which we never saw again. The foaming waves which each instant arose nearly perpendicular before and behind us were at the same time, frightful and admirable and we could not help exclaiming with the prophet. '*Mirabiles elationes maris, mirabilis in altis Dominus:* Wonderful are the surges of the sea: wonderful is the Lord on high.' (Ps. xcii. 4.) However, we possessed our souls in peace, loving to abandon ourselves to the good pleasure of Him Who leads to the door of the tomb and brings back again. He willed to bring us safe and sound through this horrible crisis. In the evening, all the missionaries recited together the litany of the Blessed Virgin, the Ave Maris Stella and the pious ejaculation 'O Mary conceived without sin, etc.' Our confidence was not in vain for scarcely had we raised our hands to the Star of the Sea when the tempest ceased. This tempest was the only remarkable event which occurred in our voyage from France to Java. We entered, on June 23, the strait of Sunda, and on the 26th we arrived at Batavia.

"Up to this, my health has continued pretty good and my two confrères are also well. Both have edified me and helped to make my voyage agreeable. I must say the same of the priests of the Foreign Missions. They and we, you doubtless know, have lived together as friends and brothers. As our ship's company was composed of honest young men and really very good boys, it seemed that we ought to try to do them some good. The missionaries could not but feel towards them some of the compassion with which Our Lord was filled at the sight of the people whom He compared to sheep without a shepherd. Several of our priests went to them from time to time in the evening, to exercise their zeal amongst them, talking familiarly with them of the truths of religion, of their principal duties and exhorting them to a Christian life. They nearly all went to confession. May Our Lord fructify the seed that has been sown in their hearts and make it produce the fruits of salvation!

"This is in a few words, Rev. and very honored Father, the history of our first voyage. It will give you cause to bless with us the heavenly Providence which is spoken of in the book of Wisdom, chapter xiv: *Tua autem, Pater, providentia gubernat; quoniam dedisti et in mari viam et inter fluctus semitam firmissimam, ostendens quoniam potens es ex omnibus salvare, etiamsi sine arte aliquis adeat mare.* 'But thy Providence, O Father, governeth it: for Thou hast made a way even in the sea, and a most sure path among the waves, showing that Thou art able to save out of all things; yea, though a man went to sea without art.' We hope that our confrères and the Sisters of Charity, who are so deeply interested in us, will still continue to join their supplications to yours to implore Our Lord to keep us under His holy protection.

"The next day after our arrival, we had the honor of seeing the Prefect Apostolic and the pastor of Batavia. They welcomed all the missionaries with as much cordiality as kindness. They hastened to offer us board and lodging. We have profited by their charity for two or three days. We returned to them toward the end of the week to celebrate with them the feast of St. Peter. Meanwhile, we will leave the ship that brought us here and go on board of an English vessel the 'Royal George' which will start sooner for China and will bring us to Macao. May Our Lord happily conduct us to the end of our voyage.

"Accept, Rev. and very honored Father, the homage and profound respect of your three children, of whom the least prays you to believe that he is, as far as he has power to be,

"Your very devoted and humble servant," etc.

We find some other details of this voyage in a letter he wrote to his brother. It is dated July 1, 1835.

"You have expected with impatience, my dear brother, and perhaps with some anxiety, some sign of life from me. Ah well! here it is. Your brother is not yet dead, what is more, he is very well. Although unworthy of my grand vocation and even of life, God has willed to preserve me; and though I shared the fatigues and the other inconveniences inseparable from a voyage like this, He was pleased so to help my feebleness that the passage has not injured my health. I have generally slept well, an essential requisite to my puny being. If my stomach can not accommodate itself to all sorts of food, especially those used at sea, it knows how to content itself with little, and did wonderfully well on a small ration of rice. The sea air has proved salutary for me; I feel, less than on land, that feverishness which has troubled me for some years. Before sailing, I could not think of the sea without a secret dread; but since I have embarked, neither the immensity of its extent, the depths of its abyss, nor the agitation of its waves has caused me the least fright. Thus, after dreading to appear before God, we must enjoy one day upon His bosom a repose until then unknown.

"It would be needless to describe to you the route we followed. To tell you that we sighted several islands and ships, saw whales and various sorts of birds and fishes, caught and ate albatross, shark and so on, would be superfluous; you can suppose this from the accounts of our predecessors. But I must tell you what perhaps you do not know, that about a month and a half ago, I fell from the top to the bottom of the staircase whose steps were covered with brass where I might have broken my head a dozen times. I escaped with some bruises on my side and a skinned thigh, but these wounds were not serious. I must tell you too, that one day we were tossed by a severe tempest from six in the morning till six in the evening when our cries of distress suddenly changed to fervent thanksgivings. *Post tempestatem tranquillum, facis, Domini* 'After a storm thou makest a calm.' (Tobias iii. 22.) God having unceasingly protectedus during all our course, we arrived in the fine harbor of Batavia three months after our departure from France. Do not doubt, my dear brother, that in this interval I have often thought of you. I love to picture to myself my good brother at different hours of the day, sometimes adoring God in church, sometimes conversing in His presence, always fulfilling his accustomed duties, always serving with joy and zeal this good Master, again prostrated before the shrine of St. Vincent recommending to his loving father the most unworthy of his children. I have not forgotten that you have promised to pray for me every day."

To complete the details John Gabriel Perboyre gave of the first part of his voyage, we add the following letter to his uncle:

"SURABAYA, July 24.

"*My Very Dear Uncle*,—I must not let the 'Edmond' leave without profiting of the opportunity to send you news. It is four months since I have had the pleasure of writing to you. Since then, as you see, I have travelled some thousands of leagues from you, but in heart and mind I have not left you. I still find myself, now and then, near you, and sometimes I surprise you praying for a poor little missionary in whom you deign to interest yourself much more than he deserves.

"Our voyage so far, has been most happy, and my companions and I, all have great cause to bless divine Providence for the special protection with which He has always favored us.

"The sea is displayed to us under all phases; sometimes tranquil, sometimes raging; sometimes, we are obliged to struggle against contrary winds; sometimes, we are borne by a strong breeze which bears us along rapidly as on a light cloud. From a dull calm to the best weather, we had all kinds, not even lacking a tempest; for, on May 31, we experienced one that our captain called the worst he had ever seen. The horizon was overclouded and darkened; a sort of roaring sound announced something wrong. An impetuous wind from behind impelled us with such violence that though we had scarcely any sails, we made nearly five leagues an hour. Continually tossed by the waves which bore us, we seemed sometimes raised to the top of a high mountain or engulfed in the deep abyss. In spite of myself, I thought I was among the precipices of Cantal and Lozere, imagining the froth to be snow and the moving waves, rocks. We could not contemplate this fearful and magnificent spectacle for more than a few moments without being exposed to a thorough drenching or, worse still, to being borne away by enormous waves that broke upon the deck like bombs. Some of our men were thrown down and rolled over by one of the waves, which engulfed in the sea, a boat that hung suspended from our ship. No one was sick and we experienced no other serious injury. In the evening, the eight missionaries who did not lose that peace, which full confidence in God gives, asked in common through the intercession of the Blessed Virgin, the cessation of the tempest which immediately began to diminish and canticles of thanksgiving succeeded our cries of distress. Thus was accomplished for us what is written in Psalm cvi. *Ipse viderunt opera Domini, et mirabilia ejus in profundo. Dixit, et stetit spiritus procellæ, et exaltati sunt fluctus ejus. Ascendunt usque ad coelus et descendunt usque ad abyssos. Et clamaverunt ad Dominum cum tribularentur et de necessitatibus eorum eduxit eos. Et statuit procellam ejus in auram et siluerunt fluctus ejus. Et laetati sunt quia siluerunt et deduxit eos in portum voluntatis eorum. Confiteantur Domine misere-cordiae ejus mirabilia ejus filiis hominum.* 'These have seen the works of the Lord, and His wonders in the deep. He said the word, and there arose a storm of wind: and the waves thereof were lifted. They mount up to the heavens, and they go down to the depths. And they cried to the Lord in their affliction:

and He brought them out of their distresses. And he turned the storm into a breeze: and its waves were still. And they rejoiced because they were still: and He brought them to the haven they wished for. Let the mercies of the Lord give glory to Him and His wonderful works to the children of men.'

"It was on June 23, that we entered the strait of Sunda. I can not describe to you the emotion we felt at the sight of these islands covered with trees bearing fruit almost within our reach; they sent forth a strong, sweet odor of cinnamon; it seemed to us that new life was imparted to our being. The next day, the feast of St. John the Baptist, my patron, I said Mass with as much ease as upon land, upon this sea, whose waters are of the color of olives and always calm. We advanced cautiously among the numerous islets and the still more numerous rocks, which were indicated to the sailors by as many crosses that arose on all sides above the surface of the water. At last, on the 26th, we were anchored in the harbor of Batavia. We passed the three following days also Sundays and the feast of St. Peter at the house of the Prefect Apostolic, where the pastor lives. Immediately after our return to the vessel, we made the necessary arrangements for changing our ship. Moving from one ship to the other should have taken only an hour, but it required three; and all this time I was obliged to work like a professional seaman. The long boat, on which I was with four or five men, and which carried the heaviest part of our luggage, was borne along so rapidly that we could not use the sail but had to fold it, because the wind blew directly against us; we made for a long time many useless efforts to resist the fury of the waves. In fact, we went back farther than we advanced. Night fell and the sea swelled while we rowed in vain. We did nothing more than attempt some long tedious curves amid the darkness, and we ran great risk of being upset or driven aground, when at last, two new rowers came with two boats which were placed one before the other in front of our boat, and attached to it by ropes in the same way as a relief horse is fixed to a carriage. This aid soon brought us happily to the ship ready to receive us. I hastened to change my linen, for being extremely fatigued from pumping and holding the helm, I was inundated with perspiration and sea-water. July 5th we left Batavia upon the "Royal George" which we thought would bring us to China but which was obliged, as well as the "Edmund," to go to take freight at the eastern extremity of Java. We have been here in the harbor of Surabaya since the 14th. We will leave August 10th. We must go back in our route to double the west coast of the Isle of Borneo; at most we shall arrive at Macao by the Feast of the Nativity. While waiting we must bear the delay with patience and try to utilize our time. We go on land on Sundays only, to say Mass. St. Vincent's day, after staying in church till noon, we dined with the pastor. In the whole island of Java there are but four priests, these are Hollanders. There are no priests at all in the neighboring isles. All these islands are peopled by Malays who follow the Mohammedan religion, at least in certain points. It is now winter in this country but the winter resembles the summers in Montauban. We are in the 7th or 8th degree of South latitude.

"At my departure from France, my health caused great anxiety even to my best friends, who now learn with surprise that I am still living. As you have shared these fears, perhaps more than any one else, I must, my very dear uncle, fully reassure you.

"Though I have suffered a little from seasickness and the heat of the torrid zone, I have not, however, been injured; and if during the first half of my trip, the state of my health was uncertain, I have since felt it grow better day by day; this makes me believe God wills that I arrive in good health at my destination. Besides 'Thy mercy is better than lives.' *Melior est misericordia tua super vitas* (Ps. lxii. 4.) I could not make this voyage to China without thinking of my dear Louis. I love to think of him walking before me and showing the way which I must follow. Alas! like the star which guided the Magi, he disappeared on the way. Oh! with what great joy shall I not rejoice when I shall see him shining with a new brightness and showing me where the Divine King Jesus is! . . . ."

---

## II.

### FROM BATAVIA TO MACAO.

We still borrow from Blessed Perboyre the account of his voyage, because it seems to us that it will be more agreeable to the reader to learn from our martyr himself, some of the impressions which he received during this long and painful trip. The first letter he wrote after his departure from Surabaya was addressed to one of the Assistants of the Congregation:

"MACAO, September 9, 1835.

"*Rev. and very honored Confrère*,—Here I am: these are the words by which I must give you my first sign of life in Macao. Yes, here I am, and blessed be Our Lord Who Himself has conducted me here! '*Si sumpsero pennas meas diluculo et habitavero in extremis maris, manus tua deducet me et tenebit me dextera tua.*' 'If I take my wings early in the morning, and dwell in the uttermost parts of the sea, even there also shall Thy hand lead me and Thy right hand shall hold me.' (Ps. cxxxviii, 9-10.)

"From the letter I wrote to the Superior-General, you have learned that, up to that time, our voyage had been most happy. It has been not less so since. We made a three weeks' stay in the harbor of Surabaya. This delay was for us what a vacation in the country is to those who have had a year of hard work. The heat of the burning climate of Java was tempered by a constant breeze from a neighboring mountain.

"Though we were occupied with study or prayer from five or six o'clock in the morning till ten in the evening, in many ways it was more pleasant on our new ship than on the other one, as we were not so much buffeted by the waves; each day we gathered new strength for the continuance of our journey. We went to town to say Mass as often as we could; that is, once or twice a week. Sometimes, but rarely, we made excursions along the shores of Java and Madeira.

"We left Surabaya, August 7. We were obliged to anchor four or five leagues from there, to await the return of the tide, for the ship ploughed the slime several feet deep. The next day, after we resumed our journey, the pilot forced us forward on a bank. Fortunately, the captain soon adjusted the sails so as to send the ship backward and turn it in another direction. In these dangers, we owe our safety to the skill of the commander and to the power of the wind, or rather, to Providence Who rules all, and Whose second causes do but execute the judgments of justice or mercy. The Monsoon from the south-east continued during the month of August in the China Sea. It favored us for some time, and on the 29th, we at last arrived at Macao.

"Though we were disposed to make a voyage a hundred times as long if ordered by obedience, I assure you, nevertheless, that we saw the end of our journey with much pleasure. Our hearts were not a little gladdened when, as we set foot on this land for which we had so long sighed, we embraced our worthy superior, M. Torrette, and his excellent co-laborer, M. Danicourt, who came to meet us at the ship. They found us and our good young Chinese confrères all in perfect health. This community has proved not only a place of repose but still more of edification and has, at the very outset, embalmed us with the good odor of Our Lord. The greatest order and most perfect regularity reign in our house at Macao; priests, seminarians, young aspirants all contribute to it. If the holy practices of St. Lazare should be lost in France, they could still be found living in full force in China.

"I know you will be offended, Rev. and very honored confrère, if I tell you nothing of my health which you saw so feeble and delicate. I am much improved. The sea air has relieved my head and delivered me from that feverishness which used to consume me, so that I have as little of it as can be expected from my temperament. My two companions are very well. As they have been always just as you knew them in Paris, I will enter into no details about them. They continued to work hard during the voyage. As to myself, my principal occupation has been reading the life of St. Vincent. Thus I consoled myself for the loss of your kind, wise discourse, by that of this good Father.

"Already I long to receive news of our confrères of Europe and particularly of the honored elders of our house in Paris. God grant that they may be long preserved to us and that He may pour forth upon them His greatest blessings. You know how deeply everything relating to our dear Congregation interests me. Among the consolations God has reserved for me, the greatest will be to learn from you that He always protects it and animates it more and more with the spirit of our holy Founder. I long to receive some letters from you; they will be more precious to me than gold or gems. I prize much your advice and fatherly reprimands—"

Some weeks later, John Gabriel wrote again to one of his relations, then a professor at the Seminary of St. Flour:

"*My dear Cousin and Confrère*:—About eight months ago, I embraced you in Paris, no doubt for the last time in life. We are now separated by seas and continents. Happily, our hearts will meet and be united in the Heart of Our Lord. My arrival in Macao can be no news to you, as I requested my brother to inform you of it. I must tell you, also, that our journey has been most happy and that you should bless Our Lord for it. You have read so many accounts of sea voyages, that it would be more than useless to give a minute description of ours. In a journey by land, there is always some new interest; the scene changes as you advance; nature presents continually a varied spectacle; the farther you proceed, the more people you meet and the more sights you see; all things combine for your enjoyment, or, at least, to vary your sensations. But, in the course of a long sea-voyage, nearly all the days are alike; what you see one day, you will see the next; always the same company, always the same isolation from the rest of men, always the same repetition of the ship's workings. The sail that rises before you is similar to the one you have just passed, and like the ones that lure you farther on. You can not pierce with a glance the depths upon which you are suspended, or promenade upon the vast plains that surround you; your horizon is but a circle of which you are the centre and whose diameter, at most, is but four or five leagues; though always changing, it seems always the same. If you now ask me how we pass the time during so monotonous a voyage, I shall tell you that, apart from the first days which were days of trial, all our time was devoted to exercises of piety and study.

"After these duties, the missionaries conversed together; sometimes, they held pious discourse with the sailors; again, they sang hymns, held a controversy or played a game of chess with the officers. After having in good weather and tempests admired the power of God in the terrible element on which we sailed, we delighted in the magnificence of beautiful nights. When we could say holy Mass, our joy was great. Our Lord's descending in our hearts, caused us forget passing sorrows and labors, and made us feel that all we did for Him was nothing compared to the price He paid for us. He has conducted us by a special providence. As for me, I see it clearly. During the first part of my voyage I had my soul in my hands; the fate of my brother Louis, the fears I felt, my inexperience of the sea, the weight of my infirmities left me but an uncertain prospect for the future. By the grace of God, I was never disconcerted. Does not the traveler, who, in the morning, finds himself enveloped in fog, continue the route, though he sees not its extent before him? But meanwhile, my health improved little by little, so that now I am very well. We arrived here August 29, that is, five months after our departure from France. If the vessel had brought us to Macao without stopping at Java, we could have arrived here in three and a half months. Beg Our Lord to send us other evangelical workmen, but let them be men whom the apostolical spirit makes all powerful, who are filled with the science in which St. Paul gloried,—the science of Jesus crucified, and who can say with him: *Scio et humiliari—et esurire—et penuriam pati;* 'I know how to be brought low—and to be hungry—and to suffer need,' (Phil. iv. 12) for our Christians are generally in great misery and poverty. Obtain for me, I beg you, this spirit and this science of which I am so destitute. Besides the memento I make for you every day, this morning I said Mass for you. I do not doubt that you will return me a hundred fold. I shall not enter China for some months; I do not yet know at what time. Recommend me to the prayers of all the confrères whom I affectionately embrace.

I am entirely yours, etc."

According to the account of one of the companions of his voyage, John Gabriel was respected and admired by all the ship's company. He did not pass his time in useless conversation. Sometimes he knelt in the cabin at prayer; again he sat on deck with breviary in hand, admiring the spectacle of sea and sky; or else, he addressed some instructions to the sailors, who listened with the greatest respect. The fortitude he showed during sea-sickness was wonderful. He suffered greatly from it during the first weeks of his voyage. It is a malady which weakens physical and moral strength, and casts passengers into a state of complete prostration. Blessed John Gabriel was so entirely master of himself that he never went to bed during the day, or interrupted his pious exercises or studies. Those alone who have suffered from sea-sickness are able to understand what violence he did to himself. When he left the French ship at Batavia, all the company hastened to bid him good-bye and the sailors and officers said among themselves, "This man is really a saint."

## III.

### SOJOURN AT MACAO.

THE writings of the saints have a certain impress which is pleasing and touching; therefore, we allow Blessed Perboyre, himself, to relate all the particulars of his sojourn in China. Besides, his account displays a pious mind for which he is to be admired. Here is what he wrote:

"SEPTEMBER 13, 1835.

"*My very dear Uncle*,—If, as I hope, you received the letter I wrote you from Surabaya toward the end of July, you have been relieved of all anxiety about my voyage which was happily accomplished. It remains only for you to learn of the continuation of our journey and of our arrival in Macao. It could not have been more satisfactory. Starting from Surabaya, August 7, we calmly sailed for China whither we arrived on the 29th, full of health and joy. We found our confrères of this distant country very well, too. Our house at Macao, where we passed some time studying the Chinese language, is a small picture of our house in Paris, having the same spirit and the same regularity. M. Torrette, who had been procurator of the seminary at Cahors, is superior and M. Danicourt, director. These two excellent Lazarists are assisted by the two Chinese confrères whom you saw in Paris and who are now priests. They teach

Latin to twelve or fifteen Chinese pupils, most of whom understand and speak it very well. They learn, too, philosophy and theology; they are training them to become good missionaries and worthy children of St. Vincent. It is by the grace of God that they have so perfectly succeeded.

"In Macao, the diocesan seminary is conducted by our Portuguese confrères and there are several others in the interior provinces. M. Torrette is visitor of all the Lazarists in China. I already know all the French confrères who have preceded me. I shall not see them all; they are mostly scattered in the different provinces which are larger than the whole of France. I shall congratulate myself no matter with whom I am sent to labor. I never cease to bless God for the grace He gives me to announce His name to the heathens. I hope that I shall with you bless Him eternally for it.

"Let me send by you a word to my brothers. I desire that my relations think, above all, of the great affair of their salvation and that they remember my distance only to pray to God for my sanctification and that of the people for whose salvation I am destined to work.

"Will you also pray, my dear uncle, that He bestow upon me this grace and blessing? Until now my existence has been barren, though I have accomplished half of a long life. This pilgrimage passes so quickly! Alas! How little use I make of it!

"The general assembly has already taken place. I have great confidence that God has blessed it; He has given so many proofs that he still cherishes the poor family of St. Vincent. Though I have always dishonored this family, I am attached to it from the bottom of my heart and would give a thousand lives for it. You know that I owe to it, as well as to you, more than I can tell. I expect still to be indebted to the community for their prayers and yours, so as to cross without shipwreck, the sea of this world and arrive at the harbor where our blessed Father, St. Vincent, awaits us."

The same day, he wrote to one of his brothers the following letter which should be preserved as a new proof of his spirit of faith :

"*My very dear Brother*,—The letter I wrote Papa from Java informed you that I have already traveled much farther than our good brother Louis. God has not judged me worthy of heaven as he was. This is to tell you that I have arrived safe and sound at the gates of China. We have been in Macao since August 29. God has protected us during all our voyage and though it has been long, my health is even better at the end than it was at the beginning. Do not think, then, that to go to China is to go to death. My confrères who have come to this country, live here as elsewhere ; though they have had some sorrows to try them, they are very well satisfied to have made the sacrifice of everything to bring the light of faith to the heathens.

"You understand that God has done me a great favor in giving me the same vocation. I hope in the end you will rejoice at it. You know true happiness does not consist in having all kinds of consolations in this world, but in doing the will of God, in serving

Him and in making as many serve Him as one can. You have told me that in leaving you I have deprived you of the good advice I could give you in France. First, I must remind you that God has especially confided your salvation to your pastor and confessor. You must often have recourse to them to receive their counsels and instructions. If, then, your spiritual affairs do not go well, you must attribute it to your negligence, not to the want of spiritual aid and my distance from you. Besides, though far away from you I will not cease to excite and encourage you to virtue and the performance of all your duties.

"I do not forget you in my prayers and I will be always, etc."

Shortly afterward the zealous missionary wrote the following letter to his successor as director of the novices:

"*Rev. and very dear Confrère,*—You have too many claims upon my remembrance for me not to give you from my distant exile some sign of life. When, on the most memorable day of our life, Our Lord deigned to associate us in His divine priesthood, He put in our hearts the seal of an eternal union, a union which has since been so well manifested in our house in Paris where Providence reunited us as colleagues. This holy friendship which ordination and the position of confrère had made so perfect, another circumstance must also increase. I must tell you that you have become dearer to me since I see the father of my spiritual children for whom Our Lord has given me so deep an affection. On the other hand, they themselves interest me so greatly that the remembrance of them unites with the memory of you and makes you share the same affection.

"On my arrival in Macao, I found M. Torrette as I expected him to be, a good friend and faithful confrère. You know well that we often talk of you; he has not forgotten that it was on the same occasion that Monsignor Dubourg ordained us three in the Sisters' chapel in presence of the body of St. Vincent. Like us, he is honored with the direction of the novices, for he performs that duty here. It is only needed that you, also, should come to China; but as we never hope to see you again, there is one compensation we propose, read *impose.* Upon all feasts of the apostles, you must offer the holy sacrifice for us. This is a settled thing.

"Though the good God has given us many spiritual favors during the course of our long voyage, I can understand the truth of this maxim. 'They that travel much abroad seldom become holy.' *Raro sanctificantur qui multum peregrinantur.* (Imitation, Book I, xxiii, 4.")

"We must, then, before beginning our great campaign in the interior of China, recover ourselves in solitude and draw thence new strength for the soul, even more than for the body. We shall obtain in Macao all that we need. The good spirit and fervor that reign in our Chinese seminary made us enjoy again with our whole hearts all the happiness we felt in Paris. Here, as there, simplicity, piety, modesty, meekness, humility and charity create a terrestrial paradise, of which only, those who have lived in it have any idea. Our young Chinamen give us great hopes for our missions; in two or three years, five or six will be ordained priests; four are about to make their vows; several other good subjects can, when desired, replace them in the seminary. Thanks to M. Danicourt, who is their professor, they have made great progress in the Latin language; they speak it much better than many pupils in the seminaries of Europe. We are really astonished when they give their conferences in Latin and repeat their prayers. You would be delighted to hear them chant Vespers and the *Miserere.* You remember hearing chanting in chapels of seminaries and religious houses: this is something like it, only better. It is a simple, solemn concert of rather musical voices, some sonorous, others childlike, which together, produced a marvellous effect. The young men work diligently; they are all taught, in different classes, Latin and Chinese, catechism of the Council of Trent and Holy Scripture, and in the more advanced, philosophy. I do not speak of the exercises of piety in common, or of the particular duties of the novices, whom you know are no less usefully employed. They have but one month's vacation and yet the greater part of it is spent in binding books, which they do with admirable skill. Later, they will print Chinese books. At the end of vacation, we all make the retreat.

"Our good health has allowed us to pursue with ardor the study of the Chinese language; but, after two months, we have scarcely begun to be familiar with it, as it is so difficult to learn. Until now, my professor has been M. Ly, but my change of dwelling has given me another teacher.

"Yes, I have changed my dwelling. Our Portuguese confrères insisted upon having some of us with them, and it is I whom Providence has sent, to find in this community new edification. In fact, the regularity of these gentlemen is as perfect as can be. By their simplicity, their goodness, their spirit of poverty they remind me of those venerable men whom God has used to transmit to the young French confrères the ancient traditions of St. Lazare. They occupy the college or seminary of St. Joseph, a large house which once belonged to the Jesuits. It has a fine church. They prepare and form the Chinese missionaries for the three dioceses of Canton, Nankin and Pekin, and educate, at the same time, the young men of Macao, to whom they teach, among others things, French and English. These pupils are not numerous, because they care little for education in this country. The five confrères who conduct this establishment are very learned. I shall have for my professor M. Gonzalves, who has prepared a Chinese-Portuguese dictionary; also a Portuguese-Chinese one, and he has in preparation a third, Latin-Chinese. He is author also of a Latin-Chinese grammar and a Portuguese-Chinese grammar, from which the missionaries from Europe study Chinese. He is, also, very learned in astronomy and mathematics --but let us speak of something else.

"Religion enjoys, for the present, great peace in the interior of China. Our missions increase in prosperity day by day, but our good confrères are killing themselves with work; their food is bad, too; they live on only a little rice and a few herbs. The Christians to whom they minister are the poorest of all. You see what devotion you must inspire in the subjects that you train for us; they must be filled with sanctity and prudence, which means they must be saints, men possessing all the virtues in a high degree of perfection. Prudence supposes great uprightness, sound judgment, a discerning mind, and good conduct and requires for the accomplishment of good, strength of soul and invincible constancy. This prudence must not only be a natural, but still more, a supernatural gift, a heavenly grace. After all, if the commission gave the authority to the apostles, it was but the communication of the Spirit of God which gave them the power to convert the world.

"And you, very dear confrère, be for us another Elias, opening heaven by your prayers and bringing down upon the unfertilized land of China, an abundant dew of graces so that the Pagans may become converted and the Christians live conformably to their faith. When you receive this letter, perhaps I will be on my way to the interior of China. My heart longs to share the work of my confrères and to join my feeble efforts to theirs. It seems that nothing will be wanting to my happiness when I shall be permitted to consecrate myself to the salvation of these poor Chinese. Have the goodness to present my respects to the Superior General, and all my confrères who wished to be remembered to me. I love them all in our Lord and I long to have a share in their holy prayers. Enlist the fervor of the good Sisters of Charity; they can acquire much merit in the eyes of God and cooperate in the salvation of souls when they remember us in their prayers."

M. Torrette, Superior at the house at Macao, thought

that he owed the new comer the attentions which his infirmities and virtues merited; but he was disappointed by the entreaties of his confrère, who sought to be treated as the last of the missionaries. Sent to St. Joseph's seminary, he left there so lasting a remembrance and so deep an impression that Monsignor Matha, afterward Bishop of Macao, could not speak of him without tears.

His sojourn in Macao was for the most part employed in prayer and the study of the Chinese language. He encountered many obstacles in this last work because of his age and his headaches which were nearly continual. "We have begun to study Chinese," said he in one of his letters, "I think it will require a long time for me to learn this language, judging from my first attempt. It is said that M. Clet could only speak it with difficulty. It used to be thought I bore some resemblance to him. May I resemble to the end this venerable confrère whose long apostolic life was crowned by the glorious palm of martyrdom!" But his industry and perseverance so well supplied for his want of fluency that at the end of three months, he could express himself passably well. He continued to devote to study all the time not claimed by his pious exercises and the duties he had to fulfil. A little while after his arrival in Ho-Nan, he was able to direct the Chinese missions, to preach and explain all the points of Christian doctrine with a facility which astonished his confrères. In the long and numerous interrogations to which he was subjected during his trial, the judges were no less surprised at the knowledge he possessed of their language, than at the

10

strength and heroic firmness he displayed during his execution.

Though he made a long voyage to work for the salvation of the Chinese, yet, having once arrived in Macao, he did not concern himself about the place he would be sent, or the time he would start for his post; he abandoned himself entirely to Providence and calmly awaited a mission to be assigned him. This is what he wrote to one of the Assistants of the house at Paris: "Do not ask me what will be my destination in this new world. I must assure you that I am in complete ignorance on this point. For a long time, my chief resolution was to practise holy indifference; upon coming here, I try to adhere to it more firmly than ever. In the first place when I would open by chance the Imitation of Christ, my eyes fell always on these words: 'My son, suffer me to do with thee what I will: I know what is best for thee.' I hasten to respond with one of the following verses: 'Lord, provided that my will remain but firm toward Thee, do with me whatsoever it shall please Thee.' (Book III, xvii, I.) I love the mysterious disposition of Providence which delights in having me live depending upon Him from day to day. When the time comes, we shall receive our mission. I shall not be troubled wherever they send me. All our confrères of China have given in our establishment in France many proofs of wisdom, piety, and zeal, and God has marvellously blessed in their works in these foreign lands; they possess in advance my entire esteem and confidence. Their charity and experience equally assure me of a kind, as well as a safe and necessary, guidance."

However, as the needs of Ho-Nan required a missionary of consummate virtue, and as Providence seemed to prepare John Gabriel for it, he was assigned this mission. On the day of his departure, he wrote his brother in Paris the following lines: "To-day I embark for the interior of China. I do not know when I shall arrive there. I hope the good God will protect me during this journey as He did in the former one. I start very well and happy. If you could get a glimpse of me now, I would present an interesting spectacle in my Chinese garb, my head shaved, my long queue and moustache, stammering a new language and eating with sticks which serve for knife, spoon and fork. It is said that I do not make a bad Chinaman. It is thus I must begin to make myself all in all. May I also gain all to Jesus Christ!"

He started in the evening so as to cross the frontier by the help of darkness; one of the missionaries who came from France with him, wished to accompany him upon the bark which would take him two or three leagues out at sea, where the Chinese junk awaited to conduct him to the shores of Fo-Kien. The holy missionary, at the very moment he was running into dangers of all sorts, seemed radiant. "This," said he to one of his companions, "is a solemn occasion which occurs but once in a lifetime." They bade farewell; their tears mingled when they embraced for the last time, and the future martyr went to the conquest of his crown.

## IV.

### FROM MACAO TO FO-KIEN.

It is still Blessed Perboyre who gives us the details of this voyage; they are contained in a letter to M. Torrette, Superior of the house at Macao.

"Fo-Kien, March 7, 1836.

"*Rev. and very dear Confrère,*—I arrived in Fo-Kien fifteen days ago. Before going further I must, as it were, look backward and return in spirit to Macao to converse a moment with you. Our voyage lasted two long months or nine full weeks. If it was not rapid, it was none the less happy, thanks be to God. You know that on December 21, towards eleven o'clock at night, amid the most profound darkness, and silence still more profound, we embarked upon this Fo-Kinese junk, sanctified by the passage of so many other Missionaries whom it conducted before us to the harvest field of Our Lord. Though the moving of our luggage was made in great haste, I missed only my pipe and fan which you had sent me by some one in the little bark, and which I suppose, will be returned to you. We passed the next night at anchor in the same harbor at Macao. The next day we went forward to Lingting where we stopped for two days. This was but a prelude to the stoppings which followed. The longest two were of eight or ten days. One was occasioned by strong contrary winds; the other which took place at Nangao, was due to a different cause. The master of the bark had relatives there and wished to see them at his leisure ; so they had the outside of the ship washed ; they drew it to the edge of the shore to profit by the ebb of the tide which drove it upon the sand. There are a good many Christians on this isle. It is on the frontier of two provinces, Kouang-Tong and Fo-Kien, lying partly in one and partly in the other; it is under the authority of both mandarins. Our officers, knowing particularly well the Fo-Kinese mandarin whose mother is a Christian, though he is a pagan, did not neglect to make, according to custom, a visit to his house, and the mandarin did not fail to come on board to see them. He arrived accompanied by his guards but they took care to enclose us in our narrow alcove, buried under the mattress and covers, which we generally use on less solemn occasions. Whilst there, we could hear the mandarin laughing and talking for nearly an hour. It was more on account of his attendants than of himself, that we were hidden. He has seen missionaries and is not ill disposed toward them. At his departure, as at his arrival, they rendered him, amid the noise of cymbals, the usual honors. We received from him a flag which bore an inscription stating that the bark had been visited by him. After this, when we entered a port or when a mandarin's boat came toward us to question us, we hoisted this flag of safety and they left us in peace. I must tell you that several times we have had to hide ourselves, especially when strangers came to our ship to sell merchandise or for anything else. The courier from Fo-Kien then put on his lettered cap and whilst his assistant attended to business outside, for our greater security he sat down at the door of our hiding place. These precautions were greater than the danger; but it is always well to take them. We are much pleased with this courier. He is an excellent Christian, wonderfully kind, and of rare prudence in speech, never saying an improper word, nor one capable of hurting the feelings of another. All the ship's company respect and love him as a father.

"We constantly sailed in sight of land; following, you know, all the windings of the coast, we dipped into all the little gulfs which are so frequent on its shores; thus making the route three times as long by these zig-zags and those necessitated by contrary winds. We scarcely ever traveled by night and often little by day, advancing always slowly and coming back, sometimes after several hours' travel, to the same port we had left in the morning, or even to the one we had left the evening before. Here a port is simply a shelter built on the shore of an island, at the foot of a mountain, near a village, where caravans of ships encamp for the night. Through fear of pirates, they prefer to sail in large companies. When they wish to start, they give one another a signal and make known their desires by hoisting a little sail which they fold according to their change in opinions. They start together and go in file, each ship imitating the continual veering and tacking of the one before it. Having the same *kouan* or store houses, they arrive at almost the same time at their common destination, where they flock together with very little caution. Once, our bark was struck in the prow by colliding with another, but it received only a slight injury. Afterwards, we had our revenge, for on another day a bark got its rope entangled in our anchor and it was extracted only with great difficulty. Notwithstanding our nearness to these neighbors, we went on deck every evening to say our beads, following the example of the ship's officers who seemed to refresh themselves after their fatigues, by closing the labors of the day with the recitation of the rosary. The sailors imitated them, and I have sometimes heard the guard sing his beads. Thus, while the pagan barks that surround us let down into the sea a blazing * trail of superstitious papers, ours sent up to the Lord of heaven the pure incense of the true faith.

"Though we traveled neither as seamen nor as observers and were, besides, strictly confined to the cell whenever it was not prudent to leave it, it was easy for us to form an idea of the southern seacoast of China. This coast is but a succession of angles jutting in and out, which form, along its whole extent, excellent natural harbors. The province of Kouang-Tong is generally bordered by high, barren mountains which are not separated from the sea except sometimes by strips of coast and piles of sand, where once the water had been. The pagan barks, in passing, offer sacrifices on several of these mountains, and upon a good many of them are erected idolatrous columns which may be seen at a great distance. China is much better defended by such ramparts than by the small fortresses which are built out at sea at certain points. We see very few houses; only now and then, some fishermen's cabins which I as-

* He refers, perhaps, to the burning of pictures of venerated objects, names and inscriptions, used in Chinese worship to propitiate the deity.

sure you are very humble. The coasts of Fo-Kien are more flat; the cultivation of the lands and the numerous habitations give them a lively air which pleases and recreates the eye of the traveler. The sea offers a no less attractive aspect. Without speaking of the ships which are coming and going in all directions, the sea is covered in certain places with innumerable fishermen's barks. When you see the sails upon the horizon, you would think it a long palisade closing our passage. But as they come nearer, you see they are really dispersed and quite far from one another. After this, it is not surprising to hear that five millions of Chinese live in the waters of the sea on which we have traveled. *Living* on the sea is the very word, since it is the only dwelling of the Chinese fishermen. He does not leave it at the close of the day, like the fisherman of Java, to light up the shores with his evening fire. He sleeps in the bark in which he works; there are all the family; there they are born, there they live, and there they die. The sea, however, is not their cemetery; they are buried on the side of the mountain. Generally these barks are of medium size. But I have no doubt there are fishermen who use other kinds of boats. You see at a short distance from you, but far from land, two men who seem to dance upon the water. Coming nearer, you perceive that they have underfoot a sort of raft made of four or five planks of bamboo, which follows the movement of the wave that bears them and often covers the raft without submerging it. It must be admitted there are some who trust their lives to very little, and yet it is their all. The sea-coasts along which we travel are studded with large rocks and numerous islands, mostly desert and sterile. We have observed one where the Chinese obtain precious stones and on this account they honor it with a special worship. It was on the shore of an island called Hai-Chan, that they solemnized the beginning of the Chinese year, February 17, the first day of the moon of Mars. They stopped for the celebration of this feast so dear to all the Chinese. On the eve, the noise of cymbals and of firecrackers from all the barks announced the beginning of the festivities. This music was heard still more on the day of the solemnity, the whole of which, as well as part of the night, is passed in amusements and rejoicings. Though there were five pagans on the ship, everything passed off without any mixture of superstitions. The courier from Chang-Tong had been engaged to offer for us, some little presents to the men, who seemed much pleased at everything that was said to them, and as each thing was presented, they cried, lowering their voices: 'Ha! Ha! Ha! Tosie, tosie, tosie, tosie.' In their turn, they wished to treat us too, that day; but as it was Ash Wednesday, we had a lawful excuse for declining with thanks. We could observe regularly the fasts and abstinences. We always managed our meals so as to follow the rules. Before Lent, we were satisfied to take a meal about nine in the morning, and another about seven in the evening, in order to have more time to study Chinese, which was generally our exclusive occupation.

"Just a word of our voyage, and I will hasten to close this letter; perhaps you are as impatient to see the end of it, as I was to see the end of the voyage.

"Our destination was the eastern extremity of Fo-

Kien, not far from Fou-Ning, a first-class town. The map shows you the left of this city, an arm of the sea which extends into the land at the mouth of the river. On February 22, after we separated from all the other ships, we entered this arm of the sea aided by a favorable wind. The two coasts presented from all points of view a most picturesque scene, and proved to us that it was not without reason that the Chinese, to denote in their language what we call a landscape, have adopted an expression composed of the two words—mountain and water, *chan chouei.* The gulf ends in a basin which is four or five leagues long and two or three leagues wide, and whose entrance is through a narrow passage. It is surrounded by hills; at their base are numerous villages which form a charming scene.

"At last, the much desired hour arrived. Towards six o'clock in the evening, we cast anchor for the last time. After waiting some time for the tide, so as to ascend the river, we sailed in a small bark, amid the darkness of night, towards the dwelling of the Vicar Apostolic of Fo-Kien, his courier accompaning us. We hid under a coverlid, as we still had a custom house to pass. The vigilance of the custom house officers was not in fault; but, satisfied by the responses given to the challenge, they dispensed with a visit. After about an hour's trip on water, we disembarked to take one nearly as long on land. God, who until this had bestowed upon us a special protection, wished also at the moment of our setting foot on Chinese soil, to work in our favor a new miracle of His care. After leaving the bark, we rushed joyfully upon a pier surrounded by water which the darkness of the night prevented our seeing well. My dear companion at sea, M. Delamarre, priest of the Seminary of Foreign Missions, made a misstep and floundered into a hole where a man had once been drowned. Imagine how shocked I was. I began calling to him, to let him know in what direction to turn. He almost immediately scrambled to the wall which he climbed while I caught hold of his coat and he readily recovered from his mishap. He ran all the danger, but the fear was all on my side. There were no injuries received except some slight wounds in our hands by cutting them against the sharp stones. Blessed be Our Lord Who has so visibly and mercifully assisted us. Can we, after this, fail in courage and confidence? 'The Lord is the protector of my life; of whom shall I be afraid?' *Deus protector vitæ meæ, a quo trepidabo?* (Ps. xxvi, 1.)

"You know with what kindness Monsignor Sebaste, Vicar apostolic of Fo-Kien, received the missionaries. He welcomed and always treated us with a goodness of heart that made us forget host and hospitality and persuade ourselves that we belonged to the family. Notwithstanding his great age, we found him enjoying perfect health, and preaching with energy to a large crowd that presses around him to hear the word of God. Your letter and little presents give him great pleasure. He has a special esteem for you; he loves also M. Laribe, whom he has several times praised for his prudence and zeal. He also eulogized a Chinese confrère whom we lost last year in Kiang-Si. As Monsignor Sebaste has lived in China for more than half a century, he has known many missionaries and among others several of our elder confrères. He saw MM. Clet, Pesné, and Lamiot, when they arrived at Macao; and on their way from Canton to Pekin, MM. Rechenet and Dumazel. It was sweet to hear from his mouth the details he gave me of these venerable confrères who have opened the way which we must follow, and prepared the harvest we must gather. He asks news of the Superior General and of the state of Congregation. All that we can tell him about the state of religion in France, the condition of the clergy, of seminarians, of religious communities, of the Propagation of the Faith, has greatly interested him. He learns with much joy of a new Congregation already evangelizing Oceanica. He told me that our country had received the gift of good works and that Providence had destined it to do much good in the world. His residence is at Tching-Theou, a village of fifteen hundred inhabitants of whom two-thirds are Christians. The flourishing church of Fo-Kien is composed of forty thousand Christians; more than thirty thousand are found in the district of the third-class town, Fou-Ngan. There are some localities, even of considerable size, where all are Christians and many, where the pagans are in the minority. In this district, also, Christians can hold up their heads, having nothing to fear. There are seven or eight large churches open to every one and well known to the mandarins. They have also two seminaries. In the large villages, every evening the rosary is sung in all the families; the neighboring mountains and valleys resound with it; it is truly admirable; you in Europe have no idea of it. Three or four thousand fishermen assemble every year with their barks, and divide themselves into three bands to receive the sacraments. A Christian of this province was appointed mandarin of Tche-Kiang. It seems that this charge is not incompatible with the duties of a Christian, provided one has enough faith and character to fulfil them. In this country there are often pagans who are possessed by the devil. They ask to receive baptism and are immediately delivered. I have had occasion to see several of the Dominican Fathers who serve this interesting mission. They seem to be much as I expected to find them, full of doctrine and virtues. There are seven or eight Europeans and an equal number of native priests. Not being far apart, they can see one another from time to time, consult together and communicate their lights, which is no little advantage.

"Now, my dear confrère, I must bid you adieu again. To-morrow we start for Kiang Si. To-day, I arrived at the seminary on the route. We shall make the journey on foot, at least the greater part of it. We shall yield ourselves more than ever into the hands of Providence. Oh, how happy we shall be when we have to depend upon God alone! I recommend myself to your prayers and those of all the confrères of our house, whom I affectionately embrace. I shall not write to France for the present. I depend on your kindness to make up for me when you write to Paris. You know how much our good superiors desire to receive frequent news from us. I am, etc.,

"PERBOYRE, Miss. Apos."

## V.

### FROM FO-KIEN TO HO-NAN.

THE reader will be glad to learn the different incidents of this voyage in a new letter from John Gabriel; it is written to his uncle, Superior of the preparatory seminary of Montauban.

"HO-NAN, March 10, 1836.

"*My very dear Uncle,*—I have not announced to you either my departure from Macao or my arrival in China. I do not doubt, however, that you have already learned both from my brother in Paris, who does not fail to communicate to you any news he receives of me, knowing how highly you prize the information, since you anxiously count each step I take in the enemy's country and, perhaps, still more anxiously await this new sign of life to entirely dissipate your fears. I owe it to the attachment I have for the best of uncles and to that which he has for me, to respond, as soon as I can, to your solicitude by relating how I began and how happily I ended a voyage equally long and perilous.

"It was on December 21, 1835, that I started from Macao with another French missionary, M. Delamarre, who was going to Seu-Tchuen and with whom I have traveled all the way to Hou-Pe. After a peaceful voyage, we landed at Fo-Kien, February 22. We stayed two weeks with the Vicar Apostolic of Fo-

Kien, who did us all sorts of kindnesses. Some points of resemblance that I observed between you and him, added not a little to my interest in him, and increased the charm of his conversation and my admiration for his apostolic virtues. When we were getting near the end of our journey, we passed some days at his seminary. Here we met several times a Dominican Father perfectly restored to health, who three years before had been seized and cruelly maltreated. He was ransomed by the power of money. A Chinese priest who had been taken a short time ago, was liberated at a cheaper rate. Though we are not protected absolutely from all such perils, religion is tolerated in this part of the province, where there are so many Christians. The mandarins can not help knowing that there are several European missionaries here. It is said that a mandarin who passed a house where the Christians were chanting prayers, said: 'These people pray for us.' This fact will prove to you to what extent the Christians enjoy liberty in this country. In some of the pagan villages of the neighborhood, the people had blasphemed against religion, and particularly against the Blessed Virgin. Immediately, a great multitude of Christians, men only, began the duty of making reparation, organizing of themselves a long procession at the head of which walked a bachelor of arts bearing the insignia of the Blessed Virgin; they made a tour of the mountains and pagan villages, singing the litanies and the praises of the Mother of God. From the seminary, we went to a large town composed entirely of Christians, where we made another stop. In this place, we visited a small mountain near by, called 'the Holy Mountain.' It is filled with the tombs of Christians. We distinguished the graves of several priests and three bishops; one of them, a Frenchman, was among the founders of the Foreign Missions and the first Vicar Apostolic of China. Near these venerable remains, we felt ourselves instantly penetrated by religious feelings and the spirit that had animated them. In this province the tombs are of a remarkable form and very ornamental. They are of a horse-shoe shape, more or less large, some fifteen or twenty feet long and half as wide. The interior, which is open, is divided into several tiers, rising one above the other, like an amphitheatre. The walls which separate these tiers are two or three feet high and sometimes ornamented with carvings. The side-walls are of the same height inside; outside they are on a level with the ground. Following the slope of the mountain, these walls unite to form a circle, in the middle of which is a sepulchral stone with a long inscription, and sometimes an engraved cross. It is under this stone that the dead body reposes. These monuments are all well made of smooth earth, firmly hardened so as to look like a single stone. They are simple and majestic, as is suitable for a tomb.

"At last, on March 15, we began in earnest our route to Kiang-Si, accompanied by four Christians who served as couriers and porters of our baggage. Traveling through a country whose language we can not speak and whose habits we badly imitate, and where entrance is forbidden under pain of death to all Europeans, we move at first with the caution and timidity of people walking upon slippery ground. But as experience increases and we go about with impunity, our assurance increases; besides we place much more confidence in the Providence of God, than in ourselves or our guides. These couriers, who are well paid to guide us, but not to tell lies about us, try to profit by the business as much as they can. In response to the questions, continually asked, of who we are, whence we come, and where we are going, they make us pass for tea merchants from Ning-Po or Nankin; they fail not to add that we do not understand the language of this province, which is certainly true. In the inns where we stop for dinner or a night's lodging, they are careful not to allow us to be too much seen. They make us cross the streets of the towns at a running pace, so the people can less easily observe us. However, we had to face everybody, not only in the towns and inns, but still more on the roads, full of comers and goers, and in the stopping places where we meet people from far and near. Sometimes, too, they eye us not unkindly, looking at us attentively, as if we were curiosities. Indeed, the Chinese differ much from Europeans; their hair is blacker and straighter, their beards less heavy, their noses flatter, their eyes usually less open and their complexion not white and red, but olive; besides, we have entirely different manners. It sometimes happens that they doubt our being strangers from the provinces of China. This is not surprising, but we pursue our way with no less safety.

Before entering Kiang-Si, we have to pass a customhouse established to examine the merchandise brought from one province to another. All our contraband was in our persons; so, while our couriers presented our goods to the customhouse officers, we glided quickly forward so as not to be reviewed by the men whose employment makes them more suspicious and whom experience has made expert. In the mean time, we found in front of us a crowd of soldiers whom we passed by, putting on a brave face and talking to them like the other travelers. Though in this trip we walked every day for fifteen hours, through great heat, over the mountains, we made nearly seven or eight leagues a day. I was no more fatigued at the end than I was at the beginning. Later, you will see that this bravery flagged a little. On the morning of March 29, we learned that we were near Kiang-Si, where our Fo-Kinese couriers would confide us to the care of others. But as they could not make themselves understood when they asked for information about the road, we made several useless twists and turns. At last, on entering a village, they were told that it contained a family of Christians; not daring to ask, they went to look for them. They were easily found because the doors of Chinese houses are covered with religious writings; and as the doors are generally open, one can see at a glance the different objects of devotion, either pagan or Christian, inside. We arrived there and seemed to breathe a purer air and to feel our hearts lightened of the weight of this pagan atmosphere which we had so long breathed. After a few moments' rest, we started for the Christian settlement that we sought, and were but a quarter of an hour on the road.

That same day we rejoiced in a new favor of Providence. To avoid the dangers which were feared on the road used by the missionaries before us, we took another route which, to our great surprise, brought us right to the place where M. Laribe was conducting a mission. I had been most desirous of celebrating the Feast of Easter with him, but I did not expect to see him for two or three weeks. This happy meeting obtained for me the pleasure of passing two weeks with him before Easter. This excellent confrère, who is Superior of the mission of Kiang-Si where he is the joy of the Christians and the happiness of the priests who live with him, is our compatriot, for he is from the diocese of Cahors. You may have seen him when he was director of the seminary at Carcassonne. I remember perfectly well that I was his guardian angel when he came from the Seminary of St. Sulpice in Paris to enter the Congregation. We were together during all Holy Week. He continued his mission, where I saw him exercise all the functions of the holy ministry and close it by receiving, during Mass, the oath which two new catechists made, on the Holy Gospels, to teach in all their purity the truths of Christianity and to fulfil well the other duties of their charge. This Christian settlement which M. Laribe attends, is newly established. Its founder died a short time ago. In his last moments he called his children around his bed and said to them: 'When we settled here, there were no Christians but ourselves, and we could not see the priest. Now the Christians, who are numerous, have the happiness of seeing the priest often. I die happy.' His eldest son, inheritor of his zeal, with fifty fervent Christians practise our holy religion with no less ardor. While I was there, a young man of twenty, came and asked for baptism. As we feared opposition from his pagan father, he was told to try to obtain his consent. The father replied that not only would he permit his son to embrace the Christian religion, but if he fulfilled well the duties of religion he himself would follow his example. In Kiang-Si, there are many things favorable to Christianity and there is great hope of extending it; every year a good number of adults are baptized. Though in this province, as in others, the Christians generally belong to the poorer class, they have among them some merchants and men of considerable fortune. One of them recently went to Pekin to become a mandarin. If the Christians of distinguished positions are rarely the most fervent, at least they are full of kindness for the missionaries and disposed to oblige them. Having finished his mission, M. Laribe kindly accompanied me to Kien-Tchang-Fou, a first-class town, about fifteen leagues distant, where M. Delamarre had arrived three days before. We first thought of separating for the rest of the route, but we concluded to continue it together. Every one agreed that we incurred no more danger. Besides, we had a double advantage; we shared the expenses of the same courier and the same ship, and each of us enjoyed the protection of our two guardian angels. While making anew our preparations for departure, we had time to receive visits and *kotheou* from the Christians of the town. The *kotheou* is a prostration by which the Chinese salute persons of high dignity and which the Christians make before the priest at his arrival and departure, when they go to see him, when they ask him a question, when they receive anything from him, when they go to Holy Communion, etc. We saw a girl who had been possessed of the devil, and several whom she had seduced and made adore her, calling herself Jesus and operating diabolical wonders. One day, uttering this horrible blasphemy, she worked one of her miracles, when a catechist said to her: 'Let us see if thou art Jesus' and he sprinkled her with holy water. She fell into a swoon and was ever afterwards delivered from the possession of the devil.

"The safest and best way to go to Hou-Pe from Kien-Tchang-Fou is by the river. When, on April 8, we resumed our journey with two couriers from Kiang-Si, we again entered the same river. Though we hired a pagan boat, we took on board without the least fear, several cases of religious articles that had come from Fo-Kien by a different route, after our departure. This time, we took the rôle of Fokinese merchants who understood little of the language of the other provinces. The four pagans who guided us, then found it quite natural for us to speak our own language, French, which they took for Fo-Kinese. We were announced as Christians, consequently were able to observe the laws of abstinence, to make the sign of the cross, to pray on our knees, to recite the rosary instead of the breviary and to read the Chinese books of religion. The course of the river and a favorable wind brought us in two or three days in front of Nan-Tchang Fou, capital of Kiang-Si. We rapidly crossed the great lake; but beyond it was a customhouse where the ships and barks which pass must always be examined by the government officers; so we provided ourselves with a *piao*, a sort of a passport. This occasioned a delay of a day, and the bad weather that followed necessitated another stop for a week. When thousands of ships were at the station with us and an infinite number of people travelling the streets of this floating town, we dared not show our faces at door or window. One day, our captain, a very good man, thinking, no doubt, that he would honor and recreate the passengers, gave us an entertainment by a kind of Chinese troubadours who recited very well and musically a long hymn in praise of the emperor. Once we set sail, we soon arrived at the confluence of a large river where we made a turn to the left and sailed up to Ou-Tchang-Fou. The river is very deep and nearly everywhere half a league wide. When, after heavy rains, it overflows its banks, it is like a sea. I saw sporting in these waters a large fish, the size of a small whale, whose flesh is not good to eat. In a certain place we met a hundred large and beautiful ships belonging to the emperor which were loaded with wood for his majesty. Upon one of these, a comedy was being performed and the shore was crowded with spectators. But when we arrived, the rain arrived, too; this broke up the performance and dispersed every one in an instant. It was also in a pelting rain and amid darkness and mud that, after eighteen days' sailing, we made our entrance in Han-Keou.

"Han-Keou is one of the greatest business places and largest cities of China. It is in front of Ou-Tchang-Fou, capital of Hou-Pe, and beside a first class town, Han-Yang Fou. These three cities are quite distinct though separated only by two rivers in the same way that Montauban is by the Tarn and the Tescou. These three cities together contain more than two millions of inhabitants, of whom not more than two hundred are Christians. We did not stop to see the people of Ou-Tchang-Fou, who are attended by priests from the Propaganda, because none of the clergy were then in the place and we wished to resume our journey. In fact, the next day after our arrival, M. Delamarre re-embarked for Seu-Tchuen with two couriers from Kiang-Si. As for me, I shall pass one more day in the Christian settlement of Han-Keou which belongs to our mission. The first office that I recited here was that of St. Cletis, Pope and Martyr. It did not require so strong a resemblance in name to remind me that I was in the very same place where our dear Martyr, M. Clet, gave his life for Jesus Christ. Oh, how ardently I desired to make a pilgrimage to his tomb! It was not more than two short leagues from the house where I lodged, but it was thought best to postpone it to some other time. I attended two sick persons in Han-Keou. M. Baldus, our confrère gave a mission there a short time ago, as well as in the other Christian sections through which I must pass and in which he had announced my arrival. In this town, I met a Christian whom M. Baldus had sent to look after the children of pagans in danger of death; and in the space of ten days, he baptized eight. I saw also one of M. Rameaux's couriers whom I had seen in Macao. In this company, upon a Christian bark, on a river smaller than the preceding one but much larger than any of those of France, I directed my course toward the northern part of Hou-Pe, having a hundred leagues to travel through immense plains. At the mouth of this river is the harbor Han-Keou, always filled with innumerable ships. The harbor Ou-Tchang Fou contains several thousand vessels used only for salt. After seeing the immense number of ships and barks in China in all its ports, it may be boldly asserted that it has many more ships than there are in the whole of Europe.

"On the fourth day of our sail, they showed me on the shore some poor hovels just rebuilt. They were the dwellings of several Christian families whose homes had been swept away the year before by the overflow of the river. I went to see them and passed part of Sunday with them. The next day I saw another Christian district, more numerous, and one of the best in the province. There I was surprised at being saluted and interrogated in French by a good-natured little man who could scarcely stammer in his own tongue. Quite recently a child of six years was drowned by falling into the river; his parents hastened to ask me what I thought about his fate; it was easy for me to console them. I attended another sick man there. I remained there only a day, though they wished me to stay until they had news of M. Rameaux. I longed too much to see him not to press forward to the meeting. As the bark could not go up the river because it was too swollen I was obliged to walk along the shore. The first march was of a dozen leagues, at the end of which we received hospitality upon two ships which stopped for commerce in a considerable place whose name I have forgotten. I found here what could scarcely be found, alas, on the ships of Europe, a holy water vase and sprinkler. The Christians begged me to give them a blessing, the first and last ceremony of a missionary when he arrives in a Christian settlement and when he leaves it. Notwithstanding the nearness of the Pagan barks on which several were not ignorant of my presence, they sang without fear the usual prayers for these occasions. In this prayer they sing of the *benefits and mercies of God, who sent to them the priest to preach to them their religion, to make them know their sovereign Lord, to bless them, to forgive them their sins, to strengthen their feebleness, to withdraw them from lukewarmness, and to fix them in the practice of good works. They implored Him to pour down His benediction on the spiritual Father; to bestow on him health, peace and wisdom, to reveal to him His will, to make him the dispenser of His graces, so that walking constantly under His conduct, in the way of the divine commandments; they may by his mediation and in virtue of his merits, arrive happily with him to the possession of eternal life.*

"A day and a half afterwards, I was in Cha-Yang, amid a young and fervent Christian settlement. It owes its origin to a dispensation of Providence, Who, without the work of man, transports from afar to this uncultivated land, a new seed to make it fruitful. A Christian from Seu Tchuen came to conduct business in this town, having no other design than to become an apostle. Little by little, he gained the confidence, the esteem, the affection of the pagans, and now he sees himself surrounded by numerous spiritual children. He related to me feelingly and with truly patriarchal simplicity, how God had used him for His work. He told how he enjoyed the good will of every one; how the mandarin, who came from the same province, honored him with his friendship and visits; how my confrères who came there to baptize adults, were pleased with his work, and how he still hoped to make new conquests for the Faith. One of these neophytes had not been called till the last hour and has already gone to receive the penny from the

Householder. For several days, they sang prayers around the dead man, which attracted a large concourse of pagans who came to see and admire so great a novelty. For fear that the inexperienced Christians might permit something superstitious in the last rites of the dead, M. Baldus sent from a Christian section, a dozen leagues distant where he was giving a mission, two young men to direct the prayers and ceremonies. When returning home, they acted as my guides. They procured me a horse but I refused it, going with my confrères, who as usual went on foot. On May 7, I had the pleasure of embracing M. Baldus and on the 8th, M. Rameaux, who gave a mission in Kin-Men-Tcheou.

"They had just begun the ministration of the seven or eight Christian settlements that compose this district. While they continued there, I stayed with them, sometimes with one, sometimes with the other, as a witness of their zeal and labors which served me as a novitiate in the art in which they excelled. To instruct, to exhort, to hear confessions and administer the other sacraments, to labor to destroy abuses, to advise the best means to make the good lasting, was their occupation every day and all day long. I loved so much to hear them preach, as they spoke not only under the impulse of grace, but with the authority of men who have a divine mission and with the simplicity of those who seek only the salvation of their brethren. The ministration of this district being finished, we went to Ngan-Lo Fou, where M. Rameaux had formerly begun a mission but had been obliged to take flight for this reason :

"The overflow of the river having broken the dike

which kept the land from being submerged, the soldiers seized this occasion to extort money from the neighboring landlords; having imputed to them this crime the soldiers imposed a fine upon them. Among them was a Christian, and this was an excellent pretext for exacting a double contribution; for in case of refusal they could denounce and pursue him on account of his religion. M. Rameaux, fearing this affair might have serious consequences, thought it best to go away. However, the catechist of the place went to the chief of the soldiers and declared, since they brought religion into the question, the Christians would not even give what the Pagans had given. The latter excused himself at the expense of his inferiors and hastened to compromise, abandoning the heavier claim to make sure of the smaller one.

"While M. Baldus ministered to the Christians of this district, M. Rameaux, alone went to show me the way to the mountains of Kou-Tching, the usual resort in vacation. I remained two weeks in Ngan-Lo-Fou, where I saw them administer the sacraments to a Turk and some adults. A good old doctor constituted himself my procurator. He went to market to buy my food and took the trouble of carrying it home himself. Generally in China, men even of highest position feel themselves honored in serving the missionaries and do not presume to take a meal with them. Usually, the priest eats alone, except in his travels, when because of the pagans, he admits the catechists to his table. But in any case to allow females to dine with him would be an unheard-of-thing and according to Chinese customs, equally ridiculous and scandalous. We do not even allow them to serve at table. In Hou-Pé women are condemned less to solitude than in the other provinces; not only do they attend to their housekeeping more openly, but frequently they are seen in troops without any men, or even with the men of their family, employed all day in working in the fields, gathering and beating the rye, hoeing the vegetables and, with feet and hands in the water, planting rice. They also take a good share of the management and labor of the barks, where you will see them sometimes turning the helm, nursing their children, doing the cooking or turning the sail.

"To continue my voyage, I had to wait for a Christian bark. I started at last in one which had just been used by a mandarin whom the viceroy of Ou-Tchang-Fou had sent to Ngan-Lo-Fou. During this sail of eight days, I was employed as in the other trips, in the study of Chinese. A mother profited by the presence of the catechists who accompanied me to have the catechism taught her son. This book and a prayer book are generally in the barks and houses of Christians who usually know how to read them, even when they do not know how to decipher any other book. We passed the night between the two large towns of Fan-Tching and Siang-Yang-Fou, so as to avoid meeting the members of the tribune who require the barks to transport them *gratis* whenever it suits their convenience. Such a meeting would be doubly trying to us. On St. John's day, we raised anchor early in the morning to go farther out in the river so that we could chant at our ease, far away from the pagans, the long prayers of the feast. On June 26, we left the river for the last time, and undertook with only the master of the bark, a new campaign on foot. As we had no baggage, we traveled briskly on our way; when we came to a brook, he had the kindness to carry me on his shoulders. We made a short halt at the house of a Christian family on our route. Having arrived early at Kou-Tching, we did not stop to salute those living there, so that we could get away immediately from so dangerous a place. For, though our residence in the mountains is under the jurisdiction of the mandarins of this third-class town, neither we nor the Christians have any great confidence in their protection: it is to them we owe our martyrs, confessors, apostates and the ruin of our houses and churches. As the want of exercise on the bark had weakened my limbs, I was very much fatigued in the evening. The next day we had to travel twelve leagues across steep mountains. With much difficulty and through repeated efforts, I arrived at the foot of the last, but I could go no further. Seeing the mountain rising before me, I suddenly remembered that I carried about me a small cross to which was attached the indulgence of the Way of the Cross. It was a good time to try to gain it. For some hours I had only dragged myself along by the help of an umbrella which I should have used as a protection from the rain which fell in torrents. I sat down on all the stones I saw on the way; then I would begin climbing again; sometimes with my hands. If you will allow me to use the expression I would if necessary have climbed with my teeth to follow the way Providence had marked out for me. My poor guide was obliged to render me the service that is given a broken-down horse which is raised up and pushed forward; he was relieved by a young man who came down the mountain. Many Christians keep their cattle on these heights. Seeing my escort, they soon guessed who I was, for I was expected, and came to my relief. As I had had nothing to eat all day, they imagined I needed food. One of them, who lived not far from home, ran thither and brought me eggs and tea. The little I forced myself to swallow I could not retain. I felt much encouraged by the news that the inclosure of the mountain contained only Christians and as were most of the people of the neighboring ones. At last I crossed the summit of this terrible mountain and, on the other side, found hidden in the bamboo thicket, our residence, where M. Rameaux and a Chinese confrère received me with open arms, and with them I soon forgot my fatigue.

"Once arrived at this house, we found ourselves buried in deep solitude; around us we saw only high mountains, which enclosed us in very narrow precincts where nature alone seemed to live, we heard only the cry of insects and the songs of birds; during the night still more silent than the day, the noise of the torrent which flowed beside us made us reflect upon the continual and incalculable rapidity of the stream which reminded us of human life. As we had seen no houses near us, we were agreeably surprised, toward nine o'clock in the evening, to hear from all sides, the music of chants and prayers, and were still more astonished, on Sunday morning, to find ourselves surrounded and saluted by four or five hundred people who came to hear Mass, and the word of God, to recite the rosary and make the Way of the Cross. Whence did they all come? From the little cabins hidden under the trees, in the windings of the mountains; many even came from a distance, crossing before day the high barriers which separated them from the Holy Sacrifice. So great a concourse in a pagan country is doubtless a shining tribute in favor of the true faith, but it is doubly striking when your own eyes see it. These are the people whom Our Lord has pleased to evangelize, to prove His divine mission; they are poor, poorer than any I have ever seen. Many are not clothed and have only rags hanging around them, less suitable to cover them than to display the most abject poverty to which a man could be reduced. Others can not come to Mass because they have not even such clothes. If you give them clothes, they hasten to sell them to escape dying of hunger. The year before, many died from want. M. Rameaux, who is a true father to the Christians of Hou-Pe, with the little means he had, could only purchase life for a certain number. Those who did not die, lived on almost nothing. The best they had was the corn and buckwheat which grew almost on the summit of the mountains. The mission possessed some poor pieces of land there and gave several people a small tract to cultivate; they reaped very little profit from them and we, still less. Our church and house, which are considered palaces in this place, are built of earth and covered with straw; there is no other pavement than beaten ground and no ceiling but the branches of bamboo which sustain the roof. This, at least, is a shelter from the rain, an advantage not enjoyed by all Chinese houses, where I have sometimes thought myself fortunate to possess an umbrella. M. Baldus came, in his turn, to breathe community air in our Chartreuse, which numbers twenty persons in all, missionaries, catechists, students, etc. We have five young men who have begun to study Latin; all study Chinese with the school children of the neighborhood. In the Chinese schools they have a singular method of studying. The scholars, sitting around a table, cry out with all their might from morning till evening, repeating the lesson given them by their master; they cease not to chant and rechant what they learn; in this way they never forget. They are so used to this method that though all have different lessons, each continues his chant, not being disturbed by his neighbor.

"My sojourn among my confrères whose company was as agreeable as it was useful to me, was not of long duration. I left them about the middle of July to go to Ho-Nan, where I must continue my studies with two Chinese confrères who belong to this province. On account of the heat, M. Rameaux obliged me to take the mule belonging to the house. The first day after crossing many mountains, rocks, and ravines, we traveled a long distance through plains. Although my dinner had been only a morsel of bread, eaten with appetite beside a stream, when I came to the hotel where we slept I did little honor to the supper. This greatly distressed the old grandfather there, who began to tell me that I must be a miser; that a gentleman who rode a horse must not begrudge his *sapeques* for two bowls of *mien*, a sort of pastry made of wheat flour and used in soup. The next day we stopped near noon at Lao-Ho-Keou, one of the largest places of commerce in Hou-Pe, after Han-Keou. Notwithstanding the extent of the two towns, the Chinese call them only markets. They contain much riches, large stores and fine shops. The streets are adorned like those of the first cities of France in days of triumph; for all along the streets, spanning them and on both sides, may be seen magnificent rows of carved pieces, well-painted and covered with gilt letters; these are used for signs. Paris has more riotous streets but none more lively; and in its shops you will not be received with more politeness and kindness, or be served with more grace. There are some Christians in Lao-Ho-Keou, but we only meet them in the barks, so as not to fall into the hands of two old apostates who are our mortal enemies. M. Rameaux was once near being taken by them. By evening, we were far from there. We lodged in an inn where we were obliged to pass the night armed, for we understood there was danger of our being robbed. We took measures accordingly and were robbed only of sleep. On the fourth day, my couriers were in a fright, because some people were observed looking at me suspiciously and it was thought best to hide me in a car. The same evening toward midnight, I arrived at our residence, at Nan-Yang-Fou, where I still remain. Although I am in the house where M. Clet was taken, I am safe and in perfect security.

"Thus, my dear uncle, from my departure from France till my arrival here, sixteen months have passed, during which I have traveled almost continually, so that I have made a journey of about eight thousand leagues. I have traveled so much that I desire to make no more long journeys till the great voyage which is made neither by land nor sea. But whilst waiting I can not help making long trips into the interior of this vast land of China. It is well; if I have come so far, it is only to run the race again in this arena; God grant that I run so as to obtain an incorruptible crown: '*Sic currite ut comprehendatis.*' 'So run that you may obtain,' (1 Cor. ix. 24.)

"It is time that I made an end to this long letter; so I will add nothing more but the recommendation of myself and ministry to your prayers and holy sacrifices. I beg you recommend me also to the prayers of charitable people, and to express the feelings of my heart to my relations at Montauban, to M. Gratacap, and to all those who wish to honor me with their remembrance and friendship.

"I am for life, my very dear uncle, your devoted and respectful nephew,

"J. G. PERBOYRE, Miss. Apos."

---

## VI.

### BLESSED PERBOYRE AT HO-NAN.

JOHN GABRIEL PERBOYRE was received with great joy by his confrères who had known him in France and who could appreciate his talents. M. Rameaux, Vicar Apostolic of Kiang-Si and Tche-Kiang, who died July 14, 1845, was then superior of this mission. Persuaded that Blessed Perboyre was more suitable than he to direct it, M. Rameaux asked permission to yield the post to him, but his humility could not overcome that of his new colaborer. Notwithstanding his repeated protests, he fulfilled the office of superior towards John Gabriel whom he would have wished to have for his master and guide; besides, M. Perboyre could not go to work at once having to learn the language. Nevertheless, thanks to his perseverance, he was soon able to work for the salvation of his dear Chinese. We are happy to find in his letters a minute account of his life at Ho-Nan. He will be his own biographer; his words are always clear, simple, precise and edifying, as we shall see.

This letter is written to the grand-vicar at St. Flour.

"HO-NAN, August 16, 1836.

"*D ar Sir*,—At the beginning of the last century, we had in China six or seven of our confrères, among whom were M. Appiani, secretary of Monsignor Cardinal de Tournon, and M. Mullener, who was Vicar Apostolic of Seu Tcheun; they came as simple missionaries of the Propaganda. Our congregation had not been firmly established here when it was given charge of the Jesuit missions, on the eve of the French revolution. The missionaries whom it sent were shared between Pekin and the provinces; Hou-Pe had four of them. The first was M. Aubin, whom the Vicars-Apostolic of Chen-Si and Seu-Tcheun desired to have appointed vicar apostolic of Chen-Si, but as he was going to Hou-Kouang he was arrested and interrogated. Doubly pleased to have an opportunity of declining the office offered him and to obtain the crown of martyrdom, M. Aubin, in all simplicity, declared what he was. He was brought to the prison in the capital of the province where he passed a year. The emperor, Kien-Long, who loved the Europeans, and who would probably have favored him, asked to have M. Aubin sent to him; but the mandarins, who preferred to get rid of him otherwise, had him poisoned. M. Clet, after a long apostolic career, was martyred in 1820. The Christians and the Chinese priests who worked under him, still speak of him with great veneration. What I have seen of his correspondence showed that he was the oracle of his confrères. The revolution which disbanded our Congregation with so many other institutions, unfortunately occasioned a sad interruption in the sending of missionaries. The evil would certainly have been greater, if their place had not been partly filled by a number of good native priests who had been trained in Pekin. Two of these priests were sent into exile where one of them still remains. M. Lamiot, at the time of M. Clet's death, being convicted of holding intercourse with him, was banished from the court and empire. He removed his Chinese seminary to Macao, where he could form new missionaries while directing those in the interior provinces. At last, Our Lord re-established in France the family of St. Vincent, which being put in a condition to fulfil all its engagements, hastened to send new aid to China. M. Torrette arrived two years before the death of M. Lamiot, to establish the succession and collect his traditions. My brother soon followed but did not arrive here. Then came MM. Laribe and Rameaux, MM. Mouly and Danicourt, M. Baldus, then your humble servant and two other missionaries. At the time I have the honor of writing you, some others must be nearly ready to come out to us. Two of our Portuguese confrères are in Kiang-Nan at the head of a numerous band of native clergy. Five or six years ago, we lost in this province M. Mirando, who died a victim to the unhealthfulness of the climate. M. Castro, who shortly after narrowly escaped the same fate, is now in Chan-Tong. The Christian districts of Kiang-Si, formerly confided to the care of missionaries of different orders, which, because of the bad times were partly abandoned, have taken on new life, reunited under M. Laribe's crosier; that of Hou-Pe has been desolated by persecution and tried by calamities of all sorts. M. Rameaux appeared there like a consoling angel; by his extraordinary zeal he succeeded in mending old ruptures, and in healing the wounds which still bled. M. Baldus, your compatriot, who is associated with him, has also shown himself a hero since the beginning of his career. Ten months have not passed since his arrival here, but in the course of his missions, he has traveled at least three hundred leagues, heard ten thousand confessions and baptized thirty-one adults.

"You know, dear sir, the missionaries have now in Pekin a very different position from that they formerly held. Then, though they were admitted into the country only as European savants, desiring to form an academy of science and art, they could in virtue of their title, exercise in the heart of the capital, all the functions of a missionary, direct a seminary, preach religion continually in their church, receive in their house more than two hundred for a retreat every year, train catechists, explain cases of conscience to the Chinese priests every day during the two months' vacation, which they take together on their return from the missions. They take care of the Christians in the different sections of the town from which they knew how to escape secretly, notwithstanding the prohibition of the Emperor against missionaries 'going into the country.'

'*Dominus dedit, Dominus abstulit.*' 'The Lord gave, and the Lord hath taken away.' (Job i, 21.) The house where these good works were started is now owned by a mandarin who built a theatre on the site of the church. The Bishop of Nankin, authorized to pass the rest of his days in Pekin, has not ceased to be the soul of the Chinese priests of the neighborhood, and to maintain secretly a correspondence with the missionaries of the four provinces under his administration. He still keeps the Portuguese church where, notwithstanding his great age and infirmities, he hears confessions regularly on the eves of Feasts and on Sundays. As to M. Mouly, Superior of the French Missions, he stays in China on the same conditions as his confrères, leading a public life only to maintain the hidden one. Our Congregation has charge of the missions in seven provinces which comprise the eastern part of China; in all these missions are Europeans, French and Portuguese. Since Providence has now procured for it greater resources than it has ever before had, it will fulfil, little by little, the different needs of its missions and strive to procure more and more their increase and prosperity.

"The ten other provinces are served, one by Spanish Dominicans, four by Missionaries of the Propaganda, generally Italian Franciscans; three by priests from the Seminary of Foreign Missions; two, Kiang-Tong and Kiang-Si, where Europeans cannot be hidden, by Chinese priests under the jurisdiction of the Bishop of Macao. In this town reside the procurators of the different missions. Each mission has a seminary for the Chinese; that of the Propaganda, at Naples; of the Foreign Missions, at Pi-

Nang; the Dominicans, at Manilla; our French Missions and the Portuguese are at Macao. At this time, the whole provinces of Nankin, Seu-Tcheun, Fo-Kien and Chen-Si which contain the most Christians, have bishops or vicars apostolic who at the same time have charge of other provinces; parts of two of these provinces are under the jurisdiction of the Vicar of Macao, which office has been vacant several years. In all China, there are scarcely eighty native priests and only forty European priests, three-fourths of whom have come here within the last ten years. In this period only two or three have died.

"You see, dear sir, that in a very short interval the Householder has sent into His vineyard a good number of laborers. As to the number of Christians in China, there seem not to be above two hundred and twenty thousand, if they even reach that number. Scattered all over the empire, they are in the crowd of pagans like a few little fishes in the sea. Estimating the total number of Chinese to be three hundred millions, in thirteen or fourteen hundred one can scarcely find a Christian. When will this leaven penetrate the enormous mass? It is the secret of Him Who has time in His power; to us has been given only the power of co-operating by our feeble efforts in this great work. '*Non est vestrum nosse tempora vel momenta, quæ Pater posuit in sua potestate; sed eritis mihi testes usque ad ultimum terrae.*' 'It is not for you to know the times or moments, which the Father hath put in His own power. But you shall be witnesses unto me even to the uttermost parts of the earth.' (Acts i, 7-8.) Yet He is pleased to depend partly for the accomplishment of this work upon the number, sanctity and zeal of missionaries. May He, then, multiply us, sanctify us and fill us with His spirit.

"The conversion of China depends also, upon the prayers of the Christians of Europe. '*Orate pro invicem ut salvemini, multum enim valet deprecatio justi assidua.*' 'Pray one for another, that you may be saved: for the continual prayer of a just man availeth much.' (Jas. v. 16.) If, then, you see from all parts, prayers arising towards Heaven, more and more multiplied, more and more fervent, you can better judge at a distance, than we who are so near, if the kingdom of God is drawing near to this great nation. What a consolation to the Church to see enter into her bosom a people so numerous and so interesting as the Chinese! For if all her children unite and do violence to the Father of mercy, they shall obtain sooner or later, this great miracle, notwithstanding the great obstacles which seems to render it impossible. The members of the 'Association for the Propagation of the Faith' have very happily undertaken this noble mission. May all their brothers in Jesus Christ become inflamed with the same zeal for the interests of the Divine King, enroll themselves in the same spiritual militia, and take up the arms of prayer to continue the ruin of the empire of satan!

"You ask me, esteemed Vicar-general, to pray that you may be useful to this good association; doubtless it has been evident to you for a long time, that this desire has been heard and it is to be hoped that you will be useful to it for a long time to come, if God deigns to receive the prayers I address to Him for the preservation and prosperity of a work so visibly His own.

"A profound peace reigns in the whole empire of China, but an innumerable army of locusts overruns nearly the whole country. You can scarcely imagine the enormous swarms which hide the ground from view. Although they scamper out of the way of the passers-by, you can hardly put foot to the ground without crushing them. They fall on your shoulders from the trees which they cover; they hang from the walls, along which they crawl, seeking food; the earth is fertilized by them; it is an astonishing sight to any one who has not seen them before. They leave only the stalk of the herbs they fancy; they devour even the leaves of the bamboo which withstands the winter's blast. Most of them are small; but some are large with long wings. When they fly it seems like flakes of snow filling the air; truly it is a terrible scourge. Families return weeping from the fields because all they have has been borne away. They hasten to gather the green corn and even the unripe rice to give it to the cattle rather than leave it a prey to these devastating insects. A kind of bean which yields a considerable crop in China will be entirely lost this year. The emperor, writing to the mandarins, deplores most earnestly the calamity which weighs upon the people; he orders them, under penalty of being deposed from office within forty days, to rid themselves of their indestructible enemies. The people go to the fields as they run to a fire; they cry out, they make a noise with rattles, they strike and kill all they can; several people go in front, driving before them a cloud of locusts till the insects are far away from their property; they begin the same thing at their neighbors; every day they do this and they talk of nothing else. When the Emperor wrote to the mandarins, only two provinces had escaped the devastation. The Chinese are chastised like the Egyptians of old; must not those who see it say, 'This is the finger of God.'" (Exod. viii. 19.)

This last incident shows the deep religious sentiments with which Blessed Perboyre was penetrated; all the other details give an exact account of the state of Christianity in the different missions in the vast empire of China in 1836.

Shortly afterwards, John Gabriel sent these tidings to a missionary, formerly Superior of the higher seminary at St. Flour and then Assistant in the Congregation.* Aside from the spirit of faith and deep piety which it expresses, this letter is of especial interest as it explains the origin of his vocation to China.

"HO-NAN, August 18, 1838.

"*Dear and very Honored Confrère*:—I should deprive myself of a great satisfaction, and it would, perhaps, be some pain to you, if after my arrival in China, I should give you no sign of life. I believe I have almost disobeyed you, so often have you requested me to write. In reparation, I must first tell you that I prize your letters no less than you do mine. I hope you will gratify me with some. However far I am from you, I often draw near to you in thought, loving to recall what you did for me and representing to myself what you still do for me. Your charity is so well known that I depend upon its not abandoning me.

* M. John Grappin, born at Besancon Dec. 8, 1790, entered the Congregation Nov. 1, 1816, died Nov. 4, 1846.

"Here I am, started upon a new career; I have serious reasons for believing firmly that the good God has destined me to follow it. He showed it to me long ago when calling me to the ecclesiastical state. I earnestly implored it of Him in a novena to St. Francis, nearly twenty years ago. The remembrance of it has often since come to me to excite my remorse, or reanimate my faith, for it seemed to me that I have been heard; I have always had it more or less in view. The way opened before me of itself when the time destined by Providence had come. It is true that you and my other directors dissuaded me from the project every time I spoke of it. But the principal reason you urged against it was my feeble health, and experience has shown that it had less foundation than was then supposed. I declare to you it seems to me a weak objection when I see ships built of frail materials make a tour of the world several times, for the petty interests of this life. I have been seized with fear at the thought that on the day of judgment they will be for me a cause of condemnation.

"I have arrived happily at my destination. Will you, honored and very dear confrere, thank God for the protection He has accorded me in consideration of your prayers and those you obtained for me? I have felt their particular effects in my long voyages, during which I have had cause to admire the inexhaustible treasures of His Providence and the innumerable gifts He showers upon all His creatures. *Domine Dominus noster, quam admirabile est nomen tuum in universa terra.—a solis ortu usque ad occasum, laudabile nomen Domini.* 'O Lord, O our Lord how admirable is thy name in the whole earth! From the rising of the sun unto the going down of the same, the name of the Lord is worthy of praise.' (Ps. viii, 1. Ps. cxii. 3.) If everywhere we are cheered by the sight, enlightened by the rays and warmed by the heat of the same sun, everywhere we find ourselves in the presence of the same heavenly Father, under the action of His almighty power, under the guidance of His sovereign wisdom, under the influence of His bounty or the weight of His justice; everywhere we see His life vivifying all creatures, so that we cry out in concert. '*Deum cui omnia vivunt, venite, adoremus.*' 'Come let us adore God by whom all creatures live.' The more we travel the earth, the more we shall be struck with the truth of these words. '*Misericordia Domini plena est terra.*' 'The earth, O Lord, is full of thy mercy.' (Ps. cxviii. 64.) but more also with this truth. '*Desolatione, desolata est terra.*' 'With desolation is all the land made desolate.' (Jer. xii, 11.) Yes, on whatever side we turn, we find it infested with vices and sullied with iniquities. There are some saints who have died from sorrow at seeing God so offended by men. This may appear astonishing, but what is really more so, is that it is not the death of all priests who are called to purge the earth of the cursed venom of sin.

"M. Baldus, who writes to you, will not fail to give information about our mission which will interest you very much. He can recount to you the success of his works, the journeys he made, the Christian families he visited, the confessions he heard, the number of adults he has baptized, the conversions he has wrought, the abuses he has corrected; in a word, the spiritual fruits of all kinds which he has produced. But, as for me, who have scarcely begun to put my hand to the plough, what can I say, if I am hereafter to be associated only with those of whom it is written: '*Ibant et flebant, mittentes semina sua.*' 'Going they went and wept, casting their seeds.' (Ps. cxxv, 6.) I do not know whether or not it is a presentiment of a bad harvest, but I am much frightened by these words: *Quae seminaverit homo, haec et metet.* 'For what things a man shall sow, those also shall he reap.' (Gal. vi, 8.) I shall be glad to glean some ears of corn to place beside my brother's large sheaves in the granary of our heavenly Father, so that I may have some slight share in their reward. This is what I beg you to obtain for me by your prayers, to which I can not sufficiently commend myself."

Humility, charity, piety and a delicacy of feeling sprang from our Martyr's heart as a brook gushes from its source, and the more we study his life the more we shall see this manifested.

To fulfil the promise he made to a distinguished priest who afterwards became bishop, M. Lacariere of St. Eustace's Church, Paris, the pious Missionary wrote the following letter:

"Ho-Nan, September 22, 1837.

"*Dear Sir,*—At my departure from Paris, you very willingly promised me your good prayers on condition that I would write you a little letter from China. This contract is too favorable to me, for me not to be eager to conclude it and see that it is put into execution. Your charity has led you to fulfil your part of the engagement every day; justice demands that I now fulfil mine.

"If you have seen my brother, or some of my confrères, you have long ago learned of my happy arrival in Macao. After a sojourn there of four months, I have started on a mission in the interior of China. By the grace of God, no serious accident has happened me in all my travels. I hope, my dear sir, that in your prayers and Masses in which I hope to have some part always, you will thank Our Lord for me for the protection He has accorded me until now, and ask Him in His goodness to continue it for the future, so that I may have the happiness of contributing a little to His glory by working out my salvation and co-operating in that of my neighbor. I am at present with two Chinese priests who teach me their language. Its construction is very different from the European tongues, and the study pleases me much more now than in the beginning; it is truly very fine when you know how to speak it well. Though full of aspirates, it is nevertheless, very sweet. All the words are monosyllables. The numerous diphthongs render it harmonious, and the five tones which vary the pronunciation of its different sounds, make it musical. For the Chinese, to read or recite is to sing. The characters are nearly infinite and it is very difficult for one man to know them all. However, with courage and a certain method you can learn many of them in a short time. The missionaries who have no leisure to devote to letters, generally know enough to understand the books of religion. They are more anxious to learn how to speak it, this being, in fact, more necessary. There are in China nearly forty European priests and about eighty Chinese priests. This number of laborers is not sufficient to take care of the Christians alone, who, however, amid this innumerable Chinese population, enslaved by the demon, seem as rare as the ears of corn which have escaped the harvester's sickle. In the different provinces, they convert, from time to time, some pagans, but one among so great a mass is almost inperceptible. It is to be hoped that God, Whose designs are impenetrable, will one day receive this great nation into the bosom of the Church. The life of missionaries in China is wholly apostolic; it is passed amid fatigues and dangers. Three-fourths of the year they have to travel over vast districts to attend to the Christian settlements, preaching, administering the sacraments etc., living frugally in a country where the rich make good cheer as elsewhere, but where the poor have not always even a little rice to nourish them.

"I pray you, dear sir, please continue your good remembrances of me before God, and believe me, etc."

At the same time, Blessed Perboyre wrote his father a letter of charming simplicity: here he mentions especially the thought that ruled him, which was to offer up his life for the cause of religion.

"CHINA, August 22, 1837.

"*My very dear Father*,—A long time ago, you learned of my arrival in good health at Macao. I have been sailing for two months more, and for five months I have been traveling by land. The good God has always well protected me and I arrived at my destination without encountering any accident. In this country, the missionaries are dressed like the Chinese, and it is only the Christians who know who we are, because strangers are not permitted to enter this empire which is perhaps ten times as large as France.

I have passed many large cities. I have traveled through longer streets, filled with more people and containing more shops than the largest streets of Cahors, and I have never been recognized as a stranger, or at least no one says anything to me. With some precaution, a missionary can stay in China; go and come and fulfil his duties without running any risk of being taken.

"We can live in this country as in any other. One part of China produces rye, another, rice, which is used for bread; there are no grapes for wine but they have many other drinks and there is no lack of vegetables. Generally, the Chinese are very kind, good children of the Church. We have some labors and sorrows to bear, but they are everywhere; besides we must gain heaven by the sweat of our brow. If we should have to suffer martyrdom, it would be a great grace for the good God to bestow upon us. It is a thing to desire, not to fear; so, my dear parents, have no other solicitude for me than to pray for my salvation and that I my contribute to the salvation of others. There are in China, missionaries not only from France but from Italy, Spain and Portugal, without counting a good number of Chinese priests. There are incomparably more pagans than Christians. You must pray for their conversion. Every year some are converted. It is to be hoped that, little by little, they will embrace our holy religion."

This letter shows that John Gabriel had a great desire to pour out his blood for the faith; but he was almost thwarted in his wish. Shortly after going to his dwelling, he was seized by a grave illness which brought him to death's door. It was thought best to administer to him the last sacraments; yet, three months afterwards, he was almost well. He resumed the study of the Chinese language, and though still weak, undertook his first mission with a Chinese priest to help him. The Christians among whom he labored had long lived in bad habits and for the most part refused to fulfil their yearly duty under another Chinese missionary who had been sent them. But they did not resist the zeal of John Gabriel and the missionary who labored with him.

After this first mission, the Servant of God immediately began his apostolic career. He shall himself, give some details about his labors and fatigues, in a letter written to the director of the novitiate of the Congregation in Paris:

"Ho-Nan, September 25, 1837.

"*My very dear Confrère*,—Last July, I received your dear letter of February 29, 1836. It was very welcome and the more so, because I have not received this year any other letters from my confrères in France. I thank you for the news you so kindly give me. Telling me of the blessings which Our Lord is pleased to pour out, more and more, upon the novitiate at Paris and our Congregation is aiming straight at the core of my heart. You desire, dear confrere, to read in your turn my letters. If I can not perfectly fulfil your desire, I shall, at least, give you a proof of my good will. I have nothing extraordinary to relate. I will tell you plainly what has been my position since I have been in China: that is all I can do. I can promise you, then, only some little details about trifles which would certainly not be worth your amiable conversation in recreation.

"It has been fourteen months since I came to Ho-Nan. This time I have passed partly at our residence and partly in the missions. I shall not speak of a three months' sickness I had shortly after my arrival here. As soon as I recovered my strength, I began with a young Chinese confrère, a mission to our Christians in Ho-Nan. To visit about fifteen hundred people scattered through twenty Christian sections, we must travel more than three hundred leagues and traverse the whole length and breadth of the province. This occurs every half year. That you may form a better idea of it, I will go over it with you.

"Let us suppose the place of our residence, the starting point, is the diocese of Cahors; there we give some missions; then we give others in the dioceses of Albi, Puy, Autun, Orleans, Versailles and Amiens; this is about the position and distances of the different districts we have to visit. As you know, this can not be done without some fatigue.

"We travel sometimes on foot, but generally in carts without springs, upon roads repaired neither by the government nor by private persons. Generally we start at night from the house of a Christian, and get home at night, with the beard whitened by the frosts of winter, the face tanned, the ears, neck and forehead skinned by the heat of the summer's sun. I shall not give you a description of the condition of the inns of China, for it could not be complete without being disgusting. I shall only say if any one is greedy for privations and mortifications, he would find enough here to make a holy fortune. Although the best bed is only a mat spread upon the ground or upon a little trestle, it does very well to sleep upon and rest oneself after the fatigues of the day.

"Arrived at an inn, we are often importuned, sometimes by a policeman who subjects us to interrogations and inscribes our names; again, by the members of the tribune who force us to give up our lodging place and seek hospitality elsewhere. To have to sustain the character of a citizen in all these travels is not the least of the European missionary's inconveniences. Not to betray himself, he must act with much reserve, leaving speech and action to the Christians who accompany him, and who, notwithstanding the precautions which their prudence or timidity makes them take, feel sometimes great anxiety, while the missionary enjoys within himself a freedom and liberty of soul which raises it above everything and fills it with joy amid dangers. You may judge from the following anecdote, how meritorious, difficult and perilous an undertaking the conducting of a European is considered by some. One of the Christians of considerable means, whose services had not been claimed, having one of his sons attacked with a serious disease, to obtain his cure, made a vow to accompany the European missionary. I gave him an opportunity to fulfil his vow, asking him to accompany me on an eight days' trip which we happily accomplished. He was not so happy on returning home, for, by order of the mandarin, he was required to go with his car on an embassy which obliged him to take a circuitous route of a hundred leagues.

"In one of my longest journeys, which took twelve days, we had no mishap except from the water, by which the road was changed into a stream from a heavy rain storm. We were drenched, as well as our luggage; and one of our guides had his eye blackened, but without grave consequences. Ho-Nan having but few mountains in the north, nearly all our traveling was through plains. In many of the towns through which I have passed, I have observed nothing remarkable; generally, they have but two streets of considerable size. I have seen a celebrated market whose streets, crossed and laid out in squares, reminded me of those of Carcassonne, the lower town. This province is less commercial, perhaps, than many others; the roads, however, are full of men carrying merchandise from one town to another upon wheelbarrows, which they put on barks when the winds are favorable; long rows of camels, asses and mules are often seen transporting merchandise from one province to another. Some of the rivers here are covered with barks. The river Jaune, which I have twice passed, is not navigable on account of the impetuosity of its waters. In crossing this river on a large ship, the traveler is exposed to the rapacity of a band of rogues who have charge of it. The largest rivers of China have no bridges; in Kiang Si only, I have seen some of a dozen arches.

"Voyages enter largely into the course of life of those engaged upon an apostolic career; this is, however, only one of the accessories and I perhaps have spoken too much about it. I still demand, dear confrère, another moment of your unalterable patience to tell you some of our principal duties. Only one word about our special manner of conducting exercises. I must speak most highly of a Chinese confrère who has accompanied me on all the campaigns. Being born in China, and having already given missions, he was of great help in a land so new to me. As in reality I have given him the greater part of the work, I must, to be just, ascribe the merit to him in proportion. He fulfilled his task with a zeal that never varied, even upon difficult occasions; preaching twice a day, giving special instructions to those who needed them, making open war on ignorance and abuses; rising before four o'clock in the morning, and retiring after ten at night, hearing confessions the whole night through in places where it was necessary, making long journeys in bad weather to bring to the sick the succors of religion, and going to visit the old apostates, or the Christians who are no better, to bring them back to their duties, getting them at first to mass, then to instructions, and to confession. Thus, by the grace of God, many sheep have re-entered the fold; prayer in common, the public worship of the Chinese Christians, is resumed with new vigor in many families, where the mother used to scarcely dare recite them in a whisper. Several Christian districts which were almost destroyed, have been re-established. Upon arriving in each mission, our first duty is to obtain an exact list of all the Christians big and little, good and bad, so as to be able to fulfil our duties better to them all. Then both of us priests, forming a board of examiners, make every one recite the catechism publicly; first, the children of both sexes from whom we judge beforehand the zeal of the parents in their regard. We have them prepared, by capable persons, to receive the sacraments. The older people recite in their turn; the aged not blushing to give in this, an example to the youngest, nor fathers or mothers, at being helped and corrected by their children. After this, we have the baptism of little children; then begins the hearing of confessions, which generally requires but a short time for the people sufficiently instructed or disposed. Every day a certain number receive Holy Communion: the most pious souls have the opportunity of repeating it before the departure of the missionaries. Baptism of adults, confirmation, marriages, admission into some confraternity is the business of the last days. The missionary cannot stay long in each Christian district for he must visit all those under his charge. The mission lasts a week, ten days or two weeks, according to the number and needs of the Christians. When one is finished, we go quickly to another, to do there what we have just done in the last one; that is, to fulfil the office of father, physician, and judge. The Chinese Christian loves to recognize these titles in a priest who can here fulfil his divine functions with all the authority and liberty proper to his sacred character.

"In the course of our visits, we generally have no other lodging or oratory than the houses of Christians in which they live the rest of the year. We have, however, a district in the north of the province, where each of the Christian districts has a fine chapel. There is one, very large, which would be a fine country church in Europe. It has a medium sized bell which calls the Christians to prayer and, besides, a large plate of the same metal with a finer sound. This they use to announce the exercises of the mission. On the feasts of St. John the Baptist, and of Sts. Peter and Paul, I sang mass in this church but without the accompaniment of the fine orchestra which is commonly used among the numerous Christian sections of the province of Pekin, and particularly in the small cathedral which M. Mouly has built in Tartary. In the time of the emperor, Kang-Hi, the Christians had churches in many towns which to-day are in the hands of pagans. The Christians especially in Ho-Nan, except the twenty people who are from Pekin, employed in commerce and clock-making in the capital of the province, are nearly all in the country, dispersed in small, obscure places. You see here, as in France, according to the expression of St. Vincent, we have the happiness of being missionaries to the poor country people.

"We are, also, dear confrère, poor ourselves. In the two provinces, we have three residences where we can pass our times of sickness and vacation. In them, we are at home. The one from which I now write you, is used this year as a stopping place by M. Rameaux on his return from the middle of Hou-Pé and by me, when I return from the north of Ho-Nan. We have divided between us almost equally a distance of more than two hundred leagues. As you may imagine, this meeting is very agreeable and useful to me; but, unhappily, too short; for the Christians of the mountains of Hou-Kouang soon took away this good confrère, who hastened to bring them spiritual help during the epidemic, fearless of the dangers which threatened him. In this place, the pagans now have a suit against the Christians before the mandarins. Three European missionaries and four Chinese have been denounced. I have not the honor to be of the number. It seems, however, that this affair will not end disastrously and will soon be settled. Still, the missionaries pursue their way as long as they have no ropes on their necks or irons on their feet.

"Thanks be to God, Who is always making new conquests for religion in the different provinces of the Chinese Empire! In Ho-Nan which, no doubt, contains the fewest, we have this year baptized twenty adults. It is consoling to see with what fervor these neophytes receive the sacrament of regeneration; but, on the other hand, it is sad to see the demon bear away his prey when we thought we had snatched it from him. Near here, lives a peasant woman of advanced age, who had been greatly edified and deeply touched by the charity and piety with which the Christian women rendered the last offices to a poor woman of her neighborhood. Seeing them praying around the coffin, she gave us great hopes that she would embrace the religion whose practices she could not help admiring. She said at last: 'I would love to be a Christian, but I fear the persecutions.'

"Some time ago, another old woman, an apostate, promised to become converted with her children who were pagans. The demon triumphed over her again, for she offered sacrifice to idols.—In a Christian district through which I passed I saw at the house of a Christian, a pagan shepherd whose mother, a widow, had married again, and embraced Christianity. He was exhorted to follow her example; he replied that he would do it later, but at present he must obtain the means to buy a wife for his deceased father. You may perhaps, think that it was a joke or a rebuke to his mother. But you should know it is customary among pagans of certain parts of China when a widow marries a second time, for the children, so as not to leave their father without a wife, even after death, to buy him a *dead unmarried girl.* She is brought to the house of her future and defunct husband, not in a funeral train, but as if she were living, with all the joys, pomps and ceremonies usual at a real wedding; after which this singular couple share the same family mourning and the same tomb in the cemetery. This is something like the Sadducees.

"Another custom generally observed in China, which the Christians share with the pagans, is that of burying the husband and wife, or wives, if there are several, in the same grave, though in different coffins; while a child dying at birth with its mother is not buried with her, but in a grave apart.

"I must not omit to tell you, that while I was at a Christian settlement, a pagan school master continually asked to see the missionary's watch, having never before seen one; he was told that he must see the missionary himself to have this beautiful machine explained, otherwise he could understand nothing. 'I fear,' said he, 'that he will only exhort me to become a Christian, or that he will make fun of my lame legs.' He was mistaken about the second point, but not about the first; for that was why his Christian friends wished to bring him to the missionary. We were told, since, that a good opportunity would overcome his fears. God grant that he will allow himself to be captured! In another Christian section, they brought a young pagan into the room where I was. He stood and looked at me with as much attention as if he wished to paint my picture; then withdrew, well satisfied, as he said, at having seen a European nose;

for, he had greatly desired all his life to see this marvel, having learned from his father, who had seen our venerable confrère, M. Clet, that Europeans have longer noses than the Chinese. This is enough of these little details; but since I have mentioned M. Clet,* I must tell you something about him more interesting than what I have just related. As in my travels I have several times followed or crossed roads, along which our venerable confrere was dragged when loaded with chains for Our Lord, and brought to the different tribunals of this province and Hou-Kouang, I assure you, it was not without emotion that I heard those who accompanied me relate their recollections of him. The very place I am now, is where he was arrested; and our nearest neighbors visited him in the different prisons, because he had been their guest. I must relate to you the following particulars which are learned from good authority:

I. "The same day that he was seized, before any one around had the least idea that he was pursued, he announced to a person who is still living, that on that day the soldiers would come to take him. This makes us think that his guardian angel must have informed him of it.

II. "At the first tribunal to which he was brought, he said, among other things, to the mandarin, 'My brother, now you judge me; in a little while my Lord will judge you.' Then the mandarin angrily said to him: 'I shall strike you and I shall see if your Lord will punish me;' and he ordered him to be beaten. M. Clet had not been martyred before the mandarin himself died miserably.

* A Lazarist missionary martyred in China, 1820, and declared venerable by Gregory XVI., July 9, 1843.

III. "At another tribunal, he said to the mandarin: 'Now, I am judged, but before three years your emperor will have rendered his account to Our Lord.' About six months after M. Clet's death, the emperor, Kia-Kin, died in Tartary, struck by lightning. The Chinese dare not tell it but in whispers.

"These little details can only add to the veneration you already have for this worthy confrère, who has sealed with his blood the faith he preached in China. On my own account, I congratulate myself upon working in that portion of the vineyard of Our Lord which he has cultivated with so much zeal and success. His memory, which they have so carefully cherished, serves only to animate me to walk in his footsteps and to continue the good he has begun.

"Now we have ended our vacation for this year, if it may be called a vacation, the time passed in studying, hearing confessions, preaching, teaching a class of future seminarians, amid a crowd of other children who come here every day to learn catechism and their prayers, etc. We are going to begin our annual retreat and then we will resume our campaign. May God bless our little labors, sanctify our efforts and make them fruitful! Trials are not lacking to the missionaries, but they are so precious in the eyes of faith, that it is worth going to the end of the earth to find them. Let not those, then, of your seminarians who may have the vocation to come and join us, fear these trials, but, rather, let them be ambitious for them. If you could only send us a good number of Francis Xaviers for China, which needs them so much! Although the most useless of all the laborers who work here, I can not help expressing frequently the desire that Our Lord will at last send the day on which this vast empire will become His inheritance, sharing in the graces which He has reserved for it in the treasures of His mercy.

"No, I can not help uniting myself to you and so many holy souls who say to Him unceasingly. *Miserere nostri, Deus omnium, et respice nos, et ostende lucem miserationum tuarum, et immitte timorem tuum super gentes quae non exquisierunt te, ut cognoscant te, sicut et nos cognovimus; quoniam non est Deus praeter te, Domine: festina tempus et memento finis, ut enarrent mirabilia tua.* 'Have mercy on us, O God of all; and behold us, and show us the light of Thy mercies. And send Thy fear upon the nations, that have not sought after Thee that they may know, as we also have known, there is no God beside Thee, O Lord. Hasten the time and remember the end, that they may declare Thy wonderful works.' (Eccli. xxxvi.)

"Permit me, reverend and dear confrère, to claim again a very special share in your holy suffrages. Recommend me to the charity of our superiors, confreres, brothers and sisters, giving my regards to them all, particularly to the Superior General."

---

## VII.

### JOHN GABRIEL IN THE MISSION OF HOU-PÉ.

In the month of January, 1838, Blessed Perboyre was sent to Hou-Pé, to work there as he had done in Ho-Nan, for the glory of God and the salvation of souls. Here, also, he was tried by labors and fatigues of all kinds. It is the future martyr who, with the charm that belongs to the words of the saints, gives us the details. He wrote to the pastor at Catus:

"HOU-PÉ, September 12, 1838.

"*My very dear Cousin,*—The most recent news you have had of me has come from Ho-Nan. I stayed a year and a half in that province. I made one visit to all the Christian sections there and even two to several of them. In January, I was called to Hou-Pé by M. Rameaux, Superior of this mission. The district I have since served and which I have left only to visit two small Christian sections a short distance away, is situated among mountains. It is two or three leagues in length and a little less, in breadth. The Christians, who compose it and among whom are very few pagans, number about two thousand, distributed through fifteen Christian districts, which, however, are so scattered that there is not one which resembles a little village. When a section is visited, entire families go every day where the missionary has established the exercises for the time. In the centre of this district, we have a residence which belongs to the mission. There, the missionary is like a pastor in the midst of a large parish, and he is in continual communication with the Christians of the whole district. He is often called on, night and day, to administer the sacraments to the sick, a consolation the Chinese Christians hasten to obtain upon the least appearance of danger. There is continually, especially before Sundays and Feast days, so great a crowd of people coming to confession that the three priests who live here have much difficulty in hearing them all. The principal Christians or catechists try, at least, to get their turn on great Feast days; there are, perhaps, few parishes in France where the Holy Table is more frequented than here. Every day, not only many girls and pious women, but also many fathers of families, assist regularly at Mass; and if they wish to obtain rain or good weather, the crowd continues and increases until they get what they desire. It it especially on Sundays and Feast days, that the flock presses around the pastor. From the beginning till the close of day, our church is continually filled. At first, they recite in common the morning prayers, the prayers of the Feast and a part of the catechism; then comes Mass, the sermon and catechism for the children; after which, those who wish, retire; some remain, others return to recite the first part of the rosary, with which they end the afternoon. The evening is taken up with the exercises of the Way of the Cross, the prayers of the different confraternities, and a conference. A week before, they choose the subject, some virtue or duty. When Sunday comes, there appear on the scene about a dozen orators, who preach, one after another, on the given subject; they are young scholars, catechists or other intelligent Christians. The priest ends this interesting colloquy by some edifying words before numerous auditors who resemble those who followed Our Lord in the desert, their relish for the nourishment of the soul making them forget the food of the body. To know how the missionaries' days are taken up, add to the confessions, baptisms, confirmations, marriages, admissions into the confraternity of the Holy Scapular or some other, the obtaining of dispensations, examinations into the difficulties that occur in the Christian districts, interrogations upon doctrine, private instructions, advice and corrections. Sometimes, even, they perform the office of justice of the peace; this they decline whenever they can, but sometimes they are obliged to exercise it. I should not, perhaps, have entered into minute details in speaking of these things to a worthy pastor like yourself who is so familiar with them in practice, and who acquits himself of them so much better than we do; but I wished, my dear cousin, to give you an idea of what a parish in China is like. There, properly speaking, we have no parishes. However, I will tell you something about our church. Ah! God forgive me, if I dare assure you that our church bears no comparison to many a barn in your country. The bare ground is enclosed within four walls of earth, covered with a roof of straw; a table serves for an altar, back of which is a hanging that extends above it like the canopy of a bed. This is a complete description of it, if I do not mention the half partition which separates the women from the men, according to the Chinese custom and the laws of propriety in all countries. If some dislike to recognize this as a church, let them come here and see it with a thousand pious faithful souls filling and surrounding, even in rain and snow, this humble inclosure, and their eyes will discover precious stones destined to compose that church of ineffable beauty which must be eternally admirable and eternally happy in the bosom of God. I beg them to consider that He Who, by being born in a stable, made it a church worthy of God, descends here every day for the happiness of those who adore

Him. He deigns often to come to abodes still more vile.

"It is impossible to give you an idea of the extreme misery of the people who live in our mountains. To describe it as it is, even in years considered good, would make you incredulous. During the months I have passed here, I have attended many sick persons; I hasten with joy to bring the consolations of religion to those who can have no other comforts; but on my way, I feel grieved when inquiring from the doctor, a catechist who accompanies me, the cause of the sickness, I hear nearly always the reply: 'There is no cause but misery and famine.' I continue my way in silence, filled with remorse at having outlived these unfortunates, not dying myself in the same manner as they do. However, our house is continually besieged by the poor, like the seminaries and religious communities of Europe, and if some tyrant desired the treasures of our church, by the grace of God the reply of St. Lawrence would be quite appropriate. One year of famine or persecution is like a whirlwind to these poor people. It sweeps them out of sight without anyone's knowing what has become of them. When better times come, they return, one by one. A few days ago, one of these poor Christians died whom God seemed to have recalled, after twenty or thirty years' absence, only that He might let him put his conscience in order and attract him to Himself. Among the small number of adults that I have baptized this year, a young man died lately, a few days after his baptism, at the time when it was least expected. I have cause to congratulate myself for having given him the sacrament sooner than I had at first intended, having more regard for his fervor than the amount of instruction he had received.

"In China, as elsewhere, the priest has often noted the loving care of Providence toward His elect, especially in regard to their passage to eternity. Here is a very striking instance; it proves that God, Who sometimes sends a priest in so extraordinary a manner, would not fail in their need to send even angel in the place of a priest. Last year at Ho Nan, as I was going to Pien-Leang, the capital of the province, to visit the Christians there, I asked the Chinese priest who accompanied me to pass through a place where formerly a great number of Christians lived, to see if there might not be need of preaching there again. Here he found a dying Christian very advanced in age, who had always been faithful to his duties. The poor man went to confession with much fervor and showed great gratitude for so precious and unexpected a grace. Two or three days after, he gave up his soul to his Creator. I could tell you of other more singular examples, well attested but not so recent.

"Let me relate to you the following fact which is told by a zealous missionary. Fifteen or sixteen years ago, Father Lamade, called in Chinese Ouan, of the Society of Jesus, died in a district next to the one in which I am now. The Christians did not dare to bury him through fear of compromising themselves, by giving burial to a stranger, and especially, a European. A family of a Christian section a short distance from here, came and claimed the body of the venerable deceased, saying that he was one of their relations from Ou Tchang Fou, who had just been to see them. But it pleased God to reveal what men so desired to hide, for during the funeral the pagans of the place heard sweet music in the air and after this miracle two families embraced Christianity. A missionary who, during long years, had visited the Christian section of which I speak, and also his catechist, have assured me that they heard this fact from the lips of several of those converted on this occasion. So, my dear cousin, Our Lord always takes care of those who abandon themselves entirely to His care when they are most abandoned by men; at the moment of death, especially, He gives them more than the promised hundred-fold. But our faith does not need these sensible proofs. A father, a mother, a brother, or a sister should have no regret for being unable to assist a loved son or brother in his last moments, if they had once known the feelings of the Divine Heart of Jesus and the heart of His holy Mother who assist with so much solicitude and ineffable tenderness all those who die in the Lord. It is in these Sacred Hearts that you have established your dwelling, my very dear cousin, and it is there you will meet me. Oh! who will give me the wings of a dove and I will fly there to fix my abode. Implore them, these very Holy Hearts, to draw to them by the odor of their ravishing perfumes, my poor and miserable heart and make it worthy of Them, like yours, to which I desire to be united in Them and for Them."

Who will not be filled with admiration in presence of the eminent virtues of Blessed John Gabriel? Now, he regrets that he can not die, like the most abandoned in the mountains of Hou-Pé; again he rises on the wings of love to the Heart of Jesus. He tells the mysterious assistance God bestows on those souls deprived of all succor in the supreme hour of death. The heart of our Blessed Martyr has known the secrets of divine charity.

We do not weary of reading his letters, where he pictures himself amid details, so pious and interesting.

In 1839, he relates to one of his confrères an account of a miracle wrought by the Blessed Virgin. He speaks also of his occupations.

"Hou-Pé, August 10, 1839.

"*My Very Dear Confrère*,—May the grace of Our Lord be with you always! You sent me a few words in my brother's letter. Though short, they are very precious in my eyes and certainly worthy of my gratitude, since they are a proof of your kind remembrance which is particularly dear to me. I can assure you for my part, that I often remember you at the foot of that crucifix which you presented at my departure from France. Your humility led you to ask to have a share in the good works of a poor man who has never done any good, and who probably will never do any hereafter; so have pity on his indigence and give him, please, a participation in your own spiritual riches.

"M. Rameaux wrote you that I had something to tell you about the effect of a miraculous medal. It is pleasant to me to fulfil the promise he made for me. When I was giving a mission in the Christian settlement of Ho-Nan, in November, 1837, the Christians of the place, brought me a young woman from another Christian section. She had been afflicted with mental derangement for about eight months. I was told that she ardently desired to go to confession and though she was incapable of this act, they begged me not refuse her what she had so much at heart. The sad state to which she was reduced made the exercise of my ministry seem useless to her; nevertheless, I heard her through pure compassion. When sending her away, I put her under the special protection of the Blessed Virgin; that is, I gave her a medal of the Immaculate Conception. She did not then comprehend the value of the holy remedy she received; but from that time she experienced its virtue, feeling better and continuing to improve till at the end of four or five days, she was entirely cured. A complete disorder of ideas, apprehensions that kept her in mortal agony, many of them, I think, coming from the devil, were succeeded by good sense, calmness and happiness. She went to confession again, and received Holy Communion with lively joy and fervor. This instance of the goodness of the Mother of Mercy will not, doubtless, surprise you, very dear confrère, who know that the whole world is filled with the mercy of Mary; but your good heart will be charmed to have this new occasion for particular thanksgiving and this is the chief motive that induced me to bring this fact to your knowledge.

"As all the news which comes from the Chinese missions passes under your eyes, I shall give you very little, fearing to repeat what you have learned from other sources. I think M. Rameaux will write to you himself; he is now in the lower part of Hou-Pe whence he will start to make a tour of Ho-Nan, after which we hope, M. Baldus and I, to meet him in these mountains. It was here he sent me nearly two years ago, and here I continue to exercise the holy ministry, whose duties leave me no time to look either backwards or forwards. From the Nativity of the Blessed Virgin last year till Pentecost this year, I have given seventeen missions or visitations to Christian sections and I can not say that I have had a moment's vacation. Really, it is scarcely possible to take any, because we are among a great number of Christians who, for the most part, love to confess often. If, for example on this Feast of the Assumption, we could hear a thousand or more, we would find that many well disposed. After the Feast, I shall go into retreat and then resume my missionary campaign for the greater part of the year. Our manner of conducting these missions, is already known to you ; I shall not speak of it. You, who in France have labored in missions with so much zeal and benediction, have but to recall your own experiences to know our entire life and all its details, to see all our actions, to hear all our words, to feel all our trials and all our consolations, to appreciate all our efforts for each soul to make him detest some sin or uproot some habit and to take him away from satan to bring him to Jesus Christ. As to the particular manifestations of the riches of the mercy of God to men, you can suppose that our vocation often makes us witness them. For example, this year, in this district, we have been consoled and edified, not only by having eight adults receive baptism with fervor, and a good number of catechumens prepare themselves soon to receive the same grace, but still more by leading back to the fold some sheep long strayed away.

Among others, a woman, given to paganism from her early youth, returned in her sixtieth year to edify the other Christians by her uncommon piety. A grey-beard, on the brink of the grave, after thirty years' apostasy, burnt the idol to which he and his family had so often offered incense, etc."

---

## VIII.

### SUCCESS OF BLESSED JOHN GABRIEL IN HOU-PE.

THE short time the Servant of God passed in Hou-Pe was crowned with great success. His virtues were admired not only by his confrères, but even by the heathens who regarded him as a saint.

He had come to China to seek for sufferings, he could now gratify his desire, for it is easy to understand how hard a missionary's life is in that country. The houses have no chimneys; daylight is seen only through very narrow windows. Generally, the dwellings are dark and unhealthy; a fire can not be lighted without causing a dense smoke which injures the chest and eyes. A little rice, some herbs boiled in water, a nourishment without seasoning and often disgusting, is what must sustain the strength of the missionary, weakened by labors and incessant travel. Often, his bed is simply a covered plank. Add to these privations, the inconveniences occasioned by the heat, hunger and thirst, etc., and it is easy to understand, as Blessed Perboyre says in his letters that the missionary in China leads an apostolic life. The Servant of God had much to suffer, too, from the weakness of his constitution and his many infirmities. But as all this did not suffice, he treated his body with great severity; he wore around his waist an iron chain. There is one penance we must mention which, however, will not surprise us. Going to different places, living among poor Christians, often covered with vermin, he could have protected himself against them; but, in a spirit of penance, after the example of many of the saints, he allowed himself to be devoured while living, and did nothing to relieve himself from the infliction.

His continual occupation was to travel through the villages where Christians were, to instruct the ignorant, to convert sinners and apostates, and to reanimate the fervor of the lukewarm. Though in very delicate health, he was always ready to brave the worst weather to bring, even in the night, the succors of religion to those who needed them.

As the Christians might at any time be called upon to confess Jesus Christ before the tribunals, he endeavored to strengthen their faith by frequent exhortations. He often read to them the Acts of the Martyrs, so as to put before their eyes the models they must imitate. At the recitation of these glorious combats, they saw that he was exalted above himself and that he burned with desire to give his life for his divine Master. A short time before he was arrested, when he was with M. Baldus, he read in the "Annals of the Propagation of the Faith" an account of the frightful tortures that had been endured by some missionaries in Cochin China. He seemed greatly impressed by this reading, and trembled as if he felt himself afflicted with all their torments. At last he said that these refinements of barbarity were horrible to nature, but when necessary, God gave the required strength to endure them. The question being asked what should be the conduct of a missionary before the mandarins, who often artfully question him about the number and names of the Christians so that they can legally try them, Blessed Perboyre replied that, in that case he would imitate the sublime silence which Our Lord opposed to the questions of Pilate and Herod.

The hour approached when the valiant champion was to descend into the arena; but before this fearful and glorious struggle, God wished to prepare him by a martyrdom still more afflicting to his heart. It is well known that St. Francis de Sales was subjected in his youth, to a great trial; it seemed to him that he was excluded from the kingdom of heaven and destined to torments for all eternity. John Gabriel passed several months in this same overwhelming tribulation. God having withdrawn from him all His lights, left him plunged in desolation, it seemed that he had nothing to expect hereafter from the divine mercy. He saw in God only a severe judge irritated against him; his innumerable sins, his constant abuse of grace, etc., terrified him. He prayed, wept and groaned much; God repulsed him with anger. His crucifix had become mute to him or, rather, he heard from the wounds of his divine Savior only threats of condemnation. If he sought consolation before the Blessed Sacrament, he found there but greater bitterness. Each time he celebrated the holy Sacrifice and received the Body and Blood of Jesus Christ, he imagined himself another Judas who ate and drank his own damnation. A profound darkness filled his soul; neither his prayers nor sighs were heard; he could say with the royal Prophet: "My tears have been my bread day and night, whilst it is said to me daily: Where is thy God?" (Ps. xli, 4.) Sleep fled from his eyelids; his food became insipid to him. It was in vain that he had endeavored to serve God from his earliest childhood; it was in vain that he had made great sacrifices to testify his love: all this was lost to him. This horrible agony caused him so much sufferings that his health was considerably affected by it. Each day he grew more pale, and wasted like a plant burnt up by the heat of the sun; he would surely have succumbed, if God had not set bounds to this trial. Jesus Christ, Whom he copied so faithfully, before making him suffer the torments of Calvary, wished him to share in His agony and dereliction in the Garden of Olives. The divine Saviour appeared to him attached to the cross; casting upon him a look of ineffable goodness He said to him affectionately "What dost thou fear? Have I not died for thee? Put thy finger into My side and cease to fear thy damnation." Then the vision having disappeared, John Gabriel felt all his terrors dissipated, giving place to the most delightful peace. The next day, there remained no trace of the extreme thinness which this trial occasioned. He no longer had any but consoling thoughts for he had received an assurance of his salvation and a presentiment of his martyrdom.

"It was he, himself," said M. Baldus afterwards, "who related this fact to me, in a conversation which I had with him in our residence of Kou-Tching, and I noticed that he related it in the third person. Not allowing him to believe that I was duped by this pious artifice, when he finished his account,

I said to him suddenly: 'I know very well of whom you speak; it was to you that this happened.' His embarrassment, and evasive responses were for me as great a proof as a complete avowal."

---

## IX.

### PERSECUTION IN HOU-PÉ.—ARREST OF THE BLESSED PERBOYRE—TORTURES ENDURED FOR THE FAITH.

WHEN the Servant of God penetrated into China, a law existed, made in 1794 by the emperor, Kien-Loung, which proscribed the Christian religion and condemned all those who professed it, to death, if they were Europeans, but only to exile if they were Chinese. The application of this law had already cost the Church several persecutions, the most violent of which, after that of 1805, took place in 1820 and procured for the Venerable Clet the palm of martyrdom.

For a long time, however, the Christians particularly in Hou-Pé, enjoyed great tranquillity. Suddenly a persecution was again started. It began in the village of Nan-Kiang where they first seized some Christians. Among them was a young man, son of the Catechist, Peng-Ting-Siang, who, frightened by the threats of the soldiers and persuaded by their caresses, miserably betrayed his brethren, told their names, their dwellings and the places where they assembled with the missionaries. Orders were immediately given by the mandarin of Kou-Tching-Hien to arrest both the missionaries and the people. A troop of soldiers, led by two commissaries of the viceroy of Ou-Tchang-Fou, two military mandarins and a lower civil mandarin, directed their steps to the residence of the missionaries at Tchang-Yuen-Keou, a small village of the province of Kou Tching-Hien near the market town of Koang-Yn-Tang. Blessed Perboyre was there with his confrère, M. Baldus, a missionary of the Propaganda on his way from Hou-Pé, Rev. Joseph Rizzolati, an Italian Franciscan, and a Chinese priest, M. Wang. These met together to celebrate the octave of the Nativity and the Feast of the Holy Name of Mary. It was, in fact, on Sunday, September 15, 1839, and the Christians of the place had come to hear Mass and assist at the other exercises of devotion which fill up the whole Sunday. The last Mass was just finished ; some of the faithful were still in church with Blessed John Gabriel, M. Baldus and Father Rizzolati. Suddenly, a Chinese Christian, named Toung-Ta-Youn, came in great haste to tell them of the breaking out of the persecution ; that the soldiers were marching to the church headed by two mandarins ; and that they were only a short distance off. He added that there was no time to lose and that each of them by swift flight should provide for his safety.

M. Baldus and Father Rizzolati made no delay in following this advice, but the intrepid Servant of God could not decide to abandon the flock so dear to him ; he wished to persuade himself and tried to convince others that the danger was not imminent. Nevertheless, the soldiers were heard approaching and every one fled but John Gabriel who thought only of escaping from danger when he saw clearly that he could no longer expose himself, without rashness. He gathered together, then, as well as he could, the sacred articles which he did not wish to have profaned, and left by a secret door the moment the soldiers entered the church. Furious at seeing that their prey had escaped, they seized the most precious things they found in the church and in the missionary's house. They burnt the papers and books with so much carelessness that every thing soon became a prey to the flames, and one of the mandarins barely escaped death.

However, the Servant of God had succeeded in hiding himself in a forest of bamboos, a short distance from the church. Night having come, he left his retreat to go to the house of a catechist, Ly-Tsou-Hoa, where he took some food he greatly needed after the fatigues and excitement of the day. His host had Blessed Perboyre's beard cut off so he could be less easily recognized as a European, and brought him three hundred paces beyond, to pass the night at the house of his cousin, the father of Ly-Tsou-Kouei, the catechist.

Not to compromise his hosts, the next day, September 16, the saintly fugitive before dawn left his new asylum to hide himself in a neighboring forest, accompanied by his servant Thomas-Sin Ly-Siang, another Christian, Wang-Kouan-King and Ly-Tse-Ming, father of the catechist Ly-Tsou-Hoa.

This was a secure retreat and he certainly would have escaped the pursuers, if Providence had not, to render him, doubtless, more like his divine Model, permitted that he too, should be betrayed by one of his own. The neophyte, Kioung-Lao-San, a new Judas, through fear or avarice, revealed to the soldiers for a reward of thirty ounces of silver, the place where John Gabriel was hidden. They immediately surrounded the forest and like ferocious beasts, ran in all directions to find their prey. Two of them, at length, found the Servant of God and his three companions, who seeing the superiority of their numbers, flight being impossible, wished at first to repulse the aggressors by force. Thomas Sin-Ly-Siang immediately proposed it to his master, but the latter remembering that Jesus in the garden of Gethsemani would not permit St. Peter to use his sword, forbade also his devoted and brave servant to use violence. Thomas obeyed, and with the exception of Ly-Tse-Ming, who succeeded in taking flight, all the other Christians hidden in this forest fell into the hands of the enemy.

These ruffians immediately rallied around the holy missionary, threw themselves upon him, seized him by his queue and dragged him to the summit of the mountain. There, they stripped off all his clothing and left him in exchange only some wretched rags; tied his hands behind his back, dealt him three heavy blows on the shoulders with a sabre and brought him, loaded with chains, to the market of Koang-Yn-Tang. The Servant of God bore patiently and with courage, all this bad treatment, not allowing the least complaint, or cry of pain to escape him.

Arrived at Koang-Yn-Tang, he appeared before the civil mandarin, Liou, of the town of Kou-Ching-Hien, who was there awaiting the prisoner. "It was pitiful to see him," says an eye witness, "with no clothes but a shirt and a pair of ragged pants, a chain around his neck and his hands tied behind his back, surrounded by soldiers who pulled him by the ears and hair, to make him look at the mandarin before whom he was kneeling."

"Are you a priest of the Christian religion?" the mandarin asked him. He replied immediately, without fearing the new torments, and death even, that this response might bring upon him: "Yes, I am a priest and a preacher of that religion." "Do you wish to renounce your faith?" "Never will I renounce the faith of Jesus Christ." "What are the motives that led you to come and propagate your religion in this country?" He did not reply to this question. The mandarin, full of anger, had him separated from his companions in captivity, loaded with chains and brought with hands and feet tied, to the house of a pagan named Heou, whose proverbial cruelty had obtained for him the surname of San-Pin-Hou; that is, three times a tiger: in his shop John Gabriel must pass the night. Eight men, chosen from the richest of the place and, consequently, less susceptible of being bribed to allow the prisoner's escape, were charged to watch near him and carefully guard him till the next day.

On the morning of Wednesday, September 17, orders were given the soldiers to lead the prisoner to the town of Kou-Tching-Hien, a short distance from Koang-Yn-Tang. But the venerable Servant of God, broken down by the cruel treatment to which he had been subjected, and weakened by hunger and fatigue, was unable to make the journey on foot. Already the sad procession began its march. The valiant Confessor of Jesus Christ stopped in a public place and was surrounded by a spiteful crowd who loaded him with all kinds of injuries and outrages, when a pagan, named Lieu-Kioun-Lin, felt himself moved with compassion at the sight. He drew near, asked and obtained permission to have the prisoner brought upon a litter whose bearers he paid and which he himself followed to town. This good action did not go without its reward. The venerable Servant of God, deeply touched, affectionately thanked his benefactor, but did not limit his gratitude to mere thanks. When he had received the palm of martyrdom, as will be related hereafter, he appeared to this charitable pagan and obtained for him, a little before his death, the grace of holy baptism.

Arrived in Kou-Tching-Hien, where still greater torments awaited him, the Servant of God appeared first before a military mandarin, who asked who he was, and what motive urged him to penetrate into the Chinese empire. "I am a European," he replied, "who came here to propagate the Catholic religion and to exhort men to fly from evil and to do good." "What route have you followed to come into this country?" He replied that he came from Kou-Tching by Nan-Chan. "In what Christian houses have you lodged?" He kept silence. "In what places have you preached? How many people have you sought to attract to your religion? Have all those who have heard your preaching, embraced the religion you taught them? Are there other Christian priests in China?" In response to all these questions he said, "I only speak for myself." "What are the advantages you hope to derive from preaching the Christian doctrine?" "I exhort men to know and serve God, so that by the practice of good works, they will strive to acquire eternal life, and avoid the fate of those who do evil and who will suffer eternal punishment." This was the second interrogation to which the Missionary had to submit in Kou-Tching. The mandarin, little touched by this solemn profession of faith, replied that it was false and that John Gabriel had no other motive than to delude the citizens of the Celestial Empire. But the Servant of God replied to this inquiry only by silence. He deigned no other reply to the proposition which was made to him to deny his faith, contenting himself with a negative shake of the head, to indicate the horror with which it inspired him, and his refusal of the proposition. The mandarin, irritated by his silence, had him beaten by the soldiers, struck a hundred blows with a bamboo rod and put into prison. But there, no repose was allowed this poor body, so tormented and enfeebled; they inflicted upon him new sufferings, which the generous Confessor supported with sweetness and admirable patience.

The next day, being brought to the tribunal of the civil mandarin, he was subjected to a new interrogation. "Are you a European? What is your occupation?" "I am a European and my employment is to preach the Christian doctrine." "Since this religion is received in Europe, why have you come to preach it in China?" "This religion is allowed to be preached everywhere, and this is why I have come to teach it in China." "What are the means which you use to spread it?" "I exhort men to the practice of good works and to serve God Who nourishes and preserves us, Who is the source of all good, and Who after death will give us in reward, the eternal glory of Paradise."

Among the goods taken from the missionaries were

different objects used for religious worship. The mandarin had them brought to the tribunal, and taking successively the chalice, the missal, the sacred vestments, all of which were used in the holy sacrifice of the Mass, he asked the Servant of God what use he made of them. The latter replied that they were used to offer sacrifice in honor of God. "Cease relating your follies; is it not rather to have yourself adored by a crowd of Christians who surround you?" "I propose no other end to myself than to give to God with the Christians, the homages that are His due." "Why does not the God Whom you serve hinder you from falling into the hands of your enemies and why has He let these calamities come upon you?" "God leaves us upon earth a prey to the greatest calamities; but these evils do not last forever and He will recompense us through all eternity for what we suffer for Him." "If you do not change your sentiments, I will make you endure severe punishment." "I pay no attention to the sufferings of the body, because I think only of eternal salvation." "I see you will not abandon your faith and that it will be vain for me to try to force you to renounce it." "You may be well assured that I will never renounce my faith." The mandarin, showing him the vessel with holy oils asked him if it did not contain water extracted from the eyes torn from the sick.* "Never," he replied, "have I committed so great a crime."

At the same time with Blessed Perboyre, the mandarin summoned before him, a Christian maiden,

*It is said that this prejudice against the Christians is the one most commonly believed by all Chinese pagans.

15

named Anna Kao, taken in the same persecution. Upon this occasion, he grossly insulted the Servant of God, who to his ignoble questions, contented himself with responding, that the missionaries and virgins vowed and preserved chastity, that they lived separate, engaged in their respective duties and that the virgins were not employed in the service of the missionaries, who were served by men who accompanied them in their travels.

At last, the mandarin tried to make him deny his faith by putting a crucifix on the ground, and ordering him to tread it under foot. But the valiant Confessor replied, "Even in death, I will refuse to deny my faith and to tread the crucifix under foot." As the mandarin added, "If you do not abjure it, I will put you to death," he replied, "Very well, I will be happy to die for the faith." Immediately he received upon his cheeks by order of the mandarin, forty blows with a strong leather strap, and his face was horribly bruised and disfigured. He was brought back to prison, where he was again delivered to the soldiers.

This was the third time the Confessor professed his faith generously before the judges, but the cruel execution to which he was subjected could draw from him no sign, no word that could be taken for apostasy. Would it not seem that God, being satisfied by these pledges of his love, would already recompense them and that the noble Servant of God, drawing near his blessed death, the object so ardently desired, would await it with calm joy? No, greater combats became his share here below, because a more glorious crown is reserved for him.

After several interrogations to which he was subjected before the civil and military mandarins of Kou-Tching-Kien and which were accompanied by the most cruel tortures, the Servant of God was brought by the soldiers to Siang-Yang-Fou, a first-class town situated about fourteen miles distant. The voyage was made by water upon the river Han-Kiang, and was for the venerable Servant of God, the occasion of new sufferings. Thrown into the bark with his hands and feet tied, he was separated from the other Christian prisoners; whilst to them were given the food and drink they needed, both were constantly refused him during all this long trip.

Arrived at last at Siang-Yang-Fou, he remained several days confined in a horrible prison, where he was spared neither insults nor tortures. Upon the appointed day, he was brought first before the tribunal of the governor of the town, who made him submit to a new interrogation, and who put to him the same question as to his character of European and Catholic missionary, and as to the motive that brought him to China, and he received the same responses. The mandarin then proposed to him to tread the crucifix under foot, but the Servant of God replied simply and with firmness, "Never will I do it." Seeing that his threats were useless, the governor thought he could more easily obtain his end by reasonings, like those sometimes heard in Europe from the pretended savants of the modern school. "What will you gain by adoring your God?" "The salvation of my soul," replied the Confessor; "and heaven where I hope to go after my death." "Fool!" replied the mandarin, "you have never seen paradise." Then turning towards the other Christian captives, "I will teach you what paradise is and what hell is. To be crowned in this life with riches and honors, that is paradise; to be on the contrary like you are to-day, condemned to lead a poor, suffering and miserable life, that is hell." At this speech truly worthy of Epicurus, he arose from his seat and had the venerable Servant of God sent back to prison.

Ten days after, he was brought before the first mandarin of the same town, who treated him with great moderation, and contented himself with asking how long it was since his arrival in China, an insidious question to which Blessed Perboyre knew how to respond so as not to compromise in any way the interests of religion.

But at the fiscal tribunal, before which he was brought in accordance with the laws of the country, a more furious tempest than any with which he had yet been tried awaited him. He was there cruelly tortured in body and soul, in his faith, as a Christian, and his dignity, as a man. Tao-Tai, president of this tribunal, and supreme judge of the city, consulting only his cruelty, ordered him beaten with a strong leather strap. Then he ordered that John Gabriel be hung from a beam by his two thumbs, firmly tied together. Then, he compelled him to remain nearly four hours amid most cruel suffering, kneeling with bare limbs upon iron chains. The venerable Servant of God supported these frightful tortures not only with fortitude but with a serene countenance and without making the least complaint.

The tyrant, nevertheless, reserved for his soul still more cruel torments than those with which he afflicted his body. He wished, but in vain, to make him abjure his faith by obliging him to tread the cross underfoot. Then he asked him what was the occupation of the *religeuses* or Christian virgins, and if they were employed in the service of the priest. The Missionary replied, that the profession of the Christian virgins was to serve God and observe chastity; that they never were allowed near the priests, who were served by the men who accompanied them in their journeys. The mandarin, who did not wish to believe this declaration, subjected the holy prisoner to new trials which became a new triumph for the Christian faith.

A month had passed amid these different interrogations, which so well displayed the heroic patience of the Servant of God, when they thought it proper to send him to Ou-Tchang-Fou, the metropolis of the province of Hou-Pé, to hear there the final judgment in his case.

---

## X.

### BLESSED PERBOYRE AT OU-TCHANG-FOU.

SHORTLY after the trial of which we have just spoken, the captive of Jesus Christ was brought to Ou-Tchang-Fou, the metropolis of the province, about fifty leagues distant. He started with about a dozen Christians who remained firm in the faith. They all had irons on their feet, hands and neck. Besides, a rod of iron about three spans in length, fixed at the top of the collar, descended upon the breast; the arms as well as the hands were attached perpendicularly to this rod. It may be imagined how painful this journey was to the Servant of God who was already suffering so much. On their arrival in Ou-Tchang-Fou, the prisoners were brought before an under mandarin who took their names; then they were taken to a horrible prison where the worst criminals were kept.

It would be difficult to form an idea of all John Gabriel had to endure in this terrible abode. There he found everything that could weary the most heroic patience and make a prison insupportable. He had much to suffer at first from the cupidity of his keepers, who were in the habit when a prisoner was brought to them to torture him with the refinements of barbarity, so as to obtain money, or to compel his relations and friends to satisfy their avarice. They would squeeze him so tightly by the arms and elbows, that the blood gushed from his fingers. As the prisoners were not allowed to leave the prison cell, they were crowded together both night and day amid filth, they could breathe only loathsome, infectious air. Their food was insufficient and of bad quality, and the atmosphere was impregnated with a fetid miasma; but what was more painful to the Servant of God, was the society of a multitude of criminals, familiar with all kinds of crimes, who used no reserve in their words or actions, whose mouths were only opened to vomit forth the most improper words, accompanied by curses, imprecations and blasphemies. The prisoners had every evening to submit to an extremely painful operation. They were fastened firmly by the feet in a sort of wooden vice, fixed to the wall. This caused them the most cruel sufferings besides the cold and their inability to move. The consequence of this treatment was that Blessed John Gabriel lost part of his foot through putrefaction and one of his fingers withered entirely away. He passed at least nine months in this purgatory, and he bore all these sufferings with admirable patience, and succeeded in softening his keepers and winning their affection. They wished to dispense him from the punishment just mentioned, but the other prisoners, when they perceived that his feet were not put in the shackles, murmured against the indulgence of the keepers. The Servant of God, to avoid all pretexts for complaint, asked to be treated like the others, saying that he bore this torture willingly for the love of God. Consequently he had to bear this punishment until death.

The town of Ou-Tchang-Fou was the scene of the combats and victories of the intrepid Soldier of Jesus Christ. It was here that his love for God was put to the most terrible proofs; it was here, also, that he bore away the palm of martyrdom. If the powers of darkness prepared themselves to inflict upon him the most painful assaults, the heavenly choirs prepared abundant aid to help him to triumph in this long and painful struggle. His first trial took place before the criminal tribunal. The supreme mandarin of justice took the lead, saying to him, "Since you are a European, why have you left your country and come to China?" "I have undertaken this voyage to spread the Christian religion in this country." "You could do that in Europe without coming to China, where entrance is forbidden by the emperor and where the people, who are instructed in a great and noble religion, can not embrace Christianity." The Confessor of the faith did not reply to this. The mandarin began to press him to abjure his religion, but, seeing that he firmly refused, he wished to try if he could compel him by suffering; so he ordered John Gabriel to be forced to kneel on iron chains and broken pottery, where he was left for several hours.

While he was in this position, a Christian having been taken to prison in the same town, passed before him and asked for sacramental absolution. Blessed Perboyre gave it to him in the presence of the whole assembly and thus filled the office of merciful judge before the iniquitous magistrates who treated him with so great injustice and barbarity. This is how it occurred: A Christian named Stanislas, an exemplary man, whose virtues gained for him the affection even of the pagan citizens, was arrested shortly after the Servant of God; the Chinese themselves wept at seeing so worthy a man in the power of his enemies. While in prison he endured all kinds of injuries from the soldiers; irons were put on his hands, feet, and neck, and he was placed near a disgusting dung-hill. The mandarin often summoned him before his tribunal and wished to make him tread upon a crucifix, but Stanislas remained immovable. After being solicited and tortured during a month and a half, they brought him back to Siang-Yang-Fou. The mandarin having asked if it was true that the Christian women were delivered up to corruption, he answered with firmness: "Not only does the Christian religion proscribe impure vices, but it is even forbidden to name them." This answer confounded the mandarin, who, in revenge, ordered thirty blows to be given Stanislas. Dragged, then, from town to town, from tribunal to tribunal, from prison to prison, this intrepid man made a journey of nearly a hundred leagues on foot, suffering from hunger, thirst, cold, rain, and the insults and cruelty of the soldiers and prison-keepers. His companion was another Christian confessor of the faith, who was blind. They were chained together; Stanislas walking first, leading the blind man. As the latter stumbled and made frequent falls and as the same chain was around Stanislas' neck, each time the blind man tripped he gave his companion so violent a jolt that the flesh of his neck was torn off and they often fell to the ground together. The soldiers had the cruelty to reproach the poor blind man for his careless walking, but Stanislas bore everything with unalterable patience; he uttered not a word of complaint, but consoled the blind Christian and exhorted him, saying: "We are sinners, let us accept this as a salutary penance." Stanislas was then brought to Ou-Tchang-Fou. He appeared several times before the mandarin, who had him tortured time and again, and always uselessly as far as making him abjure his religion was concerned. However, sufferings had so weakened him, that he could not get to the tribunal without crawling upon his hands and feet. It was on this occasion that passing before the Servant of God, he asked him to give him absolution to help him to prepare for death, which he felt was not far distant. Three days after, he expired in prison from the effects of the injuries he had endured. The Servant of God fulfilled this ministry of reconciliation for another Christian, who asked for absolution in the presence of the judges.

Shortly after the last trial of Blessed Perboyre, the same mandarin summoned him before him again, and insisted on knowing what made him come to

China. "I have not come here attracted by the thirst for riches, honors, applause or enjoyment, but with the sole desire of procuring the glory of God and the salvation of souls."—"But now you are loaded with chains and oppressed with torments; no doubt you repent of having had this design."—"I am far from repenting of it, nay more, I regard it as a great honor to bear these chains and to be afflicted with all sorts of tortures."—"But have you seen the God whom you with so great efforts seek to worship?" asked the mandarin who regarded as folly the reply so full of wisdom, which he had just heard.—"The Supreme Master of the world," said the Confessor of the faith, "is a Being who has no beginning and, being spiritual, can not be seen by the eyes of the body. Besides, we learn from our holy writings that He exists, and all the truths contained in our holy books are more certain than anything that can be seen by the eyes of the body."—"You certainly act like a madman," replied the mandarin, "in giving so great authority to your books and allowing yourself to be deceived by these fancies. You would be worthy of compassion if you had not deceived others, and done injustice to the people to whom you have taught these follies."

After having appeared twice before the criminal tribunal where he gloriously confessed the faith, the Servant of God was brought before the civil tribunal. The president, having put to him questions similar to those reported above, the Confessor gave the same answers, renewing his profession of faith, refusing to denounce the Christians and priests, whose names and dwellings they sought to learn. The mandarin urged him again, but Blessed Perboyre opposed his efforts with the most invincible resistance. He wished to try if, by new tortures, he could make him submit. He was then placed on his bare knees on iron chains, having his hands raised and loaded with a heavy piece of wood, which he had to hold up from nine o'clock in the morning till evening; moreover, the soldiers had orders to strike him every time that, overcome by fatigue and suffering, he let the piece of wood fall, or even when his arms would bend. The generous Confessor supported this long and horrible torture with the same courage and tranquillity of soul with which he bore the others; then he was brought back to prison.

In one hearing, the mandarin reproached him, with much anger and bitterness, that, by his artifices, he had deceived the people and drawn upon them all the evils that had befallen the Christians then brought before the tribunal. The mandarin ordered these Christians to spit in the Martyr's face, to curse him, to strike him, and told one of them to tear out his hair; he found five who had the cowardice to apostatize. These unhappy creatures obeyed the impious orders of the mandarin, vomiting out against the Servant of God, outrageous words, which they accompanied with cruel treatment. But another Christian, feigning to obey the judge, respectfully approached the Missionary and took some of his hair, which he preserved as a relic. As he did this before every one, without the mandarin's opposing it, the apostates blushed for their cowardice, and stopped their outrages. The other Christians remained firm in their faith, rendering a glorious testimony to religion. As to the Servant of God, he bore without complaining the insults of these unhappy renegades; he felt them more sensibly as they came from his children and brothers in the faith.

---

## XI.

### NEW SUFFERINGS OF BLESSED PERBOYRE.

THE Servant of God on re-entering prison, did not fail to thank Him in the effusion of his soul for the signal favor He had accorded him, and implored Him to sustain his courage to the end. The time he passed in prison was employed in strengthening himself more and more in charity, begging Our Lord to pardon his executioners. He often meditated upon the torments which the Son of God endured from men. When he was harassed and fatigued, he revived himself by prayer. He incessantly invoked Mary, his good mother, the angels, the martyrs and all the saints who from their thrones in heaven beheld his combats.

Till now he had suffered by the order of the different mandarins, before whom he had appeared; but he had not yet been presented to the vice-roy of Ou-Tchang-Fou, who put his patience to still greater tests and prepared for him still greater triumphs. This man, ferocious as a tiger, had gained a reputation for cruelty throughout the empire. When criminals were brought before him, he was transported with fury and treated them with a barbarity that would scarcely be believed. It is said, that sometimes carried away by passion, he forgot his rank and dignity; darting from the tribunal he would throw himself upon the accused, and with his own hands tear out his eyes. But when the Christians were concerned in the case, his fury knew no bounds; he bore them an infernal hatred and had sworn to destroy their religion in the province. The Servant of God was brought before the ferocious man, declared himself a priest and confessed his faith with a calm, firm, and generous dignity. While he made this profession, there was brought to the tribunal, a picture of the Blessed Virgin, very well painted, which had been taken when the missionaries' house was pillaged. Now, among the calumnies which the Chinese pagans raised against the Christians was one which attributed to them the custom of tearing out the eyes of the sick to extract the colors, which were used, they said, to make beautiful pictures. The vice-roy accused the Servant of God of being often guilty of this crime, and to punish him for having replied that he had never been guilty of that atrocity, he had him suspended by the hair and left for several hours in this position.

It would be impossible to describe the refinements of barbarity which the vice-roy invented to weary the patience of the missionary and force him to renounce Jesus Christ and inform on the priests and Christians whom he knew. In one of these horrible trials, he was attached by his hands to a sort of a cross and he hung thus from nine in the morning till the evening. On another occasion, the judge had engraved with iron points upon his patient's face these words, "*Tchoun-Sie-Kiao*," which means "Propagator of an abominable sect." Sometimes the executioners bound him to a large machine, which raised him in the air by means of ropes and pulleys, and let him fall with his whole weight, so that his body was bruised and his limbs dislocated. Sometimes, while he was kneeling on iron chains almost suspended by the hair from a post, his arms crossed and violently stretched and tied to a piece of wood, they placed upon the calves of his legs a beam, at the extremities of which two men balanced themselves thereby condemning the sufferer to the most frightful tortures. To vary these trials, they made him sit upon a chair so elevated that his feet could not touch the ground; they fixed him there by cords tightly tied around his thighs. Then they hung upon his feet enormous stones which occasioned him intolerable pains in the knees. At other times, the seat to which he was attached permitted him to rest his feet on the ground; but large stones pushed with difficulty under the soles of his feet caused him pains no less excruciating. During this long series of tortures, the Servant of God lost none of his calmness and serenity; not only was he never heard to utter a cry or complaint, but all saw shining in his face the joy with which his heart was filled. When he came from these barbarous trials, all his bones were broken and his strength exhausted; the soldiers had to carry him back to prison where new trials awaited him.

The frightful torments of which we have just spoken, were followed by a month's rest; the vice-roy wished probably, to allow him to gather new strength so he could exercise upon him for a longer time, his insatiable rage.

The month having expired, the Servant of God appeared before the criminal tribunal. While subjected to these tortures, his persecutor ordered him to tell by what route he had penetrated into the interior of China; in what houses he had stopped; what persons had favored his entrance; but Blessed Perboyre kept silence, knowing well that he was not obliged to answer, and, besides, the least revelation exposed the missionaries and Christians to more cruel outrages. The judge, irritated against him, ordered fifteen blows to be given him on the face with the thick leather ferule before mentioned, and as he thought it was Blessed Perboyre who had strengthened the faith of several who remained invincible amid the tortures which were employed to draw them into apostasy, he asked him what mysterious drink he had given these Christians who would not renounce their religion. The Servant of God replied that he had given them no beverage and this reply earned him ten more blows with the ferule upon the face.

Among the prisoners who were a butt for the cruelty of the mandarins was a maiden named Anna Kao, who had long edified the Christians by her virtues. She was arrested in her house whilst at prayer. She confessed the faith with a firmness and constancy which filled the faithful with admiration, and astonished the pagans and mandarins themselves. The soldiers who seized her, having proposed to her to tread on the cross with threats of death if she refused, she replied without hesitation, that she preferred to die. Then they brought her to the tribunal to make her appear before the mandarin. The latter forced her to kneel on iron chains; two soldiers, holding swords to her neck to frighten her, commanded her to tread upon the cross. But the intrepid virgin replied: "Cut off my head if you wish; never will I renounce my religion." They frequently urged her to renounce the faith, but as all these solicitations were baffled by her firmness, she was condemned to exile and sent into Seu-Tchuen.

It was about this maiden the mandarin asked Blessed Perboyre if she was employed in his service. He replied negatively. Then the mandarin had him knelt on iron chains; then he ordered him to be attached by the hands to a post while one of the soldiers seized him by the hair and moved him about, lifting him up with great cruelty. This suffering lasted an hour. The vice-roy having presented to him a vessel with the holy oils, said: "Is not this the beverage with which you fascinate Christians and strengthen their faith?" "It is not a beverage," replied the Confessor. Thirty blows with a rod upon the thighs followed this response.

Several times during this trial, the vice-roy bade him declare the names and dwelling places of the priests, catechists and Christians; he always maintained a profound silence. They beat him, they basely outraged him to force him to speak; they tortured him; and scourged him most cruelly, but nothing could make him open his mouth. A mandarin having asked him if he was a Christian, he replied immediately, "Yes, I am a Christian. It is my honor and glory." Then this mandarin, having a crucifix brought and placed before him, said: "If you will tread under foot the God whom you adore, I will give you your liberty." At this impious proposition the Confessor cried out while his eyes filled with tears. "Oh! how can you thus insult my God, my Creator and Saviour!" then stooping down painfully, for his body was all bruised, he took up the holy image, clasped it to his heart, pressed it to his lips, kissing it with the most affectionate tenderness, he bathed it with his tears. At this sight, the soldiers darted upon him, tore from his hand the sacred image of Our Saviour and, moved by an infernal impulse outraged it most atrociously. This horrible profanation broke the poor missionary's heart; he uttered a loud cry, a cry that revealed his great desolation and which showed how much more sensitive he was to this sacreligious act than to his own tortures. To punish him for having refused to profane the crucifix, they gave him one hundred and ten blows with the *pantsé*, a long rod of. bamboo used to strike criminals in China.

Another mandarin, to induce him to save himself, asked him only to tread on a cross which was painted on the floor, but he replied: "I cannot." Then, when the order was given him again, the soldiers seized him and forced him to tread on the cross, and he cried out in a loud voice: "I am a Christian, it is not I but you who profane this august sign of redemption." The impious judge had an idol brought and promised the Confessor, if he would adore it, he would set him at liberty. The Christian Hero replied with firmness: "You may, if you will, cut off my head, but I will never consent to adore this idol." Then the judge ordered him to be dressed in the sacred vestments as had already been done in Siang-Yang-Fou. After some moments' reflection, Blessed Perboyre obeyed and dressed himself before the tribunal. When they saw him in his sacred vestments, the men of the tribunal and the soldiers cried out: "*It is the living God.*"

The mandarin, having returned to the subject of the holy oils and the sacrament of extreme unction, renewed the calumnies against the Christians and added: "If you had not deceived the Christians by the hope of eternal life, they would not have made you come to China and you would not have had opportunity to tear out their eyes. If you do not admit that you are guilty of all these things, I will have you struck as you have merited." The Servant of God having replied he could not reproach himself with the crimes that had been imputed to him, the president ordered thirty blows with a rod to be given on his back. These were inflicted with so great force that blood flowed again in abundance. Wounded by this cruel treatment, having his eyes dim and closed, he could neither rise nor kneel upright; the soldiers then seized him by his hair, lifting him up and throwing him down on the ground again several times; they opened his eyes to force him to look at the vice-roy, who asked him again how many people's eyes he had taken out. He again replied that he had not been guilty of this crime and they gave him ten blows with a rod which he bore with unalterable patience. The astonished vice-roy could not understand how a man could endure so much suffering with so great calmness; and began to suspect that he had some secret means of making himself impassible. Ten other blows followed without disturbing the tranquillity of the Martyr. Then came new questions to which he did not reply, though he could speak; but he regarded it as useless to refute so often the same calumnies. The irritated vice-roy ordered the soldiers to give him again fifteen blows with a rod; but his victim remained mute; he said to him: "What! I make them strike you and you do not reply." This heroic silence confirmed him in the opinion that John Gabriel had upon him some object endowed with the virtue of raising him above the feeling of suffering; he then ordered him to be stripped of his clothing, bidding the soldiers to give him a minute inspection. On account of infirmity, the Confessor of the faith had been obliged for some years to wear a bandage. At the sight of this article, the persecutor thought he had found what he sought and doubted not that it was the instrument which blunted his feelings. The Servant of God protested, but uselessly, against the vice-roy's absurd opinion; though his weakness was evident, he wished to appear convinced that John Gabriel wore it as a talisman and took occasion from this to overload him with calumnies. Afterwards, to destroy the pretended charm which produced these marvellous effects, the vice-roy had a dog killed and forced the Confessor to drink the blood of this animal and had his head rubbed in it, then he ordered the seal of the mandarin to be printed on his legs.

After this long and painful interrogation, the Servant of God who seemed not to have a breath of life in him, was brought back to prison. However, the next day they brought him before the tribunal where a still more frightful trial awaited him. The vice-roy, furious that he could not overcome his constancy the evening before, renewed the questions which he had addressed to him, assuring him that he would force him to confess all the crimes which were imputed to him. The prisoner replied that he had nothing to add to what he had already said. Immediately at a sign from the mandarin they stripped him and made him lie on the ground while they gave him ten blows on the back with a rod. The mandarin repeated his calumnies against Blessed Perboyre, and he put to him a number of insidious questions which remained unanswered. He ordered again ten blows with a rod to be given him, saying: "It is in vain you desire to die soon; you shall endure for a long time the most violent pains; each day you shall be tortured by new torments; and this death you desire, you shall not obtain till you are weakened by the most atrocious torments." Then he ordered him to be suspended upon a rack, but as the Confessor of Jesus Christ could neither walk nor stand, he was seized by the soldiers and suspended upon the rack and his executioners were ordered to loosen and tighten the machine to which he was attached by his hair. After he had been tortured for an hour, they took him down from the rack half dead. They placed him before the vice-roy, and opened his eyes to make him look at his persecutor who during all this time mocked and insulted him, asking him if he did not feel very well.

The tyrant did not stop here. Wishing at any cost to triumph over the constancy of the Martyr, he returned to the charge, urging him strongly to reply in a satisfactory manner to the questions put to him and to avow himself guilty of the crimes of which he was accused. These solicitations remained unanswered. The judge, furious at his silence, had him cruelly struck now and then, sometimes with a rod and sometimes with a ferule of leather, but neither rod nor ferule could overcome the heroic firmness of the Missionary. It is said that at the sight of his invincible countenance, the vice-roy could no longer restrain his rage, and thinking that he had not been struck with enough force, he darted from his chair and arming him-

Blessed John Gabriel Perboyre, Commanding the Respect and Admiration of the Criminals in Prison with him.

self with the murderous instrument, discharged upon his victim so many and so terrible blows that every one thought the death of the Servant of God was inevitable and imminent. The pagans themselves trembled at the sight of the vice-roy's cruelty; they accused him of ferocity towards a man whose gentleness and patience at last excited their compassion. There were none even among the mandarins and soldiers who were not incensed at the atrocities committed upon a prisoner in whom no fault could be found. When the persecutor had satiated his implacable hatred, the invincible Martyr, almost expiring, was brought back to prison. According to the testimony of the soldiers, he had received that day more than two hundred strokes with the rod. The keepers, who saw him in this state, felt themselves moved to compassion; to prevent his clothes, which were all soaked with blood, from sticking to the bruised flesh, they hastened to take them away and wash them. The catechist, Andrew Fong, who was in the prison when they took off Blessed Perboyre's clothes, has depicted the sad state of the martyr; his face was swollen to a prodigious size; his flesh was so bruised and torn by the rod and scourge, that it hung in shreds around his body; enormous pieces had been torn off; all his limbs were but one wound; he no longer possessed the appearance of a man; he resembled his Divine Saviour, of whom it is written: "From the sole of the foot unto the top of the head, there is no soundness,—wounds, and bruises and swelling sores. We have seen him as it were a leper; there is no beauty in him or comeliness" (Isais, i and liii). In fact, the body of the generous Confessor had been bruised and broken in pieces; but sustained by the all-powerful virtue of Jesus Christ, he had supported all these torments with a serenity which beamed in his glance and upon his bruised and disfigured countenance, and showed that he esteemed himself happy to suffer for God. Amid so many tortures, scarcely a groan or sigh escaped his lips, though nature smarted under an excess of suffering. Blessed John Gabriel returned to prison and fell on his knees and began to prepare himself for the supreme hour of death.

---

## XII.

### DEATH OF BLESSED PERBOYRE.

His executioners, obliged to declare themselves vanquished, wished not to continue a struggle which would be an eternal disgrace to them. For four months they had employed against their victim all the resources which could be suggested by the most refined cruelty. Nothing had been forgotten which could weary his patience or overcome his heroic firmness. In the town of Ou-Tchang-Fou alone, he was subjected to more than twenty hearings at which he received a thousand insults and injuries, impossible to relate in detail. It was probably about the middle of January that his executioners grew tired of persecuting him; so the vice-roy ordered him to be strangled, but as this order could not be executed until ratified by the emperor, John Gabriel Perboyre remained eight months in prison. We know in what a state he was brought there and it is astonishing to find that he survived all his tortures in this place, his body having been torn in shreds and his bones laid bare. Suffering had taken away the power of speech, and he had to go to bed as he was unable to sit or stand.

While the mandarins were torturing him, no Christian could come to see him; no doubt flattering themselves with the hope that, deprived of all succor, they could more easily overcome his constancy. But after the last interrogatory, they relaxed this severe regulation. One of the first who came to see the prisoner was a Chinese Lazarist, M. Yang. What a heartrending spectacle met his eyes! It was like the sorrow of Job's friends when they saw him stretched on a dunghill, covered with ulcers, so pitiful was the state in which he found the Servant of God. When the Chinese priest saw him lying upon the ground half dead, his limbs stained with dry blood, he was deeply affected and poured forth abundant tears; it was with difficulty that he calmed himself so as to speak to him. The Servant of God desired to go to confession, but was restrained by the presence of the two officers of the mandarin, who stood constantly beside him for fear that his friends might poison him. One of the Christians, who accompanied the priest, respectfully invited them to step a little aside, so that the missionaries could talk more freely; they kindly complied and Blessed Perboyre made his confession. When the Christians were dismissed, John Gabriel with difficulty raised his voice to recommend himself to their prayers; one of them told him not to speak so loud on account of the pagan soldiers present. One of the officers said to him: "Pray have nothing to fear;" and another added: "Rest assured that we will take good care of him." When leaving the prison the missionary, M. Yang, asked one of the officers to take some money to buy everything needed for Blessed Perboyre, but the latter refused it, saying one of the Martyr's friends had already given him two hundred sapeques of which he had spent nothing, because the patient was in too much suffering; the doctor had ordered him to give him only a little rice water and salted herbs; but that he would be permitted in a few days, to have whatever he wished. This physician, though a pagan, was much impressed with the gentleness and other virtues of the sick man, showing much interest and taking particular care of him.

After this, the Confessor was often visited by the Christians and, among others, by a catechist named Fong, who did him many services. They brought to his prison, clothes, a mattress, and bed covering; thereby diminishing his sufferings. There was, however, one solace which the Servant of God desired above all others, and that was the Holy Communion; but it was impossible to obtain It for him, as the soldiers had orders to taste everything that was offered him. He was obliged to endure this privation, which was not the least of his pains, the whole time he remained in prison.

He profited by the visit of the Chinese Lazarist of whom we have spoken, to send a brief message to his confrères. His letter was in Latin and stained with blood from his hands. This is what he wrote: "The circumstances of the time and place do not permit me to give you long details of my condition; you know them sufficiently well from other sources. After being arrested in Kou-Tching, I was treated well enough the whole time I remained there, though I was subjected to two examinations. In Siang-Yang-Fou, I had to submit to four. In one of them, I remained half a day upon my knees on iron chains and suspended on the machine *hang tsé*. In Ou-Tchang-Fou, I underwent more than twenty hearings; in nearly all of which I suffered different tortures because I would not tell the mandarins what they desired to know. If I had spoken I would have started a general persecution throughout the empire; what I suffered at Siang-Yang-Fou was directly for the cause of religion. At Ou-Tchang-Fou, I received one hundred and ten strokes with the *pantsé* because I would not tread on the crucifix. Later, I shall tell you other details. Of the twenty Christians who were taken and tried with me, two-thirds publicly apostatized."

We have already said that the prison to which M. Perboyre was sent was filled with malefactors and criminals, loaded with guilt. These unfortunate prisoners, witnessing every day the holy life of the Servant of God, soon learned to appreciate him; feelings until then unknown sprang up in their hardened hearts. Admiring his virtues, they proclaimed that he had a right to every respect and consideration; all compassionated him and said that he merited much better treatment. As to Blessed Perboyre, far from considering his condition worthy of compassion he could only congratulate himself upon his good fortune. His days and nights were passed in sufferings, it is true, but they filled him with joy, because they made him comformable to his divine Model. He had nothing to expect but death, yet this death was the object of his desire, because it put him in the possession of the Sovereign Good.

At last, on September 11, 1840, an imperial courier brought the edict that ratified the sentence of death. According to the custom established in China, as soon as an edict of this kind is known, it is speedily put into execution. John Gabriel was immediately taken from prison and, like his Divine Master, was led to execution with some robbers who were put to death the same day. He walked bare-footed, with his hands tied behind him, bearing a long rod at the end of which was written the sentence of death pronounced against him. "*Et imposuerunt super caput ejus causam ipsius scriptam.*" "They put over his head his cause written." (Matt. xxvii, 37.) The Servant of God had recovered his strength and, more astonishing still, his wounds had disappeared. His face was beautiful and resplendent, his flesh had become as fresh and clear as a child's. Every one exclaimed at the miracle when seeing him in this state. As for the martyr, he pursued his way with courage and joy toward the place of triumph after the example of his divine Model. "*Proposito sibi gaudio sustinuit crucem.*" "Having joy set before him, endured the cross." (Heb. xii, 2.)

According to another Chinese custom, criminals are led to execution with haste and at a running pace. This quick march, joined to the noise of cymbals, gives the executions for capital offences, a terrible character which frightens the Chinese. Blessed Perboyre, after a long journey, arrived at last at the place where he must consummate his sacrifice. The pagans, warned by the noise of cymbals, ran there in crowds; but as they knew the example of gentleness and patience which the Confessor had given throughout his long examination, and his long sojourn in prison, they murmured because there was put to death a man so benevolent and so kind, saying that he equalled the gods in goodness.

They began with the seven prisoners who had been condemned to death, and during their execution the Servant of God knelt down to pray. The pagans were impressed by his suppliant, recollected attitude, and a Christian who, bathed in tears, stood nearby, heard voices saying, "Look at that European kneeling and praying." At last, the Martyr was attached to a gibbet in the form of a cross. His hands were thrust behind him and tied to a cross-piece of wood; both his feet were bent backwards, so that he was suspended in a kneeling posture and raised about four or five spans above the ground. His death was more painful than that of the others, who were promptly decapitated. The vice-roy ordered for the Christian priest a more cruel kind of execution; one that would last longer. The Confessor of the faith was to be strangled; after the first vigorous tightening of the rope, the executioner slackened it, so as to give the Martyr time to come to himself and realize his sufferings; then tightened it again, and stopped. It was the third jerk that proved fatal; but, as the body still retained some signs of life, a soldier approached and, having given him a severe kick in the stomach, Blessed Perboyre gave up his soul to God. It was noon on Friday; he expired at the same hour as his divine Master; he had tried during life to imitate

Him by the practice of His virtues. Our Lord gave him a greater resemblance to Himself in His passion and death.

The body of the Servant of God became immediately after his death a subject of admiration and astonishment. All who saw him, remarked that he was not disfigured; that his limbs preserved their suppleness and that he had none of the marks that are usually found upon bodies of criminals who have suffered death from strangulation; these are horrible to see. Their features are distorted, their cheeks livid, the blood running from their mouths, convulsively opened, their tongues hanging out, and their eyes starting from their sockets. No one could look at this spectacle without being filled with horror. As to Blessed Perboyre, his face was not changed; his eyes were modestly lowered towards the ground as in life; his mouth closed, his complexion ruddy; his body, in a word, had undergone no alteration and bore no trace of suffering or death; so that several who saw him did not think he was dead and advised that he should be exposed some days to the heat of the sun so as to be assured of his death. An idolator, whom Christian relatives had brought to the martyrdom, after examining the body and perceiving its flexibility was so struck by this miracle that he desired to embrace Christianity and had himself received among the catechumens.

The body of the Martyr remained a day and night upon the instrument of execution. The next day, the soldiers took it down and placed it in a coffin, bringing it to a mountain called Hon-Chen. Meanwhile, the catechist Fong, went in great haste to the harbor

Martyrdom of Blessed John Gabriel Perboyre,
September 11, 1840.

of Pin-Hou-Men, so as to consult with the other Christians to obtain from the soldiers the Martyr's clothes and the coffin which contained his body. These measures were so well arranged that everything succeeded according to their desires; by means of a sum of money they induced them to deliver to them the clothes of the Missionary, the instruments of his execution and the bier on which were his precious remains. They furnished the soldiers with a coffin filled with earth in place of the one they received, and while they seemed to bury the body of the Martyr, the Christians bore it to the chapel a short distance off. They clothed him in rich, magnificent vestments, made the preceding night, and celebrated the office of the church for these occasions; then they interred him on the slope of the Ronge mountain, beside Venerable Clet, the Lazarist missionary who had been martyred twenty years before, and whose glorious death Blessed Perboyre had envied.

God soon punished those who had pursued His servant. The mandarin of Kou-Tching, who had him arrested, was deposed from office shortly afterwards and hanged himself in despair. The vice-roy who was so cruel to him was condemned to exile on account of his cruelties and the evils he had caused in his province. It was even with difficulty that he escaped the vengeance of the people, who, thinking this punishment too light, wished to have him torn to pieces and to treat him as he had treated others.

We cannot pass over in silence the admirable conduct of the parents of our Martyr when they learned about the combats and sufferings of their son. M. Laborderie, vicar of Catus, was sent to announce this news to them. His embarrassment redoubled as he approached the house; but Blessed Perboyre's mother judged, on seeing him, that he had something painful to communicate and said to him: "I remember that when the pastor at Catus came to tell us of the death of Louis, it was at the same time, the same hour that you come now, and I have a presentiment that you have come to announce something similar about our poor Chinese son." M. Laborderie then said to her, "I have not come to bring you that news; all I have to communicate is that your son has been taken and put in prison by the idolators; truly he has been maltreated, but now they have become more kind and more humane in his regard."

These words brought no trouble to the heart of this truly Christian mother; for like the mother of the Maccabees, she heard with calm courage the account of the sufferings endured by her son. She said that ever since his departure for China she expected nothing else but to hear these tidings, and this expectation had been a preparation for it. "And," added she, "why should I lament now? I should perhaps offend God and would be distressing myself about what was the object of my son's most ardent desires; for since he has been in China, his letters show how ardently he desired martyrdom; if anything would pain me, it would be to learn that, overcome by suffering, he had scandalized, by cowardly apostasy, those whom he had converted."

She was no less calm when she learned the news of John Gabriel's death; she replied to those who told her to make the sacrifice of him with courage: "Why should I hesitate to make to God a sacrifice of my son? Did not the Blessed Virgin generously sacrifice hers for my salvation? Besides I would not truly love my son if I grieved when I knew he had attained the object of his desires."

It may be remembered that when the Servant of God was brought from Tcha-Yuen-Keou to Kou-Tching, a pagan, touched with compassion at the sight of his sufferings, and the difficulty he had in walking, had him brought in a litter, at his own expense to Kou-Tching. This good action soon received its reward. The old man, falling sick, was soon at death's door. While his life was despaired of and when he himself was absorbed in sad, gloomy thoughts, Blessed Perboyre appeared to him, in a dream, with two ladders, one red, on which he was leaning, and the other white on which he invited the sick man to come to him, saying, "You suffer extremely, do you not? Mount where I am by this white ladder and you will be happy." Then the sick man tried to mount, but the demons opposed his efforts. He remembered that the Christians used the invocation of the holy Names of Jesus and Mary to chase away the spirits of darkness, he invoked these holy Names and in an instant the vision disappeared and he felt himself entirely cured. Awakening, immediately, he hastened to send for the catechists; had himself instructed in the truths of religion and induced his family to follow his example. Having had the happiness of being baptized, shortly after, he died in three days with the most edifying sentiments of piety.

In a letter written by a Lazarist Missionary, we find the following details which are no less remarkable. "When the servant of God was martyred, a large cross, luminous, and very distinctly formed, appeared in the heavens. It was seen by a considerable number of the faithful, living in different Christian sections very distant from one another. Many pagans were witnesses of this miracle, and some of them exclaimed: 'There is the sign the Christians adore; I renounce idols; I wish to serve the Master of heaven.' They then embraced Christianity, Monsignor Clauzette, administering baptism to them. When the prelate learned the facts I have just related, he did not give much credit to them. But afterwards, impressed by the number and importance of the testimonies, he made formal inquiry, which resulted in the information that a cross, large, luminous and well formed, had appeared in the heavens; that it was seen at the same time, of the same form, the same size and in the same part of the heavens by many witnesses, Christians and pagans; that these witnesses lived in districts very distant from one another and that they could have had no communication together. Monsignor has besides questioned many Christians who had known Blessed Perboyre, and they all declare that they had always regarded him as a great saint."

# BOOK III.

## VIRTUES OF BLESSED JOHN GABRIEL PERBOYRE.

To avoid continual interruptions in our narrative, we have passed over in silence many instances of the virtues of Blessed John Gabriel Perboyre, so this third book will be devoted to showing his sentiments about the different virtues and how he put them into practice.

Though a long time has elapsed since the martyrdom of John Gabriel, and as his humility has robbed us of many of his actions, the little that has come to our knowledge will suffice, we hope, for the glory of the Martyr and the edification of souls.

---

### I.

#### HIS FAITH.

Faith, the foundation of all the perfection of a true disciple of Jesus Christ, always shone in the holy missionary; it was the principle of all the good he did during his whole life. See what is said upon this subject by a pious ecclesiastic. "Although I have had many opportunities to observe people animated by a lively, practical faith, I have never seen any one whose faith was more sincere, more ardent, more solid and more enlightened."

It might be said that St. Paul has given the Martyr's portrait in these words: "My just man liveth by faith" "*Justus meus ex fide vivit*" (Heb. x. 38.) In fact, not contenting himself with believing with a firm, unwavering faith, all that the church teaches, and submitting himself with profound humility and the docility of a child to all that she proposes to our belief, he strove, above all, to conform his actions to his belief. "Prejudices of mind and heart never biased his judgment," wrote a missionary, "others say that they ought to be guided by the spirit of the gospel, but a host of obstacles from within themselves, hinder them from applying these maxims to their own conduct. It was not thus with John Gabriel; all his sentiments sprang from a divine principle."

This spirit of faith inspired him with a great hatred for the world and for all the world esteems; made him love and seek for everything which the world rejects. He had a great idea of the dignity of man, because he regarded him, not with the eyes of the flesh, but with those of faith. He considered man in his source and model, that is, in God Who has created him to His image and likeness. His spirit of faith manifested itself especially when he spoke of man, regenerated in the blood of the Lamb, made the child of God, the temple of the Holy Ghost, and united to Jesus Christ.

These considerations excited in him lively sentiments of gratitude towards God who had allowed him to be born of Christian parents; and every year on the anniversary of his baptism, he offered to Our Lord thanksgivings for so great a benefit.

God had communicated to him many great lights

on the dignity of the priesthood. "If we had collected together all the thoughts that he has imparted to us on this subject," said a fervent priest, who for many years was intimate with him, "we would have had an interesting and instructive volume about the sublimity of this vocation and the duties it imposes."

One day, talking familiarly with an ecclesiastic who loved to consult him about his duties and the life a minister of the altar must lead, he said among other things: "A priest, receiving the same mission as Jesus Christ, and destined to work for the salvation of souls, must not only represent Jesus Christ by the divine character with which he is clothed and by the sacred functions this divine Saviour came to exercise on earth, but he must also reproduce Him in his interior and exterior; in his interior, by his thoughts, his desires, his affections; his thoughts must be the thoughts of the Man-God; his desires must be the desires of the Man-God; his affections must be the affections of the Man-God. He must be able to say with truth like St. Paul, 'I live, now not I; but Christ liveth in me.' (Gal. ii. 20.) Again, Jesus Christ must be manifested in his exterior, in his bearing, in his language and all his actions. Every one ought to know that he speaks, that he acts, from a divine principle, so that he can say to all those about him: 'Be ye followers of me, as I also am of Christ.' (1 Cor. xi. 1.)

"Jesus Christ has declared in the gospel that He is the life we must live. 'I am the life.' Whoever lives not this life dwells in death. Jesus Christ passes through our soul as the blood passes through all parts of our body to communicate life to them; and as a priest is called to great perfection, he must also possess this life in a perfect manner. But few priests truly live this life." M. Perboyre showed how much he compassionated a priest who did not live the life of Jesus Christ, and spoke with so much force that the one to whom he spoke was frightened and said: "Truly, I no longer know where I am, I shall scarcely dare, to-morrow, to go to the altar to offer the holy Victim, for my life is not the supernatural one Christ demands of me." Blessed John Gabriel, seeing he was overwhelmed by what he had just heard, consoled him by telling him not to lose courage but to have recourse to Jesus Christ to beg Him to communicate to him His Spirit, and if he prayed for this grace with fervor and perseverance, this divine Saviour, Who is goodness itself, would not fail to bestow it upon him.

He no longer saw the man in the dispenser of the mysteries of God, but a privileged creature not belonging to earth, but fulfilling here below a celestial office. Thus he could scarcely comprehend how a priest, when he fulfils his sacred functions could act in a natural manner. "Can you imagine supernatural actions done in a natural manner?" said he to the same ecclesiastic. "Is it possible for a minister of God to forget so far the sublimity of his vocation? When we are on the point of applying ourselves to our holy functions we should never fail to consider in Whose name we are going to fulfil them; the profit they will be to the glory of God, the salvation and the perfection of our neighbor; let us think what Jesus Christ would say to us if we would ask Him how we must comport ourselves and how He would acquit Himself, if He were in our place." He then applied these principles to the different functions of the holy ministry; for example, to the recitation of the divine office, to the celebration of the holy mysteries, the preaching of the word of God and the administration of the sacraments. "He spoke to me so well upon this subject," says an ecclesiastic to whom the Blessed Martyr addressed himself, "that I felt myself penetrated with a horror of purely natural conduct and filled with the desire of acting always with a spirit of faith in all the functions of the holy ministry."

The faith of John Gabriel placed him, in some sense, in another world. He saw everything in God; his superiors held to him the place of God; he obeyed them as God Himself. But it was especially in the person of the successor of St. Peter that he loved to consider Jesus Christ. Penetrated with the thought that the Sovereign Pontiffs have been established by our divine Saviour to enlighten and direct His Church, he had for everything they ordained a full and perfect deference. He would not have considered himself a disciple of Jesus Christ if he did not revere him who had received the plenitude of His authority; nor a child of St. Vincent if he had not imitated the filial devotion to the Holy See of his father, who has said that an humble submission and obedience to the decrees of the Sovereign Pontiff were a good way to distinguish the true children of the Church from the rebellious. So, on all occasions, he manifested his attachment and obedience to the head of the Church. He proved this on one occasion which naturally finds place here.

Being superior of St. Flour, he adopted the system of Abbé Lamennais, because he thought it would contribute to the glory of the Church. "The Servant of God inclined towards the ideas of Lamennais," says a learned and pious prelate who was at that time quite intimate with him, "but he acted as a saint, being deceived like the saints who sometimes happened to be deceived." He upheld his opinions under the eyes of the Bishop of St. Flour who, far from thinking it wrong, loved to talk with him on these subjects. When he learned the doctrines had been questioned by the Holy See, he ceased speaking of them, saying he must wait, and that Rome would put an end to all uncertainty by the judgment she would pronounce. We know from good authority that, some time before Abbé Lamennais had been silenced by the Pope, God had made known to John Gabriel in prayer what was false in this doctrine. By this knowledge, he told an ecclesiastic that it would be condemned; even indicating the motives on which the Sovereign Pontiff founded his objections. Afterwards, having read the encyclical of Gregory XVI, this priest was much astonished to find there, all the reasons which had been given by the Servant of God.

As soon as Blessed Perboyre knew of the sentence fulminated against the doctrine of Lamennais, he subscribed to it heart and soul, and blessed God for it. As some priests pretended the condemnation did not bear upon Lamennais, he labored earnestly to enlighten them and told them that it would be better to reject entirely all that the Sovereign Pontiff had condemned. Others were offended at certain expressions in the encyclical; it seemed to them that Lamennais and his party were treated harshly. They expressed their surprise to John Gabriel, who hastened to show them how much they were in the wrong, and ended by these words: "Let us pray to God that He may preserve us from ever finding fault with the words of the Sovereign Pontiff; it is Jesus Christ who has said to him: 'Thou art Peter; and upon this rock I will build my church; and the gates of hell shall not prevail against it.' (Matt. xvi. 18.) Let us receive the words of the Holy Father as we would receive the words of Jesus Christ, and if this divine Saviour when speaking of His disciples has said to us: 'He that heareth you, heareth me; and he that despiseth you despiseth me' (Luke x. 16), how much stronger reason has He to despise us if we receive not with respect and humility the words of him who is His living representative on earth."

To attack the prerogatives of the Holy See was to touch the apple of his eye; he would immediately defend them and did so with so much power, moderation and wisdom, and knew so well how to present his reasons, that it was difficult not to be impressed by them. Many ecclesiastics owe to his enlightened zeal their return to better sentiments. He refuted, when occasion required, with much prudence and learning, the calumnies which Fleury, in his Ecclesiastical History, has so often stated against this august See, so worthy of our love and respect. He could not bear what is called in France the liberties of the Gallican Church, which are in truth nothing but servitude. Finding himself one day in the company of priests, some of whom were imbued with these ideas and who spoke with little respect of the authority of the Sovereign

Pontiff, he showed them how far this language was from the simplicity and the purity of faith with which we must honor the authority which Jesus Christ has confided to His vicar; and he concluded thus: "Let us take care, gentlemen, never to attack the prerogatives of the Holy See; let us believe that it never goes beyond its powers in the decisions that it makes. Let us recognize in it all the authority that it takes in all questions, whatever they may be."

He had so much respect for the Sovereign Pontiff that he would not allow, even for debate, these prerogatives to be attacked, not only when they were universally held by Catholics, but even when they could be contested without going against faith. "One of the most severe lectures that ever I received from him," said one of his old seminarians, "was given me on the occasion of a discussion I had had with a confrère, about the contested privileges of the Pope. I had maintained, contrary to my conviction and only for argument, the sentiment of theologians little attached to Rome. I was earnestly reprimanded for it; he told me I must never, even in dispute, question any of the prerogatives our common Father was believed to possess."

The spirit of faith, with which John Gabriel Perboyre was animated, revealed itself on all occasions. His conduct in church preached eloquently of the real presence of Jesus Christ on our altars; when he was at prayer one would think it was one of those angels whom the prophet Isais represents to us prostrated at the foot of the throne of the Eternal, who veils his face and repeats unceasingly, "Holy, holy, holy, the Lord God of hosts." (Isais, vi. 3.) He wished to speak of God and of the things of God only with great respect, and he could not endure to have the words of holy Scripture used in jest, and several times reproved the young ecclesiastics who used them in this way. He read it on his knees and with his head uncovered; so God communicated to him great lights for the understanding of the truths and mysteries which it contains. His words were always words of faith animated by charity. Moreover, the rigors of a horrible prison so generously endured, his invincible constancy amid long and cruel tortures; the death which he endured for the faith after having heroically confessed it, show how solidly he was established in this virtue.

---

## II.

### HIS HOPE.

THE promises that God has made to men, the benefits which He ceases not to bestow upon them, animated the Servant of God with a lively joy and a great confidence in the Author of so many good things. But it was especially the sight of Jesus Christ crucified or dwelling for love of us in the sacrament of the Eucharist which gave him confidence and filled him with consolation. When he meditated upon the care Providence has for His creatures, he felt penetrated with gratitude and cast himself into the arms of God with less care than a child in the arms of its mother. He was full of joy when all human resources failed him. He exclaimed on one occasion, "Oh, what happiness to be so reduced that we can expect nothing but from God alone!"

We cannot express all that he felt in thinking that he was called to contemplate God in His glory, and to drink in the torrents of His delights. But, on the other hand, his hope was often also a source of sadness to him; for he sighed ardently for the possession of God. He often raised his eyes, all bathed in tears, towards his heavenly country and said with the prophet: 'When shall I come, and appear before the face of God?' (Ps. xli. 3.) It was often observed that his face bore an expression of pain, when in the recitation of the breviary, he found passages where the prophet expressed regrets of the length of his exile. He often wept for the blindness and indifference of so many Christians who, forgetting their sublime destiny, run after shadows and chimeras which deceive them and bring upon them the greatest misfortunes; he would have desired a thousand voices to tell everyone how much they are to be pitied who fly from heaven to precipitate themselves into hell.

Piously jealous for the honor of God, he felt very sensibly when he heard any word contrary to the respect we owe to His paternal Providence. This is related by one of the professors of the preparatory Seminary of St. Flour. "Having on one occasion a great cause for vexation, I went to complain to him of an injustice that I thought had been done me. He tried to quiet me, telling me nothing could happen without the permission of God and that this occurrence should be considered as an act of His will Who disposes all things for our greater good. But, as I was not very well disposed then to receive these representations, I replied in a hurt tone and in a manner disrespectful to Providence. Astonished at my language, he observed very sweetly it is true, but with great energy, that the words that just escaped me were out of place, especially as an ecclesiastic. I withdrew, but scarcely had I entered my room when I was impressed with what he had just said to me ; I understood that I had committed a great fault and had caused pain to my superior. I went immediately to look for him to express my regret at having spoken with so little discretion. He received me with great kindness and gave me new considerations upon the respect we should have for the will of God in our regard and the manner we should speak of it. He said, among other things, that what afflicted him most was to hear evil said of Providence ; that we should submit with love to all that God permits ; besides, we can never murmur against it without being guilty of injustice and black ingratitude, because He permits nothing but for the greater good of men. He made me feel how good and amiable Providence is, in all that happens, even the most painful things ; so that I was confused at having forgotten it. The words he addressed to me on this occasion made so deep an impression that they remain forever engraven in my heart. I seem to hear him still speaking to me with so much kindness and unusual gentleness, but also with a force and energy which seemed almost divine. What especially impressed me was the pain he seemed to feel that no one gave to the Providence of God the justice that was its due."

Blessed Perboyre always showed himself a zealous defender of the Providence of God. If any attacks were directed against it, he immediately spoke up and showed that the evils we suffer in this world are the fruit of our sins: we need not complain of God, but of ourselves; we should rather humble ourselves before the divine Majesty and confess that it is for our faults that we have been punished; that we are not chastised according to our offences because, if we were treated as we have deserved, we would be much more severely dealt with. It was thus the zealous Servant of God vindicated Providence, but with so much gentleness and prudence that he wounded no one; all who heard him speak withdrew convinced and edified.

It is not to be imagined that John Gabriel's hope was not put to great tests. Besides those we have already noted, he had others, many others, that he suffered in his soul. God is pleased to form His saints in the school of Calvary, to make them walk during nearly all their life in a way strewn with briars and thorns. His profound humility hid from him all the good that was in him; he saw only faults and imperfections in himself whom he regarded as something abominable, causing horror to heaven and earth. His slightest faults seemed monstrosities to him. He thought he did nothing to merit reward; while his virtues impressed every one, he considered himself a cause of scandal. However, this did not make him have less confidence, because if he considered his defects, he thought, too, of the mercy of God. He was long tried by dryness and frightful darkness of soul, so that he went along like a person who did not know where to put his foot and who is surrounded by precipices. It seemed to him that the number and enormity of his sins rendered him unworthy of the goodness of

God, but he went his way hoping in the divine mercy which would surpass his infidelity. Like the Royal Prophet, he felt temptations to discouragement, and reanimated his confidence by saying to himself, 'Why art thou sad, O my soul? and why dost thou disquiet me? Hope in God, for I will still give praise to Him: Who is the salvation of my countenance, and my God. (Ps. xlii.)

His hope was neither presumptuous nor rash. He was always watchful; he labored to combat his passions and mortify his senses and to work with ardor to sanctify himself. Knowing that he had everything to fear from himself and all to expect from God, he put his sole confidence in prayer, which he regarded as the source of grace and success. He often exhorted others to this holy exercise. "Pray and get others to pray," said he to one of his confrères, "nearly all depends on that. Grace alone gives true success in work." On another occasion, he expressed himself thus: "No real good is done in souls but by prayer;" a truly remarkable maxim, and one which merits to be meditated upon. There is not one of his letters in which he does not solicit the prayers of those to whom he wrote.

Full of the thought of St. Paul, that Jesus Christ intercedes for us unceasingly with His Father, he never feared to present himself before God to ask for the graces which he needed. "If our sins render us unworthy of being heard," he said, "the sanctity of Jesus Christ and the fervor with which He prays for us, makes His Father forget our unworthiness and only consider Him, whom He has appointed our advocate. Besides, by our baptism, we have become members of Jesus Christ; consequently, by this union our needs are in a manner the needs of Jesus Christ; we can ask for nothing relating to the salvation or perfection of our soul, without asking for it, as for Jesus Christ, Himself, for the honor and glory of the members is the honor and glory of the body."

---

## III.

### HIS LOVE FOR GOD.

In his earliest childhood Blessed Perboyre began to love God, and his love always continued to increase. As he advanced in age, he received new graces and lights, and he neglected nothing in his correspondence with them. He never said, "It is enough;" it seemed to him on the contrary, that all he did for his God was nothing in comparison to what he should have done. This love had such empire over him, that all his being belonged to the service of divine love. His body was a victim which he immolated each day; his intellect was continually occupied about heavenly things. He could not think of the perfections of God without being penetrated with admiration, and, as it were, transported out of himself. When in reciting the divine office, he chanced upon a passage where the prophet spoke of the divine attributes, he could no longer contain himself, he was lost in the contemplation of what faith revealed to him in God, and the faithful remembrance of the benefits he had received from Him was as a spur which urged him to give himself more perfectly to His service. His will was so intimately united to that of God, that he could have said with truth that he no longer lived, but it was God who lived in him. He felt a bitter pain at seeing that God was so little known and so little loved by the most of men; and he tried to supply for their indifference by the fervor of his love. Through the low opinion he had of himself, he thought that, far from honoring God, he outraged Him by his infidelities, so that the love he bore Him became often to him a source of humiliation, torment and agony.

The whole world was to him a mirror in which he contemplated the divine perfections. If he looked at a flower, it reminded him of Him Who has said, 'I am the flower of the field, and the lily of the valley' (Cant. ii. 1.) If he saw the sun shining, he thought of Him Who enlighteneth all men who come into the world and he begged Him to pour His light into his soul and teach him how lovable He is; he conjured Him to warm his heart and make him produce the fruits of salvation and perfection. If he saw a star shining in the blue heavens, his thoughts turned immediately to Him of Whom it is written; 'I am the bright and morning star' (Apoc. xxii. 16), and he implored Him to direct him on the stormy sea of this world. A shepherd in the country reminded him of the good Shepherd who gives His life for His flock; a lamb made him think of the Lamb without spot who has come to efface the sins of the world. If he saw a bird take a flight into the air, he exclaimed with the prophet, 'Who will give me wings like a dove, and I will fly, and be at rest?' (Ps. liv. 7.) "Do you see this little stream?" said he one day, "after it has flowed for some time it will lose itself in the sea; it is thus that our hearts should tend towards God." He saw all creatures only as the gifts of the divine munificence; this thought refreshed him in the air he breathed and nourished him in the food he ate. When anyone did him a service, he thanked God first of all, as he regarded Him as the first cause of all the good that was done him.

John Gabriel, being filled with the love of God, showed in his conversation his interior dispositions. for "Out of the abundance of the heart, the mouth speaketh." (Matt. xii. 34.) He spoke of the things of God with such simplicity, that his words had the power of inflaming hearts and leaving on them the sweetest and most salutary impressions. "When he spoke," said a priest of the mission, "it was with charming gaiety, even now I still feel the most pleasant recollections of his conversations; nothing touches me so deeply today, as the meditation upon the solid words which came from the lips of my holy friend. He knew how to turn everything to profit and his conversation was so grave and pious that we did not dare talk of temporal interests in his presence.

Blessed Perboyre, not contented with having the most affectionate sentiments for God, strove to show them by the practice of good works. It could be said of him as of the spouse in the canticles that his hands were full of precious stones, "*plenae hyacinthis*," (Cant. v. 14.) He not only did good, but he did it with all the perfection of which he was capable. He loved to quote these words of St. Vincent: "It would be better to be cast upon burning coals than to do an action to please creatures." He frequently recommended purity of intention. "In all you do," said he, "labor only to please God, without which you will lose your time and pains."

This is what he himself practised at all times. Upon awakening in the morning, he made an offering of all his actions to God and begged Him to bless them, which offering he never neglected to repeat during the day. During his meals, whilst he gave nourishment to his body which he could not do without, his heart was always united to God; it was even remarked sometimes, that his feelings of devotion so moved him that he was obliged to stop eating. If he took some recreation it was for God and in the presence of God. When fatigue and suffering obliged him, sometimes, to suspend his work, he rested himself by prayer or by walking up and down the room, singing spiritual canticles, to express his love for God. "His day," relates a priest who had known him intimately, "was but a succession of acts of love of God, almost as multiplied as the beatings of his heart, and at evening it was again in the arms of God that he took his repose.

God reigned without a rival over all his affections. He loved his parents because he made it a duty. In his intercourse with them he continually reminded them of the vanity of the things of this world and strove to bring them to God. "Do not forget," said he in a letter which he wrote his brother, "that our life disappears like a shadow and at death we will be treated as we have merited by our virtue and vices. Have a horror of the pleasures of the world. Seek always and above all your eternal interests, all the rest is but vanity." In another letter he gave the following advice. "I can not too much recommend to you, my brother, to fulfil exactly the duties of religion. Reconcile yourself to God, from time to time, by a good confession. Do not imitate other young men who generally abandon the duties of their religion and behave badly. Do not be too much attached to the goods of this earth. Never forget that the affair of salvation is the business which should occupy you always and above all. 'What doth it profit a man if he gain the whole world and suffer the loss of his own soul?' (Matt. xvi. 26.) We must strive to go to heaven, but it is only virtue and sanctity which bring us there. As we live, so we die."

His fervor was not subject to variations. In the most painful trials as in prosperity, in dryness as in consolation, he went to God with the same courage. Lukewarmness appeared to him under an extremely formidable aspect; he regarded it as one of the greatest evils which can attack a soul that tends to perfection, and he said that without great vigilance and continual mortification, it was impossible not to fall into this deplorable state. Having started one morning with a pious priest to say Mass in the country, his companion asked him if he would help him to make his prayer. The Servant of God, after recollecting himself an instant, spoke of the unseemliness of lukewarmness in a priest. "In pastoral retreats," said the clergymen, "I have heard many sermons on this subject. I have read also, very good treatises upon it; but I never read or heard anything that made so great an impression upon me."—As a means to guard against tepidity he recommended often to put in practice, the counsel given by the pious author of the Imitation: "He does much that does well what he does. *Age quod agis.*" (Book 1. xv.) "It is not necessary," he added, "to do many or extraordinary things to make ourselves agreeable to God, it suffices that we do well what we do. Let us fulfil all our duties with all the perfection we are capable of and by this means we will do much." Giving an example of what he recommended to others, he performed each of his actions as if he had nothing else to do and as if his salvation or damnation depended upon it, so that nothing hasty or confused was ever observed in his conduct. Deeply penetrated with the greatness and majesty of Him Whom he served, he took every care to avoid even the slightest negligence and never thought of pleasing himself in what he did.

---

## IV.

### HIS PURITY OF CONSCIENCE.

"*He that loveth cleanness of heart, . . . . shall have the king for his friend.*" (Prov. xxii. 11.)

From his earliest childhood, Blessed Perboyre, like the young Tobias, held himself aloof from company and frivolous amusements and took pleasure in living at the foot of the altar or in nourishing his soul with holy reading. Besides, he could never endure the slightest shadow of sin or see God offended without feeling much grieved. During his course of humanities at the preparatory Seminary of Montauban, those who saw him every day could not observe, as had already been stated, the least disobedience, even any decided imperfections. While at the Seminary during his ecclesiastical studies, there is the same testimony from those who knew him. He remained two years at Montdidier and his superiors, confrères and pupils say they never observed the slightest variation in his conduct. For five years he was superior at St. Flour, and, those who saw him frequently, proclaim unanimously that his life seemed more like that of an angel than of a man. In Paris he directed the novitiate for nearly three years and in this employment, always gave the same edification. Searching looks were fixed upon him; they attentively considered his actions; they carefully weighed his words; they sought to surprise him in some imprudence; but he showed himself always the same; that is, acting and speaking in the spirit of God. During all the time he lived in China, not only did his virtue experience no diminution but it went on increasing, as Monsignor Rameaux wrote in one of his letters. We do not wish to say that he was impeccable and, doubtless, no one will impute to us this thought. Whatever virtue a man has, he must more or less share in human infirmity; we will limit ourselves to verify here the testimony which has been given about him. The Servant of God must have committed faults, and often he accused himself of them; but they were slight and imperceptible. All that could be discovered in him, was a little emotion which he displayed on four or five occasions. Those who observed him then, said that they would not have noticed it in other persons, otherwise very virtuous, but they remarked it in him, because everything in his conduct was so holy and his face usually was so calm, that they were surprised at even a transient imperfection. The same persons declared that they have been still more edified by his humility which made him on these occasions accuse himself and ask pardon for the scandal he had given.

To establish and perfect himself in this purity of conscience, he often had recourse to God by prayer. He endeavored to study the dispositions of his heart, and when he perceived in himself any bad tendency, he strove to combat it. Born with a lively, sensitive disposition, he used every effort to make himself master of it. He spoke little because he knew a great talker is exposed to falling into many faults; and he who wishes to become perfect must watch over his tongue. Before beginning a conversation, or making a reply, it was his custom to raise his heart to God to ask of Him the grace to say nothing to displease Him. He lived in habitual recollection; the enemy could not attempt to attack him without his perceiving it immediately; but if sometimes he was surprised, he soon recognized his fault and humbled himself for it. Mortified and severe towards himself, he watched over all his senses, and his heart was like a fortress whose gates are always securely fastened.

Blessed Perboyre bestowed great care upon his particular and general examinations of conscience. Every evening, before retiring to rest he asked God's pardon for all the faults he might have committed, particularly for those he did not know. When at his examen in the evening, he discovered some fault or negligence in the service of God, he generally made it the object of his prayer the next day, and sometimes even for several consecutive days; so that he could humble himself the more before God, and guard himself against relapse. Every week he approached the sacrament of penance with the most holy dispositions, but sometimes he advanced the time because he could not allow in his soul the least shadow of a fault.

Conversing one day familiarly upon pious subjects with an ecclesiastic, this is what he said about the purity of conscience which should distinguish the priests of Jesus Christ: "We must not only guard against grave faults, but we must also avoid with the greatest care even the slightest. We can not bear a grain of dust in our eye, how is it that we can bear the least little sin in our soul? We would hasten to free our eye of the speck of dust because it makes us suffer and hinders our distinguishing objects; and yet we do not observe that our soul suffers much more when it is sullied by sin. These faults which we commit are like a whirlwind of dust which prevents our seeing the dangers to which we are exposed. As it is impossible for a blind man to enjoy the beauties of the heavens, so it is impossible for a soul, which has not purified itself from the slightest faults, to contemplate the divine perfections; as a blind man can not lead those who are like himself, so a priest who allows himself to be blinded voluntarily by sin, can no longer be useful to souls. He who, on the contrary, lives in great purity of conscience, can contemplate every day the infinite perfections of God; he enjoys great discernment in understanding souls and can apply to each what suits him. How enviable is his lot! but who pities him who is deprived through his own fault of a good so precious and desirable?"

## V.

### HIS CONFORMITY TO THE WILL OF GOD.

PERFECT love, according to St. Augustine, consists in having no other will than that of Him Who is the object of our love. It was according to this principle that our holy missionary stripped himself of his own will to live only for the will of God; this renunciation he practised not only on certain occasions but always, even until death. God was pleased to try him during a great part of his life by painful infirmities which would have disconcerted virtue less firm than his; never did he show the slightest impatience about it. He never complained; he did not even speak of his sufferings: he regarded them as a precious occasion to acquire merit and render himself more agreeable to God. He saw in them a means of testifying to God his love, and he would not have wished for the whole world to be delivered from them. When a serious indisposition or sickness forced him to remain in bed, he seemed always so gay and contented in this state that those who left his room went away much edified.

Very often John Gabriel had to submit to many contradictions, and sometimes, as he was very sensitive, he felt them keenly; but immediately he raised his heart to God to offer to Him his trials. He never uttered any complaint against the authors of them, being persuaded that nothing happens but by the permission of God. On these occasions, he represented to himself that God acted in his regard as a father or mother who induces a well-beloved child to take a bitter medicine, which would improve its health, which has been injured. When death took from him a dear relative or friend, his first act was to offer to God this sacrifice and he submitted with love to the decrees of Providence, saying with Our Lord: 'Yea. Father: for so it hath seemed good in Thy sight.' (Luke x. 21.) He proved this in a striking manner when he learned the death of his brother Louis whom he loved as himself. Far from allowing himself to murmur, he blessed Providence and induced his parents to confess that God had showed Himself all good and all merciful in the terrible trial with which they were afflicted. The vessel which brought him to China was assailed by so furious a tempest that it seemed each instant about to be submerged; nevertheless, he writes in a letter already quoted, "we possessed our souls in peace, loving to abandon ourselves to the good pleasure of Him Who brings to the gate of death and back again."

"I have never seen a person more resigned than he was to the will of God," said a Missionary; "he complained of nothing, neither cold nor heat, food nor clothing; he never spoke of these things but left them to Providence." If it rained, snowed or froze he was content; if he was despised or humiliated he was still content because God willed it, so his soul remained strong while his body seemed feeble."

He submitted with the same abandonment when God sent him interior trials. If he was attacked by the most horrible temptations or desolated by the greatest aridity, if Our Lord withdrew from him the light of His countenance to leave him plunged in darkness, it was all the same to him, provided the divine will had its accomplishment. He desired to have neither better health, more learning nor more sanctity than God willed. "We must," said he, "strive to imitate on earth the life of the angels; what distinguishes them in heaven is that they have no other will than that of God, and Our Lord in bidding us to ask every day of His Father that His will be done on earth as it is in heaven, has shown us clearly how much He desires that we should enter into these dispositions."

When he had an action to perform, he considered, first, if it was conformable to the will of God; and he begged Him to make him know how to do what was most agreeable to Him. He had often on his lips, still more in his heart, these words of Jesus Christ: "My meat is to do the will of Him who sent me, that I may perfect His work." (John iv. 34.) He pronounced them with feelings so expressive of love and happiness that one might suppose it was the divine Saviour Himself when, beside the well of Jacob, he addressed them to His disciples.

A young priest to whom he recommended the practice of seeking in everything the good pleasure of God, having asked him how he must act to accomplish it, John Gabriel said to him, "If you wish to establish yourself in this practice, you must renew every day your resolution to work at it with ardor, and begin, continue and end your days in this holy exercise. When the hour for rising comes imagine that the Holy Spirit comes to say to you as the angel once said to

St. Peter, 'Arise quickly,' '*Surge velociter.*' (Acts xii. 7.) Rise, then, without delay; offer yourself to God and testify to Him your desire of doing during this day all that you know would be most agreeable to Him. During your prayer, beg God to manifest His will; for why do we make our prayer if it is not to learn to know it? We are like the workmen whom the householder has called to work in his field, we are His servants, and is it not just that the laborers should ask him who employs them what they must do and how they must do it. You must then listen to His voice as the holy Spouse listens to that of the Spouse. If you are faithful in listening to the voice of God He will teach you what He asks of you. After this you must implore His blessing and go full of zeal to accomplish His work.

"In the course of the day, it will be well to think often that you work not for yourself, but for God, and that all your actions must be done with great perfection. I counsel, you, also, to act always in His holy presence; for just as servants are much more attentive to their work when they are under their master's eye, so even you will feel animated with much greater ardor if you consider that God has His gaze fixed upon you. By this means you imitate Our Lord who tells us in the gospel, 'I do always the things that please Him.' (John viii. 29.) He does not content Himself with saying that He did often what was agreeable to His Father, but he tells us He did it always, to show us that we must never relax in this holy practice. But as of ourselves we can do no good, we must often address ourselves to God, saying to Him, 'Lord make me always accomplish what is agreeable to

Thee; yes, always; for I desire never to stray from Thy holy will.'" "This is what he taught me about conformity to the will of God," relates this priest, "and he himself would not do the slightest action without consulting God. He continually addressed to Him the prayer he recommended to me; he repeated it nearly as often as he breathed, because he had a great desire to imitate Our Lord and to be able to say with truth like Him, '*Quae placita sunt ei facio semper.*' 'I do always the things that please Him.'" (John viii. 29.)

---

## VI.

### HIS LOVE FOR JESUS CHRIST.

Devotion towards Jesus Christ was a distinctive characteristic of Blessed Perboyre. Everything that reminded him of this loving Saviour, awakened in him the deepest feelings of love. The reading which he preferred was that which spoke to him of Jesus Christ, and it was on this account he studied continually the gospels and the epistles of St. Paul. Our Lord was always on his lips as on his heart. "His special devotion," says a missionary who had been his director in the novitiate, "was for Our Lord, Whom he loved as tenderly as a child loves his father; his soul was knit to that of Jesus as the soul of Jonathan was to David's. His thoughts and affections were so much absorbed in Our Lord that he spoke of Jesus Christ with the greatest tenderness. In all he did, suffered or undertook, his aim was to please Jesus; he studied

His life, His virtues and His heart, so as to imitate Him, and his progress was so great that he succeeded in becoming a living copy of Jesus Christ. It was in speaking of Our Saviour that he became animated and eloquent. He said of Him many sublime, deep truths; and there was quite an analogy between his manner of speaking of Jesus Christ, especially of His charity, and what was said by St. Paul, whose writings he read and meditated upon continually."

He celebrated the feasts of Our Lord with especial fervor; at the times which recall more particularly His great love for us, he felt his love for Him redouble. During the celebration of the Feast of Christmas and the following days, he was penetrated with gratitude, passing whole hours before the crib of the Infant Jesus, expressing the deepest affection for the ineffable goodness of God, Who has been pleased to descend from heaven to earth in the form of a Babe. His poverty, sufferings and humiliations touched John Gabriel deeply, and filled him with the desire to imitate the virtues of which He has given the example in coming into this world.

He never wearied of speaking of Our Lord, and as his reflections were edifying we will here repeat some of them: "Jesus Christ," said he, "is the great Master of science; it is He alone who gives true light. All science which comes not from Him or leads not to Him is vain, useless, dangerous. There is but one important thing which is to know and love Jesus Christ." The Imitation of Christ was, after the holy Scriptures, his favorite book; he delighted especially in quoting the following passage: "He to whom the Eternal Word speaketh, is set at liberty from a multitude of opinions. From one Word are all things; and this one all things speak and this is 'the Beginning who also speak to us.' (John viii. 25.) Without this Word no one understands, or judges rightly. He to whom all things are one, and who draws all things to one, and who sees all things in one, may be steady in heart and peaceably repose in God. O Truth, my God make me one with Thee in everlasting love! I am wearied with often reading and hearing many things; in Thee is all that I will or desire. Let all teachers hold their peace; let all creatures be silent in Thy sight. Speak Thou alone to me." (Imitat. Book I, Chap. III.) These passages from the Imitation delighted him exceedingly, and an ecclesiastic relates that nothing was more touching than to hear him explain the sense of these words, for he said admirable things on this subject.

The Servant of God, one day, seeing this same priest wearing glasses, asked him why he used them. He replied that it was to distinguish objects better. "Ah, well!" added his questioner, "is it not just to do for your soul what you do for your body? When we are left to ourselves we are in darkness, we are liable to confound good with evil, truth with error: but God has given us a sure means of not being deceived, this means is His Word, 'That was the true light which enlighteneth every man that cometh into this world.' (John i. 9.) It is He, consequently, Who must enlighten us amid the darkness which surrounds us, and direct our steps in the paths of truth, so that we may attain perfection. Often implore Him to enlighten you, never walk without your Light if you do not wish to wander. When you study, beg

Him to teach you Himself; if you speak to any one, ask Him to inspire you to know what to say; if you have any action to do, conjure Him to let you know what He desires of you."

Blessed Perboyre was not willing to content himself with studying and knowing Our Lord, he wished to go further, so he strove to imitate Him. Upon this subject he made the following reflections which will not be read without interest. "Jesus Christ has not come on earth solely to instruct us by His doctrines, but also to serve as our model. When His Father sent Him to us, He told us all what once was said to His servant Moses concerning the tabernacle. 'Look, and make it according to the pattern, that was shown thee in the mount.' (Exod. xxv. 40.) Jesus Christ Himself has said to us, 'I have given you an example, that as I have done to you, so do you also.' (John xiii. 15.) Observe well that he did not say, I have given the example of virtues to make them the object of your admiration, but in order that they may be the object of your imitation. 'But one thing is necessary,' (Luke x. 42) says Our Lord to us in the gospel, 'but what is this one thing necessary?' It is to imitate Him. We can not attain our salvation without conformity to Jesus Christ. After our death we will not be asked if we have been learned, if we have been engaged in distinguished employments or if we have been spoken of advantageously in this world; but God will ask us if we have been occupied in studying Jesus Christ and imitating Him. If God finds in us no resemblance to the divine Model Who has been given us we will be rejected; we will, on the contrary be glorified if we render ourselves conformable to

Him. Jesus Christ is the model of the predestined, the saints in heaven are portraits of Jesus Christ risen and glorious, even as on earth, they have been portraits of Jesus Christ suffering, humiliated and laboring. The saints who are highest in glory and nearest Our Lord, are those who have best imitated their model, who have more perfectly depicted Him in themselves. If we wish to attain to the glory of Heaven, we must become painters; the more faithfully we paint in us His humility, His obedience, His charity and His other virtues, the more assured we shall be of our salvation and the greater will be our glory in heaven. Like a painter, who burns with the desire of reproducing faithfully a valuable picture, have your eyes fixed continually on Jesus Christ. Let us not be content with having one or two points of resemblance to our Model, let us enter into all His feelings and make His virtues our own. Let us begin anew every day and keep on without growing weary.—At our rising we must represent to ourselves Jesus awakening, and begin as He did to honor God. In our prayer and other devotions, let us strive to enter into the feelings of respect and love with which He was penetrated when He began these holy exercises. We should do the same at our meals, at our intercourse with our neighbor and in all our actions. But can we succeed in expressing perfectly the features of so beautiful a model? We have only to second the operations of the Holy Ghost in our hearts: this divine Spirit will form in us the image of Jesus Christ by the effusion of His gifts, but unfortunately we put many obstacles in the way of His operations in our souls, and often we form images of the demon rather than of Our Lord. Let us not forget that if Jesus Christ is the type of our perfection; He is also the means by which we can arrive at this perfection. Let us often address ourselves to Him and say: 'Lord, Thou willest that I labor to imitate Thee and I desire it with all my heart, but Thou knowest that I am only a bad apprentice for I can do nothing without Thee; paint then for me, for if Thou take not the brush and put a hand to it, I will but daub and produce unformed features which will bear no resemblance to Thee."

On another occasion speaking on the same subject, he said, "We should especially strive to imitate Jesus Christ in the deference He had for His Father and His perfect dependence on His will. This divine Saviour shows us in a striking manner how important it is to act only by the inspiration of God. He, Who was the sovereign Master of heaven and earth, the Eternal Word, the perfect image of His Father, seemed to have no will, no judgment, no action of His own. He consulted His Father always, and acted only by His will. 'I came not of myself.' '*Non veni a meipso.*' (John viii. 42.) He says to us, 'I speak not of myself.' '*Non loquor a meipso.*' (John xiv. 10.) 'As I hear, so I judge.' '*Sicut audio, sic judico.*' (John v. 30.) He lived not, acted not, judged not; it was His Father Who lived, Who acted, Who judged in Him. Let us imitate this conduct and think and act always by the spirit of Jesus; let us always be united to Him so that we can receive unceasingly His divine influence. It is He, Himself, who counsels us when He says: 'I am the vine; you the branches.—As the branch cannot bear fruit of itself, unless it abide in the vine: so neither can you, unless you abide in me.—Abide in me, and I in you.' (John xv.) Does not this show clearly that we must always act by His spirit? But alas! we are far from this perfection. Oh! let us dread the reproaches which He addressed to a bishop in the Apocalypse. 'I find not thy works full.' '*Non invenio opera tua plena.*' (Apoc. iii. 2.)

"Let us strive," said he at another time, "to grow every day in the love of Jesus Christ. We are to be pitied, if we do not feel ourselves pressed by an earnest desire of loving Him and of loving Him alone. God, the Father, has all His delight in His Son, and we should not have indifference for Him. The angels and saints can never weary of contemplating His admirable perfections, and we have only contempt for Him. At the name of Jesus, every knee must bend in heaven, on earth and in hell, and we do not render Him the homage that is His due. If we wish to acquire this perfect love, let us often have recourse to Jesus, because He is the source of all graces. Everything comes from Him and we can have nothing but through Him. It is He Who gives life to our soul as food gives life to our bodies; let us attach ourselves to Him as a child clings to his mother, and let us draw from Him the milk of all the virtues. The child draws the purest substance from his mother with which he nourishes himself; so if we attach ourselves to Jesus we can draw from Him a life wholly divine."

"Nothing ever seemed more touching to me than Blessed Perboyre's words when he spoke of Our Lord Jesus Christ," said the priest who has preserved for us the preceding thoughts. "He returned often to this subject; he quoted continually the words and examples of Our Lord. If he gave us some advice it was always Our Lord of Whom he spoke and Whom he proposed for our model. 'Our Lord,' said he, 'did this, Our Lord did that; and will you not do as He did? Must not a priest be another Jesus Christ?' It was impossible not to be touched; he charmed us and we could say, on leaving him, like the disciples who had conversed with Our Lord when going to Emmaus, 'Was not our heart burning within us whilst He was speaking?' (Luke xxiv. 32.) Yes, I felt the same effects within me; it seemed that I was with Our Lord Himself. The hours flew by like minutes when he spoke thus in the fulness of his heart. When I left him I felt that he had put fire into my soul, and even now I cannot recall his conversation without being deeply touched. I seem to see and hear him still; I seem to breathe again this perfume of sanctity, this good odor of Jesus Christ which he always spread around him."

Another day the same priest came to him and said, "M. Superior, I have not yet made my spiritual reading, and I must confess to you that I do not feel very well disposed; I have taken the liberty to come to you in hopes that you will say some edifying words which will do me more good than all the reading I can do."—"My dear friend," replied Blessed Perboyre, "do you think me capable of saying anything edifying? You would do much better if you addressed yourself to Our Lord, and implored Him to speak to your heart. He is so good that He will not refuse to hear your prayer, and what He will tell you is much better than all you can hear or read in the best books. Or, if you like it better and desire to make a reading that will greatly profit you, take for your book Our

Lord, Himself; consider how He passed His day and how you pass yours; compare all your actions with His, from the time of your rising until now; see what resemblance there is between his disposition and yours, between the virtues He practised and those you have practised to-day. By this means you will see as in a mirror what faults you may have committed. You will know also, what dispositions you lack, and the consideration of so beautiful an example will incite you to labor with new ardor for your perfection." Blessed Perboyre spoke a long time on this subject, and though he thought himself incapable of saying anything good, his auditor was no less edified, and withdrew well pleased with the advice received.

If John Gabriel exhorted others so earnestly to imitate Our Lord, he, himself, practised in a perfect manner what he recommended. He would not dare to prescribe for another what he had not done himself and in this he remembered Him of Whom it is written 'Jesus began to do and to preach.' (Acts i. 1.) Ardently desirous of imitating Jesus Christ, he considered Him unceasingly; as the Holy Spirit never found in him any obstacle to His divine operations, he perfected more and more in his soul the image of his Saviour. Every day before going up to the holy altar, he addressed himself to Our Lord and said to Him with the greatest fervor: "Here I am, O my divine Saviour; notwithstanding my unworthiness I am going to give Thee a being which Thou hast not, the sacramental being. Ah! I beg Thee, I conjure Thee, to operate in me the same marvel which I shall operate upon this bread in virtue of the power Thou has confided to me. When I shall say 'This is my body,' say also of Thy unworthy servant 'This is my body.' Cause me by Thy all powerful and infinite mercy, to be changed and transformed into Thee. May my hands be the hands of Jesus, may my eyes be the eyes of Jesus, may my tongue be the tongue of Jesus, may all my senses and my whole body serve but to glorify Thee, but especially transform my soul and all its powers; may my memory, my intellect, my heart be the memory, the intellect, the heart of Jesus; may my thoughts and feelings be like Thy thoughts and feelings and as Thy father said of Thee: 'This day have I begotten Thee (Ps. ii. 7) mayst Thou say of me and also with Thy heavenly Father: 'This is my beloved Son, in whom I am well pleased.' (Matt. xvii. 5.) Yes, destroy in me all that is not for Thee; make me live but for Thee and in Thee, so that I can say also on my part with the great Apostle, 'And I, now not I; but Christ liveth in me.'" (Gal. ii. 20.)

This prayer which he made to God before holy Mass, with a heart burning with the desire of being heard, he renewed during his thanksgiving. "When I consider the life which he led," said one of the professors at Saint Flour, "everything made me believe that God had heard him. His heart lived but for Jesus and in Jesus. To him could well be applied what St. John Chrysostom said of St. Paul—that the heart of Jesus had become the heart of St. Paul: *Cor Christi, cor Pauli.* In seeing him it seemed to me that I saw Our Lord; when he spoke, it seemed to me I heard Our Lord conversing with men; when he walked, it seemed to me I saw Our Lord walking; it seemed that Our Lord had passed into him and filled him as a tree is filled with the sap that vivifies it, or as iron, heated in the fire, is filled with the element, which has penetrated it. I used to say to myself, 'When Our Lord was on the earth, had He another language? Had He different manners?'"

---

## VII.

### HIS DEVOTION TO THE PASSION OF OUR SAVIOUR.

WHAT especially excited his devotion to Our Lord was the remembrance of the torments which His love made Him endure for us. "Who loved me," he said, often with St. Paul, "and delivered Himself for me." (Gal. ii. 20.) This thought was like a fiery dart which inflamed his heart. He had his eyes always fixed on the author and finisher of our faith and he meditated unceasingly upon the sufferings of Our Saviour. In preparing for the holy sacrifice of the Mass, he remembered that this sacrifice is the same as the sacrifice of the cross and, clothing himself in holy vestments, he represented to himself Jesus Christ tied and bound by His enemies and clothed with a white robe in sign of derision. When he went to the altar, he imagined Our Lord going to meet His enemies or on His way to Calvary to consummate His sacrifice. In the course of the day, he still thought only of Jesus Christ Who had offered Himself on the altar as He was once offered on Calvary, and he said to himself: "Jesus Christ immolates Himself for me; I must, then, immolate myself for Him; my life must be a continual sacrifice."

The sight of the crucifix awakened in Blessed Perboyre the deepest feelings of love, and he delighted in often looking upon it. In the tribunal of penance, his eyes were fixed upon this sacred image which he held in his hands. Often he suspended his work to contemplate the crucifix placed on his table, to cover it with kisses, to press it to his heart, to bathe it with his tears. Scarcely any one ever entered his room without finding him kneeling at the foot of the crucifix, and it was observed that his eyes were wet with tears. Many a time, as has been already stated, he was surprised, in a rapture, unconscious before the cross, or weeping, groaning, and sobbing like a criminal and incapable in this state of knowing, at first, who had come. Each Friday, he honored the Passion more particularly, and besides the fast which he imposed on himself, he cherished in his soul the remembrance of the sufferings of the Man-God, whose last sigh he received with love at three o'clock in the afternoon. When he could make the Way of the Cross, he never neglected to do it. But he seemed to surpass himself during the week consecrated to the dolorous mysteries, which the Church recalls to her children's remembrance. On Holy Thursday and Good Friday he scarcely left the repository where Jesus dwelt and he remained there absorbed in deep meditation. Holy Thursday evening he prolonged his visit during many hours, when he could not pass the whole night before the repository.

A worthy ecclesiastic relates that having occasion to speak to him during Holy Week, he found him full of the thought of the Passion. Blessed Perboyre began to speak to him about the mystery of the day and particularly of the passage in the gospel where it is said Our

Lord being in the garden of Olives began to fear, to feel weariness and sadness. "Our soul is the temple of Jesus Christ, and very often we make Him feel the same agonies which He experienced in the garden of Olives on the eve of His death. This occurs when we allow ourselves to grow lukewarm in His service. Then Our Lord begins to feel fear; He fears not for Himself but for us, because He sees how much this laxity exposes us to being lost; He fears for us because of the chastisements with which we are threatened if we persevere in our lukewarmness. Not only does He begin to fear but He also begins to be weary. As long as we are faithful in maintaining ourselves in fervor, He takes great delight in living in our hearts; but from the instant that we show Him only coldness. He wearies of us, for who would not weary of the company of a person, whom he had crowned with benefits and who showed him only indifference? At length, if He sees that we persevere in this state, and resist His frequent inspirations to leave it, His Heart will be filled with sadness and His sadness will become so great that He can say with truth: 'My soul is sorrowful even unto death,' '*Tristis est anima mea usque ad mortem*,' (Matt. xxvi. 38.) The garden of Olives is not far from Calvary and if we do not take care we shall soon make Him die in our hearts."

On another occasion, he made to the same priest the following reflections on the mysteries of Holy Week: "On these days which the Church has consecrated in order to recall to our minds what Our Lord has suffered for us, it would be a great cause of shame for a Christian not to occupy himself with these mysteries of love, but it would be monstrous for a priest to be cold and indifferent. Our Lord desires to find some hearts which compassionate His sorrows and which know how to appreciate His love; but very few respond to His desire. This divine Master sees us, like His disciples, plunged in a shameful sleep; He comes to knock at the door of our souls to induce us to share His sorrows, but we deign not to pay attention to Him. He complains in holy Scripture of having vainly sought some one who would be sensible of His sorrows, and He declares that all have refused Him the consolation, He desires. Ah! Let it not be so with us: let us hasten to love Him as He merits, and let us be occupied only with consoling Him and making Him amends by our fervor for the insensibility and ingratitude He receives from the greater part of His creatures." According to the priest who heard these reflections just quoted, the Servant of God said this in so earnest a tone that he was much impressed, and withdrew with his heart filled with the same sentiments about Our Lord's Passion which animated Blessed Perboyre.

He suffered greatly at seeing God offended by the sins which are committed in the world. He was as much affected as if he had seen with his own eyes Our Lord outraged, in person, and persecuted as He was in His passion. The carnival was a time of affliction for him and his grief redoubled during the last three days, on account of the unruly disorders they occasion. Besides the penances that he imposed upon himself to appease the anger of God, he remained long hours before the holy tabernacle absorbed in deep sadness. He would have liked to be able to make Our Lord forget the outrages with which He is overwhelmed and to make amends to Him for the ingratitude of most Christians. He, then, represented to himself this divine Saviour in agony as in the garden of Olives, seeking some one to console Him, and saying principally to His ministers: 'My soul is sorrowful even unto death.—Will you also go away?—What? Could you not watch one hour with me?' (Matt. xxvi. 38., John vi. 68., Matt. xxvi. 40.) And so he was seen prolong his prayer till eleven o'clock at night, and sometimes, even till sunrise.

He often recommended meditation on the Passion of Our Lord. "People complain sometimes that they do not know how to meditate," said he, "it suffices to look five minutes at the crucifix with the spirit of faith to feel penetrated with love and gratitude to Our Lord, and better disposed to serve Him. A person who will be faithful to this practice and who will offer every day some little mortification to God, in gratitude for all He has suffered for him, will make great progress in perfection. Yes, it suffices to look upon a crucifix with faith to receive precious advantages; it is not necessary to know how to read or to have many books; the crucifix is the most beautiful and touching of all books."—"Why do we so often change the subject of meditation?" said he another time, "For one thing is necessary, *Porro unum est necessarium*, (Luke x. 42) and he would show the crucifix. On another occasion he said to an ecclesiastic: "As for me, I can mediate on one thing only," and he again showed the crucifix.—It was too little for John Gabriel Perboyre to compassionate the sufferings of Jesus Christ, he strove to crucify himself with Him so that he could say with St. Paul: "With Christ I am nailed to the cross." (Gal. ii. 19.) So, also, he received with joy all the crosses which Providence sent him. If his health was impaired, he rejoiced because it made him more conformable to Jesus Christ suffering; if he felt some humiliation, he rejoiced in thinking Our Lord was loaded with reproaches; if he met with contradiction he rejoiced again, because he remembered that Our Lord had been an object of contradiction. Everything that could give him the least resemblance to Jesus Christ was for him a subject of joy.

---

## VIII.

### HIS DEVOTION TOWARDS THE HOLY EUCHARIST.

Blessed Perboyre had no less devotion for the Holy Eucharist than for the Passion. This fervent lover of Jesus Christ had constructed for himself two tents—one at the foot of the cross and the other before the tabernacle, and he went continually from one to the other, to contemplate there the charity of God and to inebriate himself with love. "His desire for visits to the Blessed Sacrament was never satisfied," said one of his novices, "anything that would bring him to the chapel was for him an occasion to go and pour out his soul before the altar and to converse with his Saviour. There, he forgot himself and passed whole hours in adoration without moving, almost without breathing. He had to do violence to himself to retire from the chapel. He went away slowly and with regret, like a child who is taken from his mother and who naturally returns to her: thus he returned to the tabernacle where He reposed Who possessed his heart and Who was his delight. When he left the chapel, especially after a long visit, his language was more ardent, his face more joyous and beaming; then his words were full of fire. It could be perceived that his heart was burning with a heavenly flame which was reflected in his face. Thus Our Lord drew him to Himself by the cords of charity and an irresistible attraction. When he was not in his room, he was found nearly always in the chapel where he tasted how sweet the Lord is, and where he found his greatest delight."

He went often to seek refuge near the tabernacle to draw thence the graces which he needed, or to keep company with Him Who has willed through love for us to share the tribulations of our exile. "Devotion to the Blessed Sacrament," said he, "must be the distinctive characteristic of priests. They must be the guardians of this sacrament and the companions of Jesus on our altars. If they knew how much pain they have caused Our Lord and of how many graces they have deprived themselves in coming but rarely to the holy tabernacle, they would guard against keeping at a distance from Him and make much greater haste in paying their court."

His sweetest consolation was to celebrate the holy Mass and to receive Jesus into his heart. "I am never more happy," said he, "than when I have offered the sacrifice of the Mass." The greatest privation he could endure was not to be able to receive Holy Communion. Thus we read in a letter written during his voyage. "Oh! how happy we feel on this vast desert of the ocean to find ourselves, from time to time, in the company of Our Lord!" One of the professors at St. Flour, told him one day that he must abstain from celebrating because he had a severe pain in his head and feared he could not say Mass with enough devotion. John Gabriel replied, "You are wrong; God does not ask for the head, he asks only for the heart." Another priest having manifested to him his intention of not offering the Holy Sacrifice because he found himself in great dryness, received this response: "Do like those who are pressed by creditors and who have not wherewith to pay. They go and borrow it, do they not? Well, borrow, yourself, from the Blessed Virgin what you need. In her you will find faith, humility, love, in a word all that you lack; and with this you will have reason to be satisfied, for it will not be with your dispositions, but with those of Mary, that you will receive Jesus Christ."

He prepared himself for Mass with great care. Besides prayer and the other exercises of piety which he performed, he passed sometimes a whole hour before the altar conjuring Our Lord to establish in him the dispositions so holy an action requires. His interior sentiments are known best from the counsels he gave a pious ecclesiastic, who witnessing John Gabriel's fervor, begged him to give to him a method for offering up the holy sacrifice well. The Servant of God at first made some objections to complying with his desire, but being urgently pressed, gave him the following directions with the air of conviction and with the pious faith which characterized him.

"Before celebrating holy Mass, we must strive to enter into the same dispositions as Our Lord, Who offers Himself for us on our altars: even as Jesus Christ wished to immolate Himself for us, so must we offer ourselves to God and immolate ourselves to His Holy Will. 'Imitate Him Whom you have in your hands,' says the Church to us. '*Imitamini quod tractatis.*' On going to the church you must be filled with the thought that we are going to immolate ourselves with Jesus to the good pleasure of God and we must say with St. Thomas: 'Let us also go that we may die with Him.' (John xi. 16.) '*Eamus et nos, ut moriamur cum illo.*' Jesus desires us to enter into these sentiments and He seems to say to us, 'Consider how great My goodness is to you to permit you to celebrate the most holy, the most awful of all mysteries; I give Myself entirely to you, but on condition that on your part you will give yourself to Me.' This is the contract which this amiable Saviour makes with us, but a contract most advantageous to us, since we receive all the benefits and give so little.

"Besides this oblation of ourselves which we make to God, it will be very profitable to offer some special victim. This victim we must seek within our heart, and we must examine ourselves attentively to know the thing to which we are most attached, or whose sacrifice will be most agreeable to God. In this we must act with generosity and avoid imitating Cain who offered to God the worst of his flock; imitate rather the piety of Abel who offered Him the best he had, or the generosity of Abraham, who showed himself disposed to immolate his son, Isaac. Be persuaded that the time you spend in seeking this victim will be well employed, as it is one of the best means to avoid routine and to draw great fruit from the holy sacrifice. For my part, I do not think a priest can celebrate advantageously to himself if he goes to the altar without this disposition. After having determined on his victim, he must put it on the paten with the host and at the time of the offertory present it to God, praying Him to receive it as a holocaust and to annihilate it.

"After this, strive to conceive a great idea of the importance of the sacrifice which you are going to offer. Imagine to yourself that you are the only priest on earth bidden to intercede for the needs of the whole world, and that from all directions people, who are interested in the great action you are going to perform, run to you to beg you to present to God their supplications; and that these supplications are so numerous that they reach from the earth to the sky. Here are thousands of the just who have numbers of graces to demand, a much greater number of sinners, of both sexes, all ages and conditions; here are the angels and saints in heaven, the angel guardians especially, and the holy patrons who come to beg you to intercede in favor of the souls in whom they are interested. What an impression would it not make upon you if all these persons, if all these angels and saints, appeared to you in a sensible form; if you were surrounded, pressed by them, if you heard their suppliant voices which implore most eagerly your charity! Add to this the lamentable groans of the souls in purgatory who also wait to receive the advantages of the holy sacrifice of the Mass. Ah! how could we allow ourselves to become lukewarm, if we thought that by a Mass well said, we could contribute to the spiritual good of so many souls whose advocate with God we are called to be! And in your quality of mediator, it is necessary that you be in friendship with God; for how can you intercede efficaciously if you are not agreeable in His eyes. Let us understand by this, how necessary it is for us to establish in our souls great fervor and purity of conscience. It is true that we have in reality but one mediator Who is Jesus Christ, and that the principal fruit of the sacrifice of the Mass is independent of the dispositions of the priest who offers it; but we know, also, that God threatens to curse the benedictions of priests who do not serve Him with fervor and rejects their sacrifices; we know that when the saints were on earth their prayers had great efficacy with God and drew down abundant graces upon those for whom they offered them.

"After you are penetrated with the importance of the act you are going to perform, wash your hands and beg God with all the fervor of which you are capable, to accord you the purity of conscience necessary to celebrate it worthily. In putting the amice upon your shoulders, remember that in the beginning the priests put it on the head; it reminds you that you must close your eyes to all things of earth and turn all your thoughts to God. Then supplicate Our Lord to surround you with the helmet of salvation, and to shelter you from all the attacks of the demon who, knowing how much the action you are going to perform procures the glory of God and the good of your neighbor, makes every effort to have priests celebrate Mass without devotion and to handle the holy mysteries in a manner little calculated to reanimate the piety of the faithful. In putting on the alb, remember that by its whiteness it is a symbol of the purity of conscience with which you must approach God. Humble yourself profoundly and pray Him to wash you in the blood of the Lamb, so that the oblation of the holy sacrifice may be for you a pledge of eternal joys. In girding yourself with the cincture, think of the purity which must be one of the principal ornaments of the priest who represents Jesus Christ; think, also, that the grace of God must enchain and captivate all your senses as the cord keeps in place all the folds of the robe. Conjure the Lord to gird you Himself with the cincture of purity and to extinguish in you the fire of concupiscence, so that you will be all shining with chastity. The maniple was, in the beginning, only a handkerchief which priests used to wipe away the tears which devotion drew abundantly from their eyes during the celebration of the holy sacrifice; never put it on without groaning interiorly that we are so far from the fervor of those early priests. This vestment also reminds us of the obligation of being rich in good works and of passing our life in labor, penance, and tears; this is why we say to God, 'Grant, O Lord, that I may be worthy to bear the maniple of tears and of sorrow, that I may receive with joy the recompense of my labor.' The stole signifies innocence, so, in taking it, let us ask of God that He may clothe us in the stole of immortality which we have lost by the prevarication of our first parents; of prayer, which requires great sentiments of humility and contrition to obtain the grace that we implore. The chasuble is the symbol of the yoke of Our Lord. Take it with the desire of allowing yourself to be conducted by Him and of having no other will but His. Let us tremble with joy in repeating these words of Jesus Christ, 'My yoke is sweet and My burden light.' (Matt. xi. 30.) Let us not forget that if we bear it generously, interior peace will become our portion in this world, and so we shall obtain the grace of living holily and of possessing God eternally in glory.

"We must be careful of the manner in which we pronounce the different prayers required; for it is a great misfortune for a priest not to be attentive to the sense of the prayers which he addresses to God and the meaning of the vestments in which he is clothed. In applying himself more to learning the meaning of the spirit of the Church, he draws upon himself abundant graces by celebrating with fervor, whilst by his negligence he would often be a cause of sorrow to heaven, and deprive the faithful of the edification and the grace which they have the right to expect from him. To avoid this misfortune a good means would be to make a meditation upon this subject and to continue it till one has contracted the happy habit of taking these sacerdotal garments with the spirit of faith, which the Church desires in the ministers of the altar. It will be well also, to read the *Manuel des Ordinands* and to meditate on all that belongs to the holy sacrifice of the Mass, so as to conceive a great idea of the sublimity of this function as well as the manner of performing it.

"There are still other means which are proper to excite our fervor when we prepare ourselves to say Mass. Faith teaches us that the sacrifice of our altars is the same sacrifice which was once offered upon Calvary, and that we there hold the place of Jesus Christ. These vestments must remind us of what Jesus Christ suffered from His enemies, and excite in our hearts the deepest sentiments of love, gratitude and compassion for our divine Master. So, when you put on the amice, think of the outrages to which He was subjected in the house of Caiphas, when they put a veil over His eyes so as to spit more freely in His august face. In putting on the alb, think of the white robe with which He was clothed at the court of Herod, beg Him to inspire you with a great hatred for the wisdom of the world, and promise Him to esteem, hereafter, only the folly of the cross. The cincture and maniple remind you of the cords with which His hands were bound and the scourges used in His flagellation. The stole must also represent the cord which was put around His neck when He was dragged like a malefactor through the streets of Jerusalem. In putting on the chasuble, think of the purple vestment which was put on Him in derision and the cross He bore on His shoulders; represent to yourself the sad state in which the divine Master was then found, and compassionate His humiliations and pains. In clothing yourself with the holy vestments, you promise to imitate Our Lord and to suffer and to be humiliated with Him. Strive to unite yourself to His dispositions in making His sacrifice. Offer yourself to God to become, if necessary, a victim of expiation for the sins of men. Oh! if there is a time when the priest should be inflamed with zeal for the glory of God and the salvation of souls, it is when he is about to offer the holy sacrifice of the Mass, which reminds him of all that Jesus Christ has willed to suffer to redeem mankind and to repair the injury done His Father by sin.

"Before leaving the sacristy, you salute the crucifix; never fail to do it with much humility and devotion. Beg Our Lord to bless you and to be with you at the altar, so that He may act in you and for you and that His spirit may animate all the prayers which come from your mouth. When you go to the altar, do it with so much piety and modesty that, in seeing you, the faithful may think that they see Jesus Christ Himself. Your heart must then be penetrated by sentiments of both pain and joy. A sentiment of sorrow at the remembrance of the passion of Our Saviour and a feeling of joy because of the joy He, Himself felt when He went to Calvary bearing His cross. 'Having joy set before Him, endured the cross.' '*Proposito sibi gaudio sustinuit crucem.*' (Heb. xii. 2.) You must rejoice also in the thought that you are going to offer yourself to God as a victim, so that you may die to all the things of this world and live only for Him.

"At the altar, represent to yourself that you are like Jesus on Calvary; this must be your dominating thought during the whole time that the holy sacrifice shall last. On opening the missal, to say holy Mass, beg sweet Jesus to open also your heart so that it may not be with the lips only that you pronounce the prayers you have to say. Every time you kiss the holy stone, remember what St. Paul said of the stone which followed every where the Israelites in the desert, 'And the rock was Christ,' (1 Cor. x. 4.) '*Petra autem Christus*,' that is, an image of the Saviour and Legislator of men. The sacred stone of our altars is also a symbol of Christ upon Whom we have been built. Kiss it, then, with the same respect and the same affection as if it were Our Lord Himself: let us beware of imitating the conduct of Judas who kissed Our Lord and wished to betray Him. This token of affection is given only to friends, and consequently every time that we kiss the altar stone, we make to Our Lord a protestation of our love for Him.

"These words, *Dominus vobiscum*, to which the people respond *Et cum spiritu tuo*, which are frequently repeated in the Mass, are very suitable for reanimating our devotion. In fact, when we say these words, we wish Our Lord to be with all the faithful, but should you not blush if He is not with you, if your mind is dissipated, if your heart is not filled with affection for God? Observe, too, that scarcely have you pronounced these words than the people respond *Et cum spiritu tuo*, 'May He be also with thy spirit.' And why do the people respond in this manner? It shows how much interested they are in the action which you perform and how much need there is of your celebrating it with fervor. For how can you intercede efficaciously for them, if you have not the dispositions which Jesus Christ demands? Remember, too, it is not only the people present at the sacrifice, who claim these dispositions from you, but the whole world, heaven and earth, the living and the dead, come to conjure you not to forget their supplications but to be by your faith, your humility and your charity, a good mediator. Imagine, then, that you hear all these souls saying to you, 'You can avert from us the greatest evils; you can draw down upon us the most precious graces, you can snatch us from hell and open for us the gates of heaven; be, then, wholly absorbed in the action which you perform, for if you allow yourself to grow lukewarm, we will not obtain the graces which must be the fruit of your good dispositions.' Do you feel yourself preoccupied with troublesome distractions? Imagine that all these souls remind you of all the supplications which they have recommended and reproach your negligence; that their guardian angels, their holy patrons, that Mary and Jesus Christ Himself say also to you: 'May the Lord be with your spirit, may He not depart from your thoughts or your heart.'

"The Preface is especially suited to excite your devotion. First, you say to the people, *Sursum corda:* 'Lift up your hearts,' and the people answer you, *Habemus ad Dominum.* 'We have lifted them up to the Lord.' Ah! what a subject of confusion to you if your heart is still engrossed with thoughts of earth. Is it not just that we be the first to practise what we recommend to others? After the Preface, do not forget that you have just united yourself to Jesus Christ to sing the praises of God with the angels and that your heart must be burning with charity.

"At the prayer of the Canon which begins with these words, *Communicantes,* how much should we not be filled with holy fear! In fact, by these words we declare that we are in the society of the Blessed Virgin Mary, Mother of God, with the apostles, the martyrs and all the saints. Let us recollect ourselves then, and with holy and pious awe let us say, 'Who am I to enter into the society of Mary and all the saints of heaven? What affinity is there between the Queen of Angels and the vilest of sinners, between my life and that of the saints when they were upon earth. Have I the purity and humility of Mary, the zeal of the apostles, the constancy of the martyrs, the generosity of the confessors, the holiness of the priests, the spirit of penance and mortification of the anchorites? If your clothes were torn, and covered with muddy, disgusting stains, would you dare to present yourself in the palace of the king and sit down among the most distinguished people of the realm? Would you not blush to find yourself in this state amid society so brilliant and so illustrious? How much more must we not fear to go to the altar if our conscience is not purified. Let us fear that, instead of being an object of complacency to heaven, we are subjects of horror on account of the sad state of our soul; and let us beg God to give us the purity of conscience which is needed to offer up the Victim without spot. Besides, let us recognize that we are destitute of the goods which would make us agreeable to the heavenly court; let us conjure Mary to communicate to us her purity and her humility; the apostles, to pour into our hearts the fire with which they were inflamed for the glory of God and the salvation of souls; the martyrs, to make us share in their heroic constancy in suffering for the faith; finally let us beg all the saints to obtain for us all the virtues that we lack, so that we may associate ourselves with confidence with all the celestial court without having to blush for our poverty.

"As you approach the Consecration, your fervor should always increase. Devote your whole attention to what you are about to do at this solemn moment; represent to yourself Our Lord when, amid His disciples assembled in the cenacle, He instituted this sacrament of love, and act in the same spirit as this divine Saviour. It is, then, especially that we need to reanimate our faith, for it is not without reason that, in the words of the Consecration, this divine sacrifice is called a mystery of faith. I counsel you also to profit by the time of Consecration to make Our Lord a demand which will certainly be very agreeable to Him. Since the priest must be another Jesus Christ, we must ardently desire to become like Him. But how can we reproduce perfectly our model? This is done only by the help of grace. Now it seems to me that the time of the Consecration is very propitious for asking Him this favor. Address yourself then to Him with confidence and humility, beg Him to operate in you, by His almighty power, a consecration which changes you into Himself so that you may no longer be what you formerly were but that you may be transformed into Jesus Christ and that you may say with the apostle St. Paul: 'And I live, now not I; but Christ liveth in me.' (Gal. ii. 20.) You will do well to renew this petition during your thanksgiving after Mass and urge Him with much pressing to accord you this signal favor.

"After the Consecration the presence of Jesus Christ upon the altar must be more than sufficient to excite in you feelings of the most affectionate love. Remember that is He Who was before all ages, Who descended from heaven, Who was born of the Blessed Virgin Mary and Who died on the cross. Think that you are surrounded by thousands of angels who trembling, adore Him, who in His presence burn with flames of the most ardent love. When you take the Sacred Host, do it with the same faith, with the same tenderness that Mary had when she took in her arms her divine Son; when you make the genuflections, never fail to make a little pause to adore Our Lord."

When John Gabriel was asked why the Gospel of St. John is nearly always said at the end of Mass, he replied: "Nothing is better suited to give you a great idea of Him Who comes to humble Himself in so extraordinary a manner in the holy sacrifice; nothing is better suited, also, to make us appreciate the treasure that we possess in our hearts and to excite in us the deepest sentiments of gratitude. After Mass all our thoughts must be holy; we must say to ourselves, 'I have begotten Him, who has no beginning. I have given being to my Creator, I have received Him in my soul; how can I allow myself base thoughts, unworthy of God? All within me should be holy and divine.' The Church wishes to teach us also, that Jesus Christ has come to us to dissipate our darkness and to make us children of light. Let us be afraid of not profiting by what He brings us, lest they may say of us as they did of the Jews: '*Lux in tenebris lucet et tenebrae eam non comprehenderunt.*' 'The light shineth in darkness, and the darkness did not comprehend it.' (John i. 5.) Alas! how many receive every day this divine light and are no less in darkness. Let us fear lest these words be applied to us. '*In mundo erat et mundus eum non cognovit.*' 'He was in the world—and the world knew Him not.' (John i. 10.) Jesus comes into our hearts and very often we pay no attention to Him, because we live in dissipation. Let us have a horror of this conduct and receive Him in so worthy a manner that we may be of the number of those of whom it is said, 'But as many as received Him, He gave them power to be made the sons of God.' (John i. 12.) Let us pray earnestly to Him to accord us this grace, for if we become true children of God, we shall thereby be conformable to Jesus Christ.

"After Mass by our actions we must testify that we have really received Jesus Christ, that we have been renewed and transformed in Him. Let us remember that Jesus Christ has immolated Himself for us, and let us often say: 'Jesus is immolated for me but on condition that I immolate myself for Him. My life must, then, be a continual immolation of myself to His holy will.' After the holy sacrifice, Jesus Christ seems to say to us: 'Thou seest what I have just done for thee. Ah! I demand now, that thou do as much for Me. Go, then, to immolate thyself for Me, sacrifice thy irregular inclinations, this passion which enslaves thee, this sensuality, this pride, this impatience, this cowardice, these wordly desires, etc. Thou art a priest for all eternity, consequently thou art always a sacrificer. Thy heart is the altar on which thou shouldst offer Me continual sacrifices; woe to thee, if thou livest according to nature, for nature will make thee commit many sins and if thou sin it is no longer thou who immolatest, it is sin, it is the demon, it is nature which degrades and immolates thee.'"

In order to vary the method and to excite piety in offering the holy sacrifice of the Mass, this fervent Servant of God gave also the following counsels. "It is a very useful practice in the office of a holy pontiff or a holy priest, to represent to ourselves how he prepared himself to say Mass, how he put on the sacred vestments, with what piety, modesty, and with what spirit of faith he celebrated the holy mysteries. We have great reason for humbling ourselves at seeing how far we are from serving God with the fervor of these saints, and we must take the resolution of imitating them more faithfully and beg them to help us to enter into the dispositions which animated them when they offered the holy sacrifice."

"It would be impossible for me," added the priest to whom Blessed Perboyre spoke, "to recall all he said to me about the disposition required to celebrate the holy Mass, or to tell the impression which was made upon me by his words. It seemed to me, after having heard him, that I had never understood the importance of this august sacrifice and when I went afterwards to offer to God the holy Victim, my heart was filled with the thoughts he had communicated to me. I remembered principally the supplications of which he had spoken and I believed myself surrounded by thousands of suppliant souls who came to conjure me to have pity on them."

It is useless to repeat here that John Gabriel, in the counsels which he gave on this subject, recommended nothing he did not practise himself. It was wonderfully edifying to see him at the altar; his piety and modesty inspired devotion in the most lukewarm. In the liveliness of his faith, the Divinity seemed for him stripped of its veil, and of its mysterious obscurity; his face, generally ruddy, became more animated at this time and was really radiant. Often, moved by feelings of love for God, he almost suffocated and was obliged to stop for some time ; at other times, suddenly seized by a kind of ecstacy, he could scarcely continue the holy sacrifice. When he lived at the Mother House in Paris, the faithful of the neighborhood often came to know at what hour the Servant of God would say Mass, so that they could assist at it and receive edification.

One day he said to an ecclesiastic who complained to him of the little fervor which he felt during Mass: "As for myself, I never feel better disposed to celebrate than when I leave the altar." In fact, God communicated to him great lights and poured into his heart the flames of the most ardent charity. At the end of Mass, he could not sufficiently admire the goodness of God in his regard ; he then felt himself penetrated with deepest gratitude and disposed to make the greatest sacrifices for Him. This may be seen by the following words that may be repeated here and which are found in a letter he wrote during his voyage to China. "When we could say Mass on Sundays our joy was great. Our Lord's descending into our hearts makes us forget past pains and fatigues, and we feel that all we do for Him is nothing to the price He has paid for us."

After Mass, John Gabriel, generally, passed half an hour in thanksgiving before the altar, but sometimes, he forgot himself entirely in Our Lord and whole hours passed without his knowledge. What happiness, what transports! Wholly absorbed in Him Who had given Himself for him, he desired to have a thousand hearts to love Him and a thousand voices to express his gratitude. Feeling his incapacity to thank

Him for so much goodness, he invited all the creatures of heaven and earth to unite themselves with him; but, not yet satisfied, desiring to give His God an acknowledgment equal to His benefits, he begged Him to thank Himself since He alone was able to understand this great love.—A priest asked John Gabriel one day to tell him how he made his thanksgiving and how it should be made; he blushed at the demand and replied, "Do you think me capable of making a proper thanksgiving? God knows how badly I do it." "But how do you make yours?" replied his questioner. "I beg Our Lord that He would return thanks to Himself as I am incapable of doing it. Nevertheless, although we are incapable of thanking God as we should for so great a favor, let us do all in our power to show our gratitude, and, as we can only do it imperfectly, we must beg Our Lord to supply for our insufficiency. This divine Saviour, Who is goodness itself, will yield to our desires, but He does not wish to be alone in this, so He makes it with us and for us. It is only on this condition that our hearts will be inundated with grace. Those who do only, what depends on themselves, draw no fruit from Holy Communion."

It is not enough to thank Our Lord after Holy Communion; he thought that a priest who has received Jesus Christ into his heart, should employ in His service his whole spiritual and corporal life, and in a manner be consumed for Him. Having assisted a young priest in saying his first Mass, he embraced him after his thanksgiving and said to him, "Now you are a priest forever! every day you will have the happiness of receiving into your heart Him Who is the joy of the angels in heaven; but you must not forget what Our Lord has said, 'He that eateth me, the same shall live by me.' '*Qui manducat me et ipse vivet propter me.*' (John vi. 58.) Must not a servant work for him who feeds him?" This thought was always in his mind. His life was but a perpetual thanksgiving and a continual immolation of himself to the good pleasure of God.

---

## IX.

### HIS DEVOTION TO THE BLESSED VIRGIN AND THE SAINTS.

AFTER God, the Blessed Virgin possessed John Gabriel's entire affections. He celebrated her feasts with a tender, filial devotion; on Saturdays he fasted in her honor, meditated upon her prerogatives and incited himself to serve her by every motive calculated to increase his fervor. Faithful to the daily recitation of the rosary, he highly esteemed this pious practice. One day after conversing with some ecclesiastic upon doctrinal subjects, as he made ready to pay his accustomed homages to his good Mother, these words escaped from his heart: "One Hail Mary well said, is worth more than all the science in the world." A priest having asked him what he must do to say the rosary well, he answered, "Many people seek methods for saying it, but for my part, I never use any, and I say it very badly; however, I think the best method for reciting the rosary is to occupy ourselves with the words of the Hail Mary, because these words well meditated upon and well understood are suitable to excite in us sentiments which could not be imparted to us by all human words united. I think that we cannot have better intentions than those of the angel, or address Mary, a prayer more beautiful, more honorable or more agreeable to her."

His devotion to Mary consisted above all in imitating her virtues. He zealously endeavored to gain all hearts to her; he wished priests to become more ardent propagators of devotion to her, and to be her most devout clients. "We must be other Christs," said he, "but how can we become like to Jesus if it is not through Mary? It was in her bosom that Our Lord took His human form; in like manner, all those who wish to become images of Jesus must be formed in the spiritual bosom of Mary. Let us cast ourselves into her heart, as a child throws himself upon his mother's bosom; let us never leave her; let us remain continually near her; by this means we become other Christs, and we can say with truth that we are brothers of Jesus Christ and children of Mary.

"A priest who desires to do much good in his ministry, must necessarily have recourse to the august Mother of God. Our Lord Himself has shown us what we must do: there is not the least doubt that He could have saved the world without the intervention of the Blessed Virgin; however, he did not; but He willed that the world should be saved by a man and a woman, even as it had been lost by a man and a woman. Our salvation came through Mary; it is through her alone we can obtain the fruit of it. Beg her, then, to bless all your words and all your actions so that you may have success. If you preach, if you hear confessions, if you offer the holy sacrifice of the Mass, if you pray, interest Mary in your favor; do nothing without her, and you will draw down abundant benedictions upon all your undertakings."

St. Joseph, in whom he had great confidence, was, also, for him an object of especial devotion. What he admired most in him, was his entire abandonment into the hands of God, his love for silence, for retirement and for the hidden life, and these were the virtues which he strove most to imitate, so that he could make himself like so beautiful a model. Frequently, he recommended this devotion, and if he gave a souvenir to any one it was generally a small treatise on his virtues, or the "Month of St. Joseph."

He had very much at heart the glory of this great saint. This is what is related upon this subject by a missionary who was under his direction at the seminary: "Although he was of unalterable sweetness of disposition, he was almost severe to me upon the subject of St. Joseph. I had read in the *Manuel des Ordinands* a beautiful litany composed in honor of this saint, from words of scripture, and, as it seemed to me that it attributed to him some qualities, which were only proper to Our Lord, I made this observation to him. Thinking that I wished to take away from St. Joseph some of his glory, he began to defend all the glorious titles that were given him in the litany, to exalt the virtues which he had practised and the singular privileges with which Our Lord had favored him. He spoke with more animation than usual, which made me understand how much he loved and admired St. Joseph. He exhorted me to invoke him with confidence. '*Ite ad Joseph*,' 'Go to Joseph.' (Gen. xli. 55.) he said to us, and he shared the opinion of St. Teresa about the influence of St. Joseph with God. Not satisfied with invoking him, he strove to imitate him especially as the model of a hidden, interior life.

He had great devotion to the holy angels, especially the guardian angels. He often invoked his own, and never left his room without praying to this faithful, devoted guide to watch over him. Before reciting his breviary, he begged these blessed spirits to help him to celebrate the praises of God as they are celebrated in heaven. After his office, he recited again a little prayer, putting himself anew under their protection. One day a priest having asked him why he so often prayed to the holy angels, he gave him this reason: "'*Similis simili gaudet.*' When we have been raised to the sublime dignity of the priesthood, we have become according to the expression of the holy Scriptures, 'Angels of the Lord,' we must, therefore, delight in conversing with the angels of heaven and often beg them to help us to live in a manner conformable to our dignity."

The great charity of the angels for men was often the object of his admiration; he thanked them for all they did for us, and he said, with a feeling of deep sadness, that he could not understand the ingratitude of men to them. When he had to begin a difficult or important undertaking, he never failed to have recourse to the guardian angels of all those with whom he had to treat, and he said he was always well pleased with this practice.

It is proper to cite here what is related by the priests who lived with him at St. Flour. "We can not omit saying some words about his devotion to the holy Angels whom he called the fathers of the spiritual life. For it was he who introduced into the house the frequent recitation of the prayer '*Angele Sancte Dei*,' 'Holy Angel of God,' and if the masters and pupils are faithful to this pious and salutary custom, it is to him that we are indebted. His respect for these princes of the heavenly court made him, when saluting those he met, have the intention of saluting their guardian angels. 'When we have business with any one,' he told us, 'it is very useful to have as a mediator, the angel to whose care this person has been committed; often by this means, things are obtained which would be otherwise vainly solicited. We see in the scriptures, that God has often used the ministry of the angels; why should we not do the same? They give us a living example of the contemplative and active life admirably united together; they preserve imperturbable peace and calmness, notwithstanding the disorders of earth; let us try to imitate them as much as human weakness will permit us, and we will find the good of it in all respects.'"

We may be sure that he did not neglect to pay homage to all the saints whom the church honors; that he often had recourse to their intercession, and that he profited by their example to advance in virtue. Each day, he honored with special devotion, the saint whose feast the church celebrated that day. The festivals which succeed each other during the Christian year, seemed to him a shining crown all perfumed with the good odor of Jesus Christ. He prepared for them with new fervor; he meditated on their mysteries, and was deeply impressed by the sentiments with which the Church on these holy days seeks to inspire her children. At such times, he appeared more radiant; he loved to speak of these feasts on which he felt his desire to live wholly for Our Lord much increased.

---

## X.

### HIS SPIRIT OF PRAYER.

THE practice of prayer has always been the distinctive mark of the true servants of God. This is one of the points by which Blessed John Gabriel showed how much he thirsted for the love of God and His justice. Prayer was for him the first and most useful of all exercises. He never failed every morning to apply himself to it with admirable fervor. "Prayer," said he, "is the breath of the soul. Our body cannot live without the air it breathes; so our soul dies when it ceases to breathe by means of prayer. This is why the prophet says, 'I opened my mouth and panted.' '*Os meum aperui et attraxi spiritum.*' (Ps. cxviii. 131.) Our Lord recommended nothing so much as prayer and meditation and He, Himself consecrated much time to it, to give us an example."

When certain priests thought they must abridge their prayer or omit it altogether because they were overloaded with business; he said, "For my part it seems to me that in this case, far from thinking of abridging my prayer, I feel that I must on the contrary prolong it. He who has a long voyage to make or a great work to undertake, would not take less food than usual through fear of growing weak; but, on the contrary, he would take more nourishment; he would choose the most substantial dishes to fortify himself to resist fatigue more readily. But you tell me that you have not time. Believe me, you will do more in one hour with God than in four relying upon yourself. A man who lives not by prayer, may labor and think that he does a great deal; but, in reality, he does much less than he who works only after having drawn his light and strength from the bosom of God. He cited the instance of the Apostles, who labored all night without obtaining anything, and who, in an instant, saw their net filled with fish, when Our Lord was with them. He related, too, the example of the great servants of God who, notwithstanding their multiplied occupations never neglected to give a considerable time to prayer and he concluded that the means of effecting the most good was not to abridge this exercise, but to prolong it, after the example of the greatest saints."

Speaking one day of the obstacles which hinder our progress in prayer, he said: "I know of no greater obstacle to our progress in prayer than our defects, and that we do not labor sufficiently to correct them. He who wishes to make great progress in this holy exercise, must examine himself every evening upon the faults which he has committed during the day; these faults must then be made the subject of his meditation the next day. If he applies himself to meditating on his faults of the previous day for some time, and deplores them with much bitterness of heart, he will soon obtain great purity of conscience and will make great progress in prayer. Let us study to know ourselves;

it is the best means we can take to correct our faults. If we know ourselves well, we shall have a great horror of ourselves; we shall hate ourselves and be disposed to take the most efficacious means of correcting ourselves."

Being asked what was the best book of meditation, he answered: "Many people are anxious to find books of meditation which suit them; I myself know none more excellent and which costs less than our own heart and the Heart of Jesus. It may be called the book of books, and I counsel you to use it often. Yes, study yourself well; study well the Heart of Jesus and in a short time you will make great progress in virtue. In your heart, you will find an abyss of miseries; in the Heart of Jesus, you will find an abyss of mercies; in your heart, you will find an abyss of poverty, in the Heart of Jesus an abyss of riches; in your heart, you will find an abyss of pride; in the Heart of Jesus, an abyss of humility; in your heart you will find anger, impatience, want of mortification; in the Heart of Jesus, you will find gentleness, meekness, patience and mortification; finally in your heart you will find faults and sins; in the Heart of Jesus, sanctity and all the treasures of virtue. These considerations will make you humble yourself, desire to become better, and make you beg the good Jesus to give you a share in His riches. Beside the Heart of Jesus you will place the heart of the Saint whose feast the church celebrates that day and consider how this heart was filled with the spirit of Jesus and became like Him; then, take the resolution of laboring, like him to imitate Our Lord; you must endeavor especially to labor that day, to acquire the virtue which particularly distinguished this saint and invoke him often during the day."

"Why should we change so often the subject of meditation," said he another time. "There is but one thing necessary, that is Jesus Christ. Let us meditate unceasingly upon this subject, for it is inexhaustible. Our Lord has said to us, 'I am the way, the truth and the life.' *Ego sum via, veritas et vita.* (John xiv. 6.) I am the way, but what way? The way of humility, charity, obedience, patience, mortification, perfection, happiness and glory. If we wish to become perfect, if we wish to arrive at happiness and heavenly glory, it is necessary to walk in this way. But that we may not stray, we need a light to enlighten us. Ah! it is He Who we must use as a light; for He is the truth and He declares to us that he who follows Him walks not in darkness but that he shall have the light of life. We need strength also to sustain us in this way and to persevere in it. Again, it is Jesus Who will be our strength; He wished to become our nourishment in giving Himself to us in the Holy Eucharist and on this account He says to us 'I am the life.'

"In the crucifix, the gospel, the Eucharist we find all that we can desire. There is no other way, no other truth, no other life, it is to Him alone, consequently, that we must attach ourselves; it is He Whom we must study; it is to Him we must unceasingly have recourse."

"We asked him, one day," relate the professors of the preparatory Seminary of St. Flour, "how a meditation should be made. Among many other things, that our memory does not retain, he told us 'When you wish to make your prayer put aside as much as possible all books; in them human language is used more or less. Use the holy gospel and if you are embarrassed about what reflections to make upon some passages address yourself to the Holy Spirit: in Him you will have the best of commentators. We must also solicit more especially of God the gift of understanding. Often have in your mouth these words of the Prophet King: 'Give me understanding, and I will learn thy commandments. *Da mihi intellectum, ut sciam mandata tua.*'" (Ps. cxviii. 73.)

Upon another occasion, he thus instructed some one who consulted him upon the same subject. "When you go to God in prayer, present yourself before Him with sweet confidence. Speak to Him with the freedom of a child to his father whom He respects and loves. Be not like those who wish always to speak to God, but who allow Him no opportunity to speak to them; let us often say with the prophet, 'Speak, Lord, for Thy servant heareth.' (I Kings iii. 9.) There are many, who instead of making prayer are engaged only in meditation; however prayer is more useful than meditation, for that is almost useless without prayer, and often of no avail. For six thousand years, the devil has meditated and is still wicked. Do not forgot when you begin your prayer, that the heart must do more than the mind, and especially must you remember that to make progress you must labor to obtain great humility of heart, because God hides Himself from the proud and reveals Himself to the humble."

A young ecclesiastic, whose confidence he possessed, said to him one day, that he found himself embarrassed at the end of his prayer to know what resolution he should take; that in thinking over his needs, it seemed to him that he had three hundred from which to chose. He wanted to know if he must take many resolutions and if he must change them often. Here is the response John Gabriel made him: "My dear friend, be persuaded that if you take two resolutions at the end of your prayer, you take one too many, and if you take a new one each day, when the end of the year comes you will retain all your defects, and as a New Year's gift to our sweet Jesus, you will present to Him only a mountain of infidelities. If St. Francis de Sales, or St. Vincent de Paul had each day taken a new resolution, St. Francis de Sales would never have become well grounded in that admirable meekness which charmed every one; St. Vincent would never have acquired that profound humility of which he was so perfect a model. It is very important to hold always to the same resolution until you have entirely corrected the fault which you intend to combat, or have acquired the virtue in which you wish to be strengthened. Every morning, we must steep it in prayer so as to act upon it with more vigor. Besides, we must make it a subject of particular examen, so as to give an account, at noon and in the evening, of the fidelity with which we labored to correct ourselves of our faults, or to advance in the practice of virtue."

## XI.

### HIS FERVOR IN THE RECITATION OF THE BREVIARY.

BLESSED JOHN GABRIEL regarded the divine office as a second sacrifice which he offered to God in union with Our Lord Jesus Christ, and he said with the prophet, 'I will sacrifice to Thee the sacrifice of praise.' '*Tibi sacrificabo hostiam laudis.*' (Ps. cxv. 17.) He considered that it was not in his own name, but in that of the Church, that he fulfilled this august ministry, for which he had been deputed; and that just as at the altar, he then held the place of Eternal Pontiff, and a true mediator who intercedes unceasingly for men with His Father. On the one side, considering all the needs of the Church, whether militant or suffering, he looked upon himself as charged with the office of drawing down upon both, the benedictions of God; but, on the other hand, he was seized with fright at the importance of the action he was about to perform, humbled himself before God, and considered himself incapable of fulfilling this office. Then, raising himself up to heaven to associate himself with the choirs of angels, he begged the saints, and the Queen of Saints, to assist his weakness; he especially united himself with Our Lord, the sole mediator, powerful and efficacious with God. Filled with this thought of the prophet that praise is not becoming in the mouth of a sinner, he strove to purify himself by interior acts of humility and contrition.

After these preliminaries, he had recourse again to God by making the preparatory prayer with remarkable fervor, it was easy to see how much he had at heart the obtaining from God the grace to make his prayer agreeable to Him. He insisted principally upon these words: *Domine, in unione illius divinæ intentionis*, etc., expressing thus his desire of reciting the divine office with the same intention and the same fervor that Jesus Christ while upon the earth, offered His prayers to His Father. When he said, *Deus, in adjutorium meum intende; Domine, ad adjuvandum me festina*, 'O God come to my assistance, O Lord make haste and help me' (Ps. lxix), it was with a deep feeling of his needs accompanied by ardent aspirations towards God to draw down His graces. If it happened sometimes, that he was not as recollected as he wished, he humbled himself profoundly so great was his desire that his mind and heart should be disposed to publish the praises of the Eternal. Like an able musician who uses his instrument only after it is tuned and fit to produce harmonious sounds, he never began his office without wholly preparing his heart. So it may well be said that his prayers were a pleasant music to the ears of Our Lord and that he performed as well as it is possible for men, the functions of the angels who in the heights of heaven celebrate upon their golden harps, the infinite glories of the Almighty.

When alone, he always recited the office on his knees with his head uncovered. If he had to say it with others, and the time and place permitted, generally before beginning it, he conversed with them on some passage of the psalms taken at random, and his reflections helped to bring to light from the Scriptures the treasures which were unknown to his hearers. "Another time," relate the professors who had known him at St. Flour, "he gave before the recitation of the divine office, a reading from the holy Scripture or the 'Imitation,' saying to us, 'Let us refresh our souls a little.' Sometimes he added, 'The words of the psalms have been produced by the Spirit of Love, we must then recite them with the same spirit, and consequently each word as it leaves our lips should be an act of love.' At other times he said: 'Let us recite the breviary in so fervent a manner that we shall not have to blush at the example of the virtues given in the life of the saint whose office we are about to say.'"

To perform this duty, he always sought the most suitable places and avoided those which would expose him to distractions. Often, when alone, he went to say his office before the holy tabernacle and recited it in a most earnest manner in an attitude of the most profound respect and abjection.

It was remarked that he was especially attentive when at the end of each psalm, he recited the Gloria Patri. He inclined his head then with great respect and seemed impressed with unusual devotion. "We must," said he, "be especially recollected during the doxology, so as to reanimate our fervor and dispose ourselves to recite the following psalm with greater devotion. If we recited the Gloria Patri with faith and piety, it would suffice to obtain the remission of the faults committed through frailty during the recitation of the breviary; by this means, also, we shall make reparation to God for all the distractions into which we have allowed ourselves to fall."

It was not rare, that absorbed in the contemplation of a truth, he interrupted himself in the middle of a psalm or even of a verse. "Suddenly," says an eye-witness, "he would stop with his eyes fixed on the heavens. Then he no longer saw anything about him; he was all absorbed in God."—Let us add the testimony of a Missionary who made the same observation. "I had," said he, "the advantage of frequently saying the divine office with him. This was the especial occasion from which I could judge how much he lived in God. Before beginning, he was, for a long time, silent and recollected upon his knees, preparing his soul for prayer, deeply impressed with the divine presence. He then began slowly but with a tone, an expression, an exterior, which excited every one to fervor and recollection. It took us considerable time to recite the office, at least one-third more than it would have taken others, because, at intervals, he stopped suddenly in the middle of a psalm or at a Gloria Patri, and remained silent till I asked him to continue. Then, without surprise or hurry, he quietly resumed the interrupted verse. Had he at each pause an ecstasy of spirit, or was he absorbed in meditation upon some truth? I do not know. Never have I questioned him upon his long and frequent pauses. Although he did not always stop at the same places, I have observed that the verses or psalms which spoke of the attributes and perfections of God, were those which inclined him most to contemplation. Our great feasts impressed him much, and when they were celebrated, he was more rapt than upon other days."

After saying the office, he seemed full of the holy ardor, he had drawn thence. "How often have we not marvelled," said several ecclesiastics, "when after the recitation of the breviary he made us share in the lights God had given him upon some passages of Scripture."

Talking one day of the advantages resulting from the fervent recitation of the breviary, he said; "The divine office is, for those who recite it well, a source of abundant grace; besides, it is a school in which we can learn to practise all the virtues. The Master who teaches us is the Holy Spirit of whom Our Lord has said, 'He will teach you all things.' (John xiv. 26.) Besides this Master, we have also the saints whose feasts we celebrate. They speak to us in an eloquent manner, showing by their conduct in what way we must correspond to the teachings of the Holy Spirit. How is it that, reciting the breviary every day, we do not become more holy?"

"We have," said Blessed Perboyre, "two powerful means of saving souls; the breviary and the holy sacrifice of the Mass. When we say our office, we are mediators with God, the same as when we offer the holy sacrifice of the Mass. But we can only be good mediators with God in as much as we are in the good graces of Him, by Whom we are all called to fulfil this duty. Without this, we should not come to Him, for it is greatly to be feared that all our petitions will only be rejected. To say the office with fruit, we must lead a truly sacerdotal life, strive to imitate Jesus Christ and to accomplish all that is required of us by the holy Scriptures, the decrees of the Sovereign Pontiff, and the Councils. Before reciting the office, let us ask Our Lord to bring to our lips and more especially to our hearts, the burning coal with which He purified the lips of the prophet, for the purer our soul is, the more efficacious wi our prayers be. I have often thought that we could well apply to the breviary the words which the holy old man Simeon said to Our Lord, 'This child is set for the fall and the resurrection of many.' (Luke ii. 34.) Consequently, let us fear and strive to enter into the disposition which the Church requires of us, so that we may draw down upon ourselves and upon all the people the benedictions of heaven."

---

## XII.

### HIS CHARITY TOWARDS HIS NEIGHBOR.

"They love not Jesus Christ," said Blessed John Gabriel, "who refuse to love their neighbor. Charity was the motive of all that Our Saviour did for men; we cannot be His true disciples without striving to imitate Him." During his whole life, he practised this maxim with much exactness, and he seemed to have but one heart and one soul with his. A sworn enemy to slander, he hastened adroitly to turn aside the conversation when evil was spoken of his neighbor. He had a great horror of the spirit of dispute and contention: and if he. sometimes, judged it proper to maintain his opinion because the interests of God seemed to demand it, he preserved the greatest regard for those who did not share his opinions. He loved to render a service and did it with the most amiable benevolence. When he was director of the novitiate, a priest who had known him at St. Flour, sent one of his brothers to Blessed Perboyre with a letter in which he recommended the boy to his care. This is the reply he received :

"*My dear Sir*,—About your brother of whom you write to me, I hasten to tell you that he arrived to-day very well and happy. His journey did not fatigue him at all. I can not express with what pleasure I embraced the dear child. As you have the goodness to suppose, I feel for him the affection of a brother. I regret that Philemon did not respond to St. Paul's admirable epistle, it would have helped me to reply worthily to your charming letter. If I am in fault, you must blame him ; my feelings are the same as his. Your brother has too many claims upon my interest and love not to merit from me all the best care and affection. By a charitable fiction imagine that I am another you.

" It is time for the post, so I hasten to close, recommending myself to your prayers, and assuring you that you may always consider me as one of your most affectionate and devoted friends etc."

His welcome, full of cordiality, charmed every one who met him. He had a special kindness for the afflicted whose pains he soothed with admirable skill. The souls of the just, detained in purgatory, had a large share in his prayers. In reference to his charity to the poor, a priest of the Mission relates: " He listened to them, willingly conversed with them, and never sent them away without an alms. Whoever they were, they were his poor and received help from him regularly, especially counsels for living for God alone. As his words had marvellous unction and no one could come near him or hear him, without feeling their effect, the poor readily became good Christians. Although he loved all, he had a marked predilection for the timid poor, seeing in them the person of Jesus Christ. His spirit of faith was so great that all the words of Our Lord were precious; they served to regulate his affections as well as his words and actions. This is why children were objects of his special affection; he loved to be surrounded by them, like his divine Master."

His charity manifested itself especially in his sweetness towards those with whom he lived. "I have never seen any one who possessed it in so great a degree," said one of his pupils, "all his actions were stamped with this virtue of gentleness; and if, sometimes, circumstances required him to take a severe tone, it was easily seen there was nothing of passion about him and duty alone forced him to act. An old vicar at Montauban gives him this eulogy: 'M. Perboyre was not only gentle, but he was gentleness itself.'"

Faithful in remembering the services done him, he promptly forgot injuries, or, if he remembered them, it was to show more kindness to those who did him any wrong. One day, as he accompanied a canon of Montauban through the streets of Paris, some workmen passing along loaded them with gross insults. Blessed Perboyre paid no attention to them, and after walking a few steps, said to the priest: "These poor people are much to be pitied, they do not know what harm they do; it should be an especial reason for praying for them, and recommending them to God in the holy sacrifice of the Mass." If any one was prejudiced against him, although not at all to blame, he was always ready to make the first advances; several times he was seen, after the example of St. Vincent, going before Mass to find the persons whom he knew were badly disposed towards him; he fell upon his knees before them and begged them to pardon him the wrongs he might have done them, although he had nothing with which to reproach himself.

This charity proceeded from an ardent zeal for the glory of God and the salvation of his neighbor. "In the holy Scripture," he said, "our Lord compares priests to fishermen and hunters: is this not to show us clearly that we must always be occupied with the salvation of souls and never allow an opportunity for doing good to escape?" A deacon, who was soon to be ordained, came to Blessed Perboyre one day telling him of the fear he felt at seeing the time of his ordination approach. He replied smilingly: "Ah! my dear friend, what is it that you fear so much? You will be the sooner in a state to glorify God and make yourself useful to your neighbor."

According to him, all the words, all the actions of a priest must be so many baits to attract souls; he succeeded marvellously in this by his whole conduct. John Gabriel could not see a soul in sin without feeling himself urged to withdraw him from it. When he was appointed director of the novices, having perceived that the barber who came there every week, lived in entire forgetfulness of his religious duties, he immediately undertook to enlighten him upon his true interests and by his counsels, his gentleness and his prayers, converted him and strengthened him in virtue till his death. This man never spoke of his benefactor but with the deepest gratitude and declared that his gentleness had won a complete victory over him.

Prudent and enlightened in his zeal, avoiding all that might be considered precipitation, Blessed Perboyre knew what the time and circumstances demanded, whether gentleness or firmness, affection or patience; he took the measures to bring to a happy conclusion all the works he undertook for the glory of God; but he depended only upon the assistance of grace. In his prayers he often implored Our Lord to be pleased to accord to His Church ministers according to His Heart; it was the cause of deep affliction to him to see priests indifferent to the interests of God. During ember week, he redoubled his fervor and exhorted others to pray to draw down the benedictions of Heaven upon the ordinations.

When he had to preach, he prepared himself especially by prayer, and he often recommended the practice. "If Our Lord," he said, "does not inspire us what to say, if He preach not with us, it is in vain that we strive to do anything of ourselves. I do not blame those who consult books, but it seems to me the first and last book that we must consult is the crucifix; it is there we find true light and we draw the unction necessary to touch hearts. If we take care to prepare ourselves sufficiently at the foot of the cross, each word from our mouths will be a burning coal to warm and inflame hearts." They asked him one day, if it was necessary to make a long preparation for preaching; and if it was not preferable in the pulpit to follow the inspirations of zeal; he replied: "Our Lord prepared Himself during thirty years to preach His gospel; most preachers do nothing, because they do not prepare themselves enough; before going into the pulpit, he must possess the science he wishes to teach; he must, above all, pray and meditate. Time passed at the foot of the crucifix is best and most usefully employed. St. Paul wished to know only Jesus, and Him crucified: he preached nothing else. It is at the foot of the cross, the saints prepared themselves, it was thence they drew those words of fire which inflamed hearts. If preachers used the same means, they would obtain the same results."

The fervent zeal of the missionary was especially displayed in the tribunal of penance; several who came to confession to him declared that it seemed to them, that they saw or heard not a man but an angel, or Jesus Christ Himself. The kindness with which he treated penitents dissipated the shame and apprehension which accompanied the avowal of faults and he made them desire to arise from them and never to fall again.

Having consulted him upon the manner in which he should conduct himself in the tribunal of penance, a young priest received from him the advice which we reproduce here because it breathes the spirit of faith and zeal which animated Blessed Perboyre. "When you enter the holy tribunal, remember that you come to reconcile souls with God, combat hell, rejoice heaven and fulfil the most sublime function that Our Lord fulfilled in the whole course of His mortal life. Should not this penetrate you with holy fear and fill you with admiration for the powers that God has confided to you? Oh! How much ought you to humble yourself, when you are about to perform such functions! 'I go to purify others,' we must say to ourselves, 'but am I pure myself? I aim at combating sin in others, but am I faithful in combating it in my own soul? I aim at exciting others to labor to attain perfection, but am I full of zeal for my own sanctification? What a source of instruction for us! Before going to the confessional, think also what great need you have for the succors of grace. I invoke Mary, the holy patrons, and the holy angel guardians of the persons who come to confession; have recourse especially to Jesus Christ, begging Him to help you to fulfil this ministry with the same sentiments that animated Him when on earth.

"When you are in front of the confessional, imagine you see written upon the door these words, 'How terrible is this place.' '*Quam terribilis est locus iste!*' (Gen. xxviii. 17.) for if you are judge now you will also be judged in your turn, and much more severely than the people who address themselves to you. Consider that this confessional, which you are about to enter, is full of dangers for an unmortified priest, and that there is no place in which he is more exposed. The demons, who see how prejudicial this ministry is to them, make every effort to hinder the priest from fulfilling this duty profitably; they attack him in the most terrible manner and if he does not keep himself on his guard, if he does not act with the spirit of faith, not only will he do no good but he will even incur the greatest perils. Consequently, let us fear lest in seeking to save others, we allow our own souls to be lost so that the demons may say to us what was said to Our Lord Jesus Christ on the cross. 'He saved others; Himself He can not save.' (Matt. xxvii, 42.) These words, which were a blasphemy in the mouths of the Jews, will become a truth against the priest, who through want of vigilance will have lost his soul through the tribunal of penance. Nevertheless, it must not cause us too great fear; we must confide in the protection of the Blessed Virgin, the angels and saints of heaven and in the special assistance which Our Lord accords to all those who encounter dangers in His name and for His glory. Faith shows us that it is not we alone who enter the confessional but that the Prince of the heavenly court is with us, and if we seek there only the interests of God, we shall leave it full of merits and be very pleasing to His eyes.

"Once you have entered the confessional, be wholly absorbed in the ministry that you have to fulfil. When you hear your penitent give you the name of Father, assume for him a compassionate charity and when you give him the blessing, pronounce the words with faith and the ardent desire that God will bestow on the Christian present, the grace you ask of God for him. If you pray without attention, your blessing will be of no use, but if you make it with fervor you have every reason to believe that God will hear your prayer, and will accord to your penitent, the sincerity and contrition which he needs. If we knew of how many graces we deprive souls, when we do not perform the ceremonies and prayers of the Church with faith, we would be much more attentive to perform them well.

"During the whole time you treat with your penitent, I counsel you to consider him with a spirit of faith and represent to yourself the image of Our Lord disfigured in him by sin, to which you must restore its first beauty. For our neighbor is not only the image of Our Lord, but faith teaches us that, by our baptism, we have become members of Jesus Christ, consequently, all Christians united in Jesus Christ who is their chief, are made part of His mystical body. Jesus Christ has two bodies, His mystical body and His natural body. Jesus Christ in His natural body, as St. Paul says, is 'holy, innocent, undefiled, separated from sinners, and made higher than the heavens,' (Heb. vii, 26,) but He is not so in His mystical body. As sinners, as well as the just belong to Him, it is the body of Jesus Christ that is sick and disfigured in sinners. We may apply to the mystical body of Our Saviour what the prophet said of Him in His passion. 'We have seen him . . . as it were a leper.' '*Vidimus eum quasi leprosum.*' (Isai. liii.) But Our Lord suffers at seeing Himself in this state and desires ardently to be delivered from sin, which inspires Him with much horror. When a penitent comes to you in the holy tribunal of penance, reflect that Jesus Himself sends you this member of His mystical body and says to you: 'As long as you did it to one of these my least brethren, you did it to me.' '*Quandiu fecistis uni ex fratribus meis minimis, mihi fecistis.* (Matt. xxv, 40.) If you despise this soul, if you neglect it, it is I whom you despise, it is I whom you neglect *mihi fecistis.* If you do not treat him kindly, if you discourage him, it is I whom you treat badly; *mihi fecistis,* I, Who am your Creator, your Benefactor, your Father, Who have borne so many fatigues and humiliations, Who have shed all My blood for you, *mihi fecistis.* If, on the contrary you are filled with charity for this soul, I shall remember all that you have done, *mihi fecistis.* I imagine that Our Lord displays all His tenderness to you to touch your heart, that He shows you His wounds to excite your compassion in favor of His sick members; imagine that you see written on your penitent's forehead these words. 'As long as you did it to one of these my least brethren you did it to me.' *Mihi fecistis.* Remember that when you perform this duty with zeal and faith, you fulfil all the spiritual works of mercy to which Our Lord has promised the kingdom of heaven. Consider how great your joy will be, when you will appear before His tribunal and He will say to you: 'Come, ye blessed of my Father, possess the kingdom prepared for you from the foundation of the world.' (Matt. xxv. 34.) 'I was naked because I had lost the robe of innocence, and you have given it to Me again. I was hungry and thirsty in My members and you have given Me food and drink. I was in exile, because sin had driven Me from these souls which were My kingdom, and by your zeal you have re-established Me upon My throne; I was sick and suffering, and you have dressed My wounds; I was in prison and in chains, and you have visited Me, you have consoled Me, delivered Me from My chains, and set Me free.'

"Represent to yourself, also, the august Virgin Mary who comes, with her heart pierced with sorrow, to beg you to take care of the souls so dear to her; for upon Calvary, she made a sacrifice of the natural body of her Son to give life to the members of His mystical body. What sorrow she feels at seeing these members dead, or dying, or covered with wounds! Can you reject the prayers of so good a Mother or despise her tears? Represent to yourself, also, the guardian angels and holy patrons of these souls, who come to implore you to do all you can to snatch them from hell and open for them the gates of heaven.

"During the whole time you are in the confessional, do not lose sight of Jesus Christ, Whose place you hold; often ask yourself, 'If Jesus Christ were here, how would He act? What would He say?' Often raise your heart to Him to ask Him for the graces which are needed on this occasion. When you are obliged to hear anything relating to the beautiful virtue say to Him, 'Jesus, who has loved chastity so much, have mercy on us.' '*Jesu amator castitatis, miserere nobis.*' When you are tempted to impatience, say to Him, 'Jesus, meek and humble of heart, have mercy on us.' '*Jesu mitis et humilis corde, miserere nobis.*' If you are perplexed about giving a decision, implore His light and say to Him, 'Jesus, Angel of the great council, have mercy on us.' '*Jesu, magni consilii Angele, miserere nobis.*'

"When a great sinner comes to you, think that he is a sheep that the good Shepherd has sought for a long time; and that you can do nothing that will cause Him more joy than to labor to bring him back. If he is lukewarm, think that Jesus Christ sends him to you that you may efface the spots which disfigure him and make him an object of disgust to Our Lord. If it is a just soul, think that Jesus desires you to conduct him by degrees to a much greater perfection. When it is a person in a community, remember that it is especially of these persons that He has said: 'You are dead: and your life is hid with Jesus Christ in God.' (Col. iii, 3.) You must make him understand that these little faults to which the spouses of Jesus Christ yield are like so many thorns which wound their divine Spouse in the apple of His eye.

"It is a very useful practice, when in the holy tribunal to hold in the hands a crucifix and often to look upon it so as to draw thence the charity, patience, and zeal which are needed. I counsel you to use it. But beware, especially in the confessional, of listening with indifference to the account of the outrages that have been done your divine Master. One of the greatest misfortunes that can happen to a priest is to listen coldly to the sins that are confessed to him. How dare you pretend that you love Our Lord, if you cannot say with the Prophet, 'The reproaches of them that reproach Thee are fallen upon me' (Ps., lxviii, 10), '*Opprobria exprobrantium tibi ceciderunt super me?*'

"When a person who comes to you, accuses himself of some grave fault say to yourself: 'There is not a fault which I may not commit.' Endeavor to watch with greater care not to fall yourself. If you walked along a slippery road and if you saw many people fall, you would be afraid and would take greater care not to fall yourself. You must, with much greater reason, use the same prudence in regard to your own soul; for we all walk in the same path and if the way is slippery for others, it is no less so for us. There is no place where a priest may receive more useful instruction than in the holy tribunal; there is no place where he has to renounce himself more, and where he can acquire more merit."

The priest for whom the Servant of God drew up

this rule of conduct which you have just read, did not weary of asking him and hearing him speak. "This advice was not easy to obtain," added he, "for I had to urge him, and return often to the charge, to overcome his modesty. But what elevated thoughts, what beautiful sentiments he expressed in his conversation! He spoke in a gentle, affectionate tone of voice, in so impressive, convincing a manner, that one of his conversations did me more good than a whole retreat. His words dropped into my soul with the sweetness of honey, and left a deep impression there. What he told me impressed me the more as I knew that he practised it himself. It was one of his maxims, that a priest should not command anything of which he did not give the example and that there is nothing more shameful than to show others the way of perfection and not walk in it oneself."

An extract from a letter written by Blessed Perboyre when about to enter China, will alone suffice to show how pure and ardent was the zeal which inflamed his heart. We cite it here and with it ends this chapter. "This evening," said the generous Missionary, "I embarked for Fo-Kien on a Chinese junk, conducted by two Christians. Being a soldier in whom rashness held the place of courage, I felt my heart thrill at the approach of the combat. I was never more happy than on this occasion. I know not what is reserved for me in the career which opens before me; doubtless it has plenty of crosses, the daily bread of the missionary. And what can we wish better in going to preach Jesus crucified? May He make me relish the sweetness of His chalice of bitterness! May He make me worthy of my predecessors, whom I am going to join! May He not permit any of us to degenerate from the beautiful models our Congregation has given us in foreign countries! In this century, M. Appiani, that invincible confessor of fidelity to the Holy See, who in China displayed all the virtues found in the first children of St. Vincent, has already received the reward of his thirty-five years' apostolate, and a few years ago, M. Clet, full of merits, after an equally long career, had the happiness of dying a martyr; all the Christians who knew him, never weary of telling his good deeds and his virtues. We do not lack examples and motives to excite and sustain us. Nevertheless, such is my feebleness that all seem to me insufficient if I can not depend on the powerful help of your prayers and those of our confrères and our Sisters of Charity. So I shall continue to demand them with much persistency, etc."

---

## XIII.

### HIS HUMILITY AND OBEDIENCE.

As Blessed John Gabriel had his eyes continually fixed upon Him Who said to us, "Learn of Me, because I am meek and humble of heart," (Matt. xi. 29.) he had a special affection for contempt, abasement and a hidden life. Those who lived with him were struck with his humility and all delight in testifying that they never saw anyone more humble than he. He took for his motto these words of the "Imitation," "Love to be unknown and esteemed as nothing," (Book I, Chap. I). Having learned in China that his uncle had allowed some of his letters to be printed, he was aghast; he expressed to his uncle the pain it caused him and notwithstanding his respect and affection, he hinted that he would stop writing to him if he again gave publicity to his correspondence.

This is said of him by a person who had attentively studied him: "Never did he speak of himself, his country, his relatives or of anything that belonged to him, whether far or near. It was impossible to know from him where he had been, or in what employment he was engaged in the Congregation. Never did he ask what was thought of his person; never did he show himself hurt when by chance anyone said or did anything that could vex him. He always showed as much modesty in his words as in his manner, his bearing breathed only humility and religion; blame or praise found him always the same, he despised praise because he thought he was not worthy of it, he willingly accepted criticism because he thought he merited nothing else."

He could scarcely comprehend how he could be endured in the offices bestowed upon him; he was astonished that the Congregation deigned to think of him. Conversing familiarly one day with one of his sisters who was a Sister of Charity, he declared that if he had known before receiving holy orders what a priest is in the eyes of faith, he would never have consented to the imposition of hands. Writing from China to his uncle, he said, he did not consider himself a missionary, but as an abortive attempt at one. In a word, he esteemed himself as abominable and incapable of any good; these were his very expressions.

"I do not think," said one of the professors at St.

Flour, "that any sinner in the world ever took more trouble to hide his faults than John Gabriel did to hide his virtues. In familiar conversation he displayed admirable virtue but he had no idea of the impression that he made. Nothing was more touching to me than to hear him speak of the things of God. One day finding that my mind was distracted before Mass, I went to him and said, 'M. Superior, I am about to celebrate Mass; I have tried to prepare myself, but I am not recollected; you will do me a great favor if you, yourself will make your prayer with me; what you will say will do me good.' Blessed Perboyre began excusing himself, I objected that he would be the cause of my not saying Mass well. 'But do you believe that I am capable of praying? Alas! God knows how badly I pray.' He ended by yielding to my entreaty and kneeling down, took for his text, 'Peace be to you,' (Luke xxiv. 36), and speaking for nearly half an hour on the peace of the Lord, he showed how precious this peace is, how important to acquire it, and what we must do to obtain it. His words were so beautiful and touching that I was filled with admiration."

On another occasion, the Superior of the Grand Seminary was less fortunate in making a similar request. The Missionaries met together to make their annual retreat, and the Servant of God followed the exercises. The Superior gave conferences twice a day, but knowing the virtue of his confrère, and persuaded that John Gabriel could speak much better than he did, proposed that the Servant of God should take charge of the office. Blessed Perboyre, seeing in this action only an excess of humility on the part of the superior, firmly refused, notwithstanding the efforts made to overcome his own. "See now," said he, "what modesty on the part of M. Superior! And to whom does he address himself, to the most incapable of all. How I would have exercised your patience if you had been obliged to listen to me during a whole week!"

During prayer or meditation, his bearing expressed the annihilation into which he was plunged in the presence of the divine Majesty, but the sight of his miseries was for him a motive to approach God with more confidence, as the following trait will show.—A priest whom he directed, came one day to tell him that he felt a great repugnance to offering the holy sacrifice of the Mass, because it seemed to him that his conscience was not pure enough. Blessed Perboyre answered him: "You afflict yourself about what for me is a reason to approach near to God with less fear; when I go to the altar without having heard interior reproaches, I am frightened at the thought that I go to God with presumption; if, on the contrary, my conscience gives me some reproach, I have less inquietude because I come near to God with more humility."

He was always ready to receive any observation that others wished to make to him, and with him they could dispense with the choice words and artifices of speech, to which they often had to have recourse so as not to awaken the touchiness of self-love. "God Who wished to make him more holy," says a missionary, "sometimes took away from him the approbation of men, and made him walk in the way of tribulations. I saw him painfully affected on one occasion, where his zeal, in every respect so just, as events afterward proved, had drawn upon him mortifying admonitions. I admired his humility and charity to those, who with good intentions, had imprudently rebuked him.—I had also been witness of a contradiction very painful to his heart; he seemed sensible of it, too, but this trial only displayed in relief all the prudence, charity and patience he possessed and the next day he thought himself obliged to ask my pardon for this slight display of feeling. Another time, fearing that he had spoken a little shortly, in my presence, to a seminarian who had merited it, he made his excuses for the scandal he thought he had caused me; all this gave me a great idea of his humility and his purity of conscience."

A priest who knew how much Blessed Perboyre delighted in humiliations, wished, one day, to put him to the test, and addressed to him some unflattering words, which were received with much satisfaction. Then he changed his batteries and attacked the Congregation of the Mission, thinking that he would be more sensitive to criticism of the community than of his own person, but this second attempt had no more success than the first.

In support of what has already been said about the humility of John Gabriel, we cite also a letter he wrote from China to his brother, Jacques, living in Paris:

"*My dear Brother*:—" I owe you many thanks for the prayers you have said for my intention. I need them very much. Continue them, dear brother, and multiply them still more if it is possible. The good

God will keep an account of them and reward you. I must, however, inform you that your zeal goes astray upon one point. When you beg God to make me a second St. Francis Xavier, you make a demand which is not certainly in the order of His Providence; for it could not be heard without working in the first place two great miracles, one in my body and the other in my soul. On the one hand, the weakness of my constitution and my infirmities of which you know a part, render me physically incapable of great labors; on the other, my great and innumerable spiritual miseries leave me no reason to doubt that I am one of those of whom it is written 'Being abominable—and to every good work, reprobate,' (Titus i. 16.) '*Cum sint abominati et ad omne opus bonum reprobi.*' No, I will be a no more marvellous man in China than in France; it is enough, my dear brother, if I may be a good little nag. If, then, you wish to pray to God for what is agreeable to Him and useful to me, ask of Him first, my conversion and sanctification, then the grace not to allow me to spoil His work in my little sphere but to allow me to accomplish at least in part, His designs upon me and to grant me mercy for the rest. Cease not, however, to pray with all possible fervor for the salvation of the poor Chinese; every day a great number of them are cast into hell. Do not, however, trouble about what persons or means God may use; the resources are infinite in the treasury of Providence. When we pray to obtain rain for our fields, we do not ask to have it fall without clouds or that these clouds break sooner than any others on the horizon."

There can scarcely be conceived sentiments more beautiful or more elevated than his. His was a soul which sought only the glory of God and which entirely forgot self.

With a humility so profound, with a heart so filled with the love of God, and the desire of imitating Jesus Christ, the obedience of John Gabriel could not help being perfect, and of this his entire life gives testimony. From his childhood, he was distinguished for his docility, and this disposition only increased the whole time he lived in community. Abandoning himself absolutely to the guidance of his superiors in all that concerned him, he showed so great respect for them that he would not make the least murmur against them, no matter what happened him. Everything was for the best in his eyes; the orders of his superiors represented to him the dominion of God, Himself, and he was so well established in submission that after the example of his divine Master, he would have prefered to lose his life rather than to have failed in obedience.

---

## XIV.

### POVERTY, CHASTITY, MODESTY, MORTIFICATION AND PATIENCE OF BLESSED PERBOYRE.

JOHN GABRIEL took great delight in poverty because Jesus Christ had so greatly loved it and recommended it to his disciples. As we have related elsewhere different traits which show how great a lover he was of this virtue, we shall limit ourselves to citing here what is said by a missionary who knew him when he was director of the novitiate. "The Servant of

God greatly loved neatness and order in his room, his clothes, etc., but everything bore the impress of poverty. On his walls were pictures without frames or with frames of blackened wood. These represented Our Lord, the Blessed Virgin, St. Joseph, St. Vincent de Paul, etc. Engravings, famous as works of art, and books luxuriously bound were not found in his room. He generally wore during the week an old cassock which he had chosen from the clothes room, and it was only obedience which could induce him to wear any other. New clothes did not please him and he used them only on Sundays and holidays and then with some regret. He allowed nothing to be wasted, not even a sheet of paper, he collected carefully the clothes and shoes which were to be given to the poor. They also profited by his slender means, for he spent nothing on himself.

If he held poverty in great esteem, he was no less attentive in preserving the precious treasure of chastity. The grace, which in his childhood had inspired him with a love for his virtue, preserved him afterwards amid a thousand dangers, as it protected Daniel in the lion's den and the three young Hebrews in the fiery furnace. Not only would he be greatly pained by the least unbecoming word, but he wished that people would not even pronounce the words purity and chastity, saying with St. Francis de Sales, that this virtue is lost in being named. He had no intercourse with persons of the other sex, which was not rigorously indispensable, and he spoke to them in a grave, laconic manner. An instance will show his great delicacy upon this point. At the time he made a visit to his family, one of his sisters who thought of entering a religious community, asked him for a private conversation. Blessed Perboyre consented, but asked one of his brothers to remain at a distance in the room. The brother being still young, quickly forgot the request and deserted his post, which earned him a reproof from John Gabriel. Those who consider this an exaggerated precaution, must remember the example of St. Vincent and several other saints who have shown extreme delicacy about everything concerning the virtue of chastity.

Every one was impressed by the modesty which shone in his face and his whole exterior. He kept his eyes lowered and never rested them on the person to whom he spoke. In the street he walked silently with his companions; if the latter spoke to him he generally waited for another time to reply; and when he was leaving town or returning to the house he would say, "You asked me such a thing I think, etc.," then he hastened to answer the question.

To modesty, Blessed Perboyre joined a great love for mortification. Although always suffering he did not interrupt on that account either his work or his prayers. He refused his eyes many innocent little gratifications such as looking at a beautiful flower, a charming view, or a handsome monument. A priest with whom he travelled, one day showed him some beautiful landscapes and remarkable buildings, seeking to excite John Gabriel's curiosity and admiration, but his enthusiasm only obtained from the Servant of God some glances in compliance which distracted him not from the sole object with which his heart loved to occupy itself. When he was seated he did not lean against the back of his chair; he did not cross his legs, nor give his body any comfortable posture which he regarded as a sensuality. Faithful to this spirit of mortification, he went only to the parlor through necessity, and in going there, recommended himself to Our Lord, then listened kindly to what was said to him, replied modestly, entering into no conversation foreign to the subject of the visit, addressing always some edifying words to his visitor and returned with joy to his cell. This virtue was no less manifested in his conversation and recreations. "He had," said one of the pupils of the seminary, "something of the silence of St. Joseph. His conversation was not hasty or noisy, but sweet, agreeable and edifying. He proposed no questions unless to give occasion for some edifying words or to draw a soul nearer to God. Curiosity about human things was entirely extinct in him. When he was questioned, he recollected himself before responding, consulted God and begged Him to inspire him what to say, then made with gentle kindness a response always wise and animated with the spirit of faith. If others differed with him, he generally kept a modest silence but did not dispute or raise his voice or seek to have his opinion prevail. To give a decision he often used the words of holy Scripture, with which he was imbued, and when he employed his own words, there was something divine about them which gave them a great unction, making them delightful to hear while they penetrated the soul. Many believed that the Holy Ghost inspired him and spoke by his mouth. His conversation, simple, and without pretension, was in Heaven more than upon earth, and raised to God those who heard him. When he joined a group, he soon brought the conversation naturally to Heavenly things. If any one persisted in speaking of worldly affairs, he kept silence and soon quietly disappeared. John Gabriel having received all the gifts of the Holy Spirit, was like a seraph on earth before going to Heaven; he truly seemed absorbed in God, gently, without difficulty or constraint, and he always walked in His holy presence."

As to his mortification at meals, we again allow one of his old seminarians to speak. "In the refactory we saw that necessity was his only rule in eating. Some confrères having related the impression produced on them when they served at table, I began to observe him with special attention when my turn for serving at table came; and, looking at him I was reminded of this passage of St. Bernard which he had quoted in conversation, 'Let us go to dinner as to a punishment and to supper as a medicine.' '*Ad prandium tanquam ad supplicium, ad cœnam tanquam ad medicinam.*' His attitude, the expression of his face, clearly showed how much his dispositions conformed to the thought of the holy Abbot of Clairvaux. Although he took great care to avoid singularity, and to hide his mortifications, he was several times discovered putting a powder on his food to give it a bitter, disagreeable taste. When a dish was well prepared, he took but little of it, until he put the bitter powder on it, then he kept it upon his plate eating it slowly, the better to taste the bitterness. His mortification was so great that we were astonished that he could live on so little nourishment and yet he allowed himself this small refection only with sighs and regrets."

Although he was usually weak and nearly always

in an almost invalid state, he was not one for seeking remedies or employing all the little cares which unmortified persons make their study and occupation. In sickness, he took the medicines that were given him and allowed his nurse to treat him as he wished. During the last winter which he passed in Paris, the weather being very severe, one of the seminarians especially observed him. "He went about his ordinary duties," says this student, "without paying the least attention to the cold. As I pitied him, I went to the person who had charge of these matters, to ask him to have a fire lighted in John Gabriel's room. The Servant of God willingly made ready for it, but his old stove would not burn and gave out only smoke. Blessed Perboyre did not attend to it, so as to have more time to devote to prayer."

Not content with making his body suffer, he applied himself especially to interior mortification. We may judge by the following details, which are given by another seminarian, the great progress John Gabriel made in this virtue. "One of the things that impressed me most about this holy confrère, was the great dominion which he seemed to exercise over himself, his senses and all the movements of nature. Everything in his exterior, his looks, his walk, his bearing, his conversation, the tone of his voice, announced a man entirely dead to himself and continually united to God. I often considered him with close attention, examined his slightest step, scrutinized the motives of his conduct, and I have never discovered in him the least indication of self-seeking, vain complacency or impatience. My attention redoubled when some praise was given him, or if he received some mark of respect; but I observed that all this made no impression on him and he seemed to have nothing to overcome on these occasions. The same could be said of disagreeable occurrences, railleries or jokes which he endured with a calmness, serenity and forgetfulness of self which never varied. If a thing was painful or flattering to nature, he was no more moved by it than if he was acting about an affair that did not concern him."

This chapter ends with an instance of the patience of the Servant of God. Having started for Carcassonne, he intended to spend some days with the confrères who directed the Seminary of that town; he arrived there about midnight, in company with a missionary who, though endowed with many other good qualities, had not so much patience as he. When they got down from the carriage the weather was threatening and while crossing the yard, they were overtaken by a heavy rain. Arrived at the door, they had extreme difficulty in awakening the porter, who reposed peacefully while the rain poured upon them. He appeared at last, but was still half asleep, and as the darkness of the night prevented his distinguishing those who stood before him, he did not recognize them as priests, but imagined they were some night-rovers or vagabonds who wished to amuse themselves at his expense. Then without taking the trouble to examine whether he was deceived or not, he left them at the door and returned to his bed. During this scene, Blessed Perboyre said not a word and congratulated himself on having something to suffer; but his companion who was of a lively disposition, began to knock and ring with more violence.

John Gabriel exhorted him to patience, but uselessly, for his confrère was not disposed, like him, to pass the night in the rain with soaking clothes. At last, the director whose room was upon the street, was awakened, went to the window, recognized the travelers, came down and hastened to let them in. The companion of the Servant of God, greatly desired to scold the porter, but John Gabriel became his advocate, pleaded his cause and saved him from a reprimand.

---

## XV.

### HIS PRUDENCE, SIMPLICITY AND FIDELITY IN FULFILLING THE DUTIES OF HIS STATE.

"PRUDENCE is the science of the Saints." *Scientia sanctorum prudentia.* John Gabriel possessed it in a high degree. He fulfilled the different employments confided to him with a wisdom which made him the admiration of those with whom he lived. He did not begin his actions hastily. Before undertaking anything he consulted God and he did not weary of questioning His will until it was clearly indicated to him. It was necessary to be with him often to be convinced that this was a practice he never neglected. Frequently he put off till the next day, and even for a longer time, his response to questions put to him, so as to have leisure to consult God. "Before acting," he often repeated, "we must consult God, the great Master of science and say to Him with humble confidence: 'Lord, what dost Thou wish me to do? What dost Thou wish me to say? What advice dost Thou wish me to give?' If we were more faithful in consulting Him, He would never fail to illuminate us with His divine light and we would avoid many faults." When his advice was asked, he never failed, after the example of St. Vincent de Paul, to raise his heart to God and beg him to enlighten him. In the counsels he gave, a stranger to all the calculations of human prudence, he sought only the interests of God and of the persons asking his advice. A great many, who were docile to him and listened to his advice, rejoiced that they overcome their repugnance and renounced their own lights which inclined them to act differently: experience having proved that his judgment was correct.

Prudence must always be accompanied by the simplicity which Our Lord recommends and in this, also, Blessed Perboyre was distinguished. He had so well preserved candor and ingenuousness from early youth, that there was never observed in him the slightest shadow of dissimulation; this precious quality gained for him the unreserved confidence of all who knew him. In imitation of Our Lord, his divine Master, he delighted in being with children and poor country people, who, in their turn, took much pleasure in conversing with him, because his simplicity put them perfectly at their ease. When he left the ecclesiastical school of Saint Flour, the parents of the pupils said: "What a great loss he is to us! It did us so much good to talk to him." He had a great horror of everything that savored of pride, domineering or affectation. He was simple in his apparel, his manners and his language. The impress of this virtue is found in all his letters, notably in the following addressed to one of his sisters for whom he stood sponsor at the baptismal font and who was then a Sister of Charity:

"*My very dear Sister*,—Our brothers have already received several of my letters and you, not the least little note. But console yourself, my dear god-daughter, now it is, at last, your turn and this time you shall have all and they none. At the time I am writing to you, you will have received news of me from the letter I wrote in Batavia to Jacques, the early part of July. You have heard that our voyage has been a happy one, thanks to the merciful providence of Our Lord, and the protection of Holy Mary. Notwithstanding my fears, I have arrived safe and sound in China and what is more, I am in better health than when I left France. Now, you must thank God for our good voyage with as much fervor as you implored it of Him. We have been in Macao two months and a half and our health continues very good. We must again become children and begin anew the a, b, c, or rather there is no a or b or any other letter of the alphabet in the Chinese language, which on that account is no less difficult to learn. When we know a little passably well, we shall use it to make war on satan in this vast Chinese Empire, where there are still so many millions of heathens. I hope that you will pray especially for me, that Our Lord will give me the grace to labor efficaciously to extend His reign in souls and at the same time to sanctify myself a little. I do not insist much on it because I think you will do all that you can and that you will even be a begging Sister to those persons who are rich in fervor and zeal. After fulfilling this double duty, keep yourself perfectly tranquil about me, without being uneasy about my health or my dangers; do not imagine each moment that all the Chinese are at my heels and think only of destroying me. These are the men whom I love much more than I fear. I assure you that I do not fear even the emperor, mandarin or soldiers. I have always in this country, a special enemy from whom I must defend myself. From him there is really much to fear: he is the worst person whom I know; he is not a Chinese but a European. He was baptized in his infancy, and afterwards was ordained a priest. From France he came to China with us upon the same ship. I have no doubt that he will pursue me everywhere and he will certainly cause my ruin if I have the misfortune of falling alone into his hands. I will not name him for you already know him. If you could obtain his conversion, you would render him a great service and your brother would be indebted to you for his happiness.

"Remember, my dear sister, that I do not forget you and that I often recommend you to Our Lord especially in the holy sacrifice of the Mass. I feel our separation no less than you. But we must make some sacrifices for Him Who died for us, Who will recompense so generously those who abandon everything for His service. What consoles me when you are so far away from me is the confidence I have that you will always be a worthy Sister of Charity by your humility and simplicity, by your obedience to your superiors, your piety and fervor in spiritual exercises, your zeal and patience in the service of the poor. Your vocation is grand! You must have the spirit of it and this you must ask of God Who desires much more to give it to you than you desire to receive it.

"As I have not written this time to my parents, I leave to you the duty and pleasure of giving them news of me. Tell them that I embrace them with all my heart. I wish that they were as contented and in as good health as I am."

Blessed John Gabriel was no less attentive in fulfilling with fervor and punctuality all the duties of his state. He loved his vocation beyond measure; he regarded as one of the greatest graces which he had received from God, his being called to the Congregation; and he could conceive no greater misfortune that for a missionary to abandon it. He would have willingly sacrificed himself for the community, to which he was attached from the depth of his bowels, according to his own expression. He could not consider the means of sanctification which he found in it without being filled with joy and gratitude. He loved to talk of his happiness to his confrères, and incited them, by his discourse, to live conformably to their state, but we must repeat here what has been said elsewhere, his example preached more efficaciously than his words and exhibited the faithful portrait of what a good missionary should be.

One of his sweetest pleasures while he lived in China was to receive letters telling him of the blessings that God bestowed on the Congregation. You will be convinced of this upon reading the following reply addressed to a priest of the mother house of the Congregation in Paris:

"*My very dear Confrère.*—The grace of God be with you always! The dear letter you had the goodness to write me last year in the month of February, arrived this year in July. It will be impossible to tell you all the pleasure and edification it gave me. From one end to the other it breathes the perfume of simplicity. It is the odor of this blessed Congregation which God has pleased to render more and more worthy of St. Vincent. You had the kindness to tell me in detail of the young confrères whom I knew at the seminary where they endured me with so much charity. The picture you gave me of their labors and success is a suitable completion of their edifying example, the remembrance of which I shall always preserve. When you have the opportunity please do not neglect to recommend me to their prayers as I so greatly need them. Upon yours, dear confrère I always depend, more than upon my own. I depend not a little also on those of M. Lego, who still takes much interest in the last of men. I beg you to give my regards to him and to all those who have the charity to honor me with their remembrance and especially with a share in their prayers. "I am, etc."

Full of filial tenderness for St. Vincent, he could not speak or think of him without being penetrated with love and veneration. He often read his life, and his conferences to the first missionaries, conferences which breathed the spirit of Jesus Christ. Constantly studying the constitutions which this great Saint has given his children, he never wearied of admiring this master-piece of piety, prudence and truly divine wisdom, and his conduct so faithfully reproduced the heavenly teachings which they contained, that his life was nothing else but the constitutions of St. Vincent put into practice. He thought that the missionaries had no need to seek elsewhere for means of perfection, because all that could be desired in this respect they could find in the life and writings of their blessed Founder. When he was preparing to start for China, his sister Antoinette, a Sister of Charity living in Paris, came to see him and asked him to give her in writing the counsels he thought would be useful to her. Although he knew it would be a great pleasure to her if he satisfied her demand, he contented himself with replying: "You have your holy rules, the conferences and life of St. Vincent, these will be sufficient, you have only to follow their instructions." When the hour of separation came, seeing her overwhelmed by the sacrifice God required of her, he led her to the chapel, and in the presence of the precious relics of St. Vincent said to her: "You must not grieve so much for your brother since you have your Father so near you."

Observe what is said on this subject by one of his novices: "The holy director whom Providence had given me inspired me with the highest esteem, the deepest affection and entire confidence. Everything about him drew him to me; his eminent piety, his great intelligence, the knowledge I observed in him, and the assemblage of virtues which I could not enough admire. Considering him as a model placed before us, I always found in his conduct a living, perfect commentary on his lessons upon the spirit and virtues required of a true missionary. He made me love my vocation. In the assemblage of the Christian virtues, none of which he lacked, what seemed to me the most remarkable was that he possessed each virtue in a just proportion. That these qualities mix themselves with the remnants of our natural frailty, that the saints, themselves, were never entirely divested of them, I will not contest, but it was difficult to discover what fault I could find in Blessed Perboyre. Yes, the Servant of God was a holy missionary, a saint formed on the model and according to the spirit of our blessed Father. In him were the common modest virtues, without display, but in an uncommon degree. A constant evenness of disposition, grace and kindness of manner contributed to make him a faithful picture of St. Vincent."

---

## XVI.

### APPEARANCE, TALENTS AND DISPOSITION OF BLESSED PERBOYRE.

BLESSED John Gabriel was short, but well proportioned. His hair was light, his face florid, his eyes bright and sparkling, his mouth somewhat large and his lips habitually smiling. His constitution was weak and delicate. An angelic purity and amiable simplicity were depicted in his looks. His face bore the impress of innocence and happiness that denote a beautiful soul. Every virtue was expressed in his exterior which represented gentleness, humility, recollection, piety and religion.

His intellectual gifts may be appreciated by the great success and rapidity with which he made his classes. Endowed with a solid, judicious penetrating mind, filled with elevated ideas, he considered all things in their source and always went to the point by the most direct way. Whatever the subject he undertook to study, he never left it until he perfectly understood it; and having a good memory he never forgot what he had once learned. He could have appeared very learned if he had wished, but instead of listening to the suggestions of self love, his happiness consisted in having himself ignored; and he had no idea that he was making a sacrifice; on the contrary, he was much astonished when anyone consulted him. "The bent of his mind led him," said one of his pupils at the seminary, "to seek for the sense and reason of spiritual maxims and pious practices in depths of dogmatic truth. He had also, a special attraction for the great masters, particularly St. Thomas and St. Bonaventure. M. Olier pleased him very much and he counselled the reading of his works. He understood, however, that God reserved the relish and understanding of supernatural things to souls humble and truly simple in faith; it was this, if I am not deceived, which produced in the secret of his heart the strong antipathy which he long manifested for the philosophy of Des Cartes, too arrogant, he said, to be true. These different qualities were revealed in Blessed John Gabriel's language: his words, full of meaning, frequently announced ideas of a high order and always expressed solid doctrine; though free from mistakes or bad taste, they were by no means studied; his was the language of perfect simplicity. Sometimes, it is true, he was a little lacking in fire and life, but this was especially due to his temperament which could not express the force and vivacity of the conviction with which his whole conduct showed him to be penetrated."

Although Blessed Perboyre seemed naturally timid, he displayed, nevertheless, great energy of character when he labored in the service of God. He was full of condescension for everyone, but no human consideration could make him waver when his conscience warned him that he should remain firm and immovable. He had a noble, generous heart, and in it there was no room but for the love of God, truth and his duties. He wished to become a saint and labored for it with constancy and indefatigable ardor, and in this daily labor he had to sustain many combats; to impose upon himself many sacrifices and to do much violence to himself; for he felt within him, like the Apostle, the law of sin opposing the reign of God. Seeing him always so calm, so recollected, so disposed to do what was most perfect, many thought that virtue was natural to him; they did not know that if he arrived at so great a degree of perfection, it was only because he never ceased to combat every irregularity in his natural inclinations. "With our inclinations to evil," said he, "any concessions are very dangerous; we must firmly oppose nature and never yield to it."

Though still very young, he felt his heart touched by the attractions of divine wisdom and in comparison to it, fortune and all the honors and pleasures of the world were as nothing in his eyes. This wisdom developed in him as a blossom opens under the sweet influence of the sun's rays and bears fruit, whose maturity does not await the ordinary season, and flourished as a grape soon ripe, '*et efflornit tanquam præcox uva.*' (Eccl. li, 19.) So he spread along his way the perfume of sanctity which brought joy to souls, reanimated them and inspired them with the desire of attaching themselves more closely to God. He spoke little, but everyone spoke of him; all were edified by him and regarded him as a saint. This is the judgment which is expressed by all who knew him. "I am often asked," said one of his admirers, "what was his prominent virtue, and I could not answer because he possessed them all in an eminent degree without one's interfering with another, they were so well ordered. God was his sole aim, this was shown in all he did; his words and actions were so well conformed to the sentiments of his heart that simplicity could be considered as holding the first rank among his virtues. He was not like those men who in one person unite several personages. one a grave, serious man of business; another light and dissipated in recreation, and a third, modest and recollected in prayer. There was in him but one person, always the same without ever passing from joy to sadness, from dissipation to recollection, from sprightliness to gentleness. They were always sure to find him in the same disposition; gentle, kind, remarkably charitable, smiling frankly but never laughing out, blaming no one, and speaking only of his neighbor when he could say some good of him."

It sufficed to see him but once to form a high opinion of his sanctity, and the impression which he first produced was never altered by the most intimate intercourse with him. No one could closely observe and study him without recognizing in him a surprising assemblage of virtues, and this discovery increased the esteem and veneration that he inspired. But, like the king's daughter, all his glory remained hidden in his interior. One of his professors who had charge of him for several years, observed that at the age when young people are most dissipated, his soul was already intimately united to God as if grounded in Him. Moses constructed in the desert a tabernacle to the Lord which seemed despicable outside because of the skins of beasts that covered it, but within was of great value because of the gold and precious stones decorating it. Thus, in silence and recollection, Blessed John Gabriel enriched his soul with all the treasures of virtue, and prepared it to become the tabernacle of God, the place of His repose and His delight. "His life," says a missionary, "was but a common life, but with all the graces of a very perfect life. Outwardly, he was like us, for he had a great horror of singularity. I have studied him, I have observed him closely, I have known for a long time all the secrets of his heart, I can say of him without hesitation, '*Omnis gloria filiae Regis ab intus,*' (Ps. xliv, 14) 'All the glory of the king's daughter is within.'"

This interior life he learned from Our Lord, who is the source of all grace and the model of all that is perfect. He did not confine himself to meditating upon the teachings and actions of Jesus Christ, he entered into His divine heart to contemplate this deep abyss of charity, obedience, humility, meekness and all the virtues. He endeavored to examine the motives upon which Our Lord acted during his mortal life, so as to understand them, to copy in all his actions this adorable Model.

A priest, who was intimate with him for many years, asked him by what means he could attain to the interior life. "You have but to pay attention to what you say every day in the Apostles' Creed and put it in practice. We find in the creed all the states through which we must pass to attain to this life."—"I assure you," replied the priest, "I find nothing about it in the creed. I shall be very grateful to you, if you will explain to me your views upon this subject." Then the Servant of God made these reflections: "Our Lord is the model of the new man whom we must strive to form within us. To attain to the interior life we must pass through the different states through which Our Lord Himself passed. So when you say in the creed that Jesus Christ was conceived by the Holy Ghost, it must also be the Holy Ghost who forms the new man in us. You must then have recourse to Him by frequent and fervent aspirations because without Him you will always remain in your first state. You, then, say that Jesus Christ was born of the Blessed Virgin Mary; you must then like Mary bear Him within you and like her give Him a new life; have recourse, then, to her and often beg her to form in you by the operation of the Holy Ghost the image of her divine Son. Jesus Christ suffers under Pontius Pilate; you must suffer like Him all sorts of trials; it is only by suffering, mortification and patience that we can put the old man to death; Jesus Christ has been crucified; you must also crucify your flesh, your tastes and your inclinations so that you can say with the Apostle: 'With Christ I am nailed to the cross.' (Gal. ii. 19.) '*Christo confixus sum cruci.*' This is not all. Jesus is dead and you must die to the world and to yourself; you must, after His example, be buried in the obscurity of the tomb by humility, the hidden life and a hatred of yourself. But as Jesus Christ after His death rose again and ascended to heaven, so you must truly rise and become a heavenly man." Then he discoursed long upon the resemblance that a priest's life must have to that of Jesus Christ risen and glorious, and made upon this subject many very interesting considerations; but the priest who heard them cannot remember them precisely so they can not be inserted in this book.

If Blessed John Gabriel spoke in an admirable manner of the advantages of the interior life and the means of attaining it, seeing him we understood better the graces, the treasures, the consolations contained in this life and felt ourselves animated by a more ardent zeal to acquire it. He continually endeavored to imitate Jesus Christ in Whom resides the plenitude of virtues; it was not enough for him to imitate one feature of this divine model; he had the pious ambition of imitating Him entirely, so as put in practice what the apostle St. Paul recommends to the Colossians, *Sicut accepistis Jesum Christum Dominum, in ipso ambulate, radicati, et superædificati in ipso, et confirmati in fide, sicut et didicistis, abundantes in illo in gratiarum actione.* (Col. ii, 6, 7.) 'As, therefore, you have received Jesus Christ, the Lord, walk ye in Him, rooted and built up in Him, and confirmed in the faith, as also you have learned, abounding in him in thanksgivings.'

In reading the life and the account of the virtues of Blessed John Gabriel Perboyre, we must admire the perfect generosity with which the Servant of God, always faithful to the graces bestowed upon him, rose to eminent sanctity, crowned by the glory of martyrdom.

We shall see in the fourth book the honors the Church has decreed to him after a long and rigorous discussion of his life, his death, and the miracles wrought by his intercession.

We shall end this book of the virtues of Blessed John Gabriel by recounting an extraordinary fact related on several occasions by M. Pierre Marie Auber, priest of the Mission, Superior of the house of St. Anne in Amiens, who died July 7, 1887.

M. Auber, being at the seminary of St. Lazare was serving the Mass of the venerable John Gabriel Perboyre, when, at the moment of Consecration, he saw him raised above the ground and ravished in ecstasy. The holy sacrifice finished, the Servant of God was alarmed for his humility, fearing the young cleric would reveal what he had just witnessed. So, returning to the sacristry, he made him promise that he would preserve inviolable secrecy about it. "I forbid you," he said, "to reveal to any one whilst I live what you have just seen."

The happy witness was faithful to the promised silence while Blessed Perboyre lived; but, after the martyrdom of his heroic confrere, he thought for the glory of God that he ought to reveal this token of His power and goodness. The fidelity with which M. Auber kept this secret, and his inclination not to believe miracles without positive proof, are for us an assured guarantee of its truth.

# BOOK IV.

## ACCOUNT OF THE BEATIFICATION OF THE VENERABLE SERVANT OF GOD, JOHN GABRIEL PERBOYRE.

THE news of Blessed Perboyre's death had not yet been received in Europe; they had only just heard in Rome that he had been arrested, when the sovereign Pontiff, Gregory XVI. desired that all the details relative to the captivity and death of the hero who had given his life for the faith, should be carefully collected so that they could the sooner proceed with the introduction of his cause. Since then fifty years have passed; and the venerable Martyr has just been declared Blessed. It seems opportune to add a fourth book to the history of his life and there relate the most striking events which have marked these fifty years, binding so to speak, the first desire expressed in 1840, by Gregory XVI., to the solemn act which Leo XIII. has recently accomplished and which permits us to venerate publicly this holy missionary. In this last book three classes of facts must be successively stated.

I. The miraculous events by which heaven seemed to declare itself in favor of its servant and which have spread more and more the renown of his virtues and the confidence which from the day of his death many souls have placed in his intercession.

II. The exhumation of his precious remains and

their translation from the cemetery of Ou-Tchang-Fou to the Chapel of the Mother House of the Congregation of the Mission, at Paris.

III. The canonical investigations begun in China and the principal acts of the process pursued by the court of Rome which have just ended in the beatification of him whose life was so holy and whose death so glorious.

---

## I.

### MIRACLES WROUGHT BY THE INTERCESSION OF BLESSED PERBOYRE.

THE marvellous circumstances which surrounded the death of Blessed John Gabriel Perboyre, the reputation for sanctity which he left everywhere among those who had seen and known him, inspired a great many persons after he had left this world with the thought of invoking him in their needs as a patron powerful with God. Their confidence was not deceived and many graces are related, many cures obtained, contrary to all human hope, by the intercession of the valiant confessor of the faith.

It was upon the very tomb of Blessed Perboyre at the gates of the town, the theatre of his long suffering and heroic death, that this devotion to him took birth. When in 1858, Monsignor Delaplace, a Bishop of the Congregation of the Mission, Vicar-Apostolic of Tche-Kiang went to Ou-Tchang-Fou to take away the body of M. Perboyre, he was surprised to see when the digging about the tomb was begun, a great number of people, pagans as well as Christians eagerly and religiously gathering the herbs and roots that grew in the earth. He learned that these wild herbs were a universal remedy; that potions were made of them which were considered infallible, and that maladies of all kinds had been by this means instantly cured. "As many voices have told me it," added the venerable Bishop, "as there are Christians in Ou-Tchang-Fou and the neighborhood." *

The Servant of God was no less powerful, and no less fervently and confidently invoked in the country which gave him birth, and where he had given from his earliest childhood sure indications of his future sanctity. A worthy priest of the parish of Mongesty, who had collected upon the very spot the most unexceptional testimony, has certified that several extraordinary graces have been obtained in this country by the intercession of the Martyr.† Among others the cure of a young girl, a boarder with the White Sisters at Sarlat, whom a violent attack of typhoid fever had brought to death's door and who was given up by the physicians. This child, Annie Malvina Lalbenque, received the last sacraments on the morning of August 17, 1847. The chaplain of the convent exhorted her mother to make a sacrifice of her daughter to God. The girl during her sickness often expressed her confidence in the intercession of Blessed Perboyre. The mother remembered it and begged the chaplain to say on the next day, which was Sunday, a Mass for her child and to join that evening in a novena which she was going to ask the religious to begin with her in

* Letter of Mgr. Delaplace to M. Etienne, June 2, 1858.
† Letter of M. Saupiquet, pastor at Mongesty, Nov. 29, 1850.

honor of the Martyr. The next morning before daylight, the sick girl called to her mother: "Mamma," said she, "my tongue is cured, my throat cleared and I am much better." From this time the danger was warded off; the convalescence advanced rapidly and soon after the young girl, accompanied by her mother, was able to go to Puech to thank the Servant of God in the house where he was born and which was already visited by numerous pilgrims, sometimes coming long distances to make their petitions or to return thanks.*

But it is especially in the family of St. Vincent de Paul that this devotion to the memory of so worthy a son of the Founder of the Priests of the Mission and the Sisters of Charity, was to find favor and express itself in touching manifestations of faith and piety becoming an efficacious resource in the most desperate emergencies. Among all the facts that might be related here, we have chosen only three cures wrought in countries very distant from one another as if God had willed to spread everywhere the glory of his servant; we select them because they seem to us to be especially noteworthy by the details, touching or marvellous, and by the gravity of the testimony by which they are attested.

The first occurred in Paris in 1841, the year after the death of Blessed Perboyre. Sister Margaret Bouyssie was then twenty-one years old, of a lymphatic temperament and delicate health, weakened still more by several maladies. Upon April 2, during her postulancy at the Woman's Hospital for Incurables she was attacked by pleuro-pneumonia which soon assumed an alarming character. The sacraments were

* Letter of M. Saupiquet, Jan. 10, 1851.

given the young sister; and she seemed to get a little better; they thought convalescence had begun. After a short sojourn in the country she was sent to the Mother House of the Sisters of Charity where she was to take the habit. It was there that, in the month of August, she saw for the first time Dr. Ratheau, physician of the community. He wrote his first observations upon the sick sister as follows:

"The diagnosis is easy to establish; we see that we have a case of pleuro-pneumonia, judging from the obstruction of the lung and a discharge of pus which fills three fourths of the cavity of the left pleura, and this, in a subject who is weak and even threatened with tubercules at the top of the lungs—if they do not already exist; beside, there is a general state of debility, so that we must pronounce it a very doubtful case. Nevertheless, we advise the use of all the means skill can employ, etc."

None of these means succeeded. Not knowing what else to do, they wished to try again the effects of the country air. The doctor, having given his consent, she was taken on August 16, a few leagues from Paris. There, the patient grew worse, the vomiting became more frequent; a fatal result seemed imminent. After four days' stay, the young sister begged to be brought back to Paris to her hospital, where she wished to die, as she said, among her sick. Dr. Ratheau went to see her and declared that, far from being improved, her condition was considerably aggravated. Things remained thus till August 22, the day on which Sister Bouyssie wished to begin a novena in honor of the new martyr. On the 25th, in the morning, suffering more than ever, she asked to be taken up so that her bed could be made. She was seized with so violent a spell of suffocation, that in a few moments she had to return to her bed. She then became drowsy and suddenly, at a quarter before twelve, she awakened and said in a strong voice: "I am cured; give me something to eat, I am very hungry." Her companions looking at her thought her delirious; but upon her insistence, and seeing the appearance of life and health that was suddenly displayed in her whole person, they brought her some soup, a chop and a large slice of bread. The hunger that consumed her was not yet appeased. Three potatoes cooked in ashes were added; she digested everything perfectly. She then arose: she had entirely recovered her strength; and went to recreation with her companions; in the evening she ate supper with them; then she went to sleep and her slumber was calm and deep. The next day she worked all day spreading linens on the clothes lines at the hospital, and on the 27th, watched the sick the whole night.

Dr. Ratheau, who at the time had declared this cure sudden and unexpected, desired five weeks later to see Sister Bouyssie. "To-day, October 4, 1841," he writes, "I desired to see the patient again. I examined her anew. Her cure continues. Never, she tells me, has she felt so well.

"Now," adds the worthy physician, "let us glance at the facts of the case. A patient presents herself having more than the probability of tubercules at the top of both lungs, a stoppage of the left lung, a considerable discharge of pus in the cavity of the pleura on the same side. Besides, there is a general exhaustion; her fever continues with a swelling of the lower limbs. She has a cough, violent suffocation, vomiting and diarrhœa which can scarcely be endured. The medicines, varied in many ways, either do no good or cannot be taken. This is the array of facts displayed before our eyes, and it was amid these disorders which continued to increase, and which could only end disastrously that the crisis came. At a quarter before twelve, immediately after a light sleep and a profuse perspiration, the patient cried: 'I am cured; give me something to eat. I am very hungry.' She who could not retain bouillon, ate soup, a chop, a large slice of bread and three potatoes. She arose shortly after, her strength entirely restored, assisted at the recreation of the Sisters and took supper with them; slept all night, and the next day was busy the whole day, spreading linens on the lines at the hospital and on the third, watched the sick all night. I ask every honest, conscientious doctor if this is the natural termination of a malady of this nature. No doubt, some persons are cured of it; but we know, too, that it requires great care, and after a long convalescence; and where was the convalescence in this case? We see her pass from serious sickness to the most perfect health. From all these facts we must draw the following conclusion: When a malady is declared organic, and a cure is wrought by passing suddenly from a state of serious disease to perfect health this cure must be considered as the effect of a cause not natural, or to speak more clearly, as the effect of a miracle."

At the beginning of the year which followed the event of which we have just spoken, in the fourth week of January, there occurred at Constantinople another case of the same kind. Sister Antoinette Vincent suffered for some years from a pain in the side, the nature and origin of which she did not understand. For a long time she struggled against the pain not wishing to admit to herself the gravity of her condition. She continued each day to attend her class. At length, however, during December 1841, overcome by sufferings which had become more acute and insupportable, she was obliged to give up and allow herself to be put to bed. The true character of her malady was then understood and the same time the inability of man to cure her. It was an inward abscess of long standing, followed by a disease of the spleen which had burst, causing gangrene which must lead to death in the near future. The patient received the last Sacraments and quietly prepared herself to appear before God. On January 20, the Superioress thought that there should be a consultation of several physicians. Their opinion was unanimous that there was nothing to be done, nothing to be tried. The abscess had caused so great disorder in the region of the heart, the poor Sister had but a few days to live. The doctors did not wish to give their signatures to the consultation, saying that it would be only signing a certificate of death.*

However, two novenas were begun in honor of Blessed Perboyre, one by the Sisters of Charity, the companions of the dying Sister, the other by the children of the school who greatly loved her and wished at any price to obtain from heaven the cure of their dear

* Letter of Sister Lesueur, Superioress of the Sisters of Charity at Constantinople, to M. Etienne, Jan. 27, 1842.

teacher by their prayers and by their sacrifices too, for they deprived themselves of the delicacies which they would have bought for their meals and reserved the money that their parents had given them,so as to buy some wax tapers. The consultation of the doctors took place on Thursday. The next day, Friday, January 21, was the fifth day of the Sisters' novena and the third of the children's. In the morning the disease had progressed so rapidly that the doctor warned them that the Sister might expire at any moment. M. Lelen, Prefect Apostolic of the Lazarist Mission, applied to her the indulgence for a happy death which he had deferred till the last moment. In the evening they thought her time had come. The rattling in her throat, the color of her face, the corpse-like odor, all seemed to announce that the end was near. She became drowsy and her sleep lasted three hours; during it she had a dream which she recalled immediately upon awakening, and she could not help seeing in it a sign of what God was going to perform upon her. At midnight she awoke; the pain had disappeared; she dressed herself sitting upright; it seemed to her that she was cured, and she felt ravenously hungry. She ate everything that had been left in her room, the bouillon, the pieces of orange and some grapes, without feeling any inconvenience, enjoying everything with great relish. The Sister Superior who saw her first, hesitated and could not believe that Sister Vincent had really returned to life; she feared to find this one of those deceptive occurrences, which far from indicating a cure, are only an immediate forerunner of death. Sister Vincent, herself doubted; she thought she was the victim of a delusion and could scarcely believe she was going to live—so ready was she to die, happy at the thought of going to her God! Her cure however, was soon apparent. No longer the death-like odor; her face resumed its natural appearance and the colors of health. She decided to speak, and told her Superioress how she felt and what she had seen in the dream. The Superioress called the other Sisters; the news of the miracles spread through the house which became, as the worthy Superioress relates, "like it was beside itself."

Resigned to the will of God, but seeing in the miraculous cure only the glorification of Blessed Perboyre who had been the instrument of it, and a great grace bestowed on the religious family in which the miracle had been performed, Sister Antoinette Vincent asked permission to rise, so as to go to the chapel to thank Our Lord, and to begin again to serve Him by resuming as soon as possible, the duties of her office. She arose, dressed herself all alone, and even made her bed; then, without help or support, she mounted the three flights of stairs which separated her from the chapel. "There prostrated before the altar," says the Sister Superior, "her fervor seemed that of an angel." Leaving the chapel, she went to see one of her companions, Sister Marie, sick like herself in another infirmary, who when she learned the sudden cure of the dying sister, refused to believe it. When she saw Sister Vincent standing before her full of life, a kind of stupor and fright were depicted in her countenance and in her bearing. "You should be a witness of this scene," a Sister of Charity wrote a few days after, "to form any idea of it." An interview no less touching was that between the children of the school and their beloved teacher now restored to them. All, both boarders and day scholars, ran to meet her, pressing one against the other, they obstructed her progress, they stood there mute, immovable, with their eyes fixed in admiration upon the Sister, and the silence of this crowd of young children proved better than words the inexpressible emotion with which they were penetrated. At length their amazement being a little calmed, the expressions of the most touching faith and pious enthusiasm issued from their lips. "I was right in saying," cried some of them, "that our Sister would be cured;" and others exclaimed, "We must no longer say *Mr.* Perboyre but *Saint* Perboyre." And the doctors with the same unanimity with which they had given up the sister now declared her perfectly cured and that the cure was contrary to all rules of science and entirely surpassed the power of their art. All with one voice, though there was a Jew among them, declared that they had been absolutely of no help in what had occurred; one of them even refused to take his fee, saying he would consider it an injustice to receive pay when everything had been done by God, Himself.

The third cure to which we have alluded took place twenty years afterwards in a town of Central America, in Guatemala, for the name of Blessed Perboyre and the pious confidence which followed it everywhere, had then crossed the Ocean. Here we shall let M. Mariscal, priest of the Mission, witness of the event, speak for himself. Almost the next day after it occurred he relates it to one of his confrères in Paris, in a letter dated June 17, 1863.

"I have great news to announce to you, or to speak

more properly, I must prove to you how liberal God has shown Himself to us. On the first of May, Sister Broquedis was seized with fatal consumption, complicated with several other diseases, so that the best physicians of this capital despaired of her life. Following their advice, I administered to her the Holy Viaticum and Extreme Unction and applied to her the indulgence for a happy death. On the 17th, the disease assumed so alarming a character that the physicians said that in the whole town there was no human remedy that could cure her. At last, the symptoms of death appeared;—a cold sweat, absence of pulse, eyes glassy and a death-like pallor. The news spread like lightning through the town and all classes of society shared in our affliction. Monsignor, the Archbishop, the other resident bishops, the canons, the communities of religious, both men and women, members of the administration, the ministers of the government and all the poor anxiously inquired about the Sister's health. Amid our common affliction, I did nothing but receive visits and console the Sisters. Seeing that God alone could come to our aid, taking in my hand a relic of Saint Vincent and a picture of Venerable Perboyre, I assembled all the Sisters in the oratory. After a short conference on conformity to the will of God, I begged them to confide themselves to His merciful Providence, and at the same time we began a novena to Venerable Perboyre; we recited for this, nine Our Fathers, each followed by a little prayer that I had composed. We intended to do the same on each of the nine following days, if the Sister did not die before that. When the doctors returned the same day, they expected to find her dead; and what was our astonishment when we heard them say: "There is some hope; we find the nature of the disease has changed." In fact, from that time the condition of the patient improved day by day, and the progress was so rapid that her wasted body found itself able to work at the end of two weeks. Then, to fulfil the promise we had made to God, we sang the *Te Deum* before the Blessed Sacrament exposed in the Sisters' oratory. The president and his family desired to assist at it. The Archbishop, having heard of the marvellous cure of Sister Broquedis by the intercession of the Venerable Perboyre, asked in writing the name of the martyr and I gave him one of his pictures which he received with much satisfaction.

---

## II.

### THE BRINGING TO FRANCE OF THE PRECIOUS RELICS OF BLESSED PERBOYRE.

THE value, the religious veneration, which is attached to all objects which recall the remembrance of a saint and which made even a bishop of the New World receive with joy a picture of Blessed Perboyre, inspired the congregation of which he is one of the glories, with the desire to gather carefully all that may remain of the martyr upon earth. Already the relic hall in the Mother House in Paris, contained a number of objects which he had used during life or which having been used at his execution, have been consecrated by his sufferings, even by his blood, of which they bore the traces. But the most precious of his relics, what remained of his body, was still in

China on the slope of the Rouge Mountain, near the gates of Ou-Tchang-Fou, where the Chinese buried him two days after his death.

In 1858, one of the Lazarist Bishops in China, Mgr. Delaplace, Vicar Apostolic of Tche-Kiang, received from the Superior-General of the Congregation, M. Etienne, the invitation to go and look for the venerated remains. Starting from Ning-Po at the end of March, after fifty-eight days' travel through all the horrors of civil war which raged with great violence in this part of the empire, the worthy prelate arrived on Saturday, May 15, in the Vicariate Apostolic of Hou-Pé, then governed by Monsignor Spelta, the Franciscan Bishop. "On a Saturday, and in the middle of the month of May," wrote Monsignor Delaplace, "could I fail to be happy?" And yet having just escaped the perils of a long and painful voyage, he saw arise before him, at the moment he thought he had reached the end, the most unforeseen difficulties, which seemed to make his hope as distant perhaps as ever, and rendered almost impossible the accomplishment of his mission.

No doubt, he had received from Monsignor Spelta, a kind and brotherly welcome. The remembrance of the two Martyrs of the Congregation of the Mission, M. Clet and M. Perboyre, was still honored in the Seminary of which the Franciscan Bishop was president and where he lived. Every year on the anniversaries of their death, February 17, and September 11, they read in the refectory the verbal process of the life and execution of the two Confessors of the faith, and the pupils have holiday. So Monsignor Spelta, espousing the cause of his venerable visitor and his Congregation, made it his duty to assist the work with as much earnestness and zeal as could have been done by "the most devoted of his confrères," as Monsignor Delaplace himself expresses it. But at the very time that the two prelates were about to start for Ou-Tchang-Fou, they learned from the most recent and certain information that all the tombstones on Rouge Mountain had been carried off by the rebels, and that all the witnesses, whose remembrance and testimony could have supplied the place of these material guides, had disappeared and could not be heard from, one having been found dead, and the others being dispersed by the troubles of the last few years. At least, they should, it was said, first send a courier and assure themselves that there was some hope of success before undertaking a journey which was not without peril. However, the confidence of the holy Missionary did not waver, and he persisted in hoping against all hope. "Never," he wrote two weeks later to M. Etienne, "has Providence demonstrated better to me than in the last two months how much there is to hope for through faith, when, humanly speaking, everything seems desperate. All our little schemes have met from our first arrival here with obstacles which seemed insurmountable; yet all these have been overcome with admirable facility. I still felt that Providence favored me while at Monsignor Spelta's house." In fact, the next day after this discouraging news had caused him the greatest anxiety, Monsignor Delaplace saw coming to the bishop's residence, a Christian from Han-Keou, Paul Fong, son of the courageous catechist, Andre Fong, who had visited and consoled M. Perboyre in prison and who had buried him with his own hands with the help of three other Chinese Christians, in the cemetery of the Rouge Mountain. Paul Fong, himself, was present and assisted with the burial. Being thirty-two years old in 1858, he was fourteen at the time of the martyr's death. He had a very exact remembrance of it and eagerly offered to conduct the two bishops to the spot where reposed the body they wished to find. Besides, he had been praying at Blessed Perboyre's tomb a month and a half before; hearing the report that the tombstones were scattered, he declared that the stone that covered his tomb still remained intact with the inscription on it. "We breathed more freely," says Monsignor Delaplace, "after hearing these words."

The venerable Vicars-Apostolic soon decided to undertake the journey and started on May 19, accompanied by M. John Baptist Tchen, secretary to Monsignor Spelta, and a native Lazarist priest, M. Vincent Fou; three days later, Saturday, May 22, the eve of Pentecost, they weighed anchor at the entrance of Han-Keou. Monsignor Spelta and the two Chinese priests went immediately to Ou-Tchang-Fou. Monsignor Delaplace remained upon the bark, where he celebrated Mass at two o'clock in the morning. Day had scarcely dawned when in his turn he crossed the Blue River and after stopping a few moments with a Christian family named Tchen whose house at the entrance to the metropolis of Hou-Pé, being outside the city walls, offered him a secure asylum, he directed his course, when he thought he could do so without danger, towards the cemetery of the Rouge Mountain. He arrived there about half past seven. His companions on the journey, surrounded by a number of Christian men and women, furnished with all that was needed for the exhumation, soon found themselves at the tomb of the martyr. Monsignor Delaplace knelt in the midst of them; he could not help admiring and blessing Providence whose intervention seemed more and more apparent, the nearer he approached the realization of his desires. According to the report of Paul Fong, the stone placed on the tomb of the Servant of God to indicate his resting place was there and had always been there. Of these stones which covered the side of the mountain to the number of several thousands, they saw but three—that of Blessed Perboyre and two others near by. The rebels, long masters of Ou-Tchang-Fou, whose ramparts they judged insufficient, wished to fortify them. The vast cemetery of the Rouge Mountain offered them the material already prepared; they drew from it a large contribution, devastating all the tombs to repair the old walls or to build new ones. One of the principal walls of defense was situated seven or eight feet from the tomb of Blessed Perboyre, before which they passed and repassed continually when going much farther to look carefully for stones of all sorts and we cannot help being surprised that they had forgotten this one, whose size and shape suited them exactly. "Explain this, whoever can," adds Monsignor Delaplace. "The simplicity of the Christians of Ou-Tchang-Fou is contented with saying that God has taken care of His martyr whom He has reserved for special veneration in His church." We feel sure the pious bishop had no difficulty in sharing the simplicity of these humble Christians and we can understand with what pious emotion he must have read upon this stone, so providentially preserved, the following inscription engraved in Chinese characters:* "May perpetual light shine upon him. Sepulchre of the noble man; Tong, [which is the Chinese name for M. Perboyre] called Gabriel in holy baptism, religious of the Congregation of St. Vincent, who died in the twentieth year of the reign of the Emperor Tao-Kuang, the sixteenth day of the eighth month." Monsignor Delaplace would have been pleased to assist at all the details of the exhumation but the place was not very secure, being near a road much frequented, just a few steps from the new fort built by the rebels but now occupied by the mandarins who came almost immediately to observe what was going on about the tomb. So he returned to his morning's hiding place at the house of the Tchen family, going by the same road that Blessed Perboyre followed on September 11, 1840, at nearly the same hour to go to his death. He remained three or four hours praying in the place where the martyr knelt in prayer looking towards the west and whence his soul went forth to heaven. In the afternoon towards four o'clock, he was preparing to make a last visit and pay his last farewell to the Rouge Mountain when he saw M. Fou coming escorted by two Christians who bore the precious remains. Without delay, Monsignor Delaplace crossed the river, which he said never looked so beautiful as upon this evening, and regained the bark where Monsignor Spelta was waiting. They returned immediately with their treasure to the seminary of Hou Pé.

*Lux perpetua luceat ei.—Sepulchrum Nobilis Viri Tong. Sancto nomine Gabrielis. Religiosi e Congregatione Sancti Vincentii, mortui anno Imperatoris Tao-Kuang, vigesimo, lund octava, die decima sexta.

Everything was completed to their satisfaction. The morning after M. Delaplace's departure, Bishop Spelta's secretary paid fifty-five hundred sapeques to the guardian of the cemetery who had furnished the necessary workmen for disinterring the coffin. They dug for more than an hour and a half before it was obtained. The two Chinese priests found all his bones in an unusually good state of preservation, white as ivory, each in its place without confusion or mixing with earth or other foreign matter.* They were taken from the coffin and carefully placed in a new case which was taken away by Monsignor Delaplace. What added to the joy of this worthy prelate in the presence of so complete a success, was the fact that, by the least delay, all would have been lost. The coffin was not much injured by the eighteen years that it had remained in immediate contact with the earth in which it had been buried, and from which it was not separated by any kind of mason work; but everyone thought it probable that the rains of the following autumn would have injured the lid, thereby breaking and dispersing the bones and making their decay more rapid. There was another kind of danger which would have interfered if they had put off the exhumation a little later. The mandarins of Hou-Pé, who feared the return of the rebels whose presence had been observed in the neighborhood, had become suspicious; they were especially distrustful of the Christians and missionaries, whose movements were carefully watched. Some weeks later the journey that the two bishops had just

*Verbal process written out by Mgr. Spelta's notary. "Ossa venerabilis servi Dei pulcherrimae albedinis jacebant omnia et singula in suo ordine, absque ulla confusione, absque ulla terrae vel alienarum materiarum admixtione."

accomplished would, no doubt, have been impossible. Scarcely had they returned to Monsignor Spelta's seminary at Tang-Kia-Ho when visits of inspection to the houses began to be multiplied. An hour after their arrival, the room which had been occupied by Monsignor Delaplace, and where the remains of the martyr had just been deposed was inspected in its smallest nooks and corners by an officer and his escort. The Vicar-Apostolic of Tche-Kiang understood that prudence required his swift return to his province so as to preserve his precious deposit. On May 26, the day on which they returned to Tang-Kia-Ho, the two venerable travellers wished first to thank Providence for the happy issue of their pious expedition. Monsignor Delaplace said at noon a Mass of thanksgiving and Monsignor Spelta, robed in full pontificals chanted a solemn *Te Deum* surrounded by the missionaries and the young Chinese seminarians. Then they began immediately to write out the acts required by the Congregation of Rites, and to have the cases made in which were to be inclosed and brought to Europe the remains of the future beatified martyr.

When all was ready, Monsignor Delaplace resumed the journey to his province, and on July 13 wrote to M. Etienne from the bark on which he descended the Tchan-Tcheou that in four days he would be among the Christians of Tche-Kiang. He had again to escape all the dangers from which Providence had before preserved him when three months before he had gone to Hou-Pé. Again he had to cross a country infested with bands of robbers and troops of rebels, passing the same deserted towns, the same villages in ruins and to sail on rivers containing dead bodies. He felt that the martyr whose remains he bore had protected him, and when he brought his holy bones to his vicariate, he said: "May they be to Ning-Po like the ark in the house Obededom! May the Chinese Dagons fall at their approach."

Tche-Kiang was not allowed long to possess this treasure. During the next year, Monsignor Danicourt, Vicar Apostolic of Kiang-Si, left China, taking with him the remains of the Confessor of the faith which he was charged to bring to Paris to the Mother House of the Congregation of the Mission. It seemed that Providence had reserved this consoling mission for the pious bishop as the crown of a glorious career, so worthily fulfilled. A month did not elapse from the day he gave his precious charge into the hands of the Superior-General, till he slept sweetly in the Lord, February 2, 1860.

It was on January 6, of the same year, the anniversary of the birth of Blessed Perboyre, that his ashes were brought to the house in Rue de Sevres, which a quarter of a century before, he left for the last time, going with joy to the labors of the apostolate, and secretly aspiring to martyrdom. What was felt in the hearts of all the children of the great St. Vincent de Paul, M. Etienne expressed a year afterwards, in a circular dated January 1, 1861, as if still under the influence of the first emotion, with that grand and simple eloquence which was natural to him. "It would be difficult," he writes, "to express the feelings of our hearts when we saw ourselves possessed of so great a treasure. Kneeling before this coffin, which breathed forth sanctity, with what affectionate veneration we loved to show our homage!

# RELICS OF BLESSED JOHN GABRIEL PERBOYRE

**At the Mother House of the Congregation of the Mission, Paris.**

---

1.—Coverlid used by Blessed Perboyre in prison.
2.—Chinese Robe worn by Blessed John Gabriel when taken by the soldiers.
3.—His Stole.
4.—Blessed Perboyre's Chinese Pants.
5.—His Chinese Shirt, torn at the neck by the chains.
6 and 7.—*Mahoutse*, or Chinese Vest, worn by Blessed John Gabriel.
8.—Glass Tube containing Blessed Perboyre's Beard.
9—Nails from his Coffin.
10.—Ropes which tied his hands during his Martyrdom.
11.—Blessed John Gabriel's Hair.
12.—Rope used in the Strangulation of Blessed Perboyre.
13.—Bamboo Rod used to tighten the Rope in his Strangulation.
14.—Veil which covered his Face during his execution.
15 and 21.—Glass Vases containing the Blessed Martyr's Ashes.
16.—Chinese Books which he used.
17 and 19.—Linen Cloths which contained Blessed Perboyre's Bones when brought from China to Paris.
18.—His Crucifix.
20.—His Chinese Inkstand.
22.—His Stockings, torn by the Chains.
23.—Chains worn by the Blessed Martyr in prison.

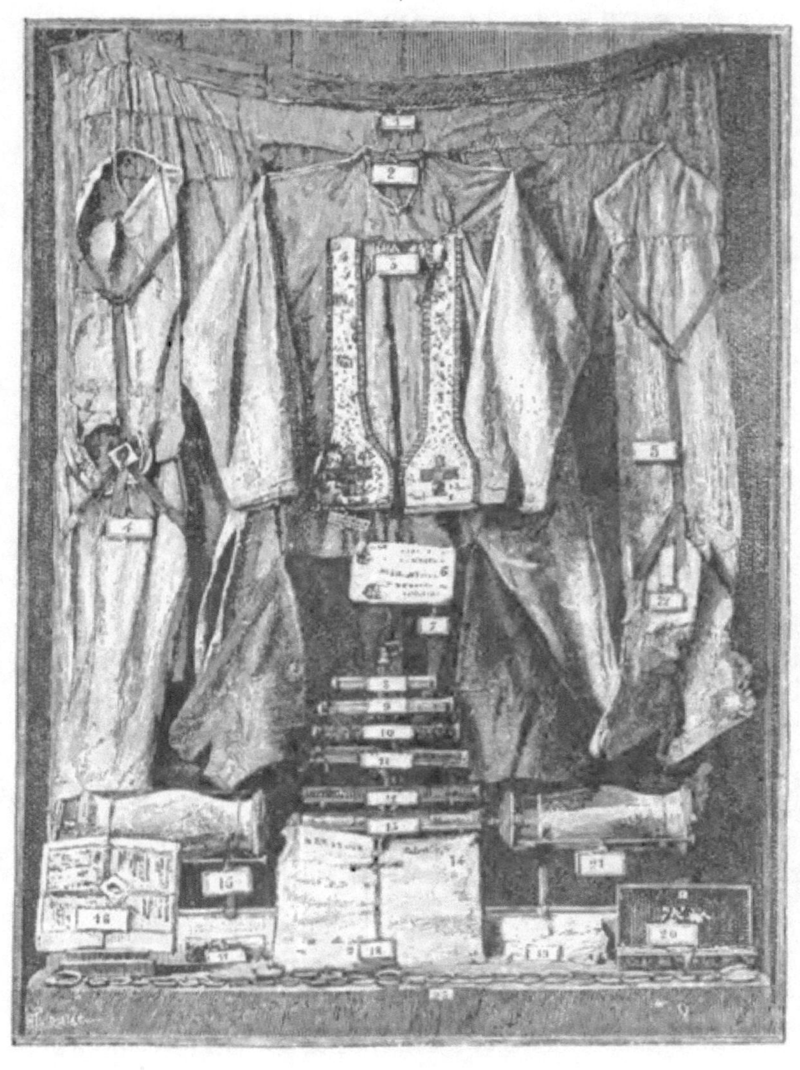

Various Relics of Blessed John Gabriel Perboyre, preserved in the Mother House of the Congregation of the Mission, Paris.

It seemed to us that from the heights of heaven he smiled on our happiness and responded to our welcome, so piously and lovingly fraternal. What joy to us all to see returned among us, surrounded by the aureola of an apostle and a martyr, him whom twenty-five years before we had seen leave this same Mother House to travel across the seas to distant shores, to which he was bringing the good tidings of salvation—to begin a career of labors, privations and sufferings for the name of Jesus Christ and to seal with his blood his faith and his love for souls! The presence of this venerable body seemed to our eyes quite a manifestation of God's design upon us, a revelation of the future which is reserved for the Congregation among heathen nations, among which are accomplished at this time events which open among them a large field for the preaching of the gospel. Formerly a director of novices, after having shown to new generations by his example as well as his teachings, what a true missionary should be, he returns again to teach them that he must know how to suffer and die for the glory of God and the salvation of his brothers."

On January 25, of this year, 1860, on the feast of the Conversion of St. Paul, the anniversary of the foundation of the Congregation of the Mission there was celebrated in the hall of the Mother House of the society, the canonical verification of the body of the blessed Servant of God in the presence of His Eminence, the Cardinal Marlot, Archbishop of Paris, accompanied by one of his vicar-generals, M. Etienne, Monsignor Danicourt, several priests of the Mission and two physicians, Drs. Hurteaux and Lemenant des Chenais, who were appointed to examine and describe the bones. These had undergone some change from the day on which they had been found entirely perfect in the cemetery of the Rouge Mountain near Ou-Tchang-Fou. Their color had assumed a yellowish tint, some bones, reduced to powder, were missing and made some of the members incomplete but the head was intact and admirably preserved; they could finally reconstruct almost the entire skeleton and they had all the elements needed to determine to a certainty the age and within a few centimeters the height of Blessed Perboyre. The identity of these remains being officially proved, they were put together again with care; and enclosed in a triple box of oak and lead were then brought into the chapel without pomp or lights and placed immediately in the vault prepared for their reception,* waiting till it please the divine Goodness to permit them to be placed on the altar so as to share the honor and glory of the body of St. Vincent." †

---

## III.

### PROCESS OF BEATIFICATION OF THE VENERABLE JOHN GABRIEL PERBOYRE.

When M. Etienne expressed the desire which we have just read, the process of beatification, which led to its realization was commenced at the court of Rome

*This vault was in an obscure place which was besides used as a passage way, where it was constantly trodden upon. In 1874, the provincial assembly of the Missionaries in France expressed the desire that the body of the Martyr be placed in a more suitable spot. They obtained in 1879 from His Holiness Leo XIII, the authority to make this translation, was given Aug. 21, 1879, by His Highness Monsignor Richard, then titular Archbishop of Larisse, and coadjutor to His Eminence Cardinal Guibert, Archbishop of Paris."

† Expressions of M. Etienne in the circular of January 1, 1861, stated above.

and gave every hope of a favorable issue. Eighteen years before, July 9, 1843, His Holiness Gregory XVI., signed the decree * which published the introduction of the cause of the Servant of God. His name did not appear alone, but with forty-three other Confessors of the faith, who, during forty-two years from 1798 to 1840, had been put to death through hatred of our holy religion in different parts of China and Cochin China, and from this date they could all receive the title of Venerable. But soon the cause of Blessed Perboyre became separated from that of these numerous martyrs to be pursued alone as promising a more sure and speedy success. Almost the next day after the publication of the decree above mentioned, M. Etienne addressed for this purpose a request to the Holy See and everything contributed to having it received; the abundance and value of the united testimony to the virtues, sufferings and glorious death of the Servant of God; the miraculous cures obtained by his intercession and attested by the gravest authorities, not to mention the undisguised favor of the then reigning Sovereign Pontiff, who was entirely won over to the cause sustained by the worthy superior of the Congregation of the Mission.

It must not be forgotten that Gregory XVI. before he had heard of the martyr's death insisted that all the documents that would hasten the introduction of his cause should be collected. After the publication of the decree of July 9, 1843, M. Etienne presented to Gregory XVI. the portrait of the newly declared Venerable Servant of God. His Holiness thanked him for his gift in a Latin letter Oct. 21, of the same year, in

* See Testimonial I.

it he expressed his admiration for "the valiant athlete of Christ who after showing himself a devoted missionary among pagans, after having displayed so much courage and constancy in the labors, perils and combats he endured for the Catholic faith, had merited by his death and the shedding of his blood, the palm of martyrdom"—"As to his canonization, the object of your most ardent desires and prayers," added the Holy Father, "we will give it every care according to the rules of the apostolic constitutions." *

Begun under such happy auspices, the first canonical inquiries were rapidly pursued; and in 1845, Monsignor Rizzolati, Vicar Apostolic of Hou-Quan, ordered by the Cardinal Prefect of the Congregation of Rites to institute in his vicariate the first process upon the martyrdom of the Servant of God, could announce that this process was ended and that he had addressed all the papers to the Secretary of the Congregation to whom he wrote on May 31, of this year.† "It is with deep and lively joy that I am permitted to inform Your Excellency, that the cause of the Venerable Servant of God John Gabriel Perboyre is, in what concerns me entirely finished and that I forward the authentic original acts to the Sacred Congregation of Rites. I must tell you that I have used the greatest diligence in the proceedings of this cause. I have neglected and even abandoned the cause of other martyrs, to conform to the pious desires of Your Most Reverend Excellency and to bring it to a conclusion with all possible promptness. And now, I think I may hope that the Venerable Perboyre will soon add new glory to the illustrious Congregation of St. Vincent,

*See Testimonial II. †See Testimonial III.

to our Vicariate, to France and to the Church herself, if the acts prepared with the greatest care, as I attest in all sincerity, in this Apostolic Vicariate, are ratified in Rome by the Holy See, I can affirm that nothing could cause me greater joy."

When this letter and the documents which it announced arrived in Rome Gregory XVI. no longer occupied the chair of St. Peter. The events which troubled the beginning of Pius IX's reign kept the cause long in suspense. It was not till the end of fourteen years, in 1860, that it was actually brought before the Congregation of Rites. But, thanks to the activity and zeal of the advocates in charge of it, thanks also, to the urging of M. Etienne, before the end of this year, December 10, the cardinals deputed by the Sovereign Pontiff under the presidency of Cardinal Patrizi, prefect of the Congregation of Rites held a special session and issued a decree proclaiming the validity of the process begun in China and of the inquiries made by the ordinary.* This decree approved on the 20th of the same month by Pius IX., was soon followed by another dated February 16, 1861, which declared that the rules prescribed by Pope Urban VIII upon *non-culte* had been obeyed, that is to say that they had not rendered to the Servant of God any of the honors reserved for the beatified and for saints.† This was nevertheless, but the preliminary of the apostolic process. Seventeen months later, on the 11th day before the Calends of August, 1862, an assembly called "ante-preparatory" was held at the residence of Cardinal Patrizi and under his presidency, in which was immediately begun the "discussion of the

* See Testimonial IV. † See Testimonial V.

martyrdom and the cause of the martyrdom" of the Venerable Servant of God. Then everything was again interrupted and for many years. With the wise and prudent slowness which the court of Rome uses in these grave questions, it was decided to wait till Providence had attested by new miracles the power and sanctity of His servant and till a second process begun in China by order of the Holy See had by new witnesses, thrown still greater light on the life and heroic death of him whose cause seemed surrounded already by so many assurances of success.

Indeed, some *remissorial* letters were, in 1855, addressed to the Vicar Apostolic of Hou-Quan, requiring him to begin a new inquiry and giving him all the powers of procedure in the name of the Sovereign Pontiff. Shortly afterwards, on account of its extent and the numerous missionary stations which it contained, Hou-Quan was divided into two distinct ecclesiastical districts, one being called the apostolic vicariate of Hou-Nan and the other the vicariate of Hou-Pé. These new arrangements delayed the proceedings of the cause, for the documents were not finished and were not sent to Rome until 1870.

Then occurred events that were painfully felt by the Holy See. It was not until ten years later 1880 that the cause was definitely taken up again by the Congregation of Rites.* All the advocates that had taken part in the process of 1860 had since died. Those appointed to replace them began the work with

* What added to the delay was that the papers sent from China had gone astray, "no doubt on account of political troubles. They were carefully searched for but it was impossible to find them. Then the postulator wrote to China to have another copy sent to Rome, the original remaining in the hands of the Vicar-Apostolic. The new writings arrived, but by the time they were read, the documents that had been lost were found." Annals of the Congregation, t. L. p. 213.

much zeal and ardor; scarcely had they examined the documents sent from China when they declared that no cause had ever been better supported and that they could rely upon a speedy and entire success.

On May 31, 1881, their Eminences the Cardinals of the Congregation of Rites examined the first doubt to be explained, which was to know "whether the process begun in China by the Vicars-Apostolic of Hou-Pé and Hou-Nan is valid and, after having heard the report and conclusions of the promoter of the faith, rendered an affirmative decree approved and confirmed the June 2 following, by the Sovereign Pontiff Leo XIII.*

In 1884, one the advocates, M. Ferdinand Morani prepared and presented a document of great importance in the history of the beatification which is the subject of these pages. It was a complete, precise and explicit summary of all the inquiries which had taken place. As it was revised by the vice-promoter of the faith, recorder of the Congregation of Rites, it might be in a manner considered as the thought of the Congregation itself. It proved at all events, with much clearness how far the process was advanced, and how near it was to conclusion at the time this document was published. The author considered the cause in all its aspects and reviewed the virtues one by one: the martyrdom of the future beatified Servant of God and the miracles wrought by his intercession.

"The miracles," he said, "by their number and the circumstances and testimonies by which is guaranteed their authenticity, are more than sufficient to establish the fact that God has willed to glorify his servant.

* See Testimonial VI.

As to the virtues: when a close inquiry was made concerning the holy missionary it was found that there was not one which he had not practised to an heroic degree. All the witnesses who were best situated to know and judge him were, successively interrogated by the advocate who classified their evidence in such a way as to leave no doubt in the mind of the reader and to make him share in the opinion of the worthy Vicar Apostolic of Hou-Pé, who wrote, when sending to Rome the acts of the process which he had just concluded, "The Venerable Servant of God by his virtues alone, without considering the account given of his martyrdom, is worthy of the honor of our altars: *Venerabilem servum Dei, absque martyrii merito, ob ejus virtutes altaris honoribus esse dignum.*"

As to the martyrdom itself, of which he gave an account as detailed and striking as possible, M. Morani showed that it was attested by witnesses, nearly all of whom were eye witnesses, being those who accompanied the Servant of God in his last voyage, and others who appeared beside him at the tribunals, shared his captivity and had been sent into exile because they were Chinese, while he, being a foreigner, was condemned to death.

We shall not proceed further with this analysis for fear of repeating here what has already been read in the preceding chapters. Allow us only, without insisting any more on the manner of Blessed Perboyre's death, to cite the summary of at least the most striking considerations by which M. Morani demonstrated that this death contained all the characteristics by which the Church recognizes a true martyrdom.

"The verity of the martyrdom of John Gabriel," said he, "rests upon the expressed design of the tyrant and the dispositions often manifested by the holy Missionary. Indeed, when M. Perboyre penetrated the interior of China, there existed an imperial law condemning to death all strangers who should be convicted of having labored to propagate Christianity in the Chinese empire. This law was made by the emperor, King-Lung; witnesses affirm that they themselves have read it in the Chinese code; this law was in force at the time M. Perboyre exercised his ministry in China; from this, we must conclude that if he was condemned to strangulation, it was because he was a Christian, the propagator of the Christian religion and a European; if he had been Chinese, according to the same law he would have only been condemned to exile. It was, besides, a notorious fact that the vice-roy who issued the sentence of death against M. Perboyre was a sworn enemy of the Christians and that his cruelty redoubled when he had to judge them. We must then say with several witnesses: 'It was for the faith, it was only in hatred of the faith that M. Perboyre was condemned; it is impossible to ascribe any other motive for his death.' '*Imperator eum in odium fidei morte damnavit; sed omnimodo haud propter aliam causam necatus est.*'

"If now, we glance at the Servant of God, the truth of martyrdom shines with still more resplendent glory. All those who knew M. Perboyre in Europe and in China, are absolutely certain that this worthy missionary went to the Celestial Empire only to make known Jesus Christ, and to propagate his religion. The Servant of God had often extolled the happiness of the Venerable Clet, who had been judged worthy of martyrdom; he had often expressed his desire of being treated like his happy confrère; but he esteemed himself unworthy of this glorious crown; and although he wished to give his life for the cause of Jesus Christ, he neglected no means which he ought to have used to avoid persecution. It is said he was seized only because his guide made his hiding place known to his persecutors, thus becoming guilty of the most infamous treachery. Indeed, several witnesses interrogated upon this important point, attest that the Venerable Perboyre did all that he could, not to implicate any of the Christians when compromised himself: he was an enlightened man and neglected none of his obligations, so all his conduct was eminently prudent. He omitted no precaution to avoid all action that might excite persecution; he stole away when it was threatened and exercised his ministry in secret; he scarcely ever went to the Christians' houses except at night and those who accompanied him were men whom he considered worthy of his whole confidence. In no sense, could be imputed to him the persecution of which he was the victim. Yet, we know that the Venerable Perboyre ardently desired to confess Jesus Christ and to sign with his blood the truths of the gospel. This was why, amid the most horrible sufferings, in spite of the most cruel tortures, he remained always firm and constant in his faith. To all the questions, to all the summonses of the pagans, presidents, and vice-roys, he replied only by testifying his attachment to our holy religion. They urged him to renounce Jesus Christ. 'No,' he replied, 'I would rather die a thousand times.' They wished him to tread upon the cross. 'That I will never do,' he replied. 'If you do not,' said the judge, 'I will put you to death.' 'That is what I wish,' he replied, 'my joy is to die for the faith.' *Usque ad mortem non fidem negabo; valde gaudeo mori pro fide mea.*' "*

Let us pause at this admirable speech, worthy of being engraved upon all the pictures of the Blessed Martyr, and which may be considered as the motto of his whole life; at the same time it defines the true character and proves the heroic sanctity of his death.

It may be divined what was the conclusion of the eloquent and solid account we just read. Venerable Perboyre is worthy to be placed among the Blessed. His influence with God, manifested by numerous and incontestable miracles, makes him the object of our most hopeful prayers; his sanctity which shows him to be a perfect model of all the apostolic virtues; his death, preceded and accompanied by the most frightful tortures endured for Jesus Christ with a truly supernatural courage, assign him a place of honor among the most illustrious confessors of the Christian faith. The conclusion of M. Morani was, from the time he published his memorial, the conclusion of the Most Reverend Cardinals and consulters of the Congregation of Rites; it was not surprising to see that each of these facts, that we shall hereafter register, marked a new and decisive step towards the desired and expected termination.

It was first on July 6, 1886, that the preparatory meeting held at the Vatican under the presidency of Cardinal Bartolini, successor of Cardinal Patrizi, as

* Extract from the Annals of the Congregation of the Mission, t. L, p. 212 and seq.

prefect of Rites, that they examined simultaneously upon one and the same question, and this by virtue of a special permission from the Sovereign Pontiff, the double doubt as to the martyrdom and the heavenly signs or miracles, which have illustrated the precious death of the Servant of God.

The eve of the day fixed for the meeting, M. Valentini, procurator of the Congregation of the Mission to the Holy See, wrote to the Very Rev. M. Fiat, Superior-General of the Missionaries and of the Sisters of St. Vincent de Paul. "I have just visited the consulters of the Congregation of Rites who will to-morrow judge the cause of our Venerable Perboyre. I found several occupied in preparing the *votum* which they must read to-morrow to the Congregation at the Vatican, but they are required to maintain the greatest secrecy. Monsignor Salluce, among others, who is, as you know, the commissary of the Holy Office, is enraptured and full of devotion for the Venerable Perboyre. He asked me as a great favor to procure for him a copy of his Life. The next day, at eight in the morning, seven carriages will come to take us, the consulters, the promoters, the sub-promoters, the advocate, the procurator, and myself, to the meeting at the Vatican. At nine o'clock the meeting will begin. The advocate, the procurator and I are to remain in the ante-chamber during the whole time of the discussion. The Cardinal promoter will read his report and his votum, each consulter will also read his votum, which must be brought to one of the three usual conclusions, affirmative or negative or suspended. The sub-promoter of the faith receives these *vota* and gives them to the *avvocato del diavolo*, that is to say to the promoter of the faith who begins his criticism *super dubio* and on each part of the doubt, and especially of everything said in favor of the cause. You know already, Father, this *avvocato del diavolo* or promoter of the faith, and you know how devoted he is to you. The Blessed Sacrament, the Mystery so dear to the heart of Venerable Perboyre, will do the rest. To-morrow it will be solemnly exposed from nine to twelve o'clock, at Rome, Paris, Naples and Turin, in the houses of the Missionaries and Sisters of Charity."

The next day, on leaving the session M. Valentini resumed his pen and wrote again to M. Fiat:

"I have just returned from the Vatican. The meeting began at a quarter after nine and ended at a quarter of twelve. It was one of the shortest that has occurred for some time. The one before this, for example, in which they treated of a Spaniard, was not finished at two o'clock. A good sign for the cause of Venerable Perboyre, which doubtless has not given much matter for discussion. The persons who assisted at this meeting were more numerous than usual. Among the Cardinals present were His Eminence, Cardinal Bartolini, prefect of the Congregation of Rites and promoter of the cause of Venerable Perboyre; His Eminence, Cardinal Pecci, brother of the Pope; Cardinal Bianchi, Cardinal Pitra, Cardinal Serafini, Cardinal Verga, Cardinal Schiaffino, Cardinal Martinelli, Cardinal Melchers, Cardinal Ricci; as apostolic proto-notary Monsignor Nussi. The prelates, auditors of the Rota, were all there, viz: Monsignor Sibilia, Monsignor Montel, Monsignor del Magno. All the officers of the Congregation of Rites, attended, namely, Monsignor Salvate, secretary; Monsignor Caprara, promoter; Monsignor Lauri, sub-promoter of the faith. Among the consulters were Monsignor Salluca, commissary of the Holy Office; Very Rev. Fr. Saccheri, secretary of the Congregation of Index; Very Rev. Fr. Zelli, Abbe-General of the Benedictines; Very Rev. Fr. Cirino, Vicar-General of the Theatines; Very Rev. Fr. Baravelli, Superior-General of the Barnabites; Very Rev. Fr. Francis de Loretto, apostolic preacher; Very Rev. Fr. Locca, Provincial of the Ministers to the Sick; Rev. Fr. Calcuzio, of the Oratorians of St. Philip Neri; Monsignor Morinella, sacristan of the Apostolic Palace; Monsignor Seppiacci, secretary of the bishops and regulars;—Very Rev. Fr. Baus, master of the Sacred Palace, and Rev. Fr. Tongiorgi, Jesuit, could not assist at the meeting but sent their *vota*. As I told you, yesterday, all that occurs at the convocation, they are obliged by oath to keep secret. I know nothing of what took place at this assembly, but I am full of hope and if I hear any special news I shall hasten to acquaint you with it." *

Two years elapsed before the general meeting, in which they considered anew the double question determined upon, but in secret, in the special convocation of July 6, 1886. It was finally on June 12, 1888, that this solemn meeting took place at the Vatican, His Holiness, Leo XIII. presiding. The question or doubt, upon which the members of this venerable assembly had to vote a second time was formulated thus: *Ad constet de martyrio et de causa martyrii, nec non de signis et miraculis, in casu et ad effectum de quo agitur?* "Whether the martyrdom, the cause of

* Annals of the Congregation of the Mission, t. LI. p. 472 and seq.

the martyrdom, as well as the signs and miracles in the case, and for the effect in question, are attested?" The same evening, the Superior-General of the Congregation received at Paris a telegram from Rome, signed by M. Valentini, bearing these words, "Complete triumph." The next day, M. Valentini wrote to M. Fiat the following letter:

*My Very Honored Father,*—The dispatch yesterday brought you the great news of the general meeting for the cause of our Venerable Perboyre and its happy result. Following the prescribed rule, the Blessed Sacrament has been exposed in our church at Monte Citorio at nine o'clock in the morning to obtain the grace so much desired. About the same hour, the Congregation of Rites went to the Vatican; for it is in the throne room that this general session must be held. The Holy Father then gave audience to the bishops, consecrated the day before. Among them was our confrère, M. d'Agostino, to whom the Holy Father addressed his congratulations upon the good cause with which he would occupy himself in a few moments. Towards half-past ten o'clock, the Holy Father entered the hall, and after the usual prayers, the cardinals seated themselves around him, the consulters and the officers of the Congregation remained standing. The members of the postulation, namely the postulator, the advocate, and the procurator were at the door ready to enter if any information was desired. You know the subject with which they were occupied. '*An constet de martyrio et de causa martyrii, nec non de signis et miraculis, in casu et ad effectum de quo agitur?*'

"This assembly is very solemn: first the Holy

Father, who is president of it, then the cardinals, as well as the consulters, give their vote in writing; besides, the vote must be either affirmative or negative, while in the other meetings it could be suspended or doubtful. If the vote is negative, *actum esset de causa usque ad tempus*, they will be through with the cause until there is a new order. At a quarter of twelve, the doors of the hall opened, and we saw the consulters come out, for they could not assist at the counting of the votes of the cardinals. As they are bound to secrecy, they passed by the members of the postulation without saying a word, scarcely saluting them; but their faces beamed with joy. It is a good omen and yet the heart still trembles. About three-quarters of an hour afterwards, the doors of the hall opened a second time, and the Holy Father called the members of the postulation. Cardinal Laurenzi hastened to meet us. He wished to tell us, but we did not take time to listen to him, we were so eager to prostrate ourselves at the feet of the Holy Father, to hear from his lips something about the issue of the cause. I have several times this year, had the happiness of seeing and hearing the Holy Father, but I do not remember, Very Honored Father, ever having seen him so joyous, so beaming; never have I heard him speak with as much freedom as upon this occasion. Prostrated at his feet, I thanked him in the name of the Congregation, in the name of the still surviving brother and two sisters of the Venerable Martyr, for whom he had the goodness to hold this session so ardently desired. The Holy Father then spoke, and in the presence of all the cardinals, said that our Congregation for a long time had desired the conclusion of this cause. 'In 1846,' added he, 'on returning from Belguim, I went to your house at Monte Citorio; M. Francois Aspetti was then superior. A portrait of the Venerable Perboyre adorned the corridor. The Superior who accompanied me, told me that he hoped to see M. Perboyre one day inscribed among the blessed. This day has come, but we have reserved the decision of the cause.' However, Leo XIII, in the audience given to the bishops before the session, for more than a half hour related the life of Venerable Perboyre, descending to particulars and details glorifying his martyrdom, exalting his virtues, in a word, he gave Blessed Perboyre's panegyric. He even added that the martyrs did not require miracles, that besides, the glorious martyrdom of our Venerable Perboyre was his greatest miracle." *

This decision, which the Holy Father reserved and which he deferred according to custom, became known before the end of the year 1888. On November 25, the day on which the Church celebrates the feast of one of her most glorious martyrs, St. Catherine, which this year fell on the last Sunday after Pentecost, occurred the solemn promulgation of the decree concerning the martyrdom and miracles of the Venerable Servant of God, John Gabriel Perboyre. Another missionary and French martyr, the Venerable Chanel, Marist, whose cause has been discussed for sometime with that of Blessed Perboyre, was the same day the subject of a like decree. These are the words in which the *Osservatore Romano* of the next day, November 26, gave an account of this double event

* Annals of the Congregation of the Mission, t. LIII. p. 315 and seq.

whose remembrance is so dear to the two Congregations and to all the Catholics of France. "Yesterday morning, there took place at the Vatican, the promulgation of the two decrees by which His Holiness has approved the martyrdom, the signs or miracles of the Venerable Gabriel Perboyre, priest of the Congregation of the Mission of Saint Vincent de Paul, and of the Venerable Pierre Louis Marie Chanel, of the Congregation of the Marists, apostle of the Isle of Futuna in Oceanica. Towards eleven o'clock, the Holy Father surrounded by his noble guard went to the hall of the throne whither he summoned His Eminence, Cardinal Bianchi, prefect of the Congregation of Rites and promoter of the cause of Venerable Chanel; His Eminence Cardinal Laurenzi, promoter of the cause of Venerable Perboyre; also Monsignor Salvati, secretary of the same Congregation, and Monsignor Caprara, promoter of the faith. He then ordered Monsignor, the secretary, to read the two decrees.

The decree concerning Blessed Perboyre offered first a short and magnificent eulogy of his life and death, then an admirable summary of the different proceedings already reviewed in the foregoing pages. * This is the translation: "Decree—China—Cause of the beatification or declaration of the martyrdom of the Venerable Servant of God, Gabriel Perboyre, priest of the Congregation of the Mission of St. Vincent de Paul. Whether the martyrdom, the cause of the martyrdom, as well as the signs and miracles in the case and for the effects in question—are attested?

"By his constancy in affirming and propagating the

* See Testimonial VII.

faith of Jesus Christ, the Venerable priest, John Gabriel Perboyre, has truly increased the honor and glory of the Church militant; by instructing nations to salvation, he has won the glorious palm of martyrdom, illustrated by God with the glory of miracles.

"He was born of parents distinguished for their piety, in the year 1802, on the feast of the Epiphany of Our Lord, in the village of Puech, diocese of Cahors. Adorned from childhood with purity and virtue, he was received when still young among the novices of the Congregation of the Mission of St. Vincent de Paul. Having become a shining model of virtue, he was sent to the Chinese Empire to labor for the conversion of the pagans to the Christian faith. Four years after his arrival in this country, a fearful persecution broke out against the Christians and seized immediately upon the evangelical laborer himself. At the approach of the soldiers, the Venerable Servant of God fled with some of the faithful, but was delivered to the enemy for thirty ounces of silver by a neophyte who betrayed him after the example of Judas; he was put in chains, beaten with rods and dragged along with his hands tied behind his back. After being inclosed in a horrible prison, he was brought forth to be tried before tribunals where he had to submit to a long trial which consisted only of cruel tortures, opprobrium, injuries, and impious interrogations. Always enchained with the tightest bonds, he was often so torn by the scourge and tortures that the flesh fell off in shreds, so that a human form could scarcely be recognized in him. Accused by false testimony of immodesty and sorcery, he was stamped on the forehead with the stigma of infamy and constrained by a superstitious custom to drink the blood of a dog. After a long year of persecution for the faith amid the greatest tortures which he bore without flinching, uniting admirable meekness with invincible strength of soul, he was at length brought to execution, to which he hastened as if to a triumph. Suspended from a post, on which was written the cause of his death, he gloriously consummated his martyrdom September 11, 1840, being executed by strangulation.

"When the news of his martyrdom was learned, the faithful, drawn by the fame of his sanctity and wonders, crowded to the place of execution and hastened forward to buy from the soldiers the precious body of the illustrious martyr. The Vicars Apostolic established in these regions, took care to draw up detailed accounts and to gather authorized testimony concerning the works of the Servant of God and the acts of his martyrdom. When these documents were brought to Rome, in view of the extreme difficulty of the time and place to establish the regular papers of the affair, Pope Gregory XVI., of holy memory, who already in consistorial allocution had declared these testimonies sufficient, permitted them to be received as information by the Ordinary, and consequently approving the sentence in the special Congregation of Sacred Rites, especially appointed by him to this effect; he signed with his own hand July 9, 1843, the commission for the introduction of the cause of this Venerable Servant of God and several other of His Servants, put to death also in China through hatred of the faith. Nevertheless, the cause of Venerable Gabriel, recommended by so many miracles, was separated from the others to be put through more promptly. But, on account of the distance of the places and political vicissitudes, it took a long time to prepare, and submit to the Sacred Congregation, the apostolic process and to treat the preliminary questions in conformity to the canonical rules. All these formalities being happily fulfilled, in the ante-preparatory meeting on the eleventh day before the Calends of August, 1862, they discussed the martyrdom and the cause of the martyrdom at the residence of Cardinal Constantine Patrizi, of illustrious memory, prefect of the Sacred Congregation of Rites, and promoter of the cause. Later, they held a preparatory reunion in the apostolic palace of the Vatican, on the eve of the Nones of July, 1886, and there, upon the report of Cardinal Dominic Bartolini, of illustrious memory, who had replaced Cardinal Patrizi, in the presence of the most Rev. Cardinals appointed to the office of the Holy Rites, they discussed, with the permission of the Pope, under one and the same question, the doubt of the martyrdom and the Heavenly signs or miracles which illustrated his precious death,—miracles wrought by the body, and at the tomb of the dead martyr, notably his marvellous apparition to the pagan, inviting him to receive baptism, and in person to many sick people who recovered their health. In the third place, in the general assembly held in the presence of Our Holy Father, Pope Leo XIII., in this same apostolic palace of the Vatican, the day before the Ides of last June, the Most Reverend Cardinal Charles Laurenzi, promoter of the cause appointed in the place of Cardinal Bartolini, taken from among the living, proposed the question: *Whether the martyrdom, the cause of the martyrdom, as well as the signs and miracles in the case and for the effect in question, have been attested.* Then, the Most Reverend Cardinals, as well as the Father consulters, each voted in turn. After counting the votes, the Holy Father wished to defer, according to custom, his decretorial judgment, advising all those present, in so important an affair, to implore assistance from God by assiduous prayer.

"Then, on the last Sunday after Pentecost, the day consecrated by the triumph of the famous Virgin and Martyr of Christ, Catherine, who attained the eternal nuptials of the divine Lamb by the same road of most cruel torments, the holy sacrifice being previously offered, he called to the pontifical palace of the Vatican, the Most Reverened Cardinals Ange-Bianchi, prefect of the Congregation of Rites, and Charles Laurenzi, promoter of the cause, Most Reverend Augustine Caprara, promoter of the faith, and myself, the secretary undersigned, and, in presence of the aforesaid, has solemnly declared that *the martyrdom and the cause of the martyrdom of the Venerable Servant of God Gabriel Perboyre, marked and confirmed by God by numerous signs and miracles, are attested.*

"The seventh day before the Calends of December he ordered the publication of the decree and the insertion of it in the Acts of the Sacred Congregation of Rites. A. Cardinal Bianchi, Prefect of the Sacred Congregation of Rites. Laurentius Salvati, Secretary of the Sacred Congregation of Rites."

After reading this decree and that concerning the Venerable Chanel, M. Fiat, Superior-General of the Congregation of the Mission, having come from France to assist at this memorable session, and the Rev. Fr. Nicolet, Procurator-General of the Marists, approached the throne of his Holiness and thanked him, each in turn. We give the translation of the words of M. Fiat, which were expressed in Latin in a lofty, graceful, elegant style.*

"*Most Holy Father*,—In this holy solemnity, a day of happiness for the children of St. Vincent de Paul, I would wish I could offer Your Holiness a worthy thanksgiving; but feeling myself entirely incapable I dare to borrow the words of the Immaculate Mother of God, the Virgin Mary, and say: 'My soul doth magnify the Lord and my spirit hath rejoiced' and so does the spirit of all the Missionaries, in receiving from Your Holiness this testimony of good will.

"We must, indeed, glorify the God of all goodness, who sends the glorious dawn of this much desired day on which the heroic faith of John Gabriel Perboyre, his constant practice of all the virtues, his unconquerable strength of soul, amid the most atrocious tortures, is proclaimed by the infallible oracle of the Sovereign Pontiff, a Martyr for Jesus Christ amid the applause of the whole church: he could also cry out 'The Almighty has done great things in me—He hath exalted my humility.'

"And now, Most Holy Father, we can, without audacity, hope that the exaltation of John Gabriel Perboyre, the most worthy child of St. Vincent de Paul, will be:

"For Your Holiness, a sweet consolation amid afflictions, so many and so great;

* Testimonial VIII.

"For the Catholic Church, an efficacious help in these calamitous times;

"For the Missionaries, who in the vast empire of China, preach the faith at the peril of their lives, a firm support and a powerful protection;

"For the members of the Congregation of the Mission, the most precious incentive for them to acquire the virtues of their vocation and to labor with ardor in the vineyard of the Lord.

"*Most Holy Father*,—In the examination of the martyrdom and the cause of the martyrdom of the Venerable Servant of God, we read 'We fear that all our praise falls short of the truth.'

"To-day we cannot feel any such fear since it has pleased Your Holiness to say with St. Ambrose:

"'I shall call him martyr; I have exalted him enough.'"

This solemn session, the most important, you might say, and the most decisive in a process of beatification, should not be terminated without a word from the Holy Father, himself. Before withdrawing, Leo XIII. pronounced the following allocution which in defining admirably the sense and the scope of the great event accomplished on this day, adds still more to the joy, the hope, the religious emotion of those who witnessed it.

"We have heard with special satisfaction the reading of the two decrees by which they had just recognized and affirmed the martyrdom of the Venerable Servants of God, Gabriel Perboyre and Pierre Marie Chanel, one an apostle in China, the other an apostle in Oceanica.

"Both of them sons of very deserving French religious Congregations are a shining glory to our century. After having spent their lives in spreading, in distant lands, among a barbarous people, the light of the gospel they have had the merit of courageously shedding their blood for the faith amid the most cruel tortures.

"Let us thank God, Who by a special design of His Providence has so opportunely permitted that at the present time there should be proposed to the faithful and also, to the ministers of the sanctuary models of so great virtue and heroism.

"In the great perils and difficult trials to which the profession of the Catholic faith is to-day exposed, these examples will be an incitement and a stimulus to us to undergo for the faith all kinds of painful labors and sacrifices; they will serve to help the laxity and torpor of the pusillanimous, and to infuse into their hearts that inflexible constancy and that invincible courage which our Martyrs have shown.

"As to us, amid our numerous sorrows and tribulations, we feel a sweet encouragement and holy joy at being able to raise to the honors of the altars these illustrious heroes and true champions of the faith. And we hope that, being admitted to the glorious phalanx of the Blessed, they will be in heaven, our mediators and intercessors with God; that the fearful war made to-day against God and the Church may come to an end; that the counsels of the impious may be brought to naught; that our enemies may be humbled and confounded, and that days of calm and peace may shine again upon the Church."

After the publication of the decree, relating to the approbation of the martyrdom and miracles of the

Servant of God, the Congregation of Rites had only, as the proceedings of the cause were entirely exhausted, to respond to the following doubt. *An tuto procedi possit ad Beatificationem?* 'Can we, in all security, proceed to the beatification?' It was on March 12, 1889, that in a general assembly of the Congregation of Rites, held in the presence of the Sovereign Pontiff, in the palace of the Vatican, the most Reverend Cardinals and consulters were called upon to pronounce upon this question. All the votes, without exception, were in the affirmative. Nevertheless, again on this occasion, as in June of the preceding year, His Holiness resolved to defer his supreme decision and to fix ultimately the date of the decrée called *de tuto* which officially makes known and sanctions the votes given in the session that has just taken place. In the meantime, and to indicate better the maturity to which the cause had already attained, a letter from Cardinal Laurenzi to the Archbishop of Paris, dated March 22, 1889, announced that the Holy Father authorized the disinterring of the body of the Venerable Servant of God, John Gabriel Perboyre, so as to obtain the relics which would be distributed during the now fast approaching solemnities of the beatification.

It was on April 25, that His Eminence, Cardinal Richard, went to the Mother House of the Lazarists to proceed with all the required ceremonies of this exhumation. The Annals of the Congregation of the Mission published two months later, give a very detailed account of it, from which we cite the principal paragraphs.

"The Archbishop of Paris arrived at two o'clock,

accompanied by M. Henri Louis Odelin, fiscal promoter, and M. Victor Charon, chancellor of the diocese. The members of the community, dressed in surplice, awaited the Archbishop, whom the Missionary priests accompanied to the chamber of relics, while the clergy took their places in the choir. The Archbishop first invoked the Holy Ghost, then mounted his throne. The fiscal promoter and chancellor above named, the instrumental witnesses, MM. Adolphe Frontigny and Armand David. M. Antoine Fiat, Superior General, M. Jacques Perboyre, brother of the Martyr, some priests of the Mother House, some Sisters of Charity, and several persons of distinction, admitted by the Archbishop, being present, there appeared M. Leon Forestier, official representative of M. Philippe Valentini, postulater of the cause, who, on March 9, had signed and forwarded the act of delegation, who urgently requested that they might proceed to the exhumation and translation of the body of the Venerable Servant of God, and that for this purpose they would choose and depute able physicians as well as the suitable persons needed for performing the necessary work. The Archbishop of Paris selected and appointed Dr. Ange Ernest Amedee Ferrand and Vincent Ferdinand Germain Alibert, physicians, to recognize and describe the remains of the Venerable Servant of God. To open the vault, to take out and open the box containing the body of the Venerable Servant of God and to do all the necessary work, His Grace appointed two lay brothers of the Congregation of the Mission, Nicholas Aubouer and Robert Haasbach, experts in masonry, carpentery and plumbing.

"After taking the usual oath, the Archbishop, accompanied by the fiscal promoter, the chancellor, the two instrumental witnesses, and the persons previously designated, went to the church, and, after adoring the Most Blessed Sacrament, approached the place where the holy body reposed. By the order of the Archbishop, the temporary stone was taken away, and they proceeded to the extraction of the triple case. To facilitate this operation, care had been taken in the construction of the outside case, to furnish both sides with rings through which ropes could be put to raise the precious deposit. The ropes having been adjusted, the case was raised with an ease which caused no little astonishment; but this soon ceased when it was discovered that on account of the dampness, the oak had rotted and that there had been raised only two-thirds of the case, the other third and the bottom remaining in the vault. On account of this break there was great difficulty in getting out the remainder of the case and the support of the other two cases of lead and oak. When all was taken out, the leaden case was placed upon a litter richly adorned and covered with red velvet. The Superior-General and MM. Jules Chevalier, Leon Forestier, and Amedee Allou, his assistants, claimed as an honor the privilege of bearing to the chamber of relics the remains of our Venerable Martyr. The community, with lighted candle in hand, reciting in a low voice the psalms common to a confessor, according to the instructions of the Sacred Congregation of Rites, preceded the litter, which was placed upon a table covered with a white cloth. Upon the order of the Archbishop, the leaden case was opened and the oak case was revealed. The physicians then began to extract with the greatest respect, the sacred bones and place them upon a table covered with a costly cloth. At the end of about half an hour, spent in verifying and registering, in the most detailed manner, all the bones that composed the precious treasure, the physicians having declared their recognition of all the bones which had been described in the verbal process of 1860, they proceeded to select the relics which must be offered on the occasion of the beatification to His Holiness, to the Archbishop of Paris, and their Eminences the Cardinals of the Sacred Congregation of Rites; they put aside, also, the bones destined to be distributed to the Houses of the Congregation, to the Sisters of Charity and to some private persons. The first cervical vertebra of the holy body was destined for His Holiness, the second vertebra for the Archbishop of Paris; eight joints of the hands and feet destined for their Eminences the Cardinal or to be shared among our Italian houses, were placed in separate boxes closed with a red silk ribbon, disposed in the form of a cross and sealed with the seal of the Archbishop. The rest of the vertebra, twelve ribs and sixteen little bones, or fragments of bones, destined for future distribution, were placed in a box which was closed in the same manner as the others. All the rest of the holy body was carefully placed in a shrine of brass, gilded inside and out. The case was lined with red silk which also covered the bones, placed on wadding and wrapped in paper. When all these means had been taken to assure the perfect preservation of the holy relics, the lid was soldered down and the shrine enclosed in wide red silk ribbon. disposed in the form of a double cross; then at the two intersections of the ribbon on the lid, the shrine was sealed with red Spanish wax, the seal of the Archbishop. This shrine which is to be placed in a red marble coffin, which will be placed under the altar to be dedicated to Blessed Perboyre, was placed temporarily with the different boxes above mentioned in in a cupboard in the chamber of relics, protected by a double lock." *

When these lines appeared in the Annals of the Mission, the decree of which we have spoken and which confirmed it by the vote of the Congregation of Rites of the preceding March 12, had already been published. On May 30, the Feast of the Ascension, the Holy Father went, at eleven o'clock in the morning, to the throne-room of his palace of the Vatican. There, surrounded by his prelates and the members of his court, the Cardinal prefect and the members and officers of the Congregation of Rites he ordered the reading and promulgation of the decree of which this is the translation.

"Decree—China—Cause of the beatification or declaration of the martyrdom of the Venerable Servant of God, John Gabriel Perboyre, priest of the Congregation of the Mission of St. Vincent de Paul; upon the question: '*Whether from the proof given of the martyrdom or the cause of the martyrdom, which God has glorified and confirmed by several signs and miracles, we may safely proceed to the solemn beatification of the Venerable Servant of God?*'"

"His strength of soul, his wonderful constancy, which having its source and receiving its form from

* Annals of the Congregation of the Mission, t. LIV, p. 319.

charity, has for its model Jesus Christ Who has died for us. This charity is the distinctive mark of the Christian martyr, has, no doubt, shone in a great number of other heroes; but in our century it has shone more brilliantly than ever amid all sorts of tortures, long endured for the faith, in the person of the Venerable Servant of God, John Gabriel Perboyre in whom the noble nation of France has every right to take great pride. This invincible hero of Christ, priest of the Congregation of the Mission, possessing the fulness of the spirit of St. Vincent, arrived in China amid a fierce persecution against the Christians, the fourth day before the Calends of September, 1835. In his ardent zeal for the propagation of the faith and the salvation of souls, full of contempt for perils and death, he embraced the labor of preaching the gospel, practised all the virtues of a true apostle and crowned his merits by sustaining for Christ a long and glorious combat, for, after the most cruel torments borne with indomitable courage and strength, he merited to shed his blood in testimony of his faith. Thus it was that he attained to glory according to the beautiful words of Saint Augustin, 'Truth finds its triumph in works of charity.' Indeed, the news of his martyrdom was soon spread abroad from the shores of Asia to all the sections of Europe and reached the Apostolic See, surrounded by all the proofs which assure certainty. The testimony, legally collected upon the martyrdom of the Servant of God, the cause of the martyrdom, the signs and miracles, were, according to custom, the subject of the most severe examination in a triple discussion before the tribunal of the Sacred Congregation of Rites. At length, by a decree promulgated on the seventh day before the Calends of December of last year, Our Holy Father, Pope Leo XIII., declared according to the prescribed rules, that the martyrdom of the Venerable Servant of God, John Gabriel Perboyre and the cause of the martyrdom, glorified and confirmed by God by several signs has been verified. Therefore, to satisfy the desires of Catholic France and especially of the members of the Congregation founded by St. Vincent, and to give to this cause its lawful termination, the question must be discussed, whether in all security, the solemn honors reserved for the blessed inhabitants of heaven can be decreed in the Church, to the Venerable Servant of God, John Gabriel Perboyre. To this end in the general assembly of the Sacred Congregation of Rites, held in the presence of His Holiness, Pope Leo XIII., in the palace of the Vatican on the fourth day before the Ides of March in the present year, 1889, the Most Rev. Cardinal Charles Laurenzi, promoter of the cause, proposed the following doubt. '*Whether,—proven the martyrdom and the cause of the martyrdom which God has confirmed and glorified by many signs and miracles, we can, in all security proceed to the beatification of the Venerable Servant of God John Gabriel Perboyre.*' The most Holy Father, after having received the unanimously affirmative votes of the Most Rev. Cardinals and the Fathers Consulters, deferred the manifestation of his supreme sentence, asking the assistants meanwhile not to neglect to implore for this special light from God. In the celebration of the Ascension of our divine Redeemer into heaven, after having offered the Holy Sacrifice in his private oratory; seated in the throne hall of the pontifical palace of the Vatican, in the presence of the Most Rev. Cardinal Charles Laurenzi, perfect of the Sacred Congregation of Rites and promoter of the cause, as well as Rev. Fr. Augustin Caprara, promoter of the faith, and the Secretary undersigned, the Holy Father decreed as follows: 'That the solemn beatification of the Venerable John Gabriel Perboyre can safely be proceeded with.' His Holiness ordered the promulgation of this decree to be inserted in the acts of the Sacred Congregation of Rites, and apostolic letters to be prepared in the form of a brief concerning the beatification which will be celebrated later. The third day before the Calends of June, 1889.

"Signed: Charles Cardinal Laurenzi, Perfect of Sacred Congregation of Rites.

"Vincent Nussi, Secretary of the Sacred Congregation of Rites."

This brief, which the Soverign Pontiff ordered to be written, could only be read in the ceremony of the beatification of the Venerable Servant of God. From the delays that usually occur in these matters, it was supposed that this celebration could not take place before the beginning of the following year in January or February of 1890. But in November, 1889, there flocked to Rome thousands of French pilgrims; thousands of workmen followed one another to the Eternal City for several weeks, led by their bishops or the generous promoters of works in the interests of the laboring class. With kind and tender consideration, Leo XIII. desired that the glorification of the French martyr should coincide with the presence of his countrymen at the tomb of the Apostles. Towards the middle of October a dispatch dated from Rome came to Paris and announced to the Superior-General of the Congregation of the Mission, that, in virtue of a definite, and henceforth official, decision of His Holiness, the Venerable Perboyre would be beatified on the 10th of the following month.

On the morning of the appointed day, at about half past nine o'clock, the Cardinals and consulters of the Congregation of Rites repaired to the Sistine Chapel, where the Blessed Sacrament was exposed. There forming a procession, composed of members of the Sacred Congregation and the bishops present in Rome, the prelates of the tribunal of the Rota, and the canons delegated by the chapter of St. Peter, they proceeded, escorted by the Swiss guard and the ushers of the palace, bearing a silver rod, to the hall of Loggia, called also the hall of Benediction, *urbi et orbi*, above the grand vestibule of the Vatican basilica. It is in this hall, transformed into a chapel, and not in the basilica itself, as formerly, that on account of the state of the times, "*ob temporum conditionem*," according to the words of the pontifical brief, it has been customary, for some years to celebrate the beatification, as well as the canonization of saints.

When the venerable cortege entered, the vast inclosure presented a truly fairy-like appearance. Amid the marble and gilding which shone in the light of a thousand tapers, the numerous emblems denoting the tortures endured by the newly beatified Martyr and an inscription in letters of gold containing the words of St. Paul about the imitators of the Son of God 'made conformable to the image of His Son.' '*Conformes imaginis Filii sui*,' (Rom. viii, 29.) recalled the distinctive characteristic of him who, in his death as in his life, was so striking an image of his Divine Model. Three pictures completed this splendid decoration. The first two represented the two miracles which accompanied or followed closely the death of the Confessor of the faith: the apparition of the luminous cross which was seen in China by a great number of witnesses at the time the holy Missionary breathed his last sigh, and the cure of the learned Chinaman to whom the Martyr appeared shortly after his death to thank him for his charitable assistance at the beginning of his imprisonment. The third picture, placed at the bottom of the hall back of the altar, representing Blessed Perboyre in heavenly glory, was covered with a veil which could not be removed until after the reading of the pontifical brief.

What was no less beautiful and striking was the immense attendance, the crowd of workmen numbering more than two thousand, to whom were joined the elite of the French colony and all the distinguished persons, priests and religious, who crowded the nave or the reserved seats. The members of the French embassy were there, near the dignitaries of the Order of Malta and numerous Roman patricians. The double family of St. Vincent was largely represented and was headed by the venerated M. Fiat, Superior-General of the priests of the Mission, and the most worthy Mother-General of the Sisters of Charity. But all eyes were directed with respectful curiosity to a worthy Lazarist, nearly eighty years of age, and to a Daughter of St. Vincent de Paul, also of an advanced age, whose eyes were filled with tears of joy and who had come one from Paris, and the other from Naples, to assist at the glorification of their blessed brother.

When the cortege entered it ranged itself in the upper part of the hall on both sides of the altar. Among the members of the Sacred College was observed His Eminence, Cardinal Langenieux, Archbishop of Rheims, president of the pilgrimage of French workmen; and among the bishops were three members of the Congregation of St. Vincent de Paul —Monsignor Bonetti, titular Archbishop of Palmyra, apostolic delegate to Constantinople; Monsignor Gallo, titular Archbishop of Patras; Monsignor d'Agostino, Bishop of Ariano, and three bishops of France, their Lordships Cocuret-Varin, of Agen, Pagis, of Verdun, and Lucon, of Belley.

Everyone being seated, the secretary of the Sacred Congregation of Rites, Monsignor Nussi, and the postulater of the cause, M. Valentini, priest of the Congregation of the Mission, went to Cardinal Aloisi Masella, prefect of the Congregation of Rites, and presented to him the brief of beatification, praying His Eminence to be pleased to promulgate it. A master of ceremonies having received the brief from the Cardinal, mounted the ambo to make the reading in a loud voice.

The following is the translation of the document, a magnificent representation of the virtues, labors and sufferings of the newly beatified martyr.

## LEO XIII.: POPE.

### "FOR AN EVERLASTING REMEMBRANCE."

"By their admirable works, the pious Missionaries,

disciples of St. Vincent de Paul, have acquired a brilliant glory in Christian society; but they are especially illustrious by their ardor for the propagation of Catholicism among the people of China, so that the remembrance of their labors and the fruits of their efforts shall not perish. In fact, in the accomplishment of this task, so arduous and laborious, this Congregation has given numerous proofs of its zeal for religion and charity towards its neighbor; therefore, God has deigned to choose from their ranks noble and agreeable victims who to the glory of all the virtues, added the triumphant palm of martyrdom.

"This glory, God has accorded to John Gabriel Perboyre, who after laboring for nearly five years with admirable charity to teach the Christian doctrine to the Chinese, was at length executed, and joyfully gave his life and blood for Jesus Christ. He was born in the hamlet of Puech, diocese of Cahors, on the eighth day before the Ides of January, 1802. His parents, Pierre Perboyre and Marie Rigal, full of attachment for their religion and solicitude for their family, trained their eight children so well to virtue, that five of them entered religion; these another of their daughters was about to imitate when taken away by death. But John Gabriel distinguished himself among them all, and from his earliest childhood gave the greatest promise. In fact, as a child, unlike the children of his age he shunned amusements and frivolities and never did anything reprehensible; so when he was but six years old his father, who raised cattle, confided a small flock to his care. But God, Who destined him to feed other sheep, willed that two years later his parents should change their plans in his regard and take him from the fields to send him to a schoolmaster to be reared and educated.

"It may easily be imagined with what ardor John Gabriel, eager to learn and develop his intellect, applied himself to study. Still he labored with no more care to increase his knowledge than to acquire the virtues, which became so eminent in him that everyone regarded him as a saint and called him one. Thus, the excellent youth advanced in piety, as in age; and there might have been applied to him with marvellous justice the words of the wise man: 'The path of the just, as a shining light, goeth forwards, and increaseth even unto perfect day.' (Prov. iv, 18.) But the designs of divine Providence soon led him to gain a ready admission into the Congregation of the Mission of St. Vincent de Paul. His brother Louis, left the paternal roof to enter the Seminary at Montauban; John Gabriel accompanied him and remained some days, his remarkable talent filled the directors and professors of the seminary with admiration; as he seemed little desirous of leaving them they did not wish to have him go away. His parents having consented to his remaining, although with regret, he was then received with joy among the pupils of the seminary and applied himself first to grammar and then to more serious study.

"In this kind of work so new to him, the young scholar showed himself marvellously endowed, full of ardor and perseverance; succeeding in everything, he soon surpassed his classmates and went beyond his masters' expectations. His success in philosophy was so great that from pupil he became professor. But modesty, the constant guardian of virtue, was so great in him that not only did he never show the least haughtiness, but would rather hide his talents than shine among his school-fellows, always exhibiting this humility of sentiment, which is conformable to the Christian precept: 'Love to be unknown and esteemed as nothing.'

"Meanwhile, feeling himself called by God to enter the Congregation of St. Vincent de Paul, for whom he had a special devotion from childhood, he asked and readily obtained admission among the novices. Two years later, he confirmed, by pronouncing his vows, the gift he had already made of himself to God, and it was this same year, that the Venerable Francis Clet had the glory of being martyred in China and thus took from John Gabriel the honor of being the first to bear away the palm. Already, young Perboyre was travelling in thought through the vast empire of China, and neglected nothing to prepare himself for his great mission. Thus, he applied himself with the greatest care to theology and the Holy Scripture; he devoted himself most ardently to the study of the doctrine of Saint Thomas of Aquin, from whose works he loved to draw, as from the most abundant source of Christian science. He had already acquired an extensive knowledge, when on the ninth day before the Calends of October, he received the order of priesthood at Paris, where he lived. What added to his joy was that, on the same day, St. Vincent had been ordained. From that time, considering that he no longer belonged to himself, but was the property of God, to Whose service he had irrevocably bound himself, he resolved to devote himself entirely to the glory of his Master and the salvation of his neighbor. Entering with ardor upon the way marked out by Christ, he resolutely followed in His footsteps, never swerving therefrom. His eminent piety, the sanctity of his life, raised him to a high degree of fervor and love of God; and when he was at the altar, all absorbed in the contemplation of this mystery of divine charity, a heavenly beauty shown in his face and attitude. It is not astonishing that his confrères had a great esteem for him, and that though still young, they conferred upon him the most important and honorable offices.

"But for a long time a great desire filled John Gabriel's soul—to evangelize barbarous nations. This he earnestly begged from the Superiors of the Congregation, and divine Providence permitted the accomplishment of his desire. As his health was feeble, the Superiors asked the advice of a physician, who declared that so long and fatiguing a voyage would be certain death to the delicate young man. John Gabriel redoubled his prayers and tears and, as it was the eve of the feast of the Purification of the Blessed Virgin, he begged and implored his Mother in heaven to obtain for him his desire. The Mother of God heard his prayers; for the physican, the night after the consultation, could not sleep, being tormented with scruples and early the next morning came again to see him and consented to the voyage.

"Without delay, the valiant hero of Christ, amid the tears of his confrères, left the Mother House of the Congregation, never to return again. He went immediately to Havre de Grace, where a merchant vessel was ready to set sail for the Orient. He embarked; his mind was filled, as he himself wrote, with the remembrance of his brother Louis, who younger than he and already ripe for heaven, had left the same port to travel to the same shores and died on the way. John Gabriel crosses the ocean safe and sound, arrives at the Eastern shore of China, the object of his desires, and at Macao leaves the vessel which brought him thither. Thence he starts for the station to which God assigned him, where at the end of two months he arrives, his courage undaunted by the fatigues of a tedious voyage.

"Beginning without hesitation a kind of life to which he was unaccustomed, he had no care, no occupation but to fulfil with zeal and exactness all the functions of his ministry. The extent of his mission, the severity of climate, the perils that threatened his life, could not deter him from visiting constantly the Christian sections confided to his care, to strengthen the neophytes in the faith and to bear the torch of truth to those who sat in darkness and in the shadow of death. Day and night, he was ready to go wherever his ministry called him and counted as nothing, fatigues, labors or journeys when there was question of the salvation of souls. Besides, as if all the labor and suffering inseparable from his position were too little, he inflicted upon himself voluntary mortification. He lived only in the most miserable huts of the poor, having boiled herbs for food and a bed of twigs for his couch; he cruelly scourged himself and wore around his waist a rough girdle of iron points. Sometimes it seemed to him that God had even withdrawn His assistance and his soul was then a prey to the most cruel agony. But, as once with Christ 'there appeared an angel from heaven, strengthening Him,' (Luke xxii. 43,) so our Saviour Himself, reassured him in a heavenly vision and inviting him to put his hand into the wound of His side pierced with the lance, brought back his courage and increased his confidence. The great day approached; in fact, the hour was not far off when the invincible martyr must give the last testimony of his virtue.

"Suddenly, there arose a violent tempest; the prefect of the province published an edict against the Christians and condemned them to death. A truly heavenly consolation, an equalled honor was reserved for John Gabriel by the Divine Bounty, Who permitted him amid the most atrocious torments which he had to endure, to bear the most striking resemblance to his divine Redeemer. For when, at the approach of his enemies he fled and sought an asylum in a neighboring forest, one of his followers like the traitor Judas, delivered him up for thirty ounces of silver. When the troop of soldiers charged upon him with fury, another of his followers, after the example of Saint Peter, wished to draw the sword and to repel force by force; but John Gabriel remembering the example of his divine Master, ordered him to put up his weapon and yield to the enemy. The soldiers, imitating the conduct of the Jews, seized their prisoner, maltreating him, striking him with their swords and to crown his humiliation, dragged him half naked through a town filled with tradesmen. Without delay, they led him to the tribunal, where with his hands tied behind him, he had to kneel before the judge who interrogated him about his country and religion. Scarcely had he declared himself a Christian, when the crowd loaded him with insults and reproaches; the judge transported with anger, commanded them to tighten his chains and sent him to a man who for his cruelty was surnamed "the tiger," with orders to guard John Gabriel, or rather to make him suffer. The next day, the soldiers took him to a town a long distance off, and he was obliged to make his way on foot. But he met an imitator of the good Cyrenean, who came to the aid of the holy missionary who was almost fainting from hunger, and his painful wounds. After his martyrdom, John Gabriel remembered his benefactor and appeared to him, speaking to him with kindness, exhorted him to embrace Christianity and obtained from God for him a Heavenly recompense. Ordered before the prefect of the military tribunal, he confessed his faith, then after the example of Jesus Christ, he made no further reply. He was buffeted and cruelly scourged and then cast into a loathsome prison.

"Yet we may say that most terrible suffering was not what he endured in his body but what he suffered in his soul. They ordered him to tread upon the image of Jesus upon the cross, but he received it with respect and covered it with tears and kisses; then these infamous men seized the crucifix and the picture of the Blessed Virgin and profaned them with the most horrible outrages. At this sight, John Gabriel felt so deep a sorrow that he seemed about to die. What also caused him much cruel suffering, was the sight of his followers who abjured the faith and, at the instigation of the judges, reproached him for the benefits he had bestowed upon them, and outraged our holy religion. Scoffed at, given over to the executioners as a butt for their insolent jests, he was cast into a narrow dungeon; his body was torn by the lash and the instruments of torture to so great an extent that his blood flowed in streams and his flesh was torn off in shreds; a red hot iron branded his forehead with the stigma of infamy; he suffered all kinds of tortures; he endured all these outrages with invincible calmness. At length, after being treated for a whole year with these refinements of cruelty, to which he ever opposed an unalterable constancy, he was brought to the place of execution, holding in his hand a rod, inscribed with the sentence of death written against him. Five criminals were to be executed with him for the most horrible crimes. The hero seemed to be going to his triumph; his face was calm and smiling; with a rope around his neck, he was attached to a gibbet in the form of a cross, and crowned his admirable virtues by suffering martyrdom, on the third day before the Ides of September, in the year 1840, on Friday, at almost the same hour that our divine Redeemer expired for us.

"The time, the manner, the circumstances, of the two deaths greatly resemble each other, and no one can refuse to John Gabriel a place among the Blessed, for whom God 'fore-knew and predestined to be made conformable to the image of His Son.' (Rom. viii. 29.)

"John Gabriel's reputation for sanctity was already great, but after his glorious martyrdom, it increased still more and spread everywhere; and Europe, like Asia, celebrated his virtues. This is why the Sovereign Pontiff, Gregory XVI., of holy memory, approving the sentence of a special assembly of the Congregation of Sacred Rites appointed by him, signed, with his own hand, June 9, 1843, the commission for the introduction of the cause of the Venerable Servant of God; and later by our will and upon our order all the necessary inquiries to form this judgment being terminated, the Congregation of Cardinals appointed by the Sacred Rites began to examine the question whether, from the judicial testimony collected, the martyrdom of the Servant of God, the cause of the martyrdom and the signs and miracles wrought by God through John Gabriel's prayers, were verified.

"All these points being subjected to the most severe investigation, and following the express vote of the Sacred Congregation, we have by the decree given the seventh day before the Calends of December, last year, solemnly declared that the martyrdom of the Venerable Servant of God, John Gabriel Perboyre and the cause of the martyrdom, illustrated and confirmed by God by many signs and miracles, are verified.

"There remained only to ask the Cardinals of the said Congregation whether, having approved the martyrdom and the cause of the martyrdom, illustrated and confirmed by God by many signs and miracles, the beatification of the Venerable Servant of God, John Gabriel Perboyre, could be securely proceeded with, and the Cardinals in the general assembly held in Our presence the fourth day before the Ides of March, this present year, 1889, responded with unanimous accord that it could be done in all security.

"We, however, in an affair of so great importance, deferred pronouncing Our Judgment, wishing beforehand to implore by the most fervent prayers the assistance of the Father of lights; this being done, We have, at last, on the solemnity of the Ascension of Our Lord into heaven, decreed that the solemn beatification of the Venerable Servant of God, John Gabriel Perboyre, could safely be proceeded with.

"Consequently, yielding to the unanimous prayers of the Congregation of the Mission of St. Vincent de Paul, in virtue of Our apostolic authority and by these present letters, We permit that the Venerable Servant of God, John Gabriel Perboyre, receive hereafter the name of Blessed; that his body and relics be exposed in public to the veneration of the faithful, but not to be borne in solemn supplication, nor his pictures to be ornamented with rays. Besides, always in virtue of Our Apostolic authority, We concede that in his honor there be said each year the office and Mass common of a martyr with the Prayers special to him approved by Us according to the rubric of the Missal and Roman breviary; We permit the recitation of this office in the diocese of Cahors and in all the houses and churches of said Congregation, to all those who are obliged to recite the canonical hours; and, as to the Mass, Our permission extends to all priests, seculars as well as religious, who go to the churches where this feast is celebrated. Finally, We grant that the solemnity of the beatification of the Venerable Servant of God, John Gabriel Perboyre, be celebrated in the above mentioned churches with the office and Mass of the rite of double major which We prescribe to be done on the day that will be designated by the Ordinary, within one year after this solemnity shall have been celebrated, on account of the condition of the times, in the upper hall of the portico of the Vatican basilica. The constitutions and apostolic ordinances and the decrees bearing upon *non-culte* and all things to the contrary notwithstanding, We wish that even to the printed copies of the present letters, provided that they are signed by the secretary of the aforesaid Congregation, and stamped with the seal of the prefect, there be given, even in judiciary discussions, absolutely the same faith that would be given to these present letters, the expression of Our will, if they were shown.

"Given at Rome, at St. Peter's, under the Fisherman's ring, November 9, 1889, the twelfth year of Our pontificate.

"M. CARDINAL LEDOCHOWSKI."

When the reading of the brief was finished, the officiating prelate appointed by the chapter of St. Peter which has jurisdiction of the hall of canonization, His Excellency, Monsignor Lenti, Vicar-general of the Vicariate of Rome, patriarch of Constantinople and canon of the Vatican basilica, entoned the *Te Deum*, which was taken up by the chanters of the Julian Chapel of St. Peter's and by all the assembly. At the same time, the veils, covering the picture of the newly beatified Missionary's apotheosis and the relics exposed on the altar, were taken away, and the joyful chimes of St. Peter's pealed forth to announce to the city and the whole world the glorification of the Venerable Martyr. After the *Te Deum*, a chanter entoned the versicle: '*Ora pro nobis, Beata Joannes Gabriel*,' 'Pray for us, Blessed John Gabriel,' and the assistants having responded: '*Ut digni efficiamur promissionibus Christi*:' 'That we may be made worthy of the promises of Christ,' the officiating prelate recited the Prayer proper to the newly declared

Blessed John Gabriel, and incensed his relics and pictures; then having laid aside the cope in which he was vested, and put on the chasuble, the solemn Mass began. It was, following the prescription of the brief just published, the Mass *In virtute* of the common of a martyr, not pontiff, with the prayers proper to him, approved by a decree of the Congregation of Rites dated September 11, 1889.

These prayers are as follows:

"COLLECT.

"Lord Jesus Christ, who hast made Blessed John Gabriel, Thy martyr in China, wonderful for innocence of life, apostolic labors and a marvellous participation of Thy Cross, grant, we beseech Thee, that, practising the lessons of his faith, charity and patience, we may be worthy partakers of his glory who livest and reignest with God the Father in unity with the Holy Ghost world without end. Amen. *Domine Jesu Christe, qui Beatum Joannem-Gabrielem, Martyrem tuum, inter Sinarum gentes, vitae innocentia, apostolicis laboribus, et præcipua tuæ Crucis participatione, mirabilem effecisti; tribue, quæsumus, ut ipsis fidei, charitatis ac patientiæ documenta sectantes, ejusdem gloriæ mereamur esse consortes: Qui vivis.*"

"SECRET.

"May this oblation, O Lord, which strengthened Blessed John Gabriel to endure the combat for the faith, obtain for us perpetual constancy in Thy service and life everlasting. Through Our Lord Jesus Christ. Amen. *Hæc oblatio, Domine, quæ Beatum*

*Joannem-Gabrielem ad subeundum pro fide certamen præparavit, perpetuam in tuo servitio constantiam conferat ac salutem. Per Dominum. . . .*"

"Post-Communion.

"May the reception of Thy Sacrament, O Lord give us the strength by which Blessed John Gabriel was enabled to live innocently and obtain the triumph of martyrdom. Through Jesus Christ Our Lord. Amen. *Cœlestem nobis, Domine, tribuant percepta sacramenta virtutem, qua Beatus Joannes-Gabriel innocenter vivere, et martyrii valuit reportare triumphum. Per Dominum. . . .*"

The feast of the beatification of the holy French Martyr was to have its completion and crown in the afternoon. Towards three o'clock, the Sovereign Pontiff, according to the usual rites on these solemnities went to the hall of the Loggia. Leo XIII., preceded by the prelates and officers of his court, and escorted by all the Bishops and Cardinals present in Rome, first adored the Blessed Sacrament, exposed since the morning in the Sistine Chapel, then the pontifical cortege went in procession to the hall of Canonization, filled as in the morning—with a dense crowd. His Holiness remained a long time kneeling in prayer before the picture and relics of Blessed Perboyre. When he arose, the members of the postulation of the cause presented to him the usual offerings, the most notable being the portrait of the martyr and a rich reliquary. Before withdrawing, the Holy Father desired to converse a few moments with M. Jacques Perboyre, the venerable Lazarist, almost an octogenarian, who had the happiness to assist at the beatification of his brother. When leaving, the Pope was the object of enthusiastic demonstrations from the immense assembly who crowded into the interior and the entrance to the chapel, and who several times broke the hedge formed around His Holiness by the palatine guards, to touch his vestments and to receive his blessing, which he gave with visible emotion. This crowd, for the most part, at least, was not that seen at the morning's ceremony. The French pilgrims were to come again the next day to assist at the Mass which the Sovereign Pontiff would say for them in the Basilica of St. Peter, at the altar of Saints Processus and Martinian, within the transept where the last council was held. These pilgrims wished to leave room for the faithful of other nations, and particularly for those of all classes of the Roman population, who by their eagerness, showed that the great act which had just been accomplished, was of interest to all Christian hearts; for if the glory of the newly beatified Martyr belongs, by special right to his religious family and his country, to the Congregation of the Mission of St. Vincent de Paul, and to France, it belongs also to the entire Church, all of whose members must take courage when they see these glorious virtues shining among them in their own day, and must find in the life and death of the Missionary and Martyr, example and encouragement, and a proof of the truth and efficacy of their faith.

THE END.

www.ingramcontent.com/pod-product-compliance
Lightning Source LLC
Chambersburg PA
CBHW031047110726
47900CB00003B/838

* 9 7 8 3 7 4 4 6 5 3 6 8 8 *